Where the Silence Calls

MJ LEE

WHERE THE SILENCE CALLS

CANELO

First published in the United Kingdom in 2019 by Canelo

This edition published in the United Kingdom in 2019 by

Canelo Digital Publishing Limited
Third Floor, 20 Mortimer Street
London W1T 3JW
United Kingdom

A CIP catalogue record for this book is available from the British Library.

Print ISBN 978 1 78863 584 4
Ebook ISBN 978 1 78863 318 5

Look for more great books at www.canelo.co

Printed and bound in Great Britain by Clays Ltd, Elcograf S.p.A.

Day One

Tuesday, April 23, 2019

Chapter One

The body sat in the chair facing the television.

He had been prepared according to the plan. All the clues were there for them to find. Eventually, they would work it all out but they would miss the most important one.

They always did.

He wanted them to know it was him; the catalyst, the instigator, the fire-starter, but not just yet. He had so much work to complete first.

Important work.

He checked the body one last time. How many hours had he spent watching that idiot box? Just staring at the screen, seeing the pictures flicker through glazed eyes.

But that was what they wanted, of course: to feed the brains of the people with enough cotton wool to deaden the pain and smother any spark that may have existed.

Morphia for the masses. Botox for the brain dead. Plastic people living plastic lives.

He adjusted the man's left arm, placing the remote control into the icy fingers. He propped up the head so it stared directly at the television. Finally he placed the slippers on the cold, bunioned feet.

Must get all the details correct, just in case somebody checked. And he liked details, his whole life had been about details.

He stood up and stepped back, staring at the tableau in front of him. Something was missing, what was it?

And then he realised the mistake he had nearly made.

The man's eyes were closed. How could he watch TV when his eyes were closed?

He searched in his briefcase. He knew he had packed it in here. Always be prepared, that was his motto, like the boy scouts.

He dabbed three dots of superglue on the man's right eyelid and then forced it open, pressing the skin back against itself. He repeated the process with the left eyelid.

Better. It looked perfect now.

They wouldn't understand, none of them would. How had he lived with this lie inside him for so long? The lie that repressed those memories, kept them hidden for all these years, beneath layers of denial as if they were swaddled in winter clothing.

The plan he had developed was good. It had a certain poetic sensibility Shakespeare would have appreciated. It was in his heart, in his hands and hammered at his head. He had a thirst, a hunger for it.

The man sitting here was part of the plan. A small step for him, but a giant leap backwards for this man.

So it goes.

He took the spray can from his briefcase, shaking it vigorously to ensure the orange paint flowed freely.

Why orange? Well, it was the colour of fire, but it was also the colour of the anorak he had stared at that day. It was a small reminder of the pain.

He tested the flow on a newspaper and then began to work on the wall. Must get the letter spacing right. It had to make a statement.

His statement, but not his words. They came from that day too, the colours, sounds and smells as sharp as if they had been branded on his brain.

He checked the clock on the mantlepiece. 22:00.

Perfect. The evening news would just be starting and the neighbours would be having one more drink before shouting at the kids to go to bed. They shouldn't have to suffer too, not tonight.

3

He smoothed down the blue gloves on his hands and took the mobile phone off the mantelpiece. Quickly making the call to the emergency services, he ended it as soon as he had delivered the information he wanted them to hear.

Now was the time to get moving. He knelt down and picked up the bottle of methylated spirits. It should be more than enough, especially if he splashed it on the armchair as well.

He unscrewed the cap, swirled the light purple contents around to mix them well, and poured the liquid over the man's head, drenching the clothes and then the chair, taking care nothing splashed back on him.

Finally, he took the green plastic lighter he had bought from the petrol station a week ago, and depressed the black lever, watching the small flame pop up from its burner. The ubiquitous cigarette lighter, so dangerous in the right hands.

So dangerous in *his* hands.

Taking the wooden spill from his bag, he lit it and watched it glow, with the flame wavering slightly in the draught from the door. He threw the spill onto the man's lap, followed by the lighter.

For a second there was nothing. Then a blue glow flowed over the body like the sea breeching a sandy shore, before erupting into a Roman candle of flame.

He felt the heat from the man's body immediately. A burning heat, like that of a just-lit barbecue.

The clock said 22:04, it was time to go.

Shame. He would have liked to watch this man burn more, hear the crackle of the flames on skin, smell the delicious aroma of roasting flesh.

He picked up his bag and checked the scene one more time. It was clean. He did like a nice clean place.

The body was burning fiercely now, the flames dancing up the wall and the armchair beginning to emit a pungent black smoke.

It was so beautiful.

Chapter Two

The phone call was logged at exactly 22:01.

'Emergency, which service do you require?'

'Fire, definitely fire.'

'Can you give me the address, sir?'

'Third floor, Roedean House, Wythenshawe.'

'And your name, sir?'

But the phone was already dead.

The call was immediately passed to the fire service and the emergency protocols went into effect. Since the Grenfell disaster, all housing blocks throughout Greater Manchester, especially high-rises, had been assessed in terms of their fire safety precautions, cladding, ability to withstand fires, and number of residents.

Dave Greene, the incident commander, assessed the data for Roedean House on the way to the fire. Above his head, the siren was bellowing its call to get out of the way.

He heaved a sigh of relief when he saw the block was one of the old ones; no cladding and no refurbishments since it was built in the 1950s, and only three storeys high. One of the old post-war council blocks, built to wonderful standards, not like the rabbit hutches of today with their plastic composites and plasterboard walls. This building was solid, built to last.

The engine raced down Stockfield Road, the siren whining over his head. They rounded the corner into the housing estate, taking another left into an internal courtyard.

An engine was already parked well back from the block.

The driver screeched to a halt, parking up behind the other engine.

Dave Greene checked his watch to make sure he knew the exact time of arrival at the incident: 22:12. The engine from Brownley Road had beaten them there. His driver would not be a happy bunny for the rest of the night.

Jumping out of the cab, followed by his team, he stared up at the third floor. Black smoke was pouring out of the flat on the right. No visible flames yet, though.

Norman Harrison, crew commander of the other engine, ran over to join him.

'You were quick, Norm.'

'Roads were clear, Dave,' he said, nonchalantly playing down the competition between the crews to see who would arrive first on the scene. 'We've started clearing residents and checked water pressure. All A–OK. No injuries reported.'

'Thanks, Norm.' Greene reached into the cab and took out the white surcoat with Incident Commander printed on the front. 'I'll take over now.' He turned back to his driver. 'Tim, check out Sector Three, rear. Any smoke or flames?'

'Sure, boss. I'm on channel one.' Tim made sure his comms were working and ran off with a crew mate to the rear of the building.

In the courtyard, residents in their nightclothes stood out on the grass in front of the block, staring up at the flat and chatting to each other. Kids wearing overcoats over their pyjamas ran around playing tag. Meanwhile, one old lady sat in her wheelchair grumbling, 'I'm missing *Naked Attraction*.'

In the distance, Greene could hear the sirens of arriving police cars, the sound bouncing off the walls of the building and seeming to come from everywhere at the same time.

After a minute, a single squad car arrived, its lights flashing, and parked on the grass. Two coppers and a middle-aged Community Support Officer stepped out of the car, pulling their stab vests down over their bellies.

Greene immediately took charge, assessing the situation from long experience.

He marched over to the local plod. 'Can you get these people to move back and ask the owners of those things to move them.' He pointed to three cars sitting in a parking bay. 'And find a resident of the block if you can. I want to know who lives in the flat.'

'No problem.' It was the PCSO who answered, but at least he knew what to do. Within a minute, all three cars began to edge out of the parking spaces and reverse slowly backwards out of harm's way.

The residents were moving backwards too, clear of the engine and pushed to the edge of the courtyard. One woman, however, was standing next to the PCSO.

'Make sure you keep the entrance and inner cordon clear in case we have to bring up more engines,' he shouted at the man, who responded with a thumbs-up and then spoke into his Airwave probably requesting backup.

He walked over to the woman. 'Do you live here, love?' he shouted over the noise of his pumps and the reversing cars.

'Aye, me and my husband and son.' The accent was typically Manchester, with a parade of flat vowels. He had to listen hard to understand her over the noise of the engines.

'All the flats occupied?'

'All six. Even Mrs Turner.' She pointed to the elderly resident in the wheelchair who was now being pushed away from the building.

'Who lived on the top floor?'

'It were Mr Brennan. Lived on his own, he did. No wife, nothing. Don't know how he got the flat, must've known somebody at the council.'

'Is he still in there?'

She shrugged her shoulders. 'Could be, but we don't see him much. Bit of a strange one is Joe Brennan.'

'Did you ring the fire in?'

'Yeah, but you lot were already on your way.'

He nodded once and moved away from her, staring up at the top floor again. The smoke was thicker now, billowing out into the night sky. A dark trail against the ambient light of the city. An orange glow from inside the flat betrayed the presence of fire.

On the ground, the team had rolled out the hoses and readied the pumps. They were a well-trained team, each man knowing exactly what he had to do.

'Get suited up, guys. You're Team Two.' He gave the order to two of his men, who immediately began to don their water-proofs and breathing equipment. 'And when you're ready, I want you to check the flats are empty, but don't enter the target flat.'

'OK, Dave.'

'Let me know when you've finished.'

The blast of a siren behind him betrayed the presence of another squad car edging its way through the crowd. More police cars had arrived now to help the two beleaguered coppers and the PCSO.

One more check of the top-floor flat. The orange glow was brighter now, the smoke thicker.

The others left him alone for a moment, knowing he was working on a risk assessment for this incident. Greene had done all the leadership training courses the fire service had to offer and had realised a long time ago he was the type known as a 'principled decision maker'. He didn't make choices, consider alternatives or assess probabilities, like all the courses said. Instead, he weighed up the risks, acting and reacting based on his experience and the needs of the situation. Like all incident commanders, he was willing to take some risk to save lives, but the safety of his men always came first.

His comms buzzed. 'Sector Three here, boss. No observable flames or smoke seen at the rear of the building. Over.'

'Thanks, Tim. Stay there until I need you. Report immedi-ately on any change. Over.'

8

He stared up at the flat on the top floor one more time before making his decision.

A siren echoing off the other buildings in the area announced the arrival of another engine. The smoke was thickening now, an acrid smell of burning plastic heavy in the air. They had to move quickly. Perhaps the resident was still inside the top-floor flat?

The new engine with its turntable ladder parked up behind his vehicle. A three-engine call-out tonight. Would he need more resources? He hoped not. John Stewart, the leader of this crew, leapt out and strode over to join him.

'Evening, Dave. What's the plan?'

Greene thought for a moment. These old blocks were brick-built and none of them had any cladding. If they could get to the fire quickly enough, they could prevent it from spreading to the roof and the other flats.

At that moment, the fire made his mind up for him. One of the windows cracked from the internal heat, sending shards of glass crashing down into the courtyard, exactly where the cars had been parked earlier. A lick of orange flame reached out through the window to kiss the night sky.

He called Harrison over to join them. 'Right, I want to go on the offensive with this incident. The fire hasn't taken hold yet and the resident may be in the building. John, get your turntable close to the top floor and pump water in through the windows. Norman, get your men into BA gear and enter the flat through the front door. At the moment, the only hazard is falling tiles from the roof and glass from the windows, so make sure all PPE is deployed. Incident Command Unit will stay here.'

'Yes, boss,' they both shouted and strode off to brief their teams.

Greene's comms crackled. 'Building clear, Incident Commander. We're exiting now. Over.'

'OK, Team Two. Come back to me. Over.'

Time to let Fire Control back at base know his decision. He walked back to the Incident Command Unit.

'Informative message from David Greene,' he said into the comms, 'Incident Commander at Roedean House, Wythenshawe. Residential flats, three floors. Top-floor flat alight in the living room, rest of the flats not yet alight. Possible resident still inside, all other residents evacuated. One pump committed to front of flat and two BA teams committed to enter flat by way of stairs. We are in OFFENSIVE OSCAR MODE.' He emphasised the last three words for the control operator.

'Message received, Incident Commander, at 22:20.'

Like the well-oiled machine it was, the turntable raised itself up to the level of the flat and began sending a stream of water through the broken window.

At the same time, Greene heard a clear message on his comms. 'Team One going in.'

Chapter Three

It took less than fifteen minutes to bring the fire under control. Luckily, they managed to confine it to the living room of the flat and it had not spread to the roof or through the front door or into the corridor.

Greene donned his own breathing equipment and marched up the stairs to the top-floor flat, followed by his two crew commanders.

A little water was running down the steps but not too much. The stairway itself was well maintained and mercifully clear of any residents' belongings, except for a bike leaning against a wall on the middle floor. He instructed one of his men to carry it down and away. He hated obstructions of any kind.

They reached the top floor. The corridor had a little smoke damage and a thin veneer of water on the cheap tiles, but other than that, seemed untouched by the fire.

The front door of the flat, however, was a different story. His men had used a fire axe to break in, leaving a heap of wood on the floor and the remnants hanging off the hinges.

Switching on his safety torch, Greene entered the flat. His men had already been through the place once, but he liked to make a final check himself. Experience taught him you could never be too sure.

Inside the entrance to the flat, the ceiling was blackened in places by smoke, but the walls remained relatively untouched, the old Anaglypta wallpaper a dirty shade of cream, as if it hadn't been changed for years. His light traversed the hall. A door on the left was closed. He pushed through it, hearing the rate of his breathing increase through his face mask.

The torchlight picked out a fridge, a small table, a gas cooker. All seemed to be fine and in working order. There was some smoke damage on the ceiling and water had seeped under the door onto the kitchen floor, but obviously the fire had not started here. The closed kitchen door had kept the fire out.

'All clear, Norman.'

'Right, boss.' His voice sounded tinny through the circuits of the comms.

They both backed out of the kitchen and opened the next door. A bedroom. A made-up bed stood against the far wall and clothes were neatly folded on the floor, but there was no other furniture.

'This man lived a spartan life, Norm.'

Again there was no fire damage.

'Can you check out the bathroom, John?'

The crew commander left to go back down the corridor.

Greene closed the door and pointed his torch towards the living room.

This was the area he was not looking forward to seeing. He moved forward cautiously, stepping over a small pile of debris lying on the floor. His breathing sounded heavy in the confined space of the face mask.

The heat increased as he entered the living room. Rivulets of sweat ran down his back. His hands felt clammy in their Tyvek gloves.

The hoses had injected water into the fire through the smashed window. Moonlight shone through it now, adding its shine to the glare of the torch. Greene stood at the entrance, letting his light play over the walls.

A scorch mark seared the far wall next to the window. The curtains were hanging in charred rags from their rails. A burnt-out TV sat in the right-hand corner, the glass of its screen shattered on the floor. A gas fire, its steel frame stark against the mantlepiece, lay on its side. Greene could feel his boots splashing through a couple of inches of water. They would have to clear it soon or it would start to seep through to the flat below.

And then his torch swung round to illuminate the body.

A man was sitting on a chair facing the burnt television, his eyes black holes in their sockets. His body was blackened and scorched with the arms raised in the classic boxer pose and his feet in their charred slippers dangling in the water as if he were paddling.

Greene stared at the corpse.

'Can we let the medical team in now, boss?' said Norman through his headset.

'More use to send in an undertaker,' Greene whispered under his breath.

'Boss?'

'Aye, send them in.'

The fireman moved off to bring up the medical emergency team. For a moment, Greene was left alone in the blackened living room with the dead body, sweat dripping off his forehead onto the glass of his face mask.

He took off his breathing apparatus and immediately inhaled the sweet aroma of burnt flesh mixed with the acrid stench of burnt polystyrene and television circuit boards. His nose detected another smell: the harsh note of petrol or something similar.

He checked for the usual burn marks where a cigarette had dropped from a hand onto the waiting polystyrene foam stuffing of the couch, but couldn't see anything. Then he checked the TV, but the plugs and wiring looked normal, with no scorch marks on the wall around the socket.

He turned around and stared at the far wall, the one on his left by the entrance.

What was that?

He inched closer, hearing his boots splash through the water.

He could see, beneath a veneer of soot and dirt and condensation, some words sprayed on it.

What did it say?

He wiped a sheen of damp from the surface, uncovering a letter followed by others. The word 'game' in bright orange paint gradually appeared.

He took a rag from his pocket and rubbed the rest of the wall. The sentence began to take shape as other words became clear. They covered the whole wall. He took one step back to look at them in their entirety.

'Oh, shit,' he said out loud.

Chapter Four

Look at them, running around like rats in a sinking ship. It was too late to save him. It had always been too late.

He stood well back from the main crowd, behind a fat man and his even fatter wife. No point in drawing attention to himself, not now. There was a big crowd in the courtyard, all the residents from the surrounding blocks had come out to see the fun.

An extended ladder revolved and slowly raised itself up to the level of the window of the flat. A spray of water issued from a nozzle on top of the ladder, soaking the interior.

The crowd raised a feeble cheer. A few of the local kids were standing still, mouths wide open, watching the men in black and yellow, with their helmets and heavy boots. He had probably done more for the future recruitment of the fire service than a thousand adverts.

The irony of the whole situation amused him.

On his right, the woman from the neighbouring flat was giving out. 'They're going to ruin the flats. Sure won't the water come right through the ceiling any moment now.' Her Irish tones cut through the roar of the pumps and the noise of the crowd.

Ah, but it was a small price to pay for the beauty he had created. Hadn't one of her own countrymen coined the phrase 'a terrible beauty is born'?

He checked his watch; time to leave. Everything was right on schedule. Nobody would notice he had gone, they never noticed people like him.

He danced his way through the crowd to the entrance of the courtyard. He took one last look over his shoulder. There were just a few wisps of smoke coming from the interior of the flat now. The fireman had doused his hose and was no longer spraying water into the interior.

Down below, at the foot of the stairs, three men were assembling, all wearing breathing gear. The leader, in a bright white surcoat, vanished into the interior and was followed by the other two.

It wouldn't be long now. Joe Brennan was dead. It was time to go to the next stage in his plan.

They would all suffer for what they had done.

They all had to suffer.

Day Two

Wednesday, April 24, 2019

Chapter Five

Detective Inspector Thomas Ridpath, temporarily assigned to the coroner's office, was having a very good day.

With the help of his new assistant, Sophia Rahman, he was now up to date with his paperwork, a first for him. The sun was shining on a bright late April morning, the coffee was still hot in his mug and United had won the night before under the new managerial regime of Ole Solskjaer. Anything had to be better than the dark days of Mourinho.

Even better, the hospital had just called to tell him he needed to book another appointment to confirm his cancer was still in remission. The myeloma, a form of bone cancer, had been defeated by a combination of his own bloody-mindedness, gallons of blood tests, the skill of the doctors at the Christie Hospital and a revolutionary combination therapy. He still needed to take one tablet of Revlimid each day, but that was nothing to hold back the spectre of the cancer.

The day had even started brightly. He had woken early to make his daughter, Eve, some coddled eggs for her breakfast.

'How are they?'

'Hmmmph,' she grunted in reply.

'That good, huh?'

'Hmmmph.'

His daughter was definitely not a morning person. But she had finished them along with a large slice of sourdough from Barbakan Deli. It was the most she had ever eaten in the morning; he must have done something right.

His wife, as usual, was running late for school.

'Where's my coffee?'

'In the flask.'

'Where're my car keys?'

'In your bag.'

'Where's my top?'

He pointed to the bright purple cardigan draped over her shoulders. 'You're wearing it.'

'Not that one, the thing that goes on the end of the marker.'

Ridpath held it up in his fingers. She snatched it away.

'Come on, Eve, we have to go. I can't be late again. I already have two demerits and Mrs Hardacre will be tut-tutting like a gecko.'

'I didn't know teachers got demerits too.'

'They don't, they get the sack. Come on!'

Eve picked up her school bag, kissed Ridpath and followed her mother out of the door.

Polly ran back, kissed Ridpath herself and said, 'Can you pick up the dry cleaning? It's my dress for the NUT conference next week.'

'No problem.'

'You'll be OK to look after Eve if I go?'

'No problem.'

'Love you,' she shouted over her shoulder as she ran out of the door.

'Love you too,' he said to the rapidly retreating back.

Then she turned, ran back to him, kissed him on the lips again and said, 'No, I mean, I *really* love you. And don't forget it's parents' night this evening at the school. You need to take Eve there by seven. I'll already be talking to my parents.'

He stroked her black hair. 'I really love you too, but you're going to be late and Mrs Hardacre will be counting down the minutes on her Swiss chronometer.'

As if to emphasise the urgency, there was a loud blast from a car horn outside, tooted by courtesy of Eve.

'Parents' night, Ridpath.'

Another kiss on the lips before Polly exited for the third time. Ridpath walked to the front door to close it, watching the Toyota Auris signal left before turning right out of their driveway.

Another day had begun with a dose of chaos. And he wouldn't miss it for the world.

It hadn't always been like that, though. After the Connolly case a year ago, Ridpath had collapsed at the coroner's court and found himself in hospital with pneumonia. The doctors were rightly worried because he had only just been pronounced in remission from myeloma, after nine months of chemo and recovery. He had gone back to work desperate to walk straight back into his job as a detective inspector on the Major Incident Team of Greater Manchester Police.

GMP had other ideas, however. He was placed in a supposedly cushy job as a coroner's officer. Nine to five, no overtime, no weekend working, and no thugs desperate to string your guts along the Mancunian Way.

Well, at least that's what they thought. Ridpath had seen it as an opportunity to rebuild his reputation as a detective after having being off sick for such a long time, throwing himself into the casework to the detriment of his health and his marriage.

Polly had left him, taking Eve with her. Lying there in hospital staring at the ceiling, he realised he couldn't continue behaving like a bloody idiot. And he couldn't live without either of them.

It had taken him six months to convince Polly to return, but he had done it. Firstly, by looking after himself: eating well, giving up the booze, building up his strength. He had also rediscovered his love of the countryside around Manchester, driving out to walk in the Peak District and later further north in Pendle Hill and the Lakes. It was on these long walks that he rediscovered himself too.

He wasn't going to be defined by an illness any more. He wasn't going to be a man in remission. He wasn't going to be hamstrung by the political games of GMP.

He was going to be Thomas Ridpath – a great husband, a better father and a bloody good copper. Easier said than done, but so far he had managed pretty well.

He was helped by two things. Polly had sat down with his two bosses, Claire Trent of the GMP, and Margaret Challinor, the Head Coroner for East Manchester. Together, they had worked out a plan which would ensure Ridpath took care of himself.

Three women looking after him. He was a lucky man.

It was the marriage counsellor, though, who finally brought them back together.

Polly had suggested it to help them iron out their differences. Ridpath thought it was a waste of time but didn't say so, agreeing to attend the sessions.

Polly researched where to go and one evening in October he turned up to meet her at the door to an old Sixties office block.

'Are you sure you want to do this, Poll? I mean talking about our problems with a stranger…'

'Listen, Ridpath, if we are going to save this marriage, we have to do something radical. Otherwise, even if we got back together it just wouldn't last. I'm not going to allow Eve or myself to go through all that again. But if you don't want to do it, I'm fine…'

Ridpath was enough of a detective to know when a woman said she was fine, she wasn't.

'No, we're here now, let's go in,' he answered. 'Anything that helps us understand each other, helps with our marriage, I'm for it.' It was the politically correct answer as well as being true.

She nodded, happy with his words, and began to climb the stairs.

As soon as he entered the consultation room, Ridpath knew it was a mistake. Inspirational posters lined the walls.

'An apple a day keeps the marriage counsellor away.'

'There is always a "we" in wedding.'

'Love is an ideal thing, a marriage a real thing.'

'It takes three to make love: you, your spouse and God.'

The last one inevitably flooded Ridpath's mind with a terrible image. Himself, God and Polly all on the same bed, smoking a cigarette after a particularly energetic afternoon.

He shook his head to get rid of the image and stared at Polly. Her mouth was wide open.

'Good evening, you must be Mr and Mrs Ridpath.' A woman appeared from nowhere, drying her hands on a thin cloth. She was dressed in a pink twinset, with mauve-grey hair, and a rope of pearls strangling her neck. 'If you'd care to sit down on the couch in front of me, we'll begin.'

Polly and Ridpath sank into a well-used couch from IKEA.

She pulled out a file. 'Now, I've read the questionnaire you both completed independently. I see you're a policeman, Mr Ridpath,' she said and smiled. 'And you are a primary school teacher, Mrs Ridpath.' A sniff this time followed by a smile. 'My name is Mrs Ransome…'

Ridpath could sense the hackles rising at the back of Polly's neck. He forced himself to stare straight ahead at the marriage guidance counsellor as his wife leant forward and said quietly, 'I use the name Polly Lam. I didn't take Ridpath's name when we married.'

Mrs Ransome smiled again. A smile painted on with a mop. 'I'm seeing that more and more these days. It's the modern way, I suppose.'

'Seeing what?'

It was starting to kick off. Ridpath kept staring straight ahead, like a mannequin in a department store.

'Wives not taking their husband's surname. It wasn't very common in my day.' She sniffed once again.

But once Polly got her teeth into something, she very rarely let go. His Chinese dragon, Ridpath called her. It was one of the many things he loved about her.

'It's because women don't want to be seen as property these days. We're not mere chattels of our husbands.'

Another sniff. 'Shall we move on?' She glanced at the clock above their heads. 'We only have an hour, and there is such a lot of ground to cover in the first session.'

First session? There were going to be more?

'So, Mrs Ridpath. I see you have highlighted two areas in the box under "areas of disagreement". Could you explain those?'

Polly coughed and began speaking. 'There are two areas where we disagree—'

'I'm sorry for interrupting, but could you speak to your husband? It's him you have to talk to, not me...'

Polly stared at Mrs Ransome, who made a little twirling sign with her fingers.

Polly swallowed and turned to face Ridpath. 'There are two areas where we disagree—'

A cough from opposite. 'Sorry for interrupting again, but you don't disagree, do you? This is how you feel about the marriage, isn't it, Mrs... Polly?'

Polly closed her eyes and began again. 'There are two areas where I have an issue. Your obsession with your job. And your inability to look after your own health—'

'So, let me get this right,' Mrs Ransome interrupted again. 'Your husband is a serving police officer, doing a difficult job. He's in remission from cancer, and you have threatened to divorce him unless he quits his job. Have I got this right?' She smiled again. 'Would you consider yourself a supportive wife, Mrs... Polly?'

Ridpath could see Polly's eyes flare for a moment and she clenched her jaw. Not a good sign. He waited for the inevitable outburst, but it didn't come.

Instead, a calm voice answered. 'Of course I will always support him, Mrs Ransome, I'm his wife. But it is more important he supports himself. We have a young daughter who loves her father and wants him to be there to help guide her through the obstacles she will encounter in life. She doesn't want a block of stone with his name on it she visits every other Sunday.'

His wife was looking at him. 'I understand, Polly,' he said, 'and I will try my best. But you know me, I can't help it. I lose myself in the investigation. The only thing that matters is the truth.'

For a moment, the marriage counsellor and her ridiculous office vanished. It was just Ridpath and Polly in the room talking to each other.

'I know, Ridpath, that's why I love you. It's just that—'

'When you say "love", Mrs Ridpath, what do you really mean?'

That was it for Polly. There followed a five-minute tirade about marriage guidance counsellors, busybodies, blatant bias, Neanderthal attitudes to marriage, and religious hypocrisy.

Ridpath loved every second of it.

Finally Polly stood up. 'Let's go, Ridpath, I can't stand another second in this place.'

As they left, Ridpath heard the counsellor suggesting she book them in for another session at the same time next week.

It never happened.

But for some reason, the marriage guidance session worked. They went for a drink afterwards and for the first time in a long time they actually talked about life, his health, what Polly wanted, and about Eve. Not long after, Polly moved back to their home with their daughter and they were a happy family again.

Dysfunctional but happy.

Ridpath promised himself he would try to change, not become so emotionally involved in his cases, care for his wife and daughter better. A promise he had managed to keep... so far.

A cough from opposite. Sophia being as polite as ever.

'Excuse me, Ridpath, but don't you have your weekly meeting at Police HQ? You looked miles away.'

Ridpath stood up and began packing his things. 'I was, Sophia, in a far, far better place.'

'It is a far, far better thing that I do, than I have ever done; it is a far, far better rest that I go to than I have ever known,' Sophia quoted the words precisely.

Ridpath raised an eyebrow. 'You surprise me, Sophia.'

'English Lit, GCSE, 2012. I got an A-star,' she said proudly. 'And how do you know the line from *A Tale of Two Cities*?'

'Pub Quiz, the White Lion, last week. We came second.'

Chapter Six

Detective Superintendent Claire Trent, the head of the Major Incident Team of GMP, had a problem. Nothing in front of her added up.

The numbers were correct, of course – she had rechecked them that morning – but still her costs far outweighed the budget she had been allocated. She would have to restrict over-time even more, but if a major investigation was initiated, it could really blow the budget out of the water.

She scratched her head with a pencil and stared at the computer screen. But no matter how hard she looked at the figures, they refused to change.

She was quite simply buggered, to put it in the latest accountant-speak.

Most people thought the life of a detective involved chasing after criminals in souped-up squad cars or making dawn raids to pick up Britain's most wanted man. A legacy of the years of *The Sweeney*, no doubt.

Even the modern stuff, with its Northern Irish superintendents chasing police corruption without a thought for costs, resources, or the latest directives from the Home Office, made her laugh every time she watched it.

Which planet were they on? Certainly not hers.

By the time a copper reached her rank they spent more time on the bureaucracy of policing – stuck in endless budget meetings, HR initiatives, and policy schemes – than on any day-to-day police work.

The latest bit of gobbledygook she had to get her head around was the allocation of resources based on data analysis by algorithms. Apparently, according to the Home Office, it was the future of policing: a cost/benefit analysis of every bloody investigation with the algorithm telling where they could allocate resources and time to justify the cost of the police force and align them with the latest governmental objectives.

Pretty soon, even certain murders wouldn't be investigated because they didn't justify the resources attached to them. Perhaps the Home Office would be more comfortable dealing with machines instead of living, breathing coppers?

She stared at the bottom line once again. The figures hadn't changed. She was still over budget for the year and savings had to be made somewhere.

'Give me a good, juicy murder any day,' she murmured to herself.

A slight tap on the door and Detective Chief Inspector Lorraine Caruso popped her head around. 'The meeting's ready for you, boss.'

She had promoted Caruso to replace Charlie Whitworth after his severe injury during the Connolly case. She now ran the day-to-day investigations of MIT, and leading the department in Trent's absence.

The interruption made her think of Charlie. A copper from the old school if ever there was one. Charlie wouldn't know an algorithm if it bit him on the arse. What had happened to him? Was his cost still on her books? She would have to check. Perhaps that's where she could make her savings on the budget? Either get him to retire or transfer him off her books. She scribbled a quick note to herself to check.

'Er... hello, boss... the meeting?'

Trent smiled and refocused. 'Thanks, Lorraine. How is everything?'

The new detective chief inspector shrugged her shoulders. 'All OK, the weekend was quiet. The thugs of Manchester must have gone on holiday for a while.'

'An Easter break?'

'Maybe. Off to Costa del Con or wherever they go.'

Trent glanced down at the long rows of budget figures and costs. As she did so, a thought crossed her mind. She paused for a moment, licking her lips. 'How's Ridpath working out?'

Without being asked Caruso pulled out a chair and sat down. 'You mean him being attached to both the coroner's office and here? To be honest, he's one of the last of Charlie Whitworth's willy-wavers and a bit of a maverick. He's got a mouth on him and he's not a team player.'

Trent smiled. 'You don't like him?'

'It's not personal. He's a bit of a clothes hanger in my opinion.'

'You mean wears the uniform but doesn't do much?'

Caruso smirked.

'He has a good reputation. Did some great work on the Connolly case. Kept at it when everyone else had given up. You think he's still one of Charlie's boys?'

'He's not one of mine…'

'You know he's still on the payroll?'

'I thought he was paid by the local authority, like all the other coroner's officers.'

The detective superintendent shook her head. 'He's a detective inspector on our books. Probationary still though, we haven't promoted him.'

'You mean I'm one person short because we're paying for him?'

Trent rose from behind her table and picked up her folder. 'I think we're late for the meeting,' she answered noncommittally as she walked towards the door.

Chapter Seven

By the time Ridpath had negotiated the traffic through central Manchester, stopped at every red light on Oldham Road, found a parking place and finally cleared the security protocols of Police HQ, the weekly MIT meeting had already started.

He entered the long room and saw the team arrayed opposite each other at two long desks, with Claire Trent sitting at the middle and Lorraine Caruso beside her.

Lorraine was speaking as he walked in.

'...the surveillance of the Moston gang hasn't shown anything of significance, boss. They're hanging out in the Trocadero Club most nights...' She stopped speaking as he slid into the room, hoping nobody would notice him.

Of course, all the team looked up from their folders and stared right at him.

It was Claire Trent who spoke. 'Good morning, Ridpath.' She stared pointedly at the clock on the wall. 'I'm so glad you could join us. Detective Chief Inspector Caruso is just going through our files and giving us an update on the progress in each one.'

'Sorry, guv'nor, traffic,' Ridpath mumbled.

She glanced around the room. 'Twenty other detectives seemed to have no problem this morning. Perhaps you need a new alarm clock, Ridpath...' she paused a second for emphasis '...or a new job.'

'Sorry, guv'nor,' Ridpath muttered again as he took the nearest available seat, removing a heavy file from it and placing it on the desk in front of him.

'Carry on, Lorraine.'

'Item three. The burglaries of old people in South Manch-ester.'

'Lorraine, people cannot be burgled, only property...' Trent said tetchily.

The detective chief inspector thought for a moment. 'Right, boss, the burglaries of the homes of old people in South Manch-ester. This case has been wrapped up by DI Makepeace and DC Carton. The Crown Prosecution Service agreed the case against the two thugs, Harold Davidson and Philip Mahoney, had merit. They have been charged with aggravated burglary and assault.'

'That's a great result, Harry and Jill. I received an email from the head of the Northwest CPS complimenting us. She thought the work collecting the evidence and putting the case together was textbook.' Trent began a round of applause that was soon taken up by the other officers.

Ridpath didn't know either of them. They were part of the new regime brought in by the guv'nor to replace Charlie's men, who had been moved on to other departments. The new broom always sweeps clean, even in the police force.

When the applause had died down, Caruso began again. 'Item four. The county lines drug investigation in Cheshire. We've called in Operation Matador...'

She was interrupted by Trent placing a hand on her arm. 'Before you go any further, Lorraine, let's hear from Ridpath on what's been happening in the coroner's office.' She stared across the table at him.

Ridpath looked around as once again all eyes turned on him. He coughed twice. 'We haven't had our work-in-progress yet. We normally do it after this meeting and I update the coroner.'

'Well, this time, update us on your work.' Trent smiled sweetly. A little too sweetly.

Ridpath realised he had walked into a trap. He thought quickly, remembering the facts compiled by Sophia that morning. 'Of course, guv'nor. Last week, there were 127 deaths in our area, outside of hospitals. Of these, the coroner has decided to open inquests on 42, with investigations underway in all of them.'

'You're investigating 42 deaths?'

'Not all of them, guv'nor. Some of them involve just checking the paperwork of the police or deciding if a post-mortem should be carried out. Or making sure the doctor who signed the death certificate has done so correctly.'

'What do you mean, "checking the paperwork of the police"?'

Ridpath took a breath. She was quizzing him. Where did this come from? 'For example, if a person dies at home, the police will be called in to check that there are no suspicious circumstances involved. Their report of the incident will be seen by the coroner and myself.'

'Has the coroner overturned a police report?' This time it was Caruso asking the question. Were they tag-teaming him?

'It happens. Recently a detective sergeant in Liverpool investigated the death of a woman. He decided the death was accidental, due to a heart attack and excessive consumption of alcohol. The Liverpool coroner, however, noticed the presence of bruising on her body. He asked the police to re-look at the case and requested a post-mortem. A Lithuanian man has since been charged with murder.'

'Have *you* ever asked for the police to re-look at a case?'

This time it was a question from Trent. They were tag-teaming him. This felt like an interrogation of a wanted criminal rather than a work-in-progress meeting. 'Not recently, no.'

Trent coughed once and scratched her nose. 'Let's continue, shall we, Lorraine?'

The meeting continued for another forty minutes without interruption. At the end, Trent wrapped up with a simple speech. 'Take care out there. We're busy people, with lots to do. But let's make sure we manage costs and overtime. I have

31

budget meetings in the next couple of weeks and I want no surprises, OK?'

'Yes, guv'nor,' the assembled detectives chorused.

As she left the room, one of the few remaining detectives from Charlie Whitworth's era, Harry Makepeace, sidled up to him. 'What was all that about, Ridpath?'

'Your guess is as good as mine, Harry. Perhaps she got out of her coffin on the wrong side this morning.'

'You heard her on about budgets again. That's all they ever talk about these days. They all know the cost of everything and value of nothing. We're the cheapest police force money can buy.'

'What's that, Harry? You were saying something?'

Lorraine Caruso had approached without either of them noticing.

Harry went bright red. 'Nothing, boss, just talking.'

'As for you, Ridpath, don't you have work to do? We all have to justify our existence these days, didn't you hear the guv'nor?'

'And how are you justifying your existence, Lorraine? Getting rid of more of coppers?' Ridpath couldn't resist winding up his supposed boss.

She just smiled and shook her head. 'You shouldn't have said that, Ridpath. You really shouldn't have said that.' She poked him in the chest. 'Remember, you work for me.' Then she turned and walked away.

Ridpath wished she had used the word 'with' instead of 'for'. He was just about to follow her and find out what was going on when his phone rang. It was the coroner, Mrs Challinor.

'Hello, Ridpath, has your meeting ending yet?'

'Just a second ago. Not the happiest of times.'

'Oh, why was that?'

'I don't know, Mrs Challinor, but something is going on here.'

'Right,' she said without enquiring any further. 'I have a case that's more important at the moment. There was a fire at

Roedean House in Wythenshawe last night. A body of a man was found in the living room. The fire investigator will be there at noon. Can you attend too?'

'You're opening an inquest on this death, Mrs Challinor?'

'I want to see your report first, Ridpath.'

'Right, I'm on my way.'

'Good. And Ridpath, be careful. I don't have a good feeling about this one.'

Chapter Eight

Ridpath shook hands with Detective Constable Ron Pleasance and the incident commander, Dave Greene, outside Roedean House. Each of them gave him a card, but of course he had left his on his desk at the coroner's office. One day he would get it right.

'Thomas Ridpath, coroner's officer for Eastern Manchester.'

'The fire investigator is on his way,' said Pleasance as he shook Ridpath's hand.

'Who are they sending?' asked Greene.

Pleasance checked his notes. 'Somebody called Terry Dolan.'

'Never heard of him, hope he knows his stuff.' Greene checked the sky. 'Better get here soon, it's gonna bucket down.'

The brilliant sunshine of the Easter weekend had given way to more typical Manchester weather: raining or threatening rain, with clouds the dirty grey of well-worn underwear.

Ridpath stared up at the three-storey block of flats. It was the classic council housing design from the 1950s. Well-built but lacking in imagination. He wondered why they had called it after the famous girls' school, he could see no resemblance at all.

Behind him, in the courtyard, four boys were playing football using a pair of jackets as goalposts, their shouts echoing off the walls of the surrounding blocks. You didn't see these games very often nowadays, but back when he was growing up it was the only thing kids did.

Pleasance stepped forward. 'Hey, you kids, can't you see the sign?' He pointed to a large council notice. NO BALL GAMES.

One of the kids gave him the finger as they picked up their jackets and the ball and ran off, shouting, 'Up yours, copper!'

Ridpath stared at the detective constable. He was sure he had never met him before. The man was young, couldn't have been older than twenty-seven. Obviously just passed his exams and on his first placement in CID. They must have been short-staffed if he was assigned to this case. 'You should have left them alone, they weren't doing any harm.'

Pleasance shrugged his shoulders. 'Breaking the law.'

'It's a council by-law, not a legal statute. They weren't hurting anyone...'

Before he finished his sentence, a white Vauxhall Vectra accelerated into the parking area and stopped in front of the flats.

'Speak of the devil,' said Greene.

A middle-aged man wearing a baseball cap over his shaven head rushed out of the car and over towards them. 'Sorry I'm late. Hope I haven't kept you waiting.' He stuck out his hand. 'Terry Dolan from Adelphi Consultants.'

'Hi Terry, shall we go in?' said Pleasance.

The others moved towards the white tent erected by the Scene of Crime team just outside the entrance, but Dolan stood where he was, staring up at the outside of the flats.

Ridpath followed his eyes and glanced up at the top floor. The windows on the right-hand side were broken and scorch marks smeared the red brick and off-white concrete.

Dolan caught Ridpath looking at him. 'You can tell a lot from looking at the outside of a fire.'

'What does this one tell you?'

Dolan pointed upwards. 'See, all the scorching of the concrete is on just one side, where the living room is. There's none outside the bedroom windows.'

'So?'

'I can tell straight away the fire probably started in the living room. I'll have to check when we go up, but I'm already pretty certain that's where it began.'

Dolan then moved away towards the tent, accompanied by Ridpath.

Pleasance met them as they approached the white Scene of Crime tent. 'Ridpath... I heard them talking in the station about you. Aren't you with the Major Incident Team?' he asked.

'I am, but on secondment to the coroner as her officer.'

The detective constable frowned. 'Bit of a comedown for an inspector from MIT. Coroner's officers are usually men at the end of their careers, not at the beginning.' Realising what he had said, Pleasance touched Ridpath's arm. 'No offence, mate, it's a bit strange, that's all.'

Ridpath was sick of explaining. It had been a year since he was placed in the coroner's office by Charlie Whitworth and he was still being asked about it. 'No offence taken, mate. I was a probationary inspector with MIT and then had a dose of cancer. In remission now, touch wood,' he tapped his temple, 'so they asked me to help in the coroner's office for a while.'

'Claire Trent still your boss, then?'

He nodded. 'Still biting my knackers on a daily basis.'

Pleasance laughed. 'I heard she was a bit of a ball-breaker. What happened to the DCI? Wilson was his name, wasn't it?'

The smile vanished from Ridpath's face. 'His name is Whitworth. Detective Chief Inspector Charlie Whitworth. He was injured in the Connolly case, run over by the perp. Broke both legs and knackered his spine.'

'I'm sure he got a big payout.' Pleasance was rubbing his fingers together.

The man was an arse. A young, inexperienced kid playing at being a copper. 'Charlie Whitworth was one of the best coppers I ever worked with. He was my boss and a great man. Next time you want to be a tit, keep it to yourself, OK, Detective Constable?'

Pleasance touched Ridpath's arm again. 'No offence meant, mate. Just a joke.'

Ridpath took a deep breath. There was no point getting upset with idiots. 'Let's get on with it,' he said with a sigh.

The crime scene manager approached them. It was Helen Charles, somebody Ridpath knew very well.

'Morning, Ridpath, I thought the vampires would be out for this one.'

'Morning, Helen. Have you finished yet?'

'Nearly. Dr Schofield was here late last night and we already moved the body to the mortuary at four this morning. I presume you'll be asking for a post-mortem?'

'Dunno yet. Depends what we see.'

'Hiya, Terry,' she said to the fire investigator. 'You're out again, must be nice to get some air.'

'Morning, Helen, can we go in?'

Helen Charles nodded. 'But make sure you suit up. We've finished in the living room and the kitchen already. Just the bedroom left.'

'You were quick,' said Ridpath.

'That's the problem with fire. Not much left for us to find. And the water used to put it out doesn't help. But most cons think us forensics can't find anything after a fire. They couldn't be more wrong. As long as we remove the soot carefully, we can use luminol to see blood or blood splatter, and even pick up fingerprints.'

'So fire doesn't destroy everything?' asked the detective constable.

'Not any more. We can even find DNA if the fire remains below eight hundred degrees Celsius. After that, it becomes difficult.'

'So did you find anything?'

'Not a lot,' she admitted with a shrug. 'But we tried.'

'We should be done quick then,' said Pleasance, rubbing his hands.

'Before you go in... I couldn't live like this man. No food in the fridge. Nothing in the cupboards. And we found a few final reminders from his electric suppliers demanding payment.'

'You've bagged them?'

'Of course. The neighbours said they hadn't seen him for ages, then spotted him yesterday morning at about eleven, pissed as a fart apparently. Kept himself to himself, hardly ever saw him. Could hear his TV, though. Loud it were, according to them.'

They put on Tyvek suits inside the small white tent and climbed the flights of stairs to the top floor.

Ridpath followed Greene and Pleasance through the wrecked front door, stepping aside as one of the Scene of Crime officers came out carrying an evidence bag with a few burnt clothes inside. The floor was still damp and everything had the bitter smell of burnt smoke. The flat had the look of a bomb site: scorch marks on the walls, soot everywhere, boot footprints on the floor.

Dolan immediately began to take photographs, lots of photographs.

'The resident was called Joseph Brennan. From the neighbours, his description matches the body we discovered,' said Pleasance.

'Any ID on the body?'

The detective constable laughed. 'If you saw what it looked like you wouldn't ask.'

'One of those, huh?'

Pleasance nodded. 'Not a pretty sight. Like a bit of steak that had been on the barbecue far too long.'

'What time did you get here?' Dolan asked.

'Just after midnight. Dave had put out the fire by then and entered the flat, discovering the body.'

'Late night?'

'All night. Gets me out of the station, though.'

'You decided to treat it as a crime scene. Why?' asked Dolan.

'None of the other rooms showed any sign of damage. Only the living room caught fire. A couple of things not quite kosher, as Dave will explain.'

'Can we look at the other rooms first?' asked Dolan.

'In any investigation of death, we normally start with the body and work out from there,' answered Ridpath.

'But this is a fire investigation. I like to move inwards, checking as I go.'

Ridpath shrugged his shoulders. 'Fine by me.'

They pushed open a door on the left. The kitchen had a small amount of smoke damage but otherwise was untouched by the fire.

'Was the door closed, Dave?'

'It was, Terry. See, there's a bit of scorching on the paint, but the fire didn't get in here.'

'Or start here.'

Ridpath glanced around the small room. As Helen said, it was spartan: one mug, one plate and one spoon lay beside the sink. A small table with one chair was pushed up against the wall.

Dolan opened the doors of a cupboard. It was almost empty: a couple of tins of soup and a few out-of-date herb jars was all that was on the shelves.

'Didn't have much, did he?'

They exited the kitchen and instead of heading across the hall to the living room turned left to walk down to the bedroom. It was as spartan as the kitchen: one single bed, clothes folded on the floor next to it. A dressing table with a single chair in front of it and an empty waste bin by the side. A small cupboard on the right.

Ridpath often thought you could learn a lot from the way a person lived, particularly their bedroom, the most personal room in any house. A cave where people escaped into the world of dreams.

This room had no personality at all. An empty room for an empty person.

Dolan opened one of the cupboards. A few dark-coloured clothes were folded neatly on shelves inside.

He was about to close it when Ridpath stepped forward. 'Hang on a minute.' He pushed the door open wider. On the shelves were two framed pictures, one above the other.

In the first, a man smiled shyly at the camera, dressed in a white coat in front of a row of test tubes.

Beneath it, another framed image. The classic photo of a kids' five-a-side football team and their beaming tracksuited coach. One of the kneeling boys was proudly holding a trophy aloft. A sign in front of them proudly proclaimed they were the Manchester champions for 1994.

Ridpath flashed back to his own childhood, playing football twice every weekend at Turn Moss, once for his school and the second game for St Matthew's Youth Club. The coach at the youth club was a roly-poly man called David McCarthy who had once been a winger for Bradford City. He couldn't jog for more than three yards without running out of breath, but he knew his football. Ridpath could have been a junior, even went for a trial with United, but his mother wasn't keen. 'Football, it's not a proper job, is it?' he remembered her saying. It may not be a 'proper job', Mum, but it pays millions and it's a whole lot easier than spending a day investigating a man who burnt to death.

He beckoned to Pleasance. 'Take a picture of the man in the lab coat, I bet it's Joseph Brennan. You'd better get Helen to bag both of the pictures too.'

Ridpath stepped back as the flash of Pleasance's camera phone activated.

'Can we go through to where the body was found now?' he asked Dolan.

The fire investigator nodded. 'It's time to get to work.'

Chapter Nine

All four of them trudged slowly down the hall into the living room. As they entered, Ridpath saw that the wall on the right, above a burnt-out armchair, was blackened heavily with smoke. A layer of water covered the charred carpet. Three of the windows were broken and the smoking skeleton of a television stood in one corner. On the mantlepiece, the clock had stopped at 10:06 p.m.

'Who reported the fire?' Dolan was asking all the questions as he shot more photographs.

Dave Greene answered. 'A phone call to 999, didn't leave a name, though.'

'I checked with the call centre, the mobile number is registered to Joseph Brennan,' added Ron Pleasance.

Dolan seemed to think about this for a moment.

'Do you think he called it in himself?' asked Pleasance.

'I'm not paid to think about stuff like that, just stuff like this. He picked up a piece of carbonised plastic and crumbled it between his fingers. 'What time did you get here, Dave?'

'22:12.'

'And what time did the call come in?'

Dave Greene scanned his log. '22:01.'

Dolan raised his eyebrows. 'Eleven minutes, pretty quick, you must have been motoring, Dave.'

Ridpath was about to say something, but decided to keep quiet.

The fire investigator pointed to the clock. 'I presume that was stopped by the heat. And you said one engine was already here when you arrived?'

'Norman Harrison's crew got here about a minute before us. Smoke was already pouring out of the top flat. We evacuated the neighbours and put the fire out quickly. Fifteen minutes after we got here, we stabilised the situation and entered the flat.'

'And this is what you found?'

'Pretty much. Except there was a body.'

'Where?' interrupted Ridpath.

'Sitting in the armchair, facing the television.' Greene pointed to the right. The armchair was now a skeleton of charred springs and a scorched metal frame. Strangely, though, some fabric on the seat and back of the chair was still attached to the metal. The fabric was in the shape of a human body. 'He was in an upright position, as if he were just watching a programme.'

'But the body was completely incinerated?' Dolan asked.

'Right. We checked for cigarette burns on the armchair, but there were none. The usual cause of death in this case is someone falling asleep while drunk with a lit cigarette in their hand.'

'And in this case?'

'Nothing.'

'Not an electrical fire?'

'No way. You can see for yourself.' Greene and Dolan moved over to the television. 'The sockets, wiring and wall above the TV set are all normal, no evidence of electrical burns at all.'

'What did you do next?

'We looked at the body again. I remember taking off my helmet and the stench of burnt meat was heavy in the air. But I could also smell accelerant.' He touched the side of his nose. 'This schnozzle, one of the best fire detectors there is. Not as good as a dog's, but smarter.'

'Accelerant?' asked Ridpath.

'Petrol, lighter fluid, something like that.'

'Methylated spirits? Kerosene?' added Dolan. 'We'll have to test which one was used.'

'Already in progress,' shouted Helen Charles from the doorway. 'Should have the results back from the lab tomorrow.'

'OK. Can you let me see them?' asked Dolan.

'No problem. Leave me your email and I'll send them on to you.'

'What do you think, Terry?' asked Ridpath.

Dolan scanned the room. 'Well, in the absence of any damage in any other room, it's obvious the fire started in here.' He walked across to the chair and examined its charred springs and fabric, as well as the scorched area on the wall above. 'I'd say it started at the chair itself.'

'What do you mean?'

'See the scorch marks above the armchair?' Dolan indicated the darker patch of smoke and soot residue on the walls. 'He either set himself alight' – a long pause – 'or was set alight.'

'It was suicide?' asked Ridpath.

Dolan laughed. 'That's for you to decide, not me. All I'm saying is, if an accelerant was used, as Dave thinks, the fire started in the area of the chair.'

'Actually, it's the coroner's decision, based on evidence from the police. My job is to advise her whether or not to hold an inquest,' Ridpath corrected him.

Pleasance laughed. 'Sounds like you have a cushy number, Ridpath. Where can I apply?'

The man was an arse. Ridpath felt the fingers of his right hand clenching to make a fist.

Luckily, Greene spoke before he could do anything stupid. 'Well, it was clear to me when I saw the body that there was accelerant present and the ignition of it was what caused the fire.'

43

'Could he have poured it on himself?' Ridpath asked.

Helen was still standing in the doorway. 'We found no metal containers on or about the body. But we did find the remains of what looked like a lighter still on his lap.'

'A lighter?'

'One of the cheap ones you buy at a petrol station. Plus there was what seemed to be carbonised ash there too.'

'That's a match, in case anybody was wondering,' said Dolan, kneeling down in front of the chair.

'A bit larger actually. Probably a wooden spill rather than a normal match.'

'But if he set himself alight, wouldn't there be a can of petrol or a bottle of meths nearby too?'

'We didn't find anything,' said Helen.

'If the liquid was kept in a thin plastic bag, that would have gone up in the fire too.' Dolan shrugged his shoulders. 'I can think of easier ways to kill yourself. Pills. Alcohol. Slitting your wrists. Jumping out of the window. But burning yourself to death? I've been a fireman for twenty years and I've heard of it, but never actually seen it myself.'

Ridpath scratched his head. 'So let me get this clear, Terry. You're ruling out an accidental death?'

'I'll know more when the tests come back on the accelerant, but I don't see how it could have been. You don't just accidentally pour petrol, or something like it, on yourself.'

Ridpath turned to the detective constable. 'You agree?'

'Makes sense to me.'

'So it could have been suicide?'

Pleasance nodded. 'He could have reported the fire to 999 and then set himself alight.'

'It's possible,' conceded Ridpath.

'If he did, he left behind a bloody strange suicide note.' Pleasance turned through 180 degrees and pointed to an alcove on the wall behind them. The soot had been cleared by the

Scene of Crime team to reveal a message in clear, bright orange letters.

PLAY THE GAME.

'Christ,' was Ridpath's only response.

Chapter Ten

'Anybody find a can of spray paint?' Ridpath asked the crime scene manager, who was hovering around the entrance.

'Yeah. Over in the corner, near the window. Probably exploded from the heat. But we'll be able to tell which colour was inside and what the brand was.'

Ridpath stood back and stared at the wall. Had this man become so depressed he had decided to take his own life? Why not just leave a note rather than spraying on the walls? And why choose this way to die? As Terry Dolan had said, taking a bunch of pills would have been much easier. But what if this was a murder? Had somebody entered the flat and set the man alight?

Ridpath found himself taking charge. 'Better hurry Dr Schofield along with the post-mortem if you can, Helen. And prioritise the accelerant tests. The sooner we know what was used, the quicker we can track where it was bought.'

'Yes, sir.' The crime scene manager saluted ironically.

'How soon can we have your report, Terry?'

'You'll have it tomorrow, Ridpath, as soon as I know what the accelerant was.'

'Great. It seems to me it's either suicide or a murder. If it's the former, we need to know more about this man—'

'Joseph Brennan,' interjected Pleasance.

'Interview the neighbours, find out where he worked, talk to his GP, check if he had any mental health issues.'

'And if it was a murder?'

'Well, then you've got a problem, Ron, a big problem.'

The detective constable sucked in his breath and leant into Ridpath, whispering, 'Could we have a word?'

They moved out of earshot of Dave Greene and Terry Dolan.

'Can you help me out here? It's my first case. I've never done anything this big before.'

He looked like somebody fresh out of school who had suddenly realised he was miles out of his depth.

'Just ring your gaffer back at the station. Tell him what we talked about and he'll send somebody more senior out to take over.'

'You don't realise, Ridpath. He's already on my case. If I go back to him with nothing, he'll know I'm useless. At the moment he just thinks I am. And besides, there is nobody else, that's why I'm here.'

Ridpath frowned.

'We're stretched at the moment. Got a couple of robberies, a missing postman and a stabbing. The boss sent me because he thought this was probably an accident.'

'Who's your boss?'

'Detective Inspector Wharton.'

'Ian Wharton?'

'You know him?'

Ian Wharton had broken more young cops than Ridpath had had hot dinners. His combination of withering sarcasm and the ability to apportion blame had caused more good policemen to leave the force than the rotten pay and antisocial hours. But somehow, as ever at GMP, Wharton had survived. It wasn't what you knew, but who you knew.

Ridpath checked his watch: 1:40 p.m. He'd promised Polly he'd pick up the bloody dry-cleaning this evening and then there was the parents' evening at Eve's school.

'Look, this is what you do. Ring Wharton and let him know exactly what you've seen here. Tell him I'm here too and then explain your next steps.'

'OK, got it, but what are my next steps?'

'Find out more about Joe Brennan. Interview the neighbours. Check out who he was and what he was doing. Find out where he worked. Also ask them if they'd seen anybody acting suspiciously in the neighbourhood.'

'Why?'

'If it was a murder, somebody must have done it, right? In these flats, people can hear you coming and going.'

Pleasance was writing all this down in his notebook.

'And I noticed it's card entry to the stairs. Get onto the council and ask them to send somebody down to check when Brennan last entered the building and if anybody unauthorised gained access. There's no CCTV on this old block, so you can't use that. But at least the card system will tell you about Brennan's recent movements.'

'Anything else?'

'Yeah, contact his GP, find out if he was under any medication or had mental health issues.'

'How do I find out who his GP was?'

'Helen,' Ridpath shouted.

The crime scene manager entered the living room.

'You bellowed, Ridpath?'

'Have you done the bathroom yet?'

'Just doing it now.'

'Any pill bottles or packets in the cabinet?'

'Quite a few, but the usuals. Valium. Sleeping tablets. Heartburn tablets.'

'Can you give DC Pleasance here the name of the pharmacy?'

'No problem.'

He swung back to talk to Pleasance. 'Give the pharmacy a call and find out who was the prescribing doctor.'

Pleasance made a note in his book. 'Got it.'

'You might want to find out who his dentist was too? Cases like this, the burns are so extensive dental records are the only way to make an ID,' Dolan added.

48

'Good idea, Terry. Another job for you, Detective Constable. Do all this and then go back to Wharton and tell him you need someone more senior to take charge. With a bit of luck, he'll see what you've done and keep you on the case.'

Pleasance put his notebook back in his pocket. 'Thanks, Ridpath, you've been a big help.'

'So what are you waiting for? Get on the blower to your gaffer and then we'll go and interview the neighbours.'

Ridpath smiled. He loved this job. And he still had time to get home and pick up Eve for parents' night.

Chapter Eleven

They knocked on the door of the neighbouring flat. It was opened by a six-year-old kid with a dribbling nose and a bag of crisps in his hands. Salt and vinegar crisps.

'Is your mum at home, son?' asked Ridpath.

'Mam,' the kid shouted over his shoulder, 'there's two coppers here to see you.' He then walked away, leaving them standing at the door.

'How did he know we were coppers?' Pleasance whispered.

'It's genetic round here. Kids can spot us from half a mile away. Think of it as the perfect example of the survival of the fittest.'

A middle-aged woman appeared at the door, wearing a faded, flowered wrap-around dress that barely covered her bosom. 'What do ye wan? I'm just getting the kids' tea. The little buggers are eating me out of house and home.' The Dublin accent was strong.

Ridpath showed her his warrant card. 'We'd just like to ask you a few questions about your neighbour Joseph Brennan, if we can. It won't take long.'

She glanced over her shoulder as the television sound increased with the noise of a kids' cartoon. 'Will ye be turning dat ting down or do I have to come in an' clip yer ears?'

The sound diminished slightly.

She turned back to the detectives. 'I don't know nuthin' about him. He was only me neighbour.'

'It doesn't matter, anything you know will help,' answered Ridpath, putting his foot across the threshold before she could close the door.

As he was already in the hall, she shrugged her shoulders and said, 'Whatever. Youse can talk to me in the kitchen while I does the chips. We don't wan' another bloody fire, do we?'

They both followed her into the kitchen. A small table with three chairs sat in one corner. A baby eating a banana in his high chair sat in the other. The woman walked over to the old Parkinson Cowan cooker and riddled the basket of chips in their saucepan. 'Don't be minding the babby, she's just after having her tea too.' The word 'tea' was pronounced like the river in Scotland.

Ridpath sat at the table and pulled out his notebook. Pleasance remained standing.

'Your name is…?'

'Mrs Finnegan. Myra Finnegan.'

'And how long have you known Joseph Brennan, Mrs Finnegan?'

She rattled the chips again. 'Well, I didn't really know him, he was just me neighbour like.'

Ridpath decided to start again. 'How long have you lived here?'

She calculated on her fingers. 'Four years now, just after I split up with my husband. The council moved us here.'

Ridpath glanced across at the baby, who couldn't have been more than a year old.

Mrs Finnegan saw where he was looking. 'She was an accident. Myself and me husband tried to get back together.' She shrugged her shoulders. 'But once a philanderer, always a philanderer. A leopard's not going to change his spots now, is he?' She took a soldier of toast with jam on it and gave it to the baby, for which she was rewarded with a banana-encrusted smile. 'Ah, but hasn't she the sweetest nature, this one. My own pride and joy, she is!' The baby was rewarded for the smile with a quick pinch of its round, reddened cheeks.

'So was Mr Brennan already living in the flat opposite?'

'He was. He moved in about fifteen years ago, bought the flat off the council soon after. Must be worth a pretty penny now.'

'How do you know he owns the flat?'

She shrugged her shoulders. 'You know, people talk. Not a lot else to do around here. And besides, the door was different. Can't be changing the door unless you own the flat, now can you?'

'Do you know where he worked?'

'Where he used to work, you mean?'

'He was unemployed?'

She nodded, folding her arms under her ample bosom. On the stove, the chips sizzled away. 'Lost his job three years ago, maybe more.'

'Where was that?'

'I dunno. Some sort of lab technician, he was. Always prancing off to work he was, in his white coat, with his long hair trailing in the breeze like an ol' girl.'

'What did he do?'

'I dunno, never asked. Used to wear a white coat all the time. Lots of stains on it.'

'How long had he worked there?'

'You'll have to ask him.' She then crossed herself, realising what she had said. 'God rest his soul.' She turned back to riddle the chips once more.

'You didn't see him much?'

'Before, we'd see him going to work in the morning and coming home at night. Like clockwork he was. Eight thirty leaving and five thirty arriving home.'

'He didn't go out?' asked Pleasance.

She shook her head. 'Stayed in all the time. We could sometimes hear his TV through the walls.'

'And after he lost his job?'

'We wouldn't see him for days on end. Don't know if he were inside or out somewhere. Only time we ever caught sight of him was Saturday mornings. He used to go to the supermarket to get his groceries every Saturday at nine o'clock, regular as clockwork.'

'Did he have any family? Any relations?'

'Not that I know of. Never saw any family visiting. Like I said, he was a bit of a loner.'

'When was the last time you saw him?'

'Yesterday morning. I heard him going up the stairs to his flat. Drunk he was. Never seen him that way before, and so early too. Swaying he was, and cursing.'

'What was he saying?'

'I dunno. Something about a message. When he saw me, he just shook his big head of hair and shouted, "Keep your bloody nose out, you old bag." Well, I just shut me door. There's nothing to be gained from arguing with a drunken man. Don't I know the truth of it from me own life.'

'What time was this?'

'Around eleven o'clock. I'd just be getting myself ready to go out.'

'Big head of hair?'

'Well, he had a mop on him. Like one of those ol' hippy fellas he was. Didn't used to be so bad, but I guess he let himself go after losing his job. A lot of them do, you know...'

She was just about to say more when Ridpath interrupted. 'Was he carrying anything?'

'A plastic bag from B&Q. Maybe he decided to do some DIY and that's what caused the fire?'

Ridpath didn't answer her.

She riddled the chips one last time and lifted the basket out of the saucepan, tipping the golden chips onto three separate plates.

'OK, Mrs Finnegan, I think we're finished. Any questions, DC Pleasance?'

The detective shook his head.

Mrs Finnegan ladled baked beans over the top of the chips.

'One last question. Did you see anybody hanging around here yesterday?'

She shook her head. 'No, not that I remember. But then I was out at lunchtime. Went to the bingo. I always go to the bingo on a Tuesday, it's the lucky dip, but I never have no luck, me.' She looked towards the kitchen door and bellowed, 'Kids, your tea is up!' She turned back to Ridpath. 'Jaysus, they'd eat me out of house and home.'

On the way down the stairs Ridpath said, 'At least you know what to do now.'

'What's that?'

Ridpath sighed. 'Get onto the local B&Q and ask their cashiers. See if a man answering Brennan's description bought something yesterday morning. Check their CCTV while you're at it. With a bit of luck, he may even have paid for it with a credit card.'

The penny finally dropped for Pleasance. 'And if he bought an accelerant, we'd know he probably committed suicide.'

'Well done, Sherlock. I'd still contact the doctor, though. Find out if he prescribed more than just Valium to Mr Brennan.'

'Thanks, Ridpath.'

'Don't forget to call your gaffer first, though. Remember the first rule of policing.'

'What's that?'

'Cover your arse.'

They reached the bottom of the stairs. Pleasance stuck out his hand. 'Thanks for all the help. Shall I let my boss know you did most of the work?'

'What do you think?'

A smile crossed Pleasance's face. 'The second rule of policing?'

'Right first time. Take the credit when you can, because there'll be another hundred coppers trying it take it before you.'

Ridpath checked his watch. 'I need to get off home. I would visit the B&Q tonight if I were you. Call me tomorrow and let me know what you discover. It will affect how the coroner treats this death.'

'OK, will do. But first I have to do something.'

'What's that?'

'Go down the local chippy. I could murder a bag of chips.'

Chapter Twelve

Ridpath's daughter was getting changed when he arrived home.

Her eyes widened in surprise. 'You're here, Dad.'

'Mum's already gone?'

'Thirty minutes ago.'

He checked his watch. The school night began at seven. If they didn't want to wait in a long line to meet the teachers, then it would be best to arrive early. 'Ok, when will you be ready to go?'

'Mum was expecting a phone call from you, so she arranged Auntie Doreen from next door to take me.'

'But I told your mum I would come back.'

Eve rolled her eyes. 'She knew that, duh, but every time there's a school night, something comes up at work for you. Last time it was a witness you had to meet, the time before that was case papers…'

'OK, OK, I get the message. But I'm here now.'

'I'll call Auntie Doreen and let her know.'

He watched as she went out into the hall to use the phone. When had his daughter become so grown-up? The years since she was a baby – gurgling away happily as she sat on his knee, clutching her rabbit while he fed her some pureed carrot, or sleeping on his chest as he watched television – those days had vanished like a flame doused in water. Where had his young daughter gone?

He already knew the answer.

A lot of it had been taken up by the daily grind of life. Visits to the supermarket. Cooking dinners. Getting dressed for school. At work, the all-consuming beast of never-ending investigations had taken him away from her. The drudgery of gathering evidence, making the case and convincing the CPS had all taken its toll in time.

And Ridpath knew his own personality. It didn't matter whether the case was a minor shoplifter or a major murder, he committed everything to it, without holding back.

Something had to give eventually and it turned out to be his health. Myeloma. Nine months of worry, pain and fear, a pharmacy of drugs and far too much time spent in isolation in hospital.

In his mind, he made the sign of the cross, the last vestiges of the Catholic education demanded by his mother. But he was in remission now, and hoped that would continue. The threat of its return was like the grim reaper with his scythe raised, frozen in mid-sweep.

Eve came back, pushing her long black hair behind one ear. 'Auntie Doreen's cool with it.'

'We need to spend more time together, Eve, to make up for lost time,' Ridpath announced.

His daughter pouted. 'OK, Dad, whatever you say.'

'I think Sugar is very cool by the way, but why does he wear make-up?'

Her eyes rolled upwards again. 'It's Suga, Dad, not Sugar. And he wears BB cream. All the boys use it, it makes your skin smoother and more even.'

He could imagine the conversation in the locker room at GMP. 'Have you discovered the latest BB cream, Sergeant Mungovan? It doesn't smear when you handcuff a suspect.' 'Not yet, Detective Inspector Ridpath, but I always use kohl eyeliner. It gives my eyes a certain *je ne sais quoi*. Puts the fear of God into criminals.'

'Dad... Dad...'

'Sorry, Eve, I was miles away.'

'But if we're going to spend time together, you are going to have to learn more about BTS.'

BTS were her favourite K-Pop band. He held out his thumb and little finger. 'Pinky promise?'

'OK.' She touched his hand with hers. 'But I'm going to test you on their albums.'

'Like *Dark and Wild* and *Youth*?'

'You've been swotting up.'

'You can never kid a kidder, kiddo. I'll be ready.' He would have to ask Polly for more stuff on BTS. Failing that, the internet would do. 'Let me take a quick shower and we'll go.'

The school night went swimmingly. Eve was doing well in all her classes and the teachers held high hopes for her in her exams. Trafford, where they lived, was one of the few school areas still operating the eleven-plus system. Eve had decided she wanted to go to Altrincham Grammar School for Girls, because that's where her friends were going. It just happened to be one of the best schools in the country, with a high pass mark and stringent entrance requirements.

Luckily the exam wasn't until September for entrance in 2020. All her teachers seemed to think she would pass with flying colours, but it seemed so unfair to him to place such pressure on a ten-year-old girl. An exam of less than two hours which would decide her future education for the next seven years, and perhaps for the rest of her life.

God, it had been so much easier in his day.

Go to school, come home, play football outside on the street for a while, eat supper and then watch TV before going to bed. His mum pushed him to study but he wasn't that interested. The absence of a father didn't help himself or his sister, perhaps that's why she had gone off the rails so badly.

Later that evening he lay in bed as Polly sat at the dressing table applying her creams and potions. Ridpath loved watching her at this moment, the precision with which she applied the eye and face cream, massaging it in with the tips of her fingers. A routine that never changed, however tired she was.

'What are we going to do about school?' he asked.

'She's enjoying it and doing well according to my colleagues. The only problem seems to be having a mum who's a teacher.'

'No, I meant about the eleven-plus.'

Polly stopped what she was doing. 'She's set her heart on Altrincham Grammar.'

'Because her friends go there.'

'Not a bad idea. At least she'll have someone she knows.'

'But it's a long way to travel...'

'Just a tram ride.' He caught her watching him in the mirror. 'Look, you know I don't agree with this whole selection business at eleven, but as long as we live in Trafford...' She shrugged her shoulders.

'Yeah, a hundred yards away is Manchester and no selection.'

She shrugged again. 'It's the stupid system. Short of moving, I don't know what we can do.'

Ridpath was quiet for a moment. 'You know, Eve is growing up so quickly...'

Polly turned towards him, her face streaked with white cream. 'And you want to spend more time with her.'

'How did you know?'

'The Dad's Dilemma. The sudden realisation that their daughter is growing up, and unless they bond now, they will lose them forever.'

'Are men so predictable?'

Polly nodded. 'But there's one thing you could do, if you wanted to be a real hero to your daughter. Actually, two things.'

'They are?'

'Take her to see the latest Avengers movie when it comes out...'

'And?'

'Book tickets for the BTS concert in London on June the first. It's a Saturday and we could make a weekend of it, go as a family I mean.'

'You almost sound as if you want to go as well.'

She smiled and got up from the dressing table to jump on the bed. 'There's nothing wrong with half-naked Korean boys dancing…'

Ridpath rolled his eyes in imitation of his daughter. 'So I'll have Eve shaking her tush to the music on one side and a wife dripping with lust on the other.'

She kissed him on the lips. 'You put it so nicely, Ridpath.'

He kissed her back. 'It's a deal, I'll book the tickets tomorrow, but let's keep this from her, our little secret.'

Another kiss, longer now.

And as Ridpath kissed his wife, he realised they hadn't talked about his cancer for a week or more. He hoped that would continue for another year at least. Scratch that. He prayed it would continue. He wanted to see his daughter grow up into a beautiful young woman. And he would give anything for that to happen.

Day Three

Thursday, April 25, 2019

Chapter Thirteen

The incident report from Ron Pleasance was sitting on Ridpath's desk when he arrived at the coroner's office.

Sophia Rahman smiled at him over the top of her computer. 'I printed it out for you. Was this the case you went on yesterday?'

He nodded and picked up the report to start reading.

'Pretty gruesome way to die.'

'There's no pretty way.' He sat down and studied the report.

Pleasance had done a good job. He had described the times of the fire and the discovery of the body. He briefly summarised Dave Greene's testimony and that of the next-door neighbour, Myra Finnegan. He described going to the B&Q store, taking a PC with him as a witness. The staff remembered an obnoxious, drunken customer with long hair and wearing a big overcoat, coming into the store as soon as they opened. Pleasance had shown them the photo of Joseph Brennan and they had recognised him immediately. They even remembered what he had bought: some plastic bags and a bottle of bleach, both items on special offer.

The detective constable was very good on his follow-up questions.

> I asked them if he had bought an accelerant ie petrol, kerosene or methylated spirits, and they answered in the negative. I also asked if he had bought any orange spray paint. Again the answer was negative. But a staff member remembered a

can of spray paint was missing from a display he had created that morning. Subsequent investigations showed that no cans of spray paint had been sold that day.

At the end, Pleasance outlined a plan of action. Check the internal CCTV of the store. Visit Joe Brennan's GP to see if he had ever been diagnosed with mental health issues. Check with the Department of Work and Pensions on Brennan's status. Find out if there was any next of kin.

The report then ended with the line: 'Detective Inspector Thomas Ridpath, the coroner's officer for East Manchester, has been informed of these enquiries'.

Ridpath smiled at the mention of his name. Not as stupid as he looked was DC Pleasance.

Along the bottom a message was scrawled in ink: 'Good report, Pleasance. Don't spend too long on this. Let Ridpath do the donkey work.' The message was signed Ian Wharton.

Seems like the leopard definitely hadn't changed his spots.

'Why are you smiling, Ridpath?' asked Sophia.

'Nothing, same old shit, different day.' Then he had an idea. 'Sophia, can you follow up on this? Find out if Joseph Brennan had any next of kin. But don't contact them yet. If he does have relatives, we'll have to let them know he's passed away.'

'No problem, Ridpath.'

'And call the mortuary and check when Schofield is doing the post-mortem on Mr Brennan.'

'He's doing a post-mortem?'

'Didn't we ask him to?'

Sophia pulled a brown folder towards her, opened it and scanned down the page. 'There's no request from us.'

Ridpath thought for a moment. Should he bother asking the pathologist to perform a post-mortem? There was considerable cost involved, as well as the pathologist's time, which may be of more use on another case.

He made a decision. 'Ask him to go ahead. We should check out the cause of death.'

'Will do.'

He stood up and put on his jacket.

'You're going out?'

'If anybody asks, I'm with Ron Pleasance checking on the death of Joseph Brennan.'

She nodded. 'OK.'

He was just leaving the office when he heard her call his name.

'Ridpath, I have a favour to ask. Could I go to the post-mortem?'

He couldn't think why anybody would want to watch a human body being reduced to a pile of skin, bones and discarded tissue. Then he remembered she was a Biomedical Sciences student. Mrs Challinor had insisted he employ somebody with medical qualifications rather than legal or police training. 'It won't be your first, will it?'

She shook her head. 'I saw lots at uni. It was one of the modules.'

'What? Cutting up dead people?'

She smiled. 'It was actually called Medical Visualisation and Human Anatomy.'

'Like I said, cutting up dead people.' He shrugged. 'OK, if you're sure?'

She smiled again. 'I'm actually looking forward to it.'

Ridpath walked out of the office, shaking his head. Young people these days. In his youth, he'd looked forward to some Northern Soul for an evening out. Now, they enjoy some Northern Liver.

Chapter Fourteen

'Can you spare some change for a coffee?' asked Soapy Sam from his seated position in front of All Saints on Market Street.

The high heels walked straight past him without pausing.

Tosser, he thought, but he said, 'Cheers, love, have a nice day.' There was no sarcasm in his voice. He had learnt years ago never to use sarcasm, the punters didn't like it. Better to be over-cheerful. It painted a more acceptable picture: the cheery chappy who's just down on his luck and asking for a bit of help to get by.

It made them feel good.

And made a few more bob for him.

Usually he worked the kebab shop next to the pubs and clubs every evening. Firstly, there was something about stuffing your face with a greasy kebab while being watched by a starving, homeless man that made the punters reach into their pockets. Secondly, the kebabs were five ninety-nine, which meant they always had a bit of change left over from a tenner. Lastly, they were pissed – you had to be pissed to eat at that scumbag's place – and there was a universal law of nature that said the more pissed you were, the more money you gave.

But something had gone wrong last night.

He'd been waylaid by Liverpool Katie and a bottle of cider which they'd shared in Piccadilly Gardens. One thing led to another and he'd never made it to his usual pitch.

How many had they drunk last night?

He checked his body. Not too bad, bit woozy, a bit hungover, but that was to be expected – he had spent most of the night on the lash.

So here he was. Outside All Saints, sitting on his blanket with the white polystyrene McDonald's cup placed within touching distance in front of him.

Hungry, hungover and broke.

Not to worry, at least it wasn't raining.

A shadow loomed over him, followed by the tinkling of coins in his cup. He always left twenty pence in there. It was his seed money. The punters didn't like to see an empty cup. By their strange way of reckoning, an empty cup meant this beggar wasn't worthy of money from other people, and therefore they wouldn't give any.

He never understood it himself. If the cup was empty, the poor bugger sitting on an old blanket definitely had no money, otherwise he would have seeded the cup. Stands to reason, don't it?

But the punters don't think like that in their world. No logic at all.

The reverse was also true. If a man like him had too many pound coins in his cup they wouldn't give either. The strange rationale being he didn't need the money. But if you live on the street, you always need money; for drugs, for alcohol, for a doorway to bed down for the night, or for your mates to share a bottle or two to chase away the time.

He would never understand the logic of the punters and their world. But you have to live in it, don't yer?

So smile. Be polite. Always say thank you, even when they don't give you nothing or look at you. And never, ever use sarcasm. A bit of wit. A bit of flirting with the girls out on the lash. That was OK.

But showing them up for the fucking hypocrites they were?

Never. Not if you wanted to get high that night.

A pair of expensive trainers stood in front of him, next to a branded shopping bag. Another few coins tinkling in the polystyrene cup.

'Thank you, guv'nor, God bless.'

He checked the cup. Two pound coins. Not bad from the young bastard. He whipped them out quickly and slipped them under his right leg. It was a start.

He couldn't remember how long he had been on the streets. Must have been two years since he lost his home to those DWP bastards. How was he supposed to remember interviews? For God's sake, he couldn't remember his name most of the time. Nowadays he was called Soapy Sam. He didn't know where that had come from. But it stuck and at least it was easy to remember for the other dossers.

'Got any gear, Soapy Sam?'

'Leave my piss alone, Soapy Sam.'

'Get your own hole, Soapy Sam.'

The name stuck. It was a good name. Easy to remember.

Another pair of shoes stood in front of him. 'Can you spare some change for a coffee?' He went into his usual routine, expecting a few coppers to be thrown in his cup.

Instead, he felt something being put into his hand. Something like paper, only stiffer, yet still flimsy. Followed by a voice. 'This is for you, treat yourself.'

Then the shoes walked away.

Soapy Sam glanced down surreptitiously at the paper in his hand.

Fifty quid.

Fifty fucking quid. He looked up to check out who had given him the money, but the man was gone. 'Cheers, guv'nor, God bless you,' he shouted anyway. Got to keep the punters happy.

He folded up the money and placed it in the special purse he wore on a string round his neck, close to his heart. You can't be too careful on the streets. A lot of bad people. Never used to be, mind. Salt of the earth used to live on the streets, but not any more.

They've all gone. Dead, some of them. Or drifted away. Or simply vanished.

He packed up his stuff in his bag, placing the old blanket in the wire shopping basket he sat on. You can't beat a shopping basket on a day like this. The cold ground is bad for you, bad for the bones and the piles. 'Gotta be comfy.' Harry the Hun had taught him that when he first went on the streets and he had never forgotten it.

Anybody who's lived on the streets will tell you the importance of being comfortable. You don't want to be packing your stuff up and moving on every five minutes. You want to find a nice doorway, with a good passing trade and preferably a boozer or three nearby. Don't move about, don't be rude, and don't ever, ever be sarcastic.

You can make a good living on the streets if you follow the rules.

He slung his bag over his shoulder, hitched his coat around his body against the cold and shuffled off.

Heaven was waiting. He looked more like a six-foot-tall black man with a dodgy red bandana and jeans hanging round his ankles, but he was heaven for Sam.

Across the tram lines, past the Caffè Nero, right after the Primark.

He spotted the man he was looking for standing in the middle of the concrete jungle. He remembered when Piccadilly Gardens was just that, a garden with flowers and sunken beds and gravel pathways. A nice place to sit and while away the hours when he was a lad.

But now it was just concrete, designed by some architect who lived in a big house surrounded by gardens, trees, birds and bees.

'Wha' you wan'?'

'One Brown and three Mamba.'

He held out his hand. 'Forty.'

Sam reached into his jumper and pulled out the folded square of paper.

'Fifty quid, you've had a good mornin'.' He signalled to a young kid, who ran off.

Sam held his hand out, the skin wrinkled with dirt and oil and bronzed by the sun. 'A tenner.'

'Wha?'

'Ten quid, my change.'

His dealer leant in closer. 'You sure you don't want one more? I can make it two 'cos I feelin' generous. You can burn all day, man.'

Sam shook his head. 'Wanna have some cider with Katie later.'

'You gotta bit of squeeze, ol' man?'

Sam shook his head. 'Me and Katie, we look after each other.'

'You married, man.' The kid ran up and tossed a small plastic bag to his boss. 'Here's your stuff and there's a little taster of something new for you, from your Uncle Tony.'

Sam checked the baggie. It was all there. He tucked the bag into the purse beneath his clothes, couldn't lose it now. 'My tenner.'

'Hold you horses, you gettin' you money. Uncle Tony, he an honest dealer.'

Sam felt the note being placed in his hand. He checked it out. An old ten-pound note. He folded it up into a small square and placed it into the purse with his gear. That was two bottles of White Lightning for himself and Katie sorted.

Now to find somewhere quiet where he could get spiced without being bothered by the cops or the plastics who patrolled the streets. And far away from the others who'd want to share his stuff.

'Get away to get away,' he mumbled to himself as he hurried across the square. Left at the corner, then first right into the

69

narrow alley. Tall brick buildings looming over him. Didn't like them, like giants ready to crush him.

Speeding up now, closer to the place, moving as quickly as he could, already tasting the acrid smoke on his tongue, feeling the jolt of Spice as it flowed over his body.

Squeeze through the graffitied gates of the building site.

Forget the past. Forget the future.

Hunker down behind the bins. A rat scurrying away.

Forget the pain.

Roll the spliff, fingers clumsy, sprinkling the Spice.

Forget him.

The lighter sparking in front of his eyes.

Forget his words as he entered me.

The smoke swirling through his body.

Warmth.

A hug of warmth.

Peace. Quiet. Nothing.

The darkness of shadow looming over him. Shoes in front of his eyes. The same shoes as before. The shoes that had given him the fifty-quid note. Perhaps he was going to get more money?

He tried to lift his head but the Spice kept him in its grip, like being at the bottom of a deep, dark well.

The shoes moved behind him. Something cold against his throat. A rapid movement and liquid flowed over his clothes.

Red liquid.

He felt himself falling sideways, the hard ground coming up to meet his head. An acrid smell. More liquid sprinkled over his body. Was it raining?

Leave me be. Leave me alone. This is my gear, my peace.

The flare of a match.

You're not having my gear.

A smell of burning. His arm on fire. Blue flames crawling up his body to his face. An aroma of roasting meat like something from his childhood, when his mother was in the kitchen cooking the Sunday roast, waiting for their dad to arrive back from the golf club.

He tried to scream but no sound came out of his throat.

Laughter from somewhere, ringing in his ears.

Then nothing.

Peace.

Chapter Fifteen

He'd shown Sam the knife before cutting his throat. Let him see the glistening steel shining in the cold light of a Manchester day.

He hadn't recognised it at all – why should he? The fact it was the same knife as the one Sam had pulled on him all those years ago simply passed him by in a haze of Spice.

The drugs had him now. Had him deep in their grip.

Giving him the fifty-quid note had been the catalyst, as he knew it would be. Within seconds, Sam was rushing off to his dealer to score. Following him back to his little bolthole on the building site was easy. Letting him settle for a few minutes while the drugs took effect, and then it was time to strike.

The area Sam had chosen for his little drug den was perfect. A small back alley not far from the city centre, surrounded by abandoned buildings. There was just one CCTV camera covering a doorway opposite. That was simple to avoid; just lift his bag to cover his face.

He doubted whether the police would even check the cameras. For them, it would be just another homeless death. A bunsen killed by his own desire for drugs. And he would leave enough clues to help them come to that conclusion.

Sam hadn't even lifted his head when he stood in front of him. He was deep in the Spice hole. A zombie in all but name.

It was time for him to burn.

It had always been time for him to burn.

He splashed the meths over the body, making sure the face was well soaked, and put the bottle down close to the body.

He remembered Sam's laughing face. The eyes sparkling, the teeth white and the mouth pink. Well, he wouldn't be smiling any more.

Not any more.

He stepped back and took out the lighter and the wooden spill from his bag. He lit the long match, watched the yellow-orange flame take hold, and then tossed it onto Sam's clothes.

The flames took hold immediately. They travelled up in a blue wave to the face and hands, feasting on the subcutaneous fat and tissue.

The scent of Sam was delicious. A wonderful aroma of roasting flesh, like the best roast pork on earth.

He tossed the lighter onto the body and waited for it to explode. The pop, when it came, was disappointing. He had expected more. Tommy Larkin had been much better.

A sound on his left. The door to the building site was being scraped against the ground.

'Hello, Sam, are you there, Sam?'

A man's voice.

He picked up his bag and ducked behind the large bin, pulling out his ball-peen hammer.

If he came too close that would be the end of him. Shame, he didn't like killing people. That wasn't part of the plan.

The sound of footsteps. Slow, dragging footsteps.

'Sam, I know you're here. You gonna share your gear?'

The footsteps stopped.

He raised the hammer and was about to jump out and bring it down on whoever was standing there.

But all he heard was a long drawn-out 'Nooooooo', followed by footsteps running away, the feet no longer dragging.

Time to get back to work before the hue and cry was raised. He could come back and finish the job later.

He had to leave the message, didn't he?

Chapter Sixteen

It was well past noon before they reached the doctor's surgery.

'We're here to see a Dr Marshall.' Ridpath and Pleasance stood in front of the reception desk. Behind them a row of seats held three patients, two of them coughing.

God, Ridpath hated going to these places. Nine months of traipsing in and out of them had put him off for life. He would have to go back soon, though, for another check-up.

The receptionist looked up from her computer. 'Do you have an appointment?'

'My name is Ridpath, I'm from the coroner's office. This is Detective Constable Pleasance. We're here about one of Dr Marshall's patients, a Mr Joseph Brennan.'

The receptionist tapped her computer. 'He's just come in, so he's very busy at the moment, but I'll try to squeeze you in before the next appointment. If you'd like to take a seat...'

Ridpath looked back again at the row of chairs and chose one that was as far away from the coughing people as possible. The last thing he needed at the moment was a lung infection. If he caught something, he would have to go back to hospital once again. It was one of the complications of having a cancer like myeloma. Doctors were always scared a minor infection might develop into something far more serious. Even if he had a cold, he was supposed to go running back to Christies.

Pleasance sat down next to him. 'Thanks for all the help yesterday. It was the first time Wharton hadn't bollocked me since I went to work at Cheadle Hulme.'

'Thanks for the credit.'

Pleasance looked shocked. 'You told me not to give you any credit. Remember?'

'I liked the line about "being informed of the enquiries".'

'I thought it was good too. Do you and Wharton have history?'

'You could say that.'

Pleasance stared at him. 'Well?'

'You can go in now, gentlemen.' The receptionist spoke before Ridpath could answer. She pointed at a door at the end of the corridor. Ridpath knocked on it, heard someone say 'Enter' and went in.

Dr Marshall was standing in front of his desk. He was a tall, elegant man in his late thirties, with salt and pepper hair extending past the collar of his white lab coat, a stethoscope hanging out of his pocket. 'You're from the police? Please sit down.'

Out of habit, Ridpath stuck out his hand.

The doctor stared down at it. 'Sorry, I never shake hands. You never know where they've been.' His voice was sharp and cutting, a voice lacking warmth. He walked behind his desk, stopping for a moment to depress the top of an antimicrobial hand gel standing next to some football trophies. As he rubbed the white foam into his hands, he said, 'What can I do for you?'

Ridpath sat down while Pleasance took out his notebook. 'My name is Ridpath, I'm from the coroner's office, and this is DC Pleasance. We're here about one of your patients. A Mr Joseph Brennan.'

'Coroner's office? I don't remember signing a notice of death form for a Mr Brennan.'

'You didn't. He died last night and we are trying to determine if the death was suicide or a possible murder.'

He swivelled round to his computer and tapped a name into it, scanning the screen. 'And how can I help you?'

'We'd like to know what you were treating him for.'

'How do you know I was treating him?'

Pleasance brought out his phone and showed the doctor the picture of the medicine bottle with the pharmacy's name on it. 'Did you prescribe these tablets for him?'

He smiled. 'As you well know, patient medical records are confidential. If you'd like to see them, you need to get a court order.'

Pleasance leant forward. 'Actually, that's not true. Under Section 29 of the Data Protection Act 2018, Mr Brennan is supposed to give his consent, but as he is deceased, I am informing you that disclosure of his medical records is in the public interest.' He reached into his jacket pocket and pulled out an envelope. 'I am providing you with written confirmation of this request and, as we are on the premises of your practice, there will be no fee for viewing the records.' He handed the envelope to Dr Marshall.

Ridpath was staring at him.

'What?'

'That was almost intelligent,' he whispered.

'Learnt it on a Data Protection Course. You should keep up to date, Ridpath.'

The doctor read the letter. 'OK, what do you want to know?'

'What were you treating Mr Brennan for?'

He scanned his notes. 'General depression. He'd lost his job...'

'When was that?'

He checked his computer again. 'The last time I saw him was just over three years ago. April 9, 2016, to be precise.'

'He hasn't seen you since?'

He shook his head. 'It would be on here if he had.'

'Could another doctor have seen him?'

'Perhaps, but not at this practice. I didn't refer him to a specialist at that time. Just prescribed Valium and an antidepressant.'

'If he saw a psychiatrist, would you know?'

'I should know. If the psychiatrist was in the NHS, he would request a copy of the medical records from me. But there's no note to that effect in my records.'

'Can you tell us anything about him?'

He stared at his screen. 'Not a lot really. I've been here twelve years and I saw him twice in that time.' He scratched his nose with his right hand. 'To be honest with you, I can't even remember what he looks like. Too many patients.' He carried on scrolling through his records on the computer.

Ridpath could imagine the footfall at a busy GP's surgery would be horrendous. But he also knew enough about body language to recognise the doctor had just lied to him. The scratch of the nose and the words 'to be honest' were such a giveaway.

Then the doctor stopped scrolling. 'That's interesting. Now I remember him.'

'What is it?'

'He had an accident when he was young, extensive scarring on his body. I remember him telling me, spent two months in hospital…'

Ridpath knew what spending a long time in hospital felt like, and there was only one word to describe it. Hell. 'Anything else?'

Dr Marshall finally looked at him. 'No, that's it, nothing more.'

'Was he disabled in any way?'

The doctor went back to his notes. 'No. In his case, there was no permanent disability. Other than the scarring, he was a perfectly normal adult suffering from depression after losing his job. Half my patients are the same.'

'Thanks for your time, Doctor. If you could print out his records, we would be grateful.'

He frowned for a moment. 'Is that really necessary?'

'I'm afraid so…' Ridpath glanced across at Pleasance before continuing. 'In the public interest, you know.'

Dr Marshall sat silently for a second before tapping on his keyboard. 'You said this man has passed away?'

Ridpath nodded.

'Can you send me a copy of the death certificate?'

'No problem, once we've completed the post-mortem.'

'Thanks. The receptionist will give you his records. There isn't much, I'm afraid.'

'Thank you once again for your time.' Ridpath reached out once again to shake the doctor's hand and then withdrew his arm quickly.

The man smiled and immediately went back to the soap dispenser, as if merely being offered a handshake would contaminate him.

Outside, Ridpath and Pleasance collected the printouts and then walked out together to their cars. 'That was a waste of time,' said the detective constable, lighting a cigarette.

Ridpath smelled the aroma of a Marlboro waft across his nostrils. The smell brought an instant hit of nostalgia combined with a quick flash of good times stood outside a pub with a pint in one hand and a cigarette in another. Despite not having smoked since his bout of pneumonia, the desire for a cigarette never left Ridpath, like a cat prowling in a corner of his mind.

He coughed and checked his watch. Should he tell Pleasance the doctor had lied about something? No point, and he might be wrong anyway. Perhaps the doctor had seen something in the records that shouldn't have been there. Never mind, he should head back to the coroner's office.

'I wonder what he was doing for the three years since he left his job.'

'I've got an appointment with the DWP at two o'clock. Perhaps they found him work.'

'Any luck finding relatives?'

Pleasance shook his head. 'Nothing so far.' He checked the medical file. 'And there's no next of kin on these. Perhaps DWP will have a name.'

'Aye, and pigs might fly. How long has Wharton given you on this?'

'Till the end of today, and then he wants me looking for the missing postman.'

'Perhaps the postie's done a runner with a parcel.'

They reached Ridpath's car. Pleasance paused for a moment before asking, 'What do you think the verdict will be?'

'About Joseph Brennan?'

Pleasance nodded.

'We'll have to wait on the post-mortem, but at the moment it looks like the coroner would probably return an open verdict. We can't prove or disprove it was suicide. It may even have been an accident.'

'And murder?'

'Doesn't look like it, unless the forensics reveal something. No suspects. No history of visitors to the flat. No reason for a murder.' Ridpath opened his car door. 'You coming to the post-mortem?'

'Dead bodies? Bits of liver? A heart on a tray? No thanks, it'd put me off my dinner.'

'OK, if he finds anything I'll let you and Wharton know.'

'Thanks, Ridpath. Fancy some lunch? There's a great little chippy round the corner.'

'Nah, I'd better get back, too much to do.' He went to shake hands and then pulled his hand back. 'As the good doctor said, I don't know where you've been, Ron.'

Chapter Seventeen

Sergeant John Bohannon wasn't having the best of days. His back was killing him, his feet hurt, his left knee was giving him gyp again, and he had a headache the size of Moss Side.

Not only that, but he was stuck with Bruce Connor as his partner. Now Bruce was a good copper and a great mate, but on a bad day they could bottle his farts and sell them to British Gas.

Today was a bad day.

Bohannon had told him not to have the curry for lunch, but did he listen? Did he buggery. And now Bohannon was suffering the consequences.

But despite this, it was about to get much worse.

They were cruising down London Road, heading away from the city centre, and had just passed Piccadilly Station. His shift had just seventy minutes left. He was planning to go straight home, take a handful of Nurofen, close the curtains and spend the rest of the day in bed, when the call came through on the radio.

'Incident reported at Back Piccadilly. Two-three-five, please respond. Over.'

'OK, Dispatch. What is the nature of the incident?'

'Unknown, over. Woman screaming, corner of Back Piccadilly and China Lane. Over.'

'We're off duty soon, Dispatch.'

'I am aware, two-three-five. Nobody else available.'

'OK, ETA five minutes. Over.' He switched the sirens on and swung the car into the outside lane.

'We got a job, Bruce.'

'But we're off soon.'

Bohannon shrugged. 'Sod's law.' He moved the car across the traffic, ignoring the large 'no U-turn' sign under the flyover. One of the perks of having the blues and twos blaring like a banshee was the rules no longer applied. Within reason, of course.

Bohannon was far too old a hand to get caught out breaking them now. Not when a comfortable retirement and pension after thirty years' service was just two years away.

He accelerated back towards town. The bloody one-way system changed every five minutes these days and the roadworks on Oxford Road had screwed things up even more.

Left along Aytoun Street, bending round to Auburn Street, cars pulling to one side to get out of his way, except for one stupid bugger in a Toyota who thought he owned the road. Bohannon gave the siren an extra buzz to wake the dozy bugger up.

Left on Piccadilly, heading towards the Gardens, picking up speed now, people stopping to watch the car as it sped past. Right along Lena Road? No, Paton Road was closer. He accelerated again, signalled right and stopped. Some stupid planner had put up two large 'no entry' signs.

'What the…' he shouted, checking his rear-view mirror. He put the gears in reverse and began accelerating back to Lena Road.

'Bloody hell, Sarge, what's got into you?'

Luckily nothing was coming the other way. He skidded to a halt and swung the car down Lena Road, turning left into Back Piccadilly. Across Paton Street to Back Piccadilly again. More bloody 'no entry' signs.

'Bugger it,' he said out loud, accelerating down the lane, hoping nothing was coming the other way.

The lane was narrow, room for only one car. A small crowd was up ahead.

He parked the car on the pavement next to a graffitied hoarding covered in posters displaying the latest acts coming to Manchester and the various DJ nights at clubs across the city: Creamfields, Fat Freddy's Drop, Juicy at the Black Dog Ballroom, Relapse at Rebellion, and even an Anarchy night at Percy Pig's, whatever one of those was. He was a Smiths man himself. Proper music, none of this drum and bass druggie stuff.

Time to be calm, take control.

'You block the road, Bruce, while I go and see what this is all about.'

'Right-o, Sarge.'

Bohannon slowly stepped out of the car, taking his time to put on his cap as he assessed the situation. The crowd, just six people actually, parted to let him see the woman in their midst, standing next to a PCSO. Her shoulders heaved as sobs racked her body. Her eyes were rimmed red and black mascara streaked her face.

'Can we stand back, please, give the lady some room,' he ordered.

The people shuffled backwards but still kept close enough to hear what was going on.

Bohannon spoke to the woman directly. 'What's up, love? What happened?'

She shuffled once more, pushing her fringe away from her eyes. 'I... I...'

'It's all right, take your time.'

'She saw something in there.' The PCSO pointed to the building site hidden by the hoardings.

'And you are?'

'PCSO Clive Tennant. I was just passing when I heard her screaming as she ran out of the alley.' The PCSO put his arm around the woman's shoulder. Bohannon was about to comment on it when she began to speak again.

'I... I...' The words seemed to catch in her throat.

'You saw something in there?'

She nodded – it was easier than speaking.

'And what's your name?'

The woman's chest heaved for a few moments as she caught her breath. 'It's… Cathy, Cathy Newman.'

Bohannon glanced down the road. Another squad car had arrived and Dave was helping them set up a row of orange-and-white traffic cones to block the entrance. He could wait or he could check it out himself.

'What did you see?' he asked the woman.

She shook her head and began to cry once more.

He tried to peer over the hoardings but they were just a bit taller than him. The gate on the left was still open. He walked over to it, trying to be deliberate and controlled in his movements. He stopped at the gate. Everybody was looking at him.

He peered in.

Nothing but a few bins overflowing with rubbish. On the right, a pile of old bathroom tiles, some rotting carpets, and weeds growing in profusion.

He leant forward. What was that smell? Like a kebab shop on a busy Friday night.

He stepped into the building site to get a better look.

Still nothing.

'I think it's beside the bins. That's what she told me earlier.' The PCSO's voice. Clive Tennant.

Bohannon stepped forward towards a pile of dirty clothes. A thin trail of grey smoke was rising from them.

'What the hell?'

He went forward one more step and then stopped. He coughed and tried to cover his nose, swallowing the bile that had risen in his throat.

A blackened body lay on its side, the flesh still smoking slightly, like a black polystyrene mannequin in a department store. A foot away, an empty bottle lay next to the blackened feet.

83

He knew then that he wouldn't be having a quiet nap this afternoon.

'Dispatch. Over.'

The Airwave crackled. 'Come in, two-three-five.'

'There's a dead body. Looks like a dosser has set fire to himself while drinking meths. Requesting assistance ASAP to keep the crowds away, and we have a highly distressed woman. Over.'

'Is he dead? Over.'

Bohannon checked out the body again. He couldn't help but notice the cigarette was still clamped between the blackened fingers of the right hand. A charred corpse of a cigarette.

'As a dodo, Dispatch,' he finally answered.

Chapter Eighteen

'Er, Ridpath, they've just called us for the meeting.'

Ridpath shook his head. Sophia was standing next to him, nudging his shoulder.

'Sure, just coming.' He picked up his coffee and followed Sophia into the meeting room. It was their regular work-in-progress meeting to catch up with the ongoing cases. Mrs Challinor was already there, sitting at the head of the table.

'So glad you could join us, Ridpath. Shall we begin?'

He could feel his face warming. That was the second time it had happened. What was it about him and meetings?

Jenny Oldfield was handing out the work-in-progress sheets. This afternoon she was wearing bright green eyeshadow and a purple gingham dress. Everybody else was dressed in various shades of black and grey.

'Can we be quick today? I have to leave early this afternoon.' Carol Oates, on Jenny's left, had her blonde hair up in a tight chignon, the colour offsetting the deep black of her jacket.

'Oh?' said Mrs Challinor, one eyebrow raised.

'I have a meeting in town.' That was it, no other explanation.

'We will try to accommodate you, but we must treat these work-in-progress meetings with the respect they deserve.'

'I just—' began Carol Oates, before being interrupted by Mrs Challinor.

'Are you OK for time, David?'

David Smail was a part-time coroner from Derbyshire. It was one of the stranger aspects of the coronial system that coroners from different districts often worked in other districts part-time, being paid extra. Margaret Challinor helped out in Central Manchester.

Although Ridpath often wondered, if they were working full-time elsewhere, how did they find the time? It was like an inspector from GMP working for Cheshire Police on his days off.

'I'm fine today. No problems.'

'And Ridpath, Jenny tells me you are finally up to date with your paperwork?'

'All thanks to Sophia.' His new assistant looked down at the table, carefully avoiding the eyes looking at her.

'Good, let's get started. The Murphy case. You're handling that, Carol?'

'The inquest is set for May 4. Should be no problem. An open and shut case of suicide.'

'You concur, Ridpath?'

'I've looked into it. The pilot had just split up with his wife, developed a gambling problem and was about to lose his job with the airline. There were no suspicious circumstances in his death.'

'The family have been notified of the inquest?'

'They will be attending with their solicitors, Dean and Bramham,' said Sophia, speaking for the first time.

'Those ambulance chasers. Make sure everything is buttoned up, Carol.'

'Will do.'

'Moving along. Treasure Trove. A metal detectorist, Scott Bevan, found a hoard of gold coins in a field between the Mersey and Chester Road. David, you're handling the hearing?'

'Yes, Margaret. It seems all above board. The trove was reported to the archaeological officer for Greater Manchester and a dig is being planned in the area for next year.'

'Keep an eye on this one, the press are onto it. Usual gold fever.'

The meeting continued in the same vein for the next couple of hours. The progress of existing cases was monitored, and decisions made on which deaths needed to be investigated and which could be disregarded.

Just before the meeting came to a close, Jenny's assistant entered the room and gave her a sheet of paper. Jenny scanned it and passed it on to Mrs Challinor.

'Something's just come in, Ridpath. One for you perhaps?'

Ridpath nodded. 'Now that I'm up to date with the paperwork, I can get on with my real job.'

'Your real job is to be up to date with the paperwork and your investigations,' said Mrs Challinor.

Ridpath stayed silent. He'd just been effectively admonished, but he knew she was right. If they weren't on top of the minutiae of the coroner's office, grieving families would suffer. Much as he hated the bureaucracy of death, it was part of his job. Luckily, Sophia was very good at it.

His thoughts were interrupted by Carol Oates. 'How is Claire Trent these days?'

Why was Carol asking him about the head of MIT? Why was she suddenly interested in his other boss?

'Fine, I think, busy as usual. I was there earlier today, and the team seems stretched. There's been a couple of armed robberies – a post office and a pawn shop – plus a stabbing in Bolton town centre between drug gangs. And they're deeply involved in the county lines investigations. Why do you ask?'

'No reason. Just curious,' she answered, pushing a stray hair that had escaped from her chignon behind her ear.

Before he could ask her another question, Mrs Challinor closed her file and stood up. 'Right, we're finished for today. Looks like you're going to make your meeting, Carol.'

Carol Oates smiled but said nothing.

'Ridpath, could you come to my office for a minute?'

'Of course, Mrs Challinor.'

As Carol Oates left the room, Ridpath could only stare after her. What was she up to?

Chapter Nineteen

Detective Sergeant Ted Jones knelt down beside the blackened body. He was wearing bright blue evidence gloves he kept in the car.

'Not a nice way to die.'

Jones glanced up at Sergeant Bohannon. 'Bunsens never are, John.'

The mortuary boys were hovering at the entrance ready to take the corpse away. Next to them, PC Bruce Connor was making sure the small crowd that had gathered stayed well back.

'Bunsens?' Bohannon asked.

'Bunsen burners. Like in the old school chemistry labs.' Jones shrugged. 'Dunno who started calling them that.'

'Subtle,' said Bohannon under his breath.

'Looks like he was drinking the meths and decided to light a spliff to give himself a bit more buzz. And poof, bonfire night in the middle of April. Where's the witness?'

'Over there. You won't get much out her. Heard nothing. Saw nothing. Smelled burning so she came in to take a look.'

'The gate was open?'

Bohannon nodded. 'A few roaches and a sleeping bag in the corner. Looks like it was one of his regular places to doss down.'

'Any ID?'

'On somebody like him? I doubt it.'

Tentatively, Jones lifted the burnt fabric of a coat with his fingertips. Flakes of blackened skin fell from the scorched face. His hand jerked back. 'Doesn't look like he's got any,' he said quickly.

He stood up and took one last look at the corpse, still with the roasted spliff between its fingers. 'You completed the incident report?'

Bohannon handed it over. Jones scanned it quickly. 'Looks good. I'd better have a quick chat with the witness, you know the boss is going to check.'

'He always does.'

Jones stuck his hands in his pockets and wandered through the gate to where Cathy Newman was sipping a Costa coffee, standing next to a PCSO. He took out his notebook, still wearing the bright blue gloves. 'You discovered the body?'

Cathy nodded. 'When can I go? I'm late back for work.'

Jones ignored the question. 'Did you see anybody else in the vicinity?'

'What? In there?' She pointed to the building site. 'No, just him.'

'Why did you go in?'

'I work in the local betting shop and thought I'd come down here for a quick ciggie. Anyway, as I got close, I smelled something...'

'What was it?'

Cathy reddened and then looked down.

Ted Jones asked again. 'What was it?'

'Well, it smelled like Sunday dinner. You know, a roast...' She stopped speaking once again.

'So you went inside the building site.'

She nodded. 'I thought it smelled so good. Reminded me of my mum's cooking. But then I went in and saw—' She looked down again and began to cry.

The PCSO put his arm around Cathy's shoulders. 'It's all right, love, let it all out.'

When she had calmed down a little, Jones continued. 'Did you see anybody else around here?'

Cathy shook her head. 'Just him. Lying there. There was still blue flames coming from the body.' She sobbed loudly.

'Thanks for your help. Clive here will take you home.' Jones nodded at the PCSO.

Cathy suddenly looked up as if remembering something. 'I did bump into somebody in the alley.'

'Who?'

'Another homeless man. He was in a hurry.'

'Would you recognise him again?'

She shook her head. 'Not really, well, they all look the same, don't they? And I never really looked at him.'

'Was he coming out of the building site?'

'No, I told you. It was at the end of the alley.'

'I think I saw somebody hanging round the alley earlier too,' interrupted the PCSO.

'Did you know him, Clive?'

'Didn't really look, I'm afraid. A lot of the homeless hang around here. Plenty of quiet places to smoke or shoot up in.'

Jones rolled his eyes. 'Don't I know it.'

'Listen, when can I go back to work?'

'You've given us your name, address and telephone number?'

'Twice already.'

'OK, you can leave now. We may need to contact you later.'

'Why?'

'Just to tidy up any loose ends. My boss is a bit of a stickler for doing stuff by the book.'

'One of those.'

'Aye, they're in the police too.'

'They're bloody everywhere.'

'Clive will walk you back if you want.'

'Nah, I'm OK. It's the betting shop just down the road.' She smiled, her eyes red-rimmed. 'Something to tell the punters, I guess.'

Jones turned away and nodded to the mortuary attendants. 'You can take him away.'

'Any name?'

'Couldn't find any ID. If you find anything, let me know.'

'Will do. We'll put him down as a John Doe.'

Sergeant Bohannon joined the group. 'We're done, Ted?'

'Aye, John. Make sure a copy of the incident report goes to my boss in Manchester Central. And don't forget the coroner.'

'No problem. Not bothering with a post-mortem?'

'No point. Just another tramp who died on the streets. Meths in one hand and a spliff in the other.'

'There'll be a lot more by the end of the year with all the Spice that's around.'

'Just hope I'm not on call next time. I'm off back to the nick, John. Don't forget the incident report or my boss will be kicking my bollocks from here to the Etihad.'

'Knowing you, Ted, you'd enjoy it.'

'He bloody would, that's for sure.'

Jones strolled to his old Audi parked behind the police squad car. He had three other cases to follow up before his shift ended and nobody was going to complete the paperwork for him.

He took one last look at the scene.

He hated bunsens. Left an awful smell on his clothes. Now he'd have to get them dry-cleaned. More bloody expense that he couldn't claim back.

He shook his head, muttering to himself as he climbed into the car and switched on the radio. An announcer was reading the news.

'*More fires have been reported on the moors above Marsden, spreading as far as Buckstones Reservoir. Firefighters are hoping the forecast rains come soon—*'

He switched it off. 'More bloody fires,' he said out loud, 'seems like they're everywhere these days.' He chuckled to himself. 'Must be that bloody global warming they're always banging on about.' He picked up the Airwave. 'This is Ted Jones, on the way back to the nick, Dispatch. The John Doe looks like an accidental death and the body has been sent to the mortuary.'

'OK, Ted, the boss is looking for you.'

'What's he want now?'

'Another burglary in the Northern Quarter. He wants you to look into it.'

'OK, give me the address, Dispatch, and can you do me a favour?'

'Sure, Ted.'

'Save me some of the roast pork from the canteen. I'm starving...'

Chapter Twenty

'Sit down, please.' Mrs Challinor pointed to the chair in front of her desk.

Ridpath wondered what he had done wrong this time. Were the forms wrong? Had he forgotten to inform a family of an inquest? Was Mrs Challinor going to send him back to MIT?

If she was, he could live with that. He missed the camaraderie of the police force: all working together to solve a case and put the perp away. But after today's meeting, he didn't know if he still had a job there with all the changes Claire Trent had introduced since Charlie Whitworth's accident.

He made a mental note to visit his old boss. He was now in a wheelchair and housebound following the accident during the Connolly case. Officially, he was still on sick leave, but there was no way he was going back to GMP, even in a desk job.

Mrs Challinor coughed. 'You're miles away, Ridpath.'

'Thinking about Charlie Whitworth.'

'How is he?'

'Not good, last time I saw him.'

'The accident?'

'Not handling it well.'

She nodded once. Ridpath knew she would get to the point now. Mrs Challinor was not one for small talk.

'I need you to do something for me.' She pushed the paper Jenny Oldfield had given her across the table. 'That case I mentioned. A body in central Manchester. Can you get on it straight away?'

The paper was from the Central Manchester coroner. On it was the notice of death with a sketchy police report. 'I thought this wasn't our patch.'

'We're helping out. They're stretched because of the inquests into the Arena bombings.'

There were few details. A death near Piccadilly, the victim a middle-aged man burnt to death.

'The bunsen?'

'What?'

'Bunsen burner. People who set themselves alight. Usually homeless living on the streets.'

Mrs Challinor looked appalled. 'That's horrible, Ridpath.'

'Gallows humour. Sorry, shouldn't have used it.'

'These are people, not just bodies or victims or bits of flesh on a mortuary slab. Always remember that, Ridpath.'

Even Ridpath knew he had crossed a line. 'Sorry, it won't happen again.'

Mrs Challinor mumbled something under her breath and then spoke directly to him. 'Look into it, will you? Make it a priority.'

'Really? These accidents happen all the time on the streets. A homeless man gets drunk and falls asleep with a fag in his hand. Or he gets out of it and forgets he's got a bottle of spirits close by…' He didn't finish the sentence, merely shrugged his shoulders.

Mrs Challinor's jaw was clenched. 'I'd still like you to look into it.'

'But the workload is pretty horrendous at the moment. I'll get on it just as soon as I'm free.'

'I'd like you to look into it now, this evening.' The order was polite but it was still an order.

'This evening? But it's nearly four already. It'll be dark in an hour or two.'

Mrs Challinor held up two fingers. 'Two reasons. David Smail told me about a similar case in Bakewell a couple of days ago.'

'Out in the Peak District?'

She nodded.

'Can't be many homeless out there.'

'You'd be surprised. These days, there are homeless everywhere.'

'Cause of death?'

'Same as this man. Burnt to death. You know I'm a stickler for deaths where we see the same pattern recurring.'

Mrs Challinor still felt guilt over the Harold Shipman case, even though it wasn't her area at that time. The doctor had managed to kill over two hundred people, mainly older women, without anybody realising and with no red flags being raised in the coroner's office. She was determined that nothing like that would ever happen again.

'And the second reason?'

Mrs Challinor pushed her glasses back onto the bridge of her nose. Her head came down and she spoke softly. 'It's personal.'

'Meaning?'

Her head whipped up and she stared straight at him. 'It's my younger brother – he's living on the streets.'

Ridpath's mouth fell open. 'You have a family member living on the streets?'

She nodded slowly.

'But… but you don't look the type…'

'And what type is that, Ridpath?'

He felt himself redden. 'I mean, these people usually come from broken homes or have suffered abuse or…'

'And I'm a typical middle-class woman with a good job, and these sort of things never happen to people like me?'

'No, I don't…'

'My brother was fine till about five years ago, then his wife left him. He went on the bottle, lost his job and his house, the kids didn't want to see him and he sort of spiralled down from there.'

Ridpath felt like an idiot. 'I'm sorry. Do you know where he is?'

'Last reports were in the centre of Manchester.'

'Couldn't you help him?'

'I tried, but people have to want to be helped. He spent three months inside Strangeways for petty larceny and managed to pick up a Spice habit as well as a criminal record.'

'Not good. Do you want me to find him?'

She shook her head. 'No point, he doesn't want to see me anyway.' Then she paused for a moment. 'You see, I was the person who turned him in. He stole from me. I thought prison would be a short, sharp shock, turn him around...'

'Most prisoners come out worse than when they went in. If they didn't have a drug habit before prison, they will have afterwards.'

'So you see, it's personal, Ridpath. I want to find out if anything is happening to these people. Two similar cases are two too many as far as I am concerned.'

'I'll take a look at it this evening. Do we have the incident report yet?'

She shook her head, checking the document. 'The Senior Investigating Officer is a Detective Sergeant Jones...'

'Ted Jones? Not the smartest tool in the woodshed, but at least he's thorough. His boss makes sure he is. I'll follow up. Can you get me details of the Bakewell death too?'

'I'll ask David Smail to send them over.'

'I'll take a look at the scene this evening, but I don't think I'll find anything. People dying on the streets don't normally leave much...'

He didn't finish his sentence. 'Thank you.'

Ridpath nodded.

Mrs Challinor pulled a file from her in tray and began to read through it.

The meeting was definitely over.

Chapter Twenty-One

After Ridpath left her office, a wave of tiredness swept over Margaret Challinor. It had been a long week. She had just finished a case that day involving the death of an alcoholic woman in hospital. The woman had somehow fallen through the cracks in the system, despite having a long history of alcohol abuse.

Everybody had followed the correct procedures in the case. The doctor had referred her to an alcohol treatment centre but not followed up. The centre had put a plan down on paper but not implemented it. Her social worker had visited her once and then resigned with the post left unfilled. A hospital case worker had made a note about the urgency of her case and then done nothing.

The woman, Elsie Richards, had collapsed in the street one Saturday morning, was taken to hospital immediately but died from liver failure the next day.

Since the 2013 Coronial Act, Mrs Challinor no longer passed a verdict at the end of an inquest. Instead she now made a 'finding of fact'. And the facts in this case were that nobody had got off their arses and done something. They had all filled in their forms, ticked their boxes, made sure their bums were covered and, in effect, achieved nothing.

It made her furious that not one person had stopped for a second to actually help this woman suffering from the sad disease of alcoholism. She began to draft a letter to the Director of Social Services, the head of the local NHS trust and Uncle Tom Cobley and all, to ensure this never happened again.

Not on her watch.

It would make her even more unpopular than she already was, but she didn't care. People mattered, not the fragile ego of some pen-pushing bureaucrat.

She rubbed her eyes, pushing the half-written letter away from her. It could wait until tomorrow when she was in a less caustic, more considered frame of mind. What she wanted was to see change, not force people into justifying their behaviour or the actions of their department. She should write something more helpful and less accusatory.

Ridpath popped into her mind. Should she ask him to use his contacts to help find Robert? Would it be an imposition on him? Even worse, would it be a misuse of her authority asking for a personal favour? She would have to think it over.

A knock on the door.

'Come,' she called out.

Jenny Oldfield, the office manager, appeared at the door. 'Just a few requisitions for you to sign before I go. We need paper, folders, and the upstairs hall light fixing.'

The usual council stuff, forms in triplicate, and boxes ticked for even the smallest expenditure. The coroner's court was not funded by central government or the Ministry of Justice. Instead, her office was paid for by the local council. And, like every other local authority in England, austerity had bitten into her funding. She had managed to find an assistant for Ridpath by asking Claire Trent to continue to pay his salary. Not the best solution, but it had worked so far.

'Can you ask Ridpath to see me before he goes?'

'He's already left, Mrs Challinor. A death in central Manchester. You asked him to look at it this evening.'

She was becoming forgetful in her old age. For a second, her mind flashed to her younger brother living on the streets, his hand held out for money, his fingers grubby with dirt, and a bottle of cheap wine by his side.

Should she look for him this weekend?

She had done it before. Walking the streets on a Sunday night in Manchester, checking on the places the homeless gathered to drink and gossip and fight. She had been shocked by the feral nature of their lives; the dirt, the poverty, the way in which drugs or alcohol dominated every waking moment.

She hadn't found him then and she doubted if she could find him now. She thought again about asking Ridpath to help find Robert. But no, it would not be ethical, she decided. This was a personal matter, not a case for the coroner's court.

Another image flashed into her mind. This time of her and Robert on the hills in the Peak District one winter long ago. Snow painting the hillsides a bright white, their mother helping them carry an old sled to the top of the hill. Her brother, six years old at most, sitting between her legs as they set off down the hill. His squeals of joy, the wind in her hair, the rush of speed as they slid down, overturning at the bottom, both ending up covered in white, wet, cold Derbyshire snow.

A perfect day.

Before he lost his life to alcohol and drugs.

Before he lost his wife.

Before he lost his kids.

Before he lost himself.

'I'll be going, Mrs Challinor.'

She shook her head and was immediately brought back to the present day. 'Fine, Jenny, see you tomorrow.'

'I'm off to my swing class tonight, the teacher moves like a dream.' Jenny batted her green-painted eyes. 'Don't work too late.'

'I won't. I'm going soon myself.'

'You have the Rafferty case tomorrow morning. I've left the brief and the notes on your desk.'

Mrs Challinor glanced down at the beige folder that was the life and death of Nora Rafferty, a pensioner who had died of hypothermia. How could such a thing happen in this day and age? 'I'll read them this evening.'

'Good night,' Jenny said breezily, closing the door.

Mrs Challinor was left alone in her office. A faint hum from the central heating system the only noise. Outside her sash window, the wind whistled through the trees. Her thoughts drifted once more to her brother.

What was he doing on this cold night?

Chapter Twenty-Two

Ridpath parked the car at Piccadilly Basin. Four pounds fifty for two bloody hours on a derelict piece of land. A rip-off and everybody knew it. But parking in the city centre always was.

He walked across the cobbles, exiting through an old crenellated gateway, a strange entrance for a car park, probably all that was left of some grand Victorian building.

This case was probably a waste of time, but in the time they had worked together, Ridpath had come to respect Mrs Challinor's instincts. She had an almost hyper awareness of possible anomalies in the deaths in Manchester. A function of Harold Shipman and his murders, he guessed.

Pulling his overcoat around him, he checked the address where the body had been found against Google Maps on his phone. The wind hustled off the Pennines and whistled through the open streets. Across the road, an old woman was pushing an empty trolley down the street. Ridpath wondered where she was going, there was nowhere to shop around here. After five o'clock, this whole area shut down, becoming a ghost town full of memories from a different era.

He tucked the scarf Polly had given him around his neck and turned right down Dale Street, past blocks of red-brick Victorian buildings, relics from the days when Manchester was the trading centre of the North.

Left along China Lane. It was dark now and there were no street lamps to mark his way. But there was enough ambient light to see what was going on. Ambient light that had an orange tinge to it, like looking through a bottle of Lucozade.

An afternoon shower had coated the road with a sheen of dirty water. Puddles pooled in the potholes and in the gaps in the flagstones. Ridpath picked his way carefully. The last thing he needed at that moment was wet feet.

He had already phoned Polly to tell her he would be back late that evening. She hadn't been happy but had said nothing. He was keeping to his promise of always letting her know where he was and she was managing (just) to avoid being too hard on him. It had worked for the last six months and the truce seemed to be holding. You had to work at a marriage, and he was determined not to make the same mistakes he had made before. Polly and Eve were far too precious for such stupidity.

He stepped over a pile of old clothes next to a large puddle. One of the homeless had staked his claim to a recess in the brick wall, placing an old sleeping bag and some rags on top of a flattened cardboard box. The man was nowhere to be seen, though. Was this the John Doe's stuff? Or did it belong to somebody else?

The windows of the building were bricked up but a large metal gate suggested that life existed in its padlocked interior. It was strange to think that just two hundred yards away was the beating heart of Manchester in Piccadilly Gardens: shops, department stores, fast-food restaurants, bookies, amusement arcades and coffee shops. All the retail outlets of a modern city.

A large rat ran across the road in front of him, jumping from the interior of a large blue and yellow bin. He shuddered. He didn't like rats. In fact, he hated them. It was their tails – long, scaly, alien.

Keep going, Ridpath, do your job.

He reached the corner of Back Piccadilly and China Lane. The building site described in the report was on the left. But calling it a building site was a bit of an exaggeration. There was no actual building going on. Just a derelict piece of ground surrounded by hoardings covered in graffiti and posters advertising bands coming to Manchester.

He noticed one advertising The Specials. Were they still going? They must all be over sixty. 'I wonder if Rudy's received the message by now,' he muttered to himself.

The whole area was as quiet as a cemetery. No passers-by walking along the alley. No workers leaving the buildings after putting in a shift. No lights anywhere.

Another shudder travelled down Ridpath's spine. 'Check it out and go straight home,' he said out loud, hearing his voice echo off the empty brick walls.

He strode to the gate. It was still open and there was no police tape preventing entry. Why would they put any up? This wasn't a crime scene, just a place where somebody had died recently.

He poked his head round the gate.

It was darker here, the ambient light didn't penetrate this far into the nether reaches of Piccadilly. He took out a torch from his pocket, shining the light on the bin on his right.

'Greater Manchester Police,' he shouted, hearing the tentative tones of his own voice.

A pair of bright, shining eyes stared at him before scuttling off into the undergrowth. He shone the light across the other bins.

No other movement.

Was this where the body had been discovered?

He shuffled slowly forward, letting the light play all around him, encouraging the rats, if there were any, to make a run for it.

He stepped in front of a bin.

At the edge of his vision, he saw something raised and then coming down towards his head. He twisted his body at the last moment, feeling the strike on the side of his neck where it met the skull.

One minute he had been awake and conscious of everything around him, the next his legs gave way and he saw himself falling in slow motion towards the rain-soaked ground.

His head hit the surface and his last thought before he lost consciousness was that was a bloody big rat.

Chapter Twenty-Three

Ridpath didn't know how long he had been out cold.

He pushed himself up into a sitting position and wiped his face with his coat sleeve. He touched the back of his head where it met the neck. There was a bump the size of Mount Everest. Luckily the skin wasn't broken, but he could already feel the headache creeping through his brain towards the temples.

Two feet away, the torch shone uselessly on the wet ground. He reached forward to pick it up and a sharp pain shot through his elbow. He must have hurt it when he fell. He grasped the torch and shone it all around.

Nobody there.

Moving gingerly, he got up from the ground, wiping down his coat and his suit trousers with his right hand. Black, wet gunk clung to it.

Shit. This is what you get for searching a crime scene in the dark: a sore head and a filthy suit.

He walked slowly back to the gate, rubbing his head the whole time. Back Piccadilly was quiet, not a soul to be seen. China Lane was empty too. His attacker had vanished into thin air.

Should he call it in?

No point. There was little chance of any police responding quickly enough to catch somebody. He wouldn't recognise whoever did it again. He didn't even have an idea of their age or height. He had only caught a glimpse of a raised arm before he had been hit over the head. If he was asked for a description, what could he say? A dark arm had attacked him.

He would be a laughing stock.

Ridpath shone his spotlight on the old building opposite. A CCTV camera pointed straight down on him. If the bloody thing was working and not a dummy, it would have filmed the perp as he left the scene.

Not for the first time, Ridpath thanked the gods for CCTV, the best thing to happen in crime enforcement in the UK for the last twenty years. And it had happened almost by accident.

He would check the footage tomorrow. With a bit of luck, he would see the person who attacked him.

What had they been doing at the building site?

Was it related to the death that afternoon or something completely different? Maybe it was just somebody looking for somewhere to doss down for the night. But if that were true, why hit him? He had identified himself as a police officer. They must have heard him.

He went back into the building site to check that nothing had dropped from his pockets when he fell over.

There was a patch of scorched ground to one side. That must have been where the John Doe had burned. But there was nothing else to be seen. Not a single indicator that a human being had died here today.

Ridpath turned to go. As he did, the torch played on the inside of the hoardings surrounding the site.

In bright orange letters, somebody had spray-painted PLAY THE GAME.

Ridpath stepped forward and touched the bottom of the last letter.

An orange smudge appeared on his fingers.

Chapter Twenty-Four

It was past eight o'clock when Ridpath reached home. As soon as he walked in the door, Polly stood up from her lesson planning and rushed to his side.

'What happened?'

'I fell over.'

She leant in and sniffed him. 'In a sewer? You'd better give me the coat, I'll take it to the dry-cleaner's tomorrow. Talking about dry-cleaning, did you pick up my dress?'

He slapped his forehead with his palm. 'Sorry, I forgot.'

'No worries, I'll pick it up tomorrow during my lunchtime and drop off this… thing.' She held the coat at arm's length. 'You'd better give me your suit too. The trousers look like they've been swimming in mud.'

'Where's Eve?'

'Upstairs, supposedly reading, but I bet she's on YouTube again.'

'Watching BTS.'

'Right first time.'

'I thought this Korean boy band stuff was just a phase she was going through.'

'You mean like me and Take That?'

'Exactly.'

'My "phase" went on for five years. And I definitely want to go to their reunion tour when it hits Liverpool. So, by my reckoning, it's lasted twenty-four years and counting…'

'We have to put up with another twenty years of girly glee about V, J-Hope and Jungkook?'

'If we're lucky. Did you book the tickets for the concert in London?'

Ridpath stayed silent.

'You forgot that too, didn't you?'

He smiled sheepishly. 'I'll do it tomorrow. Hopefully there'll be some left.' He pointed upstairs. 'I'll go and say hello.'

'Don't stay too long, I'll reheat the fish cakes. There's still a bottle of Sauvignon Blanc in the fridge too, if you want a glass or three.'

He kissed her on the lips. 'Sounds delicious. I'll just pop up to see the monster. And sorry about the tickets and the dry-cleaning.'

'Are you sure you're OK?'

He thought about telling Polly the truth about the attack but decided not to. She would only worry and that wouldn't be good for either of them. 'Me, I'm right as rain, never felt better,' he lied and ran up the stairs to see his daughter.

Ridpath stopped for a moment outside the door with a picture of BTS and a sign saying 'Keep out on pain of death', listening for movement inside.

Nothing.

He tapped on the door.

No answer.

He pushed it open. His daughter was sitting in front of her computer with her back to him, the Christmas present of purple Beats headphones clamped to her ears. He crept forward and pinched her just below her ribs. She jumped six inches into the air.

'Dad,' she shouted, whipping off her headphones, 'don't do that!'

'Do what?' he said, holding his hands up in the air as if to say it's a fair cop.

'Don't creep up on me like a perv.'

'A perv? Where did you learn that?'

'Sex education. Mum teaches it.'

'And she taught you to call people pervs, did she?'

'Well, not exactly, but she said to watch out for inappropriate behaviour from adults.'

He glanced over her shoulder, deciding to change the subject. 'What are you watching?'

She clicked the laptop and the screen went to black. 'Nothing.'

'I thought you were supposed to be doing your homework, not watching BTS?'

'Who said I was watching BTS?'

Ridpath reached over her shoulder and tapped another key. The latest video from the Korean boy band was playing.

'I've already finished my homework, it was so easy. Mum said I could watch before I went to bed.'

'She did, did she?' Ridpath pretended to leave the room. 'Shall I ask her?'

Eve sat where she was.

Ridpath was left holding the door, not exiting the room.

'You can't kid a kidder, Dad. Is that one of your police interview techniques?'

He nodded. 'One of them.'

'You're not very good at it, are you?'

He laughed. 'I suppose not. Come on down and chat with me while I eat my fish cakes.'

'Mum's specials? I would watch for the bones, she always forgets to take them out.'

'Come on.'

She glanced at the video playing on YouTube and switched it off. 'You should really get into BTS, Dad,' she said, getting up from her seat. 'They're mint.'

'Mint? Is that Trebor's or the Royal?'

She shook her head. 'Sometimes, Dad, I really don't know what you're on about.'

They went downstairs. Ridpath devoured the fish cakes, he hadn't realised how hungry he was. Eve told them all about

Jungkook and how the girls, even Molly Beamish, thought he was so dreamy. Polly sat with them both and drank two glasses of Sauvignon Blanc.

Ridpath loved being a family again, all the highs and lows of it.

But as he sat there, he couldn't stop his mind going back to the moment at the building site when he'd felt something strike his head. And it wasn't just the bump that he could still feel on his skull.

Three questions kept running inside his brain.

Who had hit him?

What the hell were they doing there?

And why had they been spraying the same words as he'd seen in Joseph Brennan's flat?

Questions that were to haunt his dreams later that night.

Chapter Twenty-Five

Using a ruler and a thick orange pen, he marked Sam's face with a large cross. Stepping back, he checked his progress. Four down, just two left.

He was nearly there, not long left now, just the adults to go.

He placed a large map of Manchester over the pictures, in case his landlady came nosying around his room when he was out, and then lay down on the boarding house's rickety bed.

On the table next to him, some stupid comedy was flickering on an old television. A comedy where the only laughter came from a machine and always sounded the same. He had turned the sound down, bored by the inanity of it all.

Still, he couldn't switch it off. Maybe after he had finished the plan he would be able to, but not at the moment.

He didn't like sleeping in the dark.

Not since that time so long ago.

His mother had always understood, never criticising him or forcing him to switch it off.

She understood. She always understood. But now she was gone, leaving him all alone.

His mind flashed back to earlier in the day. He had enjoyed killing Sam. The knife across his throat. The flames searing his skin. The intoxicating smell of burning flesh. He remembered it all.

It was beautiful.

But he would have to be more careful next time.

That copper returning to the scene had surprised him. Who would have expected him to come back, especially when it was going dark and the night was threatening rain? What was he doing there? What was he checking out? Surely they hadn't linked the deaths yet?

Never mind, he had taken care of it. A quick strike to the back of the head and the man collapsed like a house of cards.

He remembered looking down at the prostrate body for a few seconds, thinking whether to finish him off with the hammer to make sure he was dead.

But he stopped. He didn't like killing people unless it was absolutely necessary. He raised his head from the pillow, checking the bag that lay next to the TV. He had forgotten to use it to protect his face when he ran out from the building site. Hitting the copper had spooked him. He wasn't thinking clearly. Next time, he would plan it better, leave nothing to chance.

Would they check CCTV?

Probably.

But never mind. He would be finished soon. Just two left to go and then he would be free.

And so would they.

Day Four

Friday, April 26, 2019

Chapter Twenty-Six

The next morning chaos reigned in the Ridpath household yet again. Eve couldn't find her special BTS hair clip. Polly couldn't find her lesson plans and the boiler decided it didn't want to have anything to do with any of the taps in the house.

Ridpath spent twenty minutes turning it off and on, fiddling with the burner switch and checking the electrics. It still wouldn't work.

'I'll give British Gas a call to come and check it,' he told Polly.

'Won't that cost us a fortune?'

He shook his head. 'It's part of their HomeCare package. We pay a fortune for it every month, to make sure we don't pay a fortune when it goes wrong.'

Polly and Eve made do with washing their faces. Ridpath took a cold shower, enjoying the refreshing feel of the icy water across his body. A decision he was to regret as soon as he stepped out of the house. The wind was howling and Storm Hannah was blowing in from the west.

As he drove to Stockfield, he wondered how they came up with such innocuous names for such evil bouts of weather. Did they think that by calling it something fluffy, the ordinary man in the street would think the weather wasn't so bad after all?

He parked and went into the old Victorian building where the coroner's court was situated. Mrs Challinor was in already. 'Good morning,' he called out as he walked into her office.

'Morning, Ridpath,' she said, without looking up from her paperwork.

'I went to the building site last night where the body of the homeless John Doe was found.'

'How was it?'

'Dirty, decrepit, ugly. Like building sites everywhere. If you hadn't told me somebody had died, I wouldn't have known.'

'The area wasn't cordoned off?'

He shook his head.

'I'm not surprised.' She passed over an incident report. It was signed at the bottom by DS Ted Jones. The John Doe's cause of death was written as 'presumed accidental, but waiting on post-mortem report'. And later on, he seemed to have made up his mind: 'A lethal combination of drinking methylated spirits and smoking illegal drugs led to an unfortunate accident'.

'Looks like we were barking up the wrong tree, but we were right to check it out,' Mrs Challinor said.

'I'd like to carry on working on it.'

Mrs Challinor frowned. 'Why?' She tapped the incident report. 'You've read this. The SIO thinks it was an accident.'

Ridpath sat down in front of her. 'For some reason, it doesn't feel right.'

'Copper's instinct?'

Ridpath rubbed the back of his head. 'That and a bump the size of Old Trafford.' He could still feel the large, sore bruise at the back of his head.

Mrs Challinor rushed out from behind her desk. 'What happened? Are you OK?'

'Somebody decided to whack me last night when I went to the building site.'

He felt her fingers running over his head gently. She had a nice touch, a soft touch.

'Have you had this checked out, Ridpath? You need to go to hospital, you could have concussion.'

'I've seen enough hospitals to last me a lifetime. I'm OK, just a bump.'

She picked up her phone. 'I'm ringing for an ambulance.'

'Please don't, I'm fine and we have so much work to do.'

Reluctantly she put the phone down. 'What happened?'

He told her exactly what had taken place at the building site the previous evening and described the wet paint of the message.

'Interesting. You think there's a link?'

He shrugged. 'I don't know, but it doesn't smell right.'

'What are you going to do?'

Ridpath thought for a moment. 'First, I need to see Charlie Whitworth at eleven a.m.'

'Is he still suffering?'

'Using a wheelchair and a walking stick, and not a happy man. I promised I would see him this morning. I'll tap his brains about this too, if that's OK with you?'

'Fine, the more help the better. After that?'

'We need to order a post–mortem on the John Doe from the building site.'

'I'll get a note to Schofield. I hope our pathologist isn't too busy at the moment.'

'I'll also have a chat with Ted Jones. Find out why he thinks it was an accident.' Ridpath felt the bump on his head again. 'Listen, the attack on me might have nothing to do with the John Doe's death…' Ridpath didn't finish his sentence.

'Or?'

'It might have everything to do with his death. I'll check out the CCTV from the area, see if I can see my attacker on it. There might even be footage of the time our John Doe died.'

'Won't the police have already done that?'

'Not if they think it was an accident. Why waste the time?'

Mrs Challinor was quiet. 'Don't forget the other arson death in Derbyshire. I'll give David Smail a call to make sure he sends the file through. And there's one more thing I have to ask you, Ridpath. I'm afraid it's a personal favour.'

'Ask away, Mrs Challinor.'

'Remember I told you about my brother living on the streets?'

'Of course.'

'Is there any way to find him? It would have to be informal, and I couldn't ask you to do it during office hours.'

Ridpath thought for a moment. 'I could put the word out on the street, ask a few coppers if anybody has come across him.'

'His name is Robert Challinor. You understand this is completely unofficial, Ridpath? Nothing to do with your work in this office.'

'Of course, Mrs Challinor, I'll ask around.' He stood up. 'I'd better get moving.'

'Ridpath,' she called to him as he was going out the door, 'shouldn't we let Claire Trent know what's going on?'

Ridpath thought for a moment. 'Not yet. She has enough on her plate and this could just be an accident, like Jones says.'

'What about the message on the wall? Surely that indicates the deaths are linked?'

'I know, but how? From my experience with Detective Superintendent Trent, we need to be absolutely sure before we approach her.'

'Be careful, Ridpath, something smells about this one.'

He nodded. 'This one stinks like a dead fish.'

Chapter Twenty-Seven

Ridpath settled in his car and immediately put *Aladdin Sane* into the disc player. It was definitely a 'Jean Genie' and a Bowie kind of morning. He always found the driving rhythms of the guitar riff helped him think.

He put the car in gear and drove away as Mick Ronson's guitar destroyed the speakers. Were the two cases linked? He didn't know, but it couldn't be a coincidence that the same message was found at both locations. And if they were linked, why? He shrugged his shoulders, even though there was nobody else in the car to see the action.

And if they were linked, the deaths couldn't have been accidents. Somebody else must have been present.

He passed Lyme Park on the right. Here, Colin Firth had famously waded out into the middle of the lake during an episode of *Pride and Prejudice*, sending most of the nation's women into a collective swoon. It was his wife's favourite BBC series. The DVD even had scratch marks on the cover. From his wife's nails or from overuse, Ridpath was yet to discover.

He glanced across at the bottle of Glenmorangie sitting on the passenger seat. It was taken from the cabinet at home, left over from his illness, when he found a glass or three in the evening helped him sleep. He had fussed over what to take Charlie. Flowers? Chocolates? Something to read? He finally settled on the single malt whisky, the sort of present he would want if he was confined to his home.

He signalled left to drive down Charlie's road. Just as he began to pull around the corner, a young man ran out from the left to cross the road. Ridpath jammed on his brakes and waited for the man to run in front of his car. For a moment, he had a quick flashback to another young man doing exactly the same on the M60 last year. A man whose death had started the Connolly investigation.

He shook his head to clear the memory and put the car in gear again, accelerating to park outside Charlie's bungalow on the left.

Ridpath glanced over to the single-storey house. All was quiet. Time to see his old boss again; why was he so nervous? He stepped out of the car, making sure to lock the doors. It would never do for a copper to have his car nicked, especially not outside the home of a former detective chief inspector. He would never live it down in the canteen.

He paused for a moment, hoping his ex-boss was better than last time he saw him.

Taking a deep breath, he walked down the driveway.

Ridpath rang the bell at the front door, carrying the bottle of Scotch like a baby. He waited a minute or so, then rang it again. A voice came from inside: 'Coming.'

Thirty seconds later, a distorted shadow appeared through the window panes and the door opened wide. 'You're late, Ridpath, you were supposed to be here ten minutes ago.'

The same old Charlie, still as cantankerous as ever, but now hobbling around with a walking stick.

'Well, what're you standing there for? Come in, before the wind decides to blow me over. And I'll take that.' He reached up to grab the Scotch. 'Mustn't let Maureen see it, or she'll put it out of my reach.'

Ridpath could smell Scotch already on his breath, even though it was only eleven in the morning. Perhaps the Glenmorangie wasn't such a good idea. 'Where is Maureen anyway?' he said, following Charlie down the hallway, peering into the lounge.

Charlie carried on down to the large kitchen at the back. 'She's away at her mother's. The old trout has had a heart attack. I never thought she even had a heart,' he said over his shoulder.

He went into the kitchen and plonked the bottle down on the table, sitting heavily on a chair and leaning his walking stick against the wall. 'Can't get around without this bloody thing any more. Hopalong bloody Cassidy, that's me.'

In front of him an array of pill bottles, tablets and capsules was strewn haphazardly on a plate. He saw Ridpath staring at it. 'Just having breakfast. I swallow more tablets these days than the Happy Mondays. Shaun Ryder and Bez have got nothing on me.'

'I'm sure they're necessary. The doctors wouldn't prescribe them otherwise.'

'Doctors,' he grunted. Then he fixed Ridpath with a stare. 'I forgot, you know all about doctors, don't you, Ridpath?'

'More than I should and more than I want.'

'You're telling me. Anyway, make yourself useful. Pass me a glass down and get one for yourself. I need something to wash these down with.'

'I can't, I'm working.'

'Well, I'm not, so pass me one.'

Ridpath reached up to a shelf and grabbed a glass, handing it to Charlie. 'How are you?'

His former boss cracked open the seal and poured a large measure of the golden liquid, yellow light through the glass reflecting onto the St Christopher medallion Charlie always wore around his neck. 'Much better when I get a drop of this inside me. The wife hides it, you know.'

'Hides what?'

'My whisky, says I drink too much.'

'She may have a point. It's only eleven o'clock, Charlie.'

'What are we now, Ridpath? The fucking alcohol police? I seem to remember you being fond of a drink when you were ill.'

Ridpath immediately flashed back to the time when he had cancer. The only thing that would dull the pain from the chemo was a few shots of whisky.

'Are you in pain?'

Charlie shook his head. 'Exactly the opposite. I feel nothing from here downwards.' He measured from his stomach to his feet. 'You can't imagine what this has done to my sex life. Not that I had much of one to start with.'

Ridpath didn't know what to say. He ended up with, 'How you keeping? Eating well?'

Charlie Whitworth grimaced, taking a long drink from his glass before picking up his phone. 'Inside here are some of the best restaurants in Manchester. Italian, Chinese, a curry, all on speed dial. I don't know what I'd do without it.'

Ridpath had the impression that Charlie's wife had been away for a while. He looked around the kitchen. A black plastic bag stuffed with takeaway boxes sat in the corner.

Charlie followed his eyes. 'You can take that out for me before you go. It's bloody difficult carrying stuff and hobbling around with a walking stick.'

'I'm sure it is.'

Suddenly Charlie's mood changed. 'Don't patronise me, Ridpath. I was your bloody boss, remember that?'

Ridpath held up his hands. 'No offence, Charlie. How's everything else?'

'Well, I don't sleep much any more. And I watch a lot of telly. Jeremy Kyle has a lot going for him.' He held up the glass. 'And I drink, when the wife lets me. And I take lots of pretty coloured tablets. But other than that I lead a fruitful and rewarding life. What are you up to, Ridpath? Still brown-nosing Claire Trent?'

'Still working between the coroner's office and MIT. Don't know how long it will continue. Claire Trent has been muttering a lot in my ear recently about resource allocation and budget cuts.'

'She's just keeping you on your toes, Ridpath, keeping you hungry. I used to love winding you up too.' He was silent for a moment then stared down at his lap. 'Sorry for not bringing you back to MIT after your illness. I know what it feels like now, being thrown on the scrapheap just because you've been ill.'

Ridpath tried to improve his mood. 'I thought they'd offered you a new job?'

Charlie guffawed. 'A job in the call centre answering the bloody phone! I'm a detective chief inspector with twenty-five years' experience, for God's sake, and they offer me that?' He took a large swallow of whisky. 'Nah, it's just to salve their bloody conscience. I'm gonna take their payoff and never see the inside of a bloody nick again.' A pause as Charlie stared into his glass. 'I was a bloody good copper, Ridpath, one of the best and look what happened.' He held his arms out, pointing to his useless legs.

'They offer you any counselling?'

'After the accident?'

Ridpath nodded.

'Yeah, they were worried about PTSD. For fuck's sake, that bastard in his car shattered my pelvis, broke my right leg in three places, fractured three ribs and broke an ankle, and all the fucking police could do was worry if I was "handling" it. I nearly bloody died and all the trick cyclist cared about was asking me what my childhood was like. If I had my way, I'd burn the lot of them. There's so much fat there, it'd make the best bonfire night ever.'

Ridpath checked his watch.

'Am I keeping you?' Charlie snarled sarcastically.

'I have to meet Ted Jones at noon.'

'That arsehole. The best box ticker I ever worked with, but useless as a detective. Couldn't detect his way out of a wet paper bag. Anyway, what you seeing him about?'

Ridpath detected the first flicker of interest in Charlie's face. 'A homeless John Doe set himself alight near Piccadilly.'

'It happens. "Bunsens" we used to call them when I was in Central. A lethal mixture of meths and fags. Poof, up in smoke.'

He stopped talking and thought for a moment. 'But I thought meths was long gone. Don't tell me they're going back on it?'

'Not that I've heard.'

'So why are you interested?'

'There may be a link with another death the night before in Wythenshawe.' Ridpath considered telling Charlie about the message written on the wall but decided against it. Instead, he said, 'Mrs Challinor is also concerned about a death by burning in Derbyshire.'

'How is our friendly neighbourhood coroner? Still trying to save the world, is she? Still worrying there may be another Harold Shipman out there?'

'She's fine…'

'Oh, we are defensive. Got the hots for her, have you? Didn't know you were into cougars.'

The Scotch was beginning to talk. Ridpath checked his watch again.

'You'd best be on your way if you're going to get into town before noon.' He splashed another large measure of Glenmorangie into the glass, spilling some on the table. The stench of it was strong in Ridpath's nostrils.

The detective stood up. 'I'd best be going, Charlie. Look after yourself and see you soon.'

'Not if I see you first, Ridpath. Close the door on your way out.' He pointed to the front door.

'Bye, Charlie.'

'Don't forget to check HOLMES. Only thing the Home Office was good for was that program. I'd check deaths of the homeless and correlate it against deaths by fire. You never know what might come up. Go and see Rob Johnson. He's the only one I'd trust to operate the system. Tell him Charlie sent you.'

'Thanks, Charlie, that's a great idea.'

But Charlie wasn't listening. He was already filling his glass one more time.

Chapter Twenty-Eight

Ridpath had arranged to meet up with Detective Sergeant Jones at the building site rather than in his office. Jones hadn't been happy, but Ridpath had insisted. There was no better way to understand a scene than being there; feeling it, seeing it, touching it, smelling it. Looking at pictures was worse than useless.

As he drove towards the centre of town, the sky was the dirty grey of an old dishcloth; louring over the city, threatening rain at any second.

A typical spring day in Manchester.

The atmosphere at the site, though, was completely different from the previous evening. For a start, there were more people around, using Back Piccadilly as a shortcut. And the buildings overlooking the site had lost their threat in the cold light of day. The area still smelled, though, with full bins lining the alleyway.

Why did nobody notice a man had burnt to death?

Jones was waiting for him when he arrived. 'You're early, Ted. Glad you got my message.'

'No, you're late, Ridpath. Why have you dragged me out of my warm, cosy, fart-filled office back to this dump?'

'The homeless person that died here yesterday—'

'The bunsen? What of it?'

'What can you tell me about him?'

Jones's eyes narrowed. 'What's it to you? I thought you were with MIT. Heard you were on sick leave, though. Cancer, wasn't it?'

At the mention of his illness, Ridpath blanched. He hated being reminded of his cancer. It was like this wraith standing over him waiting to strike at any minute. 'Well, I'm back at work and working for the coroner. She asked me to look into it.'

'Didn't they get my report? Open and shut case. An accident. Life on the streets, innit.'

The catch-all for a multitude of sins. It was just life on the street. The concrete jungle where the survival of the fittest ruled and the police were a thin blue line holding back the forces of anarchy.

'For her, it's still open and definitely not shut.'

'You really gonna waste my time with this, Ridpath?'

'That's Detective Inspector Ridpath to you, Ted. And yes, I'm going to waste your time until I'm satisfied this was an accident.'

Jones began to walk away. 'Take it up with my gaffer. I'm not staying here any longer.'

Ridpath pulled his phone from his pocket and redialled the last number. He held it out to Jones. 'You can talk to him now, if you want.'

He had taken the precaution of ringing Detective Inspector Harris, Jones's boss, this morning. Harris was old school, a copper who was aware the coroner knew Claire Trent, who knew the chief constable. As ever in GMP, it wasn't what you knew, but who you knew.

Jones was listening to his boss and nodding his head. 'But… but… yes, sir.'

He clicked off the phone and stared at the screen before handing it back to Ridpath.

'It didn't have to be this way, Ted.'

'That's Detective Sergeant Jones to you,' he said, walking through the gate into the building site. Ridpath followed him.

Beside the bins, Jones pointed to a dark patch on the ground. 'This is where we found the bunsen. An empty bottle of meths at his feet and a spliff still between his fingers. Wasn't much left of him. You know those pictures of the victims of the first nuclear bombs in Hiroshima?'

Ridpath nodded.

'Like that, only worse.'

'Witnesses?'

'None came forward. As you can see, the place isn't over-looked.' He pointed to the next building with its bricked-up windows. 'The woman who was the first responder said he was still glowing when she found him.'

'Why did she come in here? It's just a building site.'

'The smell. She thought somebody was cooking a roast dinner.'

Ridpath turned around in a circle. He could see the surrounding buildings but no cameras. He hurried back to the gate. The camera on the building opposite would have caught anybody entering or leaving.

If it was working and recording and switched on.

He pointed to it. 'Did you check CCTV?'

'Why waste time doing that? I told you, he had a bottle of meths at his feet and a lit cigarette. He burnt himself to death.'

Ridpath didn't say anything but walked back to the area behind the bins, looking down at the dark patch on the ground. 'Did you keep the bottle of meths?'

Jones shook his head.

'Well, where is it?'

'I don't know. Perhaps one of the ghouls took it as a souvenir.'

'There were people watching?'

'A few. Police investigating a death always attracts the ghouls, you know how it is.'

Ridpath knew only too well people's morbid fascination with death. 'Did you dust it for fingerprints?'

Jones threw his hands up in the air. 'It was a bunsen, for Christ's sake. One of the homeless. If he didn't die here, it would be somewhere else. In a doorway surrounded by cider bottles or covered in Spice roaches. You know how it is, Ridpath – people don't last long on the streets.'

Ridpath pointed to the graffiti. PLAY THE GAME in its bright orange letters. In the full light of day, it was even clearer. Only the final 'E' displaying signs of being rushed.

Jones shook his head. 'Definitely wasn't here yesterday.'

'You sure?'

'Read my lips. It wasn't here yesterday.'

Ridpath checked the time. 'Right, you can go now.'

'Wasted enough of my time, have you?'

Ridpath had had enough. 'Listen, a man died here yesterday. Our job is to find out what happened, not to rush back to our nice warm office and a friendly chat with some PCSO.'

'I did my job, OK? He was a Spice-head who killed himself drinking meths. He won't be the first and he won't be the last. If you actually did some coppering in Manchester instead of enjoying a cushy number with the coroner, you'd know it.'

'Finished?'

Jones nodded.

'You can leave. I'll let your boss know how co-operative you were.'

Jones stalked out of the building site, shouting, 'Don't bother, I can look after myself,' over his shoulder.

Ridpath was left staring down at the dark patch on the ground. A man had died. Somebody's son, perhaps a father. A man who once had dreams of happiness and love and life. Now he was just a mark on the ground.

Nobody should live like that and nobody should ever die like that.

At that moment, Ridpath decided he had to do three things.

Find out who the man was.

Discover how he died.

And work out who was the bastard who'd hit him over the head last night.

He wasn't going to let this one go. John Doe deserved better.

Chapter Twenty-Nine

Ridpath was just about to start his engine and drive back to Stockfield when the phone rang.

He had tried to get the CCTV from the building opposite the site, owned by a company called Charest Fashions, before he left Back Piccadilly. But despite him ringing the bell three times and shouting through the letterbox, nobody had answered the door.

He would try again later. Or perhaps Sophia would. Time to get her to do something.

He had grabbed a quick Big Mac, large fries and a Coke and raced back to the car. Five bites later and with sauce dribbling down his chin, the Big Mac was no more, sitting heavily in the pit of his stomach. The fries were still waiting for him, ready to be washed down by the Coke.

He thought about letting the phone go to voicemail, but after four rings he gave up and decided to answer. 'Ridpath.'

'Hi there, it's Margaret Challinor. I've just got off the phone with Schofield. He has a window now.'

A window. Why did Ridpath care what his office looked like? 'I'm sure it will throw some light on the dead.'

'What's that?'

'A window, light, in his office.'

'No, Ridpath, a window; time to do the post-mortem on our John Doe.'

'Oh, that sort of window.' Ridpath wished he'd never opened his mouth.

'If you go there now, you'll catch him in the middle of it.'

Did he really want to see the pathologist cutting open a burnt body after his lunch? He felt the Big Mac in his stomach and answered, 'I'm on my way, Mrs Challinor. I'll try to debrief you later back in Stockfield. And could you ask Sophia to meet me at the mortuary? I promised her she could attend a post-mortem.'

'Why would you do that?'

'She asked.'

'Ugly things, post-mortems.'

'Don't I know. I'm on my way now.'

'OK, I'll tell her.'

The phone clicked off abruptly. Ridpath put the car in gear and pulled out of the car park. Luckily, or unluckily, he was only ten minutes' drive from the mortuary. He just hoped his stomach was up to whatever was waiting for him there.

Of course it wasn't. He gagged just as soon as he walked into the examination room. The combined smell of disinfectant, preserving solution and burnt flesh got to him immediately. He put his hand over his mouth and swallowed just as Dr Schofield greeted him in his high-pitched voice.

'Good afternoon, Ridpath, I thought you'd never make it.'

The doctor's eyes, sandwiched between the top of his surgical cap and the bottom of his mask, were shining. He suffered from hypergonadism and so had the demeanour and appearance of a seventeen-year-old boy, despite being one of the best forensic pathologists in the country. He was standing next to a polished stainless steel table with a half-dissected body lying on it.

Ridpath's gaze shifted from the body back to the doctor. 'I hoped I wouldn't have to.'

'And you're in luck. Just for today, this mortuary is offering a two-for-one special.'

Ridpath shook his head, not understanding.

The doctor stepped backwards slightly to reveal another white sheet covering a large lump lying on the neighbouring table. 'I performed a post-mortem on your other burn victim, a Mr Brennan, this morning. Two deaths by fire in a short amount of time, most unusual. It meant I had to read up on the procedures.'

Schofield's assistant removed the white sheet covering Joseph Brennan's body to reveal a completely burnt, dismembered corpse.

The smell was overpowering. A mixture of burnt toast, roast pork and decayed flesh filled the room. Ridpath swallowed again. *Keep it together.*

He adjusted his face mask. Not one but two burnt corpses to stare at. He hoped the Big Mac would stay in the depths of his stomach. He opened his mouth to speak and the words almost dribbled out of it. 'We haven't confirmed the identification of Brennan yet. We're waiting on a DNA match.'

Dr Schofield picked up his notes. 'The crime scene manager seemed to think it was him.'

'All the indications point that way, but there's been no confirmation yet.'

'No matter. The DNA has gone to the lab, plus we took fingerprints, even though with the condition of the body, I doubt they will be of much use.'

Ridpath raised an eyebrow.

'Burning often causes sloughing of the skin, making finger-print information worse than useless. However, the forensic team found a dental bridge close to the body. We should be able to match the dental records.' Schofield gestured back towards the other body in front of him. 'Shall we finish this client first, though? He's revealed some rather interesting nuggets of information.'

'The SIO, Ted Jones, thinks it was an accident. The man was drinking meths and smoking Spice. He set himself alight.'

'He might have made that presumption. However, I came to this customer with an open mind and have reached a very different conclusion.'

Ridpath was suddenly interested. Ignoring the smell, he stumbled over to where Dr Schofield and his assistant were standing in front of the mortuary table. The doctor was holding a scalpel in his hand. He leant forward and made a long incision.

'I'm afraid we started without you and have made a fair amount of progress already.'

'No worries,' mumbled Ridpath, 'but why do you think this wasn't an accident?'

'All in due time. Let me take you through my reasoning first. Then we may reach the same conclusion, or a different one, together.'

Dr Schofield stepped aside to allow Ridpath to see the body in its full horror for the first time. The face and hands were shades of black with patches of raw red and yellow flesh. The skin in one place had split, as if it had been slashed open with a knife. The hair and eyebrows had mostly burnt away, but tufts still remained poking through the blackened skin.

The body itself was a pure white beneath the shoulder line. A body that hadn't seen the light of day for a long time.

The doctor glanced down at the cadaver lying on the stainless steel table. 'Burn victims are never the most appealing things to look at, and in a post-mortem present a number of challenges.'

'Such as?' Ridpath mumbled, covering his mouth.

'Most contact elements and trace elements are destroyed in the fire, so Locard's exchange principle no longer applies. Plus any other evidence – skin epithelials under the nails, hair samples, bruising on the skin – is also destroyed. As long as the temperature of the corpse remains under 800 degrees Celsius, we can still obtain DNA, though.'

Ridpath glanced across at the two corpses lying next to each other. One had a black head and hands but the rest of the body was white. The other was completely blackened from head to toe. Both had their arms up like boxers getting ready to fight. Ridpath found himself staring at the two bodies. These men had once been living, breathing human beings, but now they just looked like specimens from a barbecue. The image appalled him and he quickly jerked his head away.

'Why do they have their arms up?'

'The pugilist's pose. Common among fire victims. It's the effect of heat on the muscles of the arms. Invariably, the victims end up looking like boxers ready to fight.'

'And why is the John Doe's body unburnt?'

'Ah, but he is no longer a John Doe, Ridpath.' Schofield held up a crocheted purse about five inches long and four inches deep. 'We found this hidden beneath his clothes. It contained a ten-pound note, two letters from the Department of Work and Pensions, three wraps of what I presume to be heroin, another bag of a herbal mixture which is probably Spice, and an expired credit card. The card has the name Sam Sykes on it. I'm sure you will check if this is his identity, but until you do we will be calling this customer Mr Sykes.'

Ridpath made an entry in his notebook. As he did so, Sophia burst into the room dressed in whites. 'Sorry I'm late, I just got your message.'

'Who is this?' asked Schofield.

'My name is Sophia Rahman. I'm Detective Inspector Ridpath's new assistant at the coroner's office.'

'It is usual, young lady, to ask for permission before entering a post-mortem. This is not a spectator sport.'

'Sorry, Dr Schofield, I should have told you. I asked her to attend,' responded Ridpath.

Schofield sniffed once. 'As you are here as a guest of the detective inspector, you will be allowed to remain, Ms Rahman, but please do not speak or interrupt my examination. And if you want to be sick, please go outside. You will find a bucket in reception.'

'There's no chance of that, Dr Schofield,' she answered defiantly.

He sniffed again. 'Let us begin.'

Ridpath wanted to get back to the post-mortem. 'Why is the torso of Sam Sykes unburnt?' he asked again.

'Our Mr Sykes lived on the streets and was wearing six layers of clothing. The clothes, particularly the overcoat, acted as a barrier to the fire.'

'So his hands and face burnt but the body itself remained untouched?'

'Exactly. The overcoat was so ingrained with dirt it refused to burn, despite having some sort of accelerant on it. We've sent samples off to the lab for testing.'

'And the purse?'

'We found it hidden beneath the layers, hanging around his neck from a piece of string. The string had burnt in the fire, but the purse itself had become lodged close to his body. It's obvious he kept his valuables there.'

'Living on the streets, he had to hide stuff. What better place than close to his skin?' Sophia spoke but Dr Schofield ignored her, carrying on with his examination.

'Let's not waste any more time, shall we?' He then adopted his best lecturer tone, though the sound was still that of a teenage boy. 'Deaths caused by fires are not uncommon in forensic practice but can be amongst the most difficult to investigate. Post-mortem evaluations have to be adapted for each situation and may be complicated by issues with identification, and the determination of the cause and manner of death.

'Deaths in house fires, such as Mr Brennan over there, where there may be low intensity burning of household effects, often occurs from the inhalation of the products of combustion. This usually involves carbon monoxide at more than fifty per cent saturation, but may also include cyanide if plastics have been burnt.'

He paused for a moment to take a breath. His speech had been quick and the voice had risen even higher as he spoke. 'Bodies may show characteristic cherry-pink discolouration typical of carbon monoxide exposure, and the upper airways show evidence of smoke inhalation. This may take the form of soot soiling of the nares and oropharynx with soot-stained mucus lining the trachea and main bronchi.'

As he spoke he pointed out the main areas on Brennan's body for Ridpath, before returning to the neighbouring mortuary table.

'Unfortunately in cases like this one involving Mr Sykes, where there has been extensive burning and charring, the integrity of the airways is compromised and soot may be present purely from external contamination and not from inhalation.'

He paused for a moment and looked up from the body. 'Are you with me so far?'

'Yes,' said Ridpath.

'Pretty basic stuff,' said Sophia.

Dr Schofield sniffed once and then continued. 'A major issue in fire deaths lies in determining whether a decedent was dead before a fire started. It should also be appreciated that abnormal levels of carbon monoxide, above twenty-five per cent, that are not normally regarded as lethal, may still have fatal consequences in those with significant underlying cardio-vascular disease. In other cases where there has been very rapid burning with fast consumption of environmental oxygen, a lack of carbon monoxide in the peripheral blood should not be taken as evidence death had occurred before the fire began. Intense heat also results in fracturing of bones and in epidural heat haematomas, where a collection of heated blood accumulates between the dura and skull. An additional forensic problem that is created by intense temperature is splitting, when heated skin contracts and tears. This most often occurs over the head, extensor surfaces and joints, and may be mistaken for ante-mortem wounding.' He pointed to an area on Sam Sykes's head that looked like it had been slashed by a knife.

Again, he stopped and looked up. 'To put it bluntly, it's bloody difficult in most cases to state whether death occurred before or after the fire.'

'In most cases?'

Schofield nodded. 'But we're lucky in both these cases. The most interesting part of this body is the throat.' He pointed to

Sam Sykes's neck. 'See there, a thin indentation. A less diligent pathologist may have put this down to the skin splitting through the effect of heat. However, after careful examination, I am convinced this man had his throat cut before he died.'

Ridpath peered over to where the doctor was pointing with his metal baton. There was a thin line on the blackened skin, almost undetectable. He concentrated on the line, controlling his reaction to the body in front of him. 'Could this have been self-induced?'

'Well, no knife was found at the scene. Plus Mr Sykes would have had to slit his own throat, then pour the accelerant on his body and set himself alight before he bled to death.' The doctor inserted the tip of the baton beneath the skin of Sam Sykes's neck. 'Both carotid arteries are severed. The general rule in medicine is if the heart stops, the victim will lose consciousness in about four seconds if standing, eight if sitting, and twelve if lying down. This simply reflects the effects of gravity on blood flow. These numbers would also mostly hold true if both carotids were suddenly severed. To the brain, the complete interruption of blood flow through the carotids would look the same as it would if the heart had stopped. So the short answer is no, this couldn't have been self-inflicted.'

'Could it have been done after the burning?'

Schofield stared at Sophia Rahman as she finished her question.

'No, impossible. The haemorrhaging around the wound is fresh. There is no sign of healing at all.'

'Indicating it was done before the victim died,' said Ridpath.

'You're catching on.'

Ridpath still found it weird looking at Schofield. It was as if a teenager was patronising him.

'Even more contrary to the assumption on the police report, I would lay ten pounds to a hundred we will find no methylated spirits in this man's stomach.'

'Why?'

'Meths has a quick and profound effect on the body. Once ingested, the body changes it into formaldehyde and formic acid. Formic acid begins to build up in the organs and when it does, serious damage to the central nervous system and the liver occurs. I can see no such build-up of formic acid in this man's organs.'

'So what are you saying, Doctor?'

'My conclusion is this death wasn't an accident. This man had his throat slit and then he was set on fire to destroy the evidence. Even worse, he was probably still alive when he was set on fire. There are smoke particles in his lungs. Whilst this is not conclusive, it suggests he was still breathing as he died. In other words, he was still inhaling the fumes.'

There was a silence in the mortuary as everybody digested the impact of these words.

Finally Ridpath spoke. 'We have a murder investigation, not an accident, Doctor?'

'Correct, Detective Inspector. I'll know the exact accelerant used when the lab reports come back.'

Ridpath nodded once. He would have to break this to Ted Jones. The man would not be pleased.

'Shall we move on to our second customer?' The pathologist moved to the next table as his assistant draped a sheet over Sam Sykes. 'This man has been catalogued as Mr Joseph Brennan of Wythenshawe in Manchester. We have taken DNA samples to help with identification but unfortunately the fingerprints have been burnt away. Luckily, he possessed a distinctive dental bridge. This should give us a positive ID when compared with his dental records. He supposedly died yesterday evening at approximately 22:00 in a fire.'

'Why do you say "supposedly"?'

'Three reasons. First, from the condition of the body when it was brought in, I would estimate he died at least six hours before the time the fire started. The precise time of any death can never be exact, but when this is paired with other evidence, I reach a conclusion I will be stating in my report.'

'And what is it?'

'This was not an accident or suicide. I intend to show you this was also murder.'

Ridpath stayed silent.

The doctor continued speaking as if lecturing a room of attentive students. 'How did I reach this conclusion? As well as the questions about the time of death, there are other factors that make me think this man was murdered.'

'Such as?' Ridpath was used to playing the straight man. Ernie Wise to the doctor's Eric Morecambe.

The assistant tilted the corpse so the burnt and blackening back was showing. It had a deep incision down its centre. 'Despite the charring of the epidermis, there is still evidence of the pooling of blood along the back and the back of the legs, suggesting—'

'The body lay on its back for a long time after death, before it was moved into the sitting position where it was found,' said Sophia.

Dr Schofield sniffed again. 'I would ask you not to interrupt me again, young lady, or perhaps you would prefer to perform this post-mortem?'

Ridpath deflected the tension by asking a question. 'So the body was definitely moved?'

'Definitely is not a word in my lexicon, Ridpath. But that is my conclusion from the available facts. It is most unusual for corpses to get up from a horizontal position and then walk over to sit down on a chair.'

Ridpath thought for a moment. 'You said there were other factors, Dr Schofield?'

The doctor pointed to the head. Obligingly the assistant pointed to the left side of the face, and rolled down the skin to reveal the bone beneath. 'See there, just above the occipital bone in the area where it meets the temporal and parietal bones. Three depressions from a hammer or some other blunt object.'

Ridpath could see the three round depressions in the bone just behind the ear. The depressions were surrounded by flakes of blackened skin, scrapes of hair and a reddy-yellow open blister of a wound. Ridpath's gorge filled with bile again and he retched, but didn't vomit.

The doctor carried on, oblivious to Ridpath's discomfort. 'Such a wound is normally caused by a ball peen hammer, the one with the rounded end. A small one, though, less than three-quarters of an inch in circumference. You know, I've seen the post-mortem reports from the Yorkshire Ripper case. His victims displayed similar injuries and we know he used such a weapon to render them unconscious.'

'Enough to cause death?' asked Ridpath.

'Possibly. Certainly bad enough to give Mr Brennan an extremely painful headache. And there's more.'

Ridpath raised his eyebrows.

'A total absence of soot and smoke in the lungs suggests he was already dead when the fire was started.'

'No longer breathing?'

'Exactly. Again, this is not conclusive. According to the literature, about twenty per cent of all burn victims have no soot in their lungs, but when taken with the other factors, it means I can only reach one conclusion.'

'He was already dead when the fire was started.'

'I'm so glad we agree, Ms Rahman.'

Chapter Thirty

Ridpath stood on the pavement outside the mortuary, dying for a fag. The queasiness from the Big Mac had long since vanished to be replaced by a strong desire for nicotine.

This was the first time he had felt this way for a long time. Ever since he had come out of hospital after his bout with pneumonia, he had told himself then he was never going to smoke again and, so far, he had kept his promise.

Until now.

He needed something to fill his lungs and rid them of the stench of the mortuary. It was all over him; in his hair, on his skin, all over his clothes.

He checked his jacket pockets, searching for a dimp that may have secreted itself in the lining.

Nothing.

He was tempted to ask one of the doctors walking by if they could spare him a fag, but didn't. He had already sent Sophia back to the coroner's office with the excuse he wanted her to chase up the lab results on the Joseph Brennan case. In reality, he wanted to be alone to think.

He forced himself to take three deep breaths. He really wanted to talk to somebody now, to help him clarify his thoughts. What he really needed was Charlie by his side. With his single-minded message of 'evidence, evidence, nothing else matters but the evidence'.

But Charlie was miles away, stuck at home and halfway through a bottle of whisky. He could ring Mrs Challinor, but better to talk to her in person. And Claire Trent would just blow him off unless he brought her something more concrete than the murder of a homeless man, possibly killed by a person or persons unknown. And the death of an unemployed worker, again possibly killed by a person or persons unknown.

Was there a link between the two deaths? They both died in a fire and they both had a message in orange paint near the bodies, but was that enough?

The MO for both deaths was very different; one died from a blow to the head and the other from a slashed throat. Was the message just a coincidence? If he looked around Manchester, would he find thousands of spray-painted PLAY THE GAME messages? Was it the signature of a particularly ghoulish graffiti artist? A sort of 'Kilroy was here' with an attitude?

In his bones, Ridpath felt sure the deaths were linked. But feelings weren't evidence as Charlie always told him. 'Feelings don't stand up in a bloody court of law.'

It was at times like this he really missed working with a team. Normally, he would go back, tell his boss or one of the other team members the post-mortem findings and they would work out a plan of action.

But here he was stuck outside a mortuary on his own. He even regretted sending Sophia back early. She had a good brain and at least he could have bounced some ideas off her.

The phone rang.

He looked down at the screen. Polly. 'Hi, Poll, what's up?'

'I just thought I'd remind you I have another parents' evening tonight. This time it's the Year 4s. You will be back in time to look after Eve, won't you?'

'Of course, and I hadn't forgotten.' He crossed his fingers. It didn't count if you told a white lie with your fingers crossed. At least that's what his mum had said when he was growing up.

'Good, I have to be at the school by six thirty, so can you be back before then?'

'OK,' he tried to make his voice sound excited.

'Are you OK, Ridpath?'

He decided to tell Polly the truth. 'Just finished a post-mortem. A man burnt to death.'

'Sounds awful. Why don't you go home now? Mrs Challinor won't mind, surely. Take a long bath and relax.'

'Just a few things to do and then I'm heading straight back.'

'Good, see you later. Love you.'

'Love you too.' The phone went dead.

What should he do?

Stop feeling sorry for himself for a start. Act, don't react. Another one of Charlie's mantras. Christ, he should compile a book of them.

He dialled Sophia's number. 'It's Ridpath. I need you to do something. Can you find the number of a Charest Fashions of Back Piccadilly? I want the CCTV footage from the camera mounted on the wall above their door.'

'What if they won't give it to me?'

'If they're difficult, just remind them you can get a court order. It's one of our powers as coroner's officers.'

'Oh, I like that, Ridpath, feels almost powerful.'

'Don't let it go to your head, Sophia. We hardly ever use them. Simply asking politely is usually more effective.'

'Are you coming back tonight? There's some stuff you have to sign.'

'Can it wait until tomorrow?'

'I suppose so, nothing is urgent.'

'I'll do it tomorrow then. Can you get onto Charest Fashions ASAP?

'Will do. Oh and Ridpath, thanks for the invite to the post-mortem. I really enjoyed it, but Dr Schofield is a piece of work, isn't he?'

He would never understand young people. How could a post-mortem be 'enjoyable'?

'He may be a "piece of work", Sophia, but he's the best forensic pathologist we have. If you want to be invited again, I suggest you send him a note thanking him for allowing you to attend.'

'Message understood, Ridpath.'

'Get the CCTV footage ASAP, Sophia.' He clicked off the phone. This was a good test for her. Did she have the moxie for an investigation? She was wonderful at the bureaucracy of the coroner's court, but he needed something more. Somebody who got their teeth into an investigation and just wouldn't let go. A clone of him, basically.

Now he was moving forward, he felt much better. Didn't need a cigarette any more. He pulled out the phone again and called Mrs Challinor this time.

'It's Ridpath. Your suspicions were correct. It looks like the homeless man in central Manchester was murdered. It may also be tied into the death of Joseph Brennan in Wythenshawe. Dr Schofield believes that was murder too. We'll know more when the lab results come in. I'll call Ted Jones and Ron Pleasance to give them a heads-up.'

'I won't ask them to reopen the case until we receive the post-mortem reports from Dr Schofield, just in case he changes his mind.'

Ridpath thought for a moment. 'That's probably best, no point in stirring up the hornet's nest until we can be certain. And one more thing, Mrs Challinor…'

'What's that?'

'I won't be coming back in this evening.' He paused for a moment thinking whether to tell another white lie but pushed on with the truth instead. 'I stink after the post-mortem, so I need a bath, plus Polly has to do another parents' evening tonight. I hope it's OK. Call me if you want more. If not, I'll see you tomorrow morning and give you a full briefing. I know it's Saturday, but you're usually in.'

'See you tomorrow, Ridpath. I think we'll have work to do.'

'The understatement of the year, Mrs Challinor.' He switched off the call and hunted through his contacts list for Jones's and Pleasance's numbers.

He made the calls. Neither of the detectives was pleased with the news. Jones managed only two words in response. 'Fucking hell.'

It was time to go home, but he knew that evening the questions wouldn't go away. They would just keep whispering to him through the long, cold darkness of the night.

Were the two murders linked? If they were, why?

Which of course would lead him onto the biggest question of all.

Who?

Day Five

Saturday, April 27, 2019

Chapter Thirty-One

'Morning, Ridpath.'

'Is it?' Ridpath had spent a sleepless night thinking about the case. His brain turning over question after question but finding no answers.

Sophia Rahman sat in front of her monitor, staring at it intently. She pressed pause on her keyboard. 'I talked to Charest Fashions yesterday. They record each day on DVD, then recycle the DVDs at the beginning of the week.'

'Please tell me they hadn't recycled them yet?'

She smiled. 'They hadn't recycled them yet. This is the one from yesterday. I've marked a few spots which you might find interesting.'

Ridpath hurried round to her side of the desk. She rewound the DVD. A black-and-white image, slightly distorted from the fish-eye lens of the security camera, appeared on the screen. It showed the alley in front of the gate to the building site but not inside the site itself. At the top right-hand corner a clock showed time ticking forwards.

A man dressed in rough, ragged clothes carrying a bag and a wire basket came in from the bottom right, stopped in front of the gate, checked over his shoulder and went into the building site.

'I think that is Sam Sykes, our homeless man,' Sophia said, pointing to the screen.

'Can you freeze-frame it when he looks back?'

'No problem.' She rewound and stopped the CCTV just as the man looked back. The picture juddered and went out of focus. 'Unfortunately, they must have used this DVD a million times. The quality is knackered, I'm afraid.'

'Is that the technical phrase?'

'Learnt it at uni. It's why I got a 2:1.'

'Never mind, perhaps somebody at the police lab can enhance it.' Ridpath checked the time in the top corner. 'Ten fifty a.m. At least we have a time now.'

'We've got more.' She resumed playing the DVD. Two minutes later another man also came in from the bottom right. He was holding up a bag to cover his face. He was wearing dark clothes: a long black coat, Nikes and a dark baseball cap. He didn't look back before stooping slightly to slip inside the gate.

'I've replayed this four or five times. We never see his face. His bag is always covering it.'

'Looks like he knew there was CCTV there. Can you rewind it?'

She quickly went back to the point where he entered.

Ridpath followed the action on the screen. 'See, he moves his bag to his head just as he comes into frame. And watch how he stoops slightly to go through the gate. I had to do the same thing, which puts him around six foot, one inch, same as me.'

'But we can get a more accurate measurement...'

'Go on.'

'Simple trigonometry. If I measure the gate and another point where he passed, for example the lamp post, we can calibrate his height.'

'Another thing you learned at uni?'

'Nah, Year 9, basic trig, isn't it?'

It wasn't basic to Ridpath. He had a grade G in GCSE maths, about the worst it was humanly possible to get.

'Let it run on.'

The DVD carried on. The wind sent an old crisp packet tumbling down the deserted lane but there was no other movement.

Then a white flare at the top left-hand corner of the screen, as if a torch had been shone at the camera.

'Did you see that? Stop it and rewind,' said Ridpath.

Sophia did as she was told. A flare of light flashed on the screen for a second then died down to a fainter glow.

'Is there no sound on this bloody thing?'

She shook her head. 'Only picture.'

The screen continued to glow faintly. In the corner, the digital clock counted down the time.

10:56:22

10:57:34

10:58:05

'Jesus, you know what this means, don't you?'

Sophia shook her head.

'It means our perp stood there and watched Sam Sykes burn to death.'

'Wait, Ridpath, there's more.'

Chapter Thirty-Two

Sophia's finger hovered over the keyboard.

The clock continued to tick over in the top corner.

10:59:13.

10:59:45.

10:59:53

A shambling figure came in from the bottom, walked slowly to the gate and pushed it open. The man was another tramp, but this time the beard was longer and the clothes even more dirty.

'See,' said Sophia, 'somebody else goes in, but ten seconds later he comes running out.'

On the screen, the tramp was running out through the gate, no longer shambling but racing as if the life had been scared out of him.

'We have a witness. This man saw everything.'

Ridpath jabbed the screen. 'Did he see the perp too?'

'He certainly looks like he's seen a ghost.'

'Can you make a copy of the DVD?'

'Not here, but I can at home. The PCs here are from the dark ages.'

'OK, we need to show this to Mrs Challinor.'

'Just wait a minute, you haven't seen everything yet.'

'There's more?'

'The camera was still working when you visited the building site later.'

She skipped forward to another point in the recording. The image was exactly the same as before, except this time the alley was sleek with rain and the light of dusk was throwing shadows across the building site.

'The cameras are not really equipped for night vision. If somebody approaches the door a light goes on, but if you avoid it, then…' She left the sentence unfinished.

A man came in from the bottom right, again holding up a black case to cover his face. He avoided the door with its light, went to the gate and slipped into the building site. The time in the corner of the screen ticked over to 19:16.

'Is it the same man? He's dressed differently,' said Ridpath.

The long black coat had been replaced by a short Harrington jacket and jeans. He was still wearing the baseball cap, though.

'We can measure again. It's not foolproof but it should tell us whether the man's height was the same.'

'Do it.' Ridpath continued to watch the screen.

Nothing was happening.

'What's he doing in there?'

Sophia didn't answer him.

The clock in the top right corner flipped on, remorseless.

19:16:54

19:17:23

19:18:12

Another man came in, from the left this time. He was checking his phone.

'That's me.'

'You take good CCTV, Ridpath.' She was looking up at him and smiling.

On the screen, Ridpath looked all around him, checking the area before approaching the gate and leaning in without entering.

'This is where I shouted and rattled the gate. There was a massive rat in one of the bins.'

Slowly, cautiously, the Ridpath on the screen vanished from view into the building site.

Ten seconds later a man came running out, not trying to hide his face this time. Instead of running back the way he came, he turned left and dashed up Back Piccadilly, away from town.

'That's after he hit me.' Ridpath rubbed the back of his head. The bump was still there, smaller now but still painful.

The clock ran on. Two minutes later, Ridpath appeared at the entrance, leaning heavily on the gate.

'You were out for over two minutes. You should have gone to hospital.'

'It wasn't much, I've had worse. And anyway, I avoid hospitals like the plague.' He pointed to the screen. 'Can you go back to where he exited the building site?'

She found the point on the DVD, just after Ridpath entered. Again they waited fifteen seconds and the man appeared.

'Freeze-frame it here.'

The DVD stopped but the picture juddered. In it they could see the jawline of a man and his mouth, but the rest of the face was in shadow or hidden by the baseball cap.

'What's he carrying in his hand?' asked Sophia.

Ridpath peered at the screen. The picture stayed still for a second and then started to judder, before freezing and juddering again.

'Is it a can or some kind of metal tube?' she asked.

But Ridpath knew what it was. A can of spray paint. And he knew 'PLAY THE GAME' had been written by this man.

'Why take the chance of returning to a crime scene simply to spray a message on the wall? And why didn't he do it earlier? He had plenty of time,' said Ridpath.

Sophia Rahman stared at him.

'It's time we took this to Mrs Challinor.'

Chapter Thirty-Three

'You're sure, Ridpath?' The coroner frowned.

Mrs Challinor sat back as Sophia paused her laptop. They had just rewatched the footage from the CCTV together, pausing it to the places they had marked to show her.

Ridpath nodded. 'And that's not all. This footage confirms Dr Schofield's post-mortem. Somebody killed Sam Sykes before he was set alight.'

'When is his report coming in?'

'He promised me he would send his preliminary findings this morning. Toxicology will follow.'

'And what about the death of Joseph Brennan?'

'He said the man's body was also burnt after he was murdered.'

'Are the two cases connected?'

'He doesn't know. But the fact that both were attacked before being set alight...'

'...suggests a pretty strong connection,' Mrs Challinor finished. 'Surely the clincher is the message written at both sites. What was it again?'

'Play the game.'

Mrs Challinor had reached the heart of the matter with her usual speed. 'There was also the man I saw when I went to the scene. It felt as if he were returning to the crime. Reliving it one more time.' He paused for a moment. 'And I'm pretty sure he spray-painted the wall. Like a dog marking his territory.'

'Or an artist signing his work.' Mrs Challinor sat forward, pointing with her pencil. 'We've got a problem, Ridpath.

Actually more than one problem. Firstly, we now need to make this a murder investigation. As a coroner, that is not in my scope. All murder investigations have to be conducted by the police. I have opened an inquest on our homeless man, but I will have to postpone it until the police have completed their enquiries.'

'Understood, Mrs Challinor. But you can see from the tape, he watched the man burn. He poured an accelerant over a man, stood there for at least five minutes and watched the body of another human being burning without lifting a finger to help him.' As he spoke, Ridpath's voice rose.

'We have to notify Manchester Central, request they reopen the Sykes case.'

'Jones wasn't too pleased when I told him this might happen last night.'

'I don't care what Detective Sergeant Jones thinks. What was the name of the head of the CID?'

'Detective Chief Inspector Harrison.'

'I'll call him later. And I'll follow up with Dr Schofield. We need the DNA, fingerprints, toxicology, trace results and report on the accelerant used as soon as possible.' She paused for a moment. 'We also need to know more about Sam Sykes.'

'If he lived on the streets, I bet he has a record for something.'

'That's a bit damning, Ridpath.'

He shrugged. 'It's reality. Most of the people on the streets have either been in prison or in a care home. Or they have a drug habit or have been picked up for prostitution. It's a life that comes into contact with the police for one reason or another eventually.' Ridpath noticed a distant look in her eye as he spoke.

'Can you find out, Sophia? Next of kin, home address, schools, whatever you can?'

'Yes, ma'am.'

'It's "Coroner" or "Mrs Challinor", Sophia.'

'Yes, ma… Coroner.'

'We'll make a copy of this CCTV and pass it onto DCI Harrison. I presume you have a proper chain of evidence.'

Ridpath looked at Sophia.

She said, 'What?'

Ridpath sighed. 'My fault, I should've briefed her correctly.'

'I don't understand, what's wrong?'

'Did you give Charest Fashions a receipt for the DVDs, placing them in a sealed bag with the time of their acquisition, the date and your signature on it?'

'No.'

'OK, can you go back and do it now? It's not valid but at least we'll be covered.'

'I don't understand, what's the problem?'

Mrs Challinor explained. 'In a court of law, there is a chain of custody. We have to be certain before any evidence is introduced into court that it hasn't been tampered with in any way.'

'But I took it home to look at it. The PCs here are too old.'

'It's OK, Sophia. Go back to Charest Fashions and get a signed statement from them saying when you received the DVDs and then keep them in an evidence bag.'

'OK.'

The glass rattled in its frame as Storm Hannah gusted through the centre of Stockfield and a surge of rain beat against the sash windows.

'There's one more thing, Ridpath. I think you should take everything we have to Claire Trent.'

Ridpath paused for a moment, frowning. 'Strictly speaking, the homeless man's death was in Central's area. DCI Harrison has to decide if it warrants the involvement of MIT. And Joseph Brennan's death was investigated by a different division too. Detective Superintendent Trent won't want to step on the toes of the other police districts.'

'You know I don't give a toss about police protocol, Ridpath.'

He thought for a moment. 'And the MO is different in both cases. Joseph Brennan was struck over the head and Sam Sykes had his throat cut. Plus, we have no evidence of a link between the victims.'

'I still think you should show her what we have discovered.'

'She won't like it.'

'Why?'

Ridpath held up his hand, extending the fingers. 'Three reasons. We don't have enough evidence without the toxicology and the accelerant reports. Second, no copper likes to be told they have a possible serial killer on their patch they knew nothing about. And third, you're going to add more unsolved deaths to her stats.'

'Sod the stats. We're talking about the death of a homeless man here, plus a possible link to another death in Wythenshawe, and perhaps one in Derbyshire. We could be dealing with a serial killer. Will he kill again?'

'I can't answer that. I don't know.'

'What do you believe, Ridpath?'

'Beliefs are not evidence, Mrs Challinor.'

The coroner rolled her eyes. 'Then based on all your police experience, what do you think?'

Ridpath looked down but stayed silent.

'What do you think?'

He paused for a moment before answering. 'I think he will kill again.'

'Then it's our job to step on toes to stop that happening.' It was Mrs Challinor losing her cool now, the first time Ridpath had ever seen her so animated.

He tried to explain police operations one more time. 'She will only get involved if she is ordered to do so by a senior officer or she is convinced there is the possibility of the involvement of a serial killer. The death is the responsibility of another SIO at the moment.'

'I don't care. I want you to brief her today. Remember our job in the coroner's office is to represent the dead in the court of the living. You need to convince her, Ridpath. I know we are dealing with a serial killer.'

Chapter Thirty-Four

'A serial killer? You've got to be joking.'

Ridpath switched off the DVD player he had attached to his computer, having just shown Claire Trent and Lorraine Caruso the footage of the murder of the homeless man. He had explained to them why he thought the deaths of Joseph Brennan and this man were linked.

'That's what it looks like, guv'nor.'

'You dragged us into work on Saturday morning for this...' Caruso glanced across at Trent. 'And what were you doing at a crime scene? You're a coroner's officer.'

'Mrs Challinor asked me to go.'

'But it's got nothing to do with you... or her.'

'The coroner can investigate any suspicious deaths in her jurisdiction...' Ridpath began to raise his voice.

Trent held her hands up. 'What he was doing there doesn't matter. We have a murder.' She clicked a page on her desktop. 'It seems Manchester Central has already classed this as an accidental death. You need to show them this footage, Ridpath.'

'What? You haven't shown the SIO yet?' Caruso glared at Ridpath.

He looked down. 'Mrs Challinor wanted me to show you both first. We believe we are dealing with a serial killer, not a single murder.'

'What do you think, Lorraine?'

'I'm not convinced. Manchester Central is handling the death of this dosser. They should have this CCTV footage and all the information Ridpath has collected. Why should we take it off them and add it to our workload? It's not a major case and it won't help our stats. These sorts of thrill murders happen and are notoriously difficult to solve.'

'Is that what you think this is? A "thrill" murder?'

'I can't see anything else, Ridpath. The links between the two deaths are tenuous. As you said yourself, the MO is different and there seems to be no connection between the two victims.'

'But I haven't seen the pathologist's report yet.'

'Neither have we.' She pointed to herself and Trent.

'I was at the post-mortems for both victims. The MO was different, but don't you think it's too much of a coincidence two people are burnt within a day of each other?'

Caruso shook her head. 'People die all the time, Ridpath. Where's your evidence the deaths are linked?'

'You're forgetting the messages written near the victims.'

'"Play the game",' Caruso sneered. 'Sounds like an Eighties song title. I've read the Manchester Central report. There was no message on the walls when they first discovered the body. The message only appeared after you visited the crime scene...'

Ridpath's mouth dropped open. 'What are you saying, Lorraine?'

'I'm just saying I find the timing very interesting. Myself and the guv'nor were just talking about what you bring to the team, and the day after, we're suddenly being presented with a mysterious serial killer...'

Ridpath stood up, pushing back his chair. 'I don't have to take that from anyone. Are you saying I planted the message?'

Trent scratched her head. The scalp was flaking just above her right ear. Her hairdresser had given her a new shampoo but it was no help; the problem was getting worse, not better. 'Sit down, Ridpath. Lorraine has raised a valid concern.' She paused for a moment. 'Forgive me for being cynical, but where's your evidence? It strikes me as an immense coincidence the same week I criticise you for your lack of results, suddenly a serial killer turns up on my doorstep.'

Ridpath stared out of the window of Trent's office, taking three deep breaths and counting beneath his breath. 'It was only confirmed by the post-mortem yesterday. You've seen the CCTV footage. The man watched another human burn to death.'

'I don't doubt that, Ridpath, and Central were wrong to ascribe this death as accidental. I believe Mrs Challinor in her role as coroner has asked them to reopen the case, which I am sure Chief Inspector Harrison will do.' She sat back in her chair and rested the urge to scratch her head. 'So the only link you have is the spray-painted message on the wall—'

'And the fact both were doused in an accelerant before being set on fire.'

'But both men were very different. One lived in a flat in Wythenshawe, the other lived on the streets. Are you sure both offences were committed by the same man?'

Ridpath thought for a moment. Was he sure? Were the two deaths linked? He decided to trust his gut. 'I'm sure they are linked. Even worse, I have a feeling there will be more.'

Trent stared at him as if looking right through him. 'We can't run this department based on your feelings, Ridpath.'

He knew that response was coming. He should have kept his mouth shut about 'feelings'. He tried one more time. 'The two deaths are linked, I know they are.'

'But we don't know for sure. We may just have two deaths by fire. Both can be handled by the local plod unless they specifically request our help,' said Caruso.

'But Jones is cocking it up, moving too slowly...'

Trent spread her arms wide. 'They are suffering, as we all are, through lack of resources and the necessity for their proper allocation at this time.'

'So the murder of a homeless man on the streets of Manchester doesn't really matter.'

Caruso's eyes rolled.

Trent's reaction was much more controlled. 'Such emotive language doesn't help, Ridpath. Manchester Central and Cheadle are handling two separate enquiries into deaths by fire over the last couple of days.'

'But the detective in Cheadle has already been pulled from the case!' Ridpath was losing his cool.

'My point exactly. Neither station has asked for help from the Major Incident Team. Lorraine's officers are already stretched. We have two major investigations going on at the moment: one gang-related and the other helping Cheshire CID in a county lines drug case. Unless Central or Cheadle ask for our help, we are not getting involved.'

'But, guv'nor—'

'And one other thing. Do you know how much it costs to mount a murder investigation?'

Ridpath shook his head.

'At least one million pounds. Three million if it becomes a major case.'

'But guv'nor, money shouldn't be our concern—'

'Read my lips, Ridpath. We are not getting involved. Correct case management is the allocation of the three precious resources – time, money and people. We are short of all three at the moment, so the respective CID departments will continue to handle the investigations. I'll inform Mrs Challinor of my decision personally.' She turned ostentatiously to her number two. 'Lorraine, I'd like to discuss the Moston gang case with you.'

Ridpath got the message. He was being dismissed.

He packed up his notes and put the CCTV discs back into their boxes, standing up to go out.

'Make sure Ted Jones gets the CCTV and your notes, Ridpath,' said Caruso as he closed the door.

Outside, he leant back against the wall and took a deep breath. Why didn't they understand?

The deaths had to be linked, there was no other explanation. And there was a serial killer at large in Manchester.

Then an idea struck him with absolute certainty.

Unless he did something, they were going to be faced with a lot more deaths.

Chapter Thirty-Five

After a minute of calming himself and collecting his thoughts, Ridpath walked back through the MIT office.

Everywhere was a hive of activity. Detectives sat at their desks on the phone, others were typing reports, still more were researching information on the Police National Database. Some of them he knew well, others he was on nodding terms with. There had been so many changes of personnel since Charlie's time. Most of the old guard had gone, to be replaced by newer, younger officers, many of them on the fast track scheme; bright bunnies but with little experience of practical policing.

He waved to Chrissy Wright. At least she was still here, and still behind her desk wearing her City scarf. The one indispensable member of MIT who managed to survive every new DCI and guv'nor.

He pressed the button to open the security door. As he did so, Harry Makepeace came through, one of the last survivors from Charlie Whitworth's time as guv'nor.

'Hello, Ridpath, what are you doing here? Don't often see you outside of our weekly meetings.'

'Work, Harry, what else? How're you doing?'

'Don't ask! Up to my bloody eyeballs in it. Even worse, I have to go off to Liverpool in a minute...'

'The county lines drug case?'

Makepeace's eyebrows raised. 'You know? Bit of nightmare. I don't mind working with Cheshire, but the worst part is dealing with all the whining and moaning Scousers... and that's just those in the police. You heard I passed my probation? I'm full inspector now.'

Ridpath hadn't heard, but it was a sore point with him. He had been appointed probationary inspector before Makepeace, but the cancer scare and then the transfer to work with the coroner had meant that was exactly where he stayed. And without somebody actively fighting his corner, that's where he would stay for the foreseeable future. 'Congratulations,' he finally mumbled.

'Anyway, got to go. See you for a pint sometime.'

Ridpath knew this was the usual meaningless offer never meant to be taken up. 'Sure, would love to. When you get back from Scouseland. Check your pockets before you leave, though.'

'What do you mean? Check I still have some?'

They both laughed and Makepeace began to move away. Ridpath had a thought. 'Harry, can you do me a favour? You don't know where I can find a Rob Johnson, do you?'

'Rob, the HOLMES liaison man? He's on the fifth floor with all the other nerds, boffins and IT guys. Watch out, though, you don't know what you might catch there. Sticky palms, you know what I mean?'

Ridpath left the MIT office and took the lift to the fifth floor, where he bumped into a female support officer. 'Is Rob Johnson working today?'

'He's second on the left, but I warn you he's busy.'

Ridpath strolled down the grey carpeted corridor and knocked on the door, going straight in.

A large man with a full beard was sitting in front of a computer, hastily opening a new screen. He glanced back as Ridpath entered the tidiest office he had ever seen in HQ.

'Are you Rob Johnson?'

'I am, but I'm busy now. If you want to come back later, Mr…?'

'Actually, it's Detective Inspector Ridpath, I'm with MIT but temporarily assigned to the coroner's office.' That was stretching it a little as it was probably the other way round these days. 'And I'd close the *Game of War* if I were you. The icon is still flashing on your desktop.'

Rob Johnson reddened as he clicked his mouse and the icon vanished.

'Charlie Whitworth sent me, said you were the best.'

'Charlie was always a good judge of character. We worked together a few times. Good man, Charlie, shame what happened.'

'He said you knew how to operate HOLMES.'

The man nodded. 'I know my way around the system. It's not very well coded and the graphics are Neanderthal. Anything the Home Office touches is screwed up before they start, but it's still the best system we have.'

'Could it help with my enquiry?'

'Depends what you want it to do. The Home Office Large Major Enquiry System is hopeless at finding out who did it, but if you want it to crunch large amounts of data from all across the country and make links between the data, nothing beats it. What's your problem?'

Ridpath liked this man. Like all experts, he made what he did sound easy. 'At the moment it's a detective superintendent and a detective chief inspector who don't believe we have a serial killer in our midst.'

'And you do? Why?'

Ridpath took him through the two deaths he had discovered.

'So you want me to see if there are any others with the same MO?'

'Got it in one.'

'You've come to the right man. You see, HOLMES is great, but if you put rubbish in you get rubbish out. That's where I come in. My speciality is reading the language from different police reports across the country and categorising it correctly so HOLMES can work its magic. Nobody better at it than me.'

'And nobody more modest.'

The bearded mouth smiled. 'Aye, that too. It's why they pay me the big bucks. When do you want it?'

'Yesterday.'

'That slow, huh. I'll get on it straight away. You got a case number for this?'

Ridpath shook his head.

'Thought so. Seeing as you're a mate of Charlie's, I'll put the hours down as testing the system. Nobody ever checks anyhow.'

'Thanks, Rob.'

'I'll call you when I've got anything. You want the whole of England?'

'No, just check the north for now, anything above Birmingham. Should be elementary for you.'

'OK, the north it is, makes my job easier.' Then Rob Johnson did a second take. 'Haha, but I've heard them all before. "The game's afoot." "Elementary, my dear Johnson." You're not the first, Ridpath, and you won't be the last. Thank God my name isn't Watson.'

Ridpath stood up and made a gesture of holding a phone to his ear. 'Call me, Rob.'

'Actually, I'll call you Thomas, if that's OK.'

'I prefer Ridpath. Thomas always makes me think of the tank engine.'

'I know, my real Christian name is Boris…'

'Poor man.'

'At least I didn't go to Eton.' A pause. 'If you see Charlie, wish him well from me. A bloody good copper was Charlie.'

As Ridpath left the room, his phone rang. 'Hello, Mrs Challinor.'

'Ridpath, I just received a report from the West Yorkshire coroner. They've found another burnt body.'

'Where?'

'Just off the A62 near Huddersfield, place called Marsden.'

'Where they had the moorland fires recently?'

'Exactly.'

'Ridpath, they found a can of spray paint next to the body.'

A slight pause. 'I'm on my way.'

Chapter Thirty-Six

It took Ridpath forty minutes to drive to Marsden. Sophia texted him the address of the incident and he entered it into his satnav.

As he got closer to the small town, he realised he didn't need the address. Three Scene of Crime vans and even more police cars were parked in a small lay-by on a sharp right-hand turn on the A62, near a place called Close Gate.

Ridpath had been walking around here, where the Pennine Way crossed the escarpment known as Standedge, a beautiful place to just sit and watch the clouds scud across the sky, listen to the skylarks and imbibe the beautiful solitude of it all.

There was no chance of any solitude now, though. Police in wellingtons and Scene of Crime officers in their white suits milled around the area. Ridpath showed his warrant card and signed in at the outer cordon.

He was met by an Inspector Grange. 'You'll be the chap from Manchester?' he said in a heavy Yorkshire accent as he shook Ridpath's hand. 'What's tha doing all the way out here?'

'Checking out a theory.'

'You'd better come with me then.'

Ridpath was led down a path and across an old bridge, turning immediately right up a steepish hill. The area looked like a moonscape: blackened and charred vegetation crunched underfoot, a few drifts of smoke still rose from dark patches of scorched earth. The acrid smell of burning suffused everything. At least it wasn't raining.

'Three days ago this was an inferno. Burning moorland in springtime? Unheard of in my lifetime. All the moor from here t'reservoir burnt to cinders. Shocking it is, shocking.'

They walked up a black path snaking through the burnt vegetation, their feet giving off little puffs of soot with every step. Up ahead, Ridpath could see a white tent erected beside a stream.

'Our forensic pathologist is just examining the body. We should be able to close the scene down soon.'

'When was it found?'

'This morning around eleven o'clock. A couple of fire fighters were checking the moor, making sure the fires were out, and they spotted a large shape leaning against a tree.'

'It wasn't seen before?'

'Too much smoke, and anyway, the fire burnt this area three days ago. We've been over near Buckstones Reservoir fighting the bloody thing, trying to make sure it stops spreading. The winds of the last few days didn't help, but at least we had some heavy rain last night.'

As they walked up, the pathologist stepped out, accompanied by the crime scene manager. He was an old man with a tired, creased face and grey hair. 'You can close it up now, Inspector. The mortuary lads are removing the body.'

As he spoke, four men carrying a shape covered by a white Tyvek cover on a stretcher came out of the tent. Ridpath recognised the shape. It had the same raised arms as the others. What had Schofield called it? The pugilist's stance, that was it.

They crept slowly down the hill, carrying the body carefully, making sure they didn't drop it.

Ridpath approached the coroner. 'My name is Ridpath, I'm with the East Manchester coroner's office.'

'How is Margaret? Still dancing the Charleston?'

Ridpath made a mental note to ask Mrs Challinor about her dancing skills. There were so many things he didn't know about her. 'She's fine. We're just checking if this death had any links to others in Manchester recently. I believe you discovered a can of spray paint.'

The crime scene manager answered. 'We did. Right next to the body. It had exploded of course, the pressurised contents couldn't stand the heat, but strangely the metallic label did. It was orange spray paint.'

'Do you know who he is?'

'We haven't discovered an identity yet. No documents or wallet survived the blaze. We're hoping he's on the DNA database. If he isn't, we'll have to work on his dental records.'

'We're checking missing persons as we speak,' said Grange.

'You might want to include Manchester in the search.'

The inspector nodded, making a note in his book.

'And did you test for the presence of accelerants?'

'Accelerants?' asked Inspector Grange.

'Petrol, kerosene, methylated spirits, turps, anything like that.'

'I do know what an accelerant is, Inspector Ridpath, but why are you asking about them?'

'We've found two bodies recently with messages sprayed in orange paint next to them. Perhaps this death is linked—'

'That explains it,' interrupted the crime scene manager.

'Explains what?'

'The streaks of orange paint we found on some unburnt gorse next to the stream. The can had been used before it was discarded.'

'Was there a message?'

The crime scene manager shook his head. 'Couldn't see one. But the area was completely burnt in the fire. Only the one patch of gorse survived.'

'Hang on.' The pathologist held up his hand. 'If there was a message and the possible use of accelerant, are you telling me this man committed suicide?'

Ridpath shook his head slowly. 'No, I'm not telling you he killed himself. I'm telling you this man was murdered...'

'But... but...' stammered Inspector Grange.

Ridpath ignored him, '...and we are now looking for a serial killer.'

Chapter Thirty-Seven

It had been a long drive home for Ridpath, accompanied only by the sounds of the Casualeers, the Impressions and Jamo Thomas. There was nothing like a bit of Northern Soul when you were feeling troubled. His fingers tapping the steering wheel as he drove through the industrial wasteland that was Oldham Road, a place where people had once lived and loved and brought up kids, but was now just a desolate corridor of car parks, warehouses, fried chicken joints and traffic lights. Modern England at its worst.

He had briefed Mrs Challinor on the day's events before he left Marsden, including the refusal of Claire Trent to get involved.

'Are you certain we are dealing with a serial killer, Ridpath?'

'After seeing the body on the moors, I'm more convinced, Mrs Challinor. But the question is why?'

'Why what?'

'Why is he killing these people? An unemployed man, a homeless man, and now a John Doe out on the moors.'

'You know that's not our remit, Ridpath. Our sole concern in the coroner's office is to find out who the victim was, where they died and how they died. The motivation of the killer is not our concern. That is the police's problem.'

'And what if the police refuse to recognise it is a problem?'

There was silence on the other end of the phone. 'Then we need to make them aware it exists.'

'And how are we going to do that, Mrs Challinor?'

'I don't know, but I'm sure you are going to tell me, Ridpath.'

'By using the only language they understand. The language of evidence. You often mention the Shipman murders in Hyde, Mrs Challinor.'

'I do, but what's it got to do with this case?'

'Shipman was allowed to carry on killing because nobody joined up the dots that elderly women were dying under his care. The hospitals, other doctors, the police, even the undertakers, all missed the signs.'

'And so did all the coroners.'

'Exactly. We need to join up the dots to show Claire Trent and MIT that something is happening. And the only way we can do that is with evidence.'

'OK, so what are the next steps, Ridpath?'

'Three things. First, we need the chemical analysis of the accelerant used. Was it the same one in each case? Second, we need to get the picture of my attacker enhanced and check if any witnesses saw him at the crime scenes in Wythenshawe and Marsden. Third, we need to find out more about the victims, what links them together.'

'It's too much work for us alone.'

'I know, that's why we need MIT.'

'Do you want me to call Claire again?'

'No, we can't risk alienating her further unless we have more evidence. Let's wait for the report on the accelerant first. Have we told the parents of Sam Sykes of his death yet?'

'Jenny has just found their address. I was going to do it tomorrow.'

'Why you? Surely Carol Oates or myself should do it?'

'No, Ridpath. I want to be there. I understand what it's like to have somebody you love living on the streets.'

'We'll go together tomorrow morning?'

'It's Sunday, Ridpath, don't you want to be with your family?'

He thought about Polly and Eve for a second. 'I'm sure they won't mind as long as it's just the morning. They don't ever emerge much before eleven anyway.'

'OK then.' A pause for a moment. Then she spoke again, a sharpness and determination in her voice. 'But let me make it clear, Ridpath, the feelings and emotional well-being of these grieving parents is the major concern of the coroner's office. It is not the needs of your investigation. Am I clear?'

'Ye-es,' answered Ridpath uncertainly.

'If I feel you are stepping over those limits, I will shut it down.'

'Of course, Mrs Challinor.'

The rain had become much stronger the closer he drove to Manchester, with gusts of wind making it fall almost horizontally.

Ridpath realised he had been driving on automatic for the last few miles. He was now turning into his own road. This was happening more and more often these days. He suddenly found himself at a destination without remembering how he had driven there. It was as if ten per cent of his mind was driving and the rest working on a problem or simply remembering something that had happened in the past. Was this a function of the tablets he was taking? Or part of the ageing process? Or the metronomic action of the windscreen wipers causing him to go into some sort of dream state?

Whatever.

He would ask the doctor next time he went to Christies. He would have to check the calendar when the next one was due. They no longer held the power over him they used to. He remembered being damp with sweat before each one, his pulse racing, his heart pounding. All in dread at hearing the words 'The cancer has returned'.

But it had been a year now he had been in remission. He felt great. Long may it bloody continue.

He parked outside the house and went in.

Polly sat at the table marking some exercise books. He went over and kissed her on the cheek. 'Have I told you I love you recently?'

She checked her watch. 'Not for ten hours, Ridpath. You are definitely failing as a husband.'

He put his arms around her neck and held her close, inhaling the sweet smell of her.

'I've booked the BTS concert in London in June,' she said. 'The tickets weren't cheap, but we'll make it a family trip, take in a show, some shopping, see the sights. Do the whole tourist bit for a weekend.'

'Good. She'll love it, but let's not tell her yet. She'll start packing immediately and I couldn't stand being told about BTS every five minutes. I know far too much about them already. How is she?'

'Fine, listening to BTS probably. No point in going out in this weather. It'd drown a dolphin. How was your day?'

'Not great. I think I'm on the trail of a serial killer, Polly.'

She frowned. 'Watch your health, OK? I know what you're like. You become so emotionally involved in your cases any common sense goes out the window. When you get your teeth into something, you won't let go. Your passion, it's one of the things I love about you. But be careful this time, I don't want you to be one of the victims of this man too.'

He bit her ear.

'Ouch, that hurt.'

'Perhaps I've bitten off more than I can chew...'

'With me? Of course you have, Ridpath, haven't you realised that yet?'

Day Six

Sunday, April 28, 2019

Chapter Thirty-Eight

The Sykes home was on a quiet, tree-lined street in Bowden, not far from Altrincham town centre.

'Worth a bob or two, these people.'

'We don't know that, Ridpath. Perhaps they bought the property long before the surge in house prices in the late Nineties.'

'True, but not a bad place to live. And certainly not a place I could afford.'

They pressed the bell on the outside gate. Instantly a dog started yapping from inside the detached house.

'Best alarm system known to man – a little dog who thinks he's a Rottweiler.'

The door opened and an old woman appeared, shoving a little Lhasa apso back with her foot. 'Stay there, Stewart, be a good boy, stay inside.'

The dog, of course, ignored her commands and tried his best to get out into the garden.

Eventually she closed the door and limped down to the gate. 'Hello, how can I help you?'

'Sorry to disturb you on a Sunday. I'm Margaret Challinor, from the coroner's office. I believe my office manager, Jenny Oldfield, rang you yesterday to tell you we were coming.'

'But she didn't say why. I did ask, but she wouldn't tell me.'

'We prefer to tell people in person, Mrs Sykes.'

There was a pause as the information registered. 'It's about Samuel, isn't it?' For a moment her chest sagged and her legs began to give way. She grabbed the stone gate post for support. 'I always dreaded this day...'

'It *is* about Samuel. Can we come in?'

She opened the gate and they walked together to the front door. 'Father will be upset. We haven't seen Samuel for three years now. He used to come back but not any more. He never comes back any more...'

Her voice trailed off as she opened the front door and the dog began yapping again. 'Don't worry about Stewart, he makes a noise but he hasn't bitten anybody for ages. You wait here while I put him in the kitchen.'

They were left in the hall as Mrs Sykes herded the reluctant dog backwards.

Ridpath looked around. The wallpaper was faded and the carpet looked like it was a relic from the Fifties. An old dresser stood in the hallway with a sad bunch of plastic flowers sitting in a Coalport vase.

'Looks like we stepped back in time,' said Ridpath.

'Some people don't want to be modern, they can't abide change...'

'Or they can't afford it. Asset rich and cash poor.'

'That's a withering assessment, Ridpath.'

'Sorry, Mrs Challinor, the policeman inside me is always there. You can tell a lot about people from their houses.'

Just as Ridpath finished speaking, Mrs Sykes returned. 'There, that's him sorted. He won't be happy and he'll sulk for the rest of the day, but at least we can talk in peace. Please come this way.'

She showed them into a large lounge. An old man was sitting in an armchair at the far side, close to a gas fire. Near him a television was on with the sound turned down. The rest of the room had photographs and pictures on the walls, along with a row of flying ducks and wallpaper beginning to yellow with age. The whole room had an air of fustiness, as if the windows hadn't been opened for decades.

'This is Father – Mr Sykes.'

Mrs Challinor stepped into the room. 'Good morning, Mr Sykes, sorry to disturb you.'

The old man ignored her, continuing to stare at the flickering television. Even this was an older model, not even a flat screen, Ridpath noticed.

'Father has been diagnosed with dementia. Sometimes he's with us and sometimes he isn't. Today he isn't,' said Mrs Sykes. She glanced at the television screen. 'Sorry, I can't turn it off. He gets upset if I do.'

'Not a problem, Mrs Sykes, but we'd like to talk to your husband as well, if we can.'

The woman frowned. 'But Father is my husband. We've been married forty-one years in May.'

'But you both...'

'He was much older when we married. I was a fresh young thing of twenty when we tied the knot. Anthony was just past forty, but then age didn't matter. Please sit down.'

Mrs Challinor and Ridpath sat on an old couch that immediately sagged under their weight. They shifted forwards to perch on the frame.

'I'm afraid I have some bad news, Mr and Mrs Sykes.' Mrs Challinor glanced in the direction of the old man. He was still staring at the television. 'I'm afraid we have to report the death of your son, Samuel.'

The woman looked down. Ridpath could see her hands were clasped tightly in her lap.

'When did he die?'

'Two days ago.'

A swallow and tears began to appear in her eyes. 'How did he die?'

'The details are not good, Mrs Sykes. You know he was living on the streets?'

She nodded. 'We tried to help but it was no good...' Her voice trailed away.

'I know, sometimes people don't want to be helped.'

A clock ticked loudly on the mantlepiece. The dog had stopped yapping. The television hummed in the corner. Ridpath wished he were anywhere but here right now. He had received training on how to break bad news to a grieving relative, but hated doing it. For some reason it never got easier.

The woman looked up and said softly, 'How did he die?'

'We believe the cause of death was the inhalation of smoke.'

'Inhaling smoke?' The woman looked at both of them.

'I'm afraid there is no easy way to tell you this, Mrs Sykes. Your son burnt to death.'

The woman's eyes registered shock and her hand went up to cover her mouth. 'My poor Samuel,' she mumbled.

Mrs Challinor continued speaking. 'We are still investigating how he died as we haven't yet ascertained whether this was an accident or something else.'

'Something else?'

'There are some inconsistencies in your son's death, Mrs Sykes.' Ridpath spoke for the first time. Mrs Challinor glanced across at him. 'We believe your son may have been murdered.'

The old man continued to stare at the television, not moving his head.

'Murdered. My poor Samuel was murdered?'

Ridpath glanced at Mrs Challinor. 'We believe it's a possibility and that's why we would like you to tell us about him.'

'Tell you about him?' Mrs Sykes repeated the question as if she was trying to understand what was happening.

'For instance, what he was like as a child. Let's start there.'

The woman smiled, her eyes moving upwards and to the right as she recalled her son's early years. 'He was a beautiful boy, blonde hair, bright green eyes, an easy-going, active boy. He was our only child, I couldn't have any more after him. We tried for a girl, but it just never happened, did it, Father?' She touched the old man's arm.

For the first time he looked away from the TV, then down at his arm before focussing on his wife. 'Is it time for tea yet?' he asked in a strange, childlike voice.

'Not yet, Father. Soon, it will be time for tea soon.'

The old man nodded once and turned back to stare at the television again.

'They loved each other did Father and Sam. Played football together, went fishing together, played tennis together.' She paused. 'Then it all changed, we don't know why. He became quiet and withdrawn, wouldn't speak to us and wouldn't do anything with Father any more. Used to stay in his room all day.'

'When was this?'

'When he was thirteen. It was not good afterwards. His schooling suffered and he started missing days…'

'Not attending school?' asked Mrs Challinor.

The woman nodded. 'Then he was arrested for shoplifting. Father had to take time off work to go down to the police station to bail him out. He never said thank you or anything.' She began to cry, tears dripping softly down her face.

'Then what happened?' Ridpath probed.

The woman sat up straight and took a deep breath. 'He left school, and soon after, he moved out. We found out later he had stolen money from us by forging Father's signature on a cheque. We think he went travelling to India, Thailand, that sort of thing. We didn't see him or hear from him for five years until he turned up on our doorstep one morning.' A long pause. 'A bit like both of you.' Another pause. 'After that, it was periods of staying with us and then vanishing. Staying here again. Stealing money. Vanishing. Stealing things to sell and vanishing again. We realised pretty quickly he was using drugs. Tried to stop him and help him stop. But it didn't work. Nothing worked.'

Once again, her head went down and she started to sob. The husband noticed his wife was crying, reached into his pocket to bring out a handkerchief and placed it gently on her lap, before returning to watch his television again.

'I think we've asked enough questions for now, Ridpath, Mrs Sykes is obviously upset,' said Mrs Challinor.

She looked up. 'No, I have to talk about him. If I don't he'll be forgotten, nobody will remember him.'

'We will remember,' said Ridpath. 'It's our job to find out what happened and remember him.'

'Thank you. I want to help.'

Ridpath glanced across at Mrs Challinor, receiving a quick nod. 'Please continue, Mrs Sykes?'

'Samuel came back once more. But this time, Father had had enough. He made Samuel promise he would stay and seek treatment. We would give him money to help him off the drugs, help him get well again.'

'What happened?'

'He tried for three days. Tried really hard, but I suppose it was too much. We woke up one morning and found he had stolen the car.'

'Did you report it?' asked Mrs Challinor.

Mrs Sykes shook her head. 'We couldn't report our own son, could we?'

Mrs Challinor's head went down and she stared at the old carpet.

'And next we heard he was in prison for burglary. In and out of prison for the next ten years. We visited him the first couple of times, but after...' Once again, her voice trailed off.

'When did you last see him?'

'Three years ago in Strangeways. He had been living on the streets, he told us. He was thin and dishevelled and he looked old, so old.' Then she took a deep breath. 'I couldn't see my little boy any more. He had vanished...'

Then she began sobbing quietly once more, her shoulders heaving.

Her husband noticed as if seeing her for the first time. He held his arms out to hold her and said, 'Don't cry, little bird, it'll soon be over, don't cry.'

'I think we've asked Mrs Sykes enough now, Ridpath. It's time we should leave.'

'But—'

'It's time, Ridpath,' she said firmly. Turning back to Mrs Sykes, her voice became softer. 'Is there anybody you could call to come and sit with you?'

Mrs Sykes shook her head. 'My sister lives down south. She always said this would happen one day.'

'Would you mind if I came back this afternoon? Sometimes it helps to have somebody to talk to.'

'You don't have to.'

'I'd like to, if you'd have me. Just for a chat.'

Mrs Sykes nodded. 'That would be good. Sometimes it's not so easy with Father.'

'I know. I'll come at five, OK?'

The woman nodded once again.

Mrs Challinor stood up. 'We need to go back to the coroner's office now.'

Ridpath stood up too, realising he could ask no more questions today.

'I'll see you out.'

'It's not necessary, Mrs Sykes, we can do it ourselves.'

'No, I'll help you. I have to release Stewart anyway.'

She stood up and walked with them to the door of the living room, stopping before she reached it. 'When can I see his body?'

'I wouldn't advise it, Mrs Sykes, the burning...'

Mrs Sykes nodded once, opening the door.

'But when I come back this afternoon, I can help you with the details of the funeral.'

'The funeral? I hadn't thought about the funeral. What shall I do?'

'Don't worry, we'll talk about it this afternoon.'

As he was leaving the living room, Ridpath noticed a framed photograph high up on the wall. 'What's that, Mrs Sykes?'

She looked upwards, following Ridpath's pointing finger. 'It's Samuel and his five-a-side team the day they won a tournament. He was a good footballer was Samuel.'

'Could I borrow it?' Ridpath asked, already reaching up to unhook it from the wall.

'I suppose so, but please return it, won't you?'

'Of course, Mrs Sykes.'

They were ushered out into the hall.

'I hope the funeral won't cost too much, we just live on Father's pension.'

Mrs Challinor turned round in the doorway. 'Don't worry, there are things we can do. I'll take you through them when I come back.'

Mrs Sykes closed the front door and they walked down the driveway to the gate.

'What was all that about, Ridpath? Why did you want the photograph?'

'Because I saw exactly the same one in Joseph Brennan's house.'

Chapter Thirty-Nine

As soon as Ridpath arrived back at the coroner's office, he went through the email sent by the crime scene manager, Helen Charles, after the Wythenshawe fire, finding the picture almost immediately.

He placed the printouts side by side. 'See, this one is cropped more tightly, but it's the same picture.' He pointed to the one they had taken from the Sykes house. It showed five boys dressed in a football kit of red shirts and white shorts, with two adults standing behind them. Only the right arm and shoulder of one of the adults was visible. Above them was a banner with the initials 'NAGBC F—' but the rest was cut off. In front of the team was a handwritten placard: 'Manchester and District Under-13s Five-a-Side Champions 1994.'

Mrs Challinor leaned across. 'Sam Sykes is in the centre holding the trophy. Is that Joseph Brennan on his right?'

They compared the thirteen-year-old Brennan with a picture of him as an adult. 'I think so,' said Ridpath. 'He certainly looks the same around the eyes.'

Ridpath began to remove the frame from the Sykes picture. 'If the mother is anything like mine, she writes names on the back.' He took the photograph out of the frame and turned it over. 'Mothers seem to be the same the world over.'

In positions corresponding with the team's pose were written five names:

Tony Doyle

Tommy Larkin

Sam

Joe Brennan

Harry McHale

In the space at the top was written:

Coach: David Mulkeen

There was no name given for the other adult.

'Is this the link, Ridpath?' asked Mrs Challinor.

'I don't know, but it's a bloody big coincidence two children in the same photo are found dead just one day apart, and both had their bodies burnt.'

A knock on the door.

'Enter,' called out Mrs Challinor.

Sophia came in. 'Sorry to disturb you, but I thought Ridpath should see this.' She held out an envelope. 'It came in last night.'

'You're working too?' asked Mrs Challinor.

'I knew Ridpath was going to be here so I thought I'd come in. Either that or stay at home and listen to my aunties asking why I'm not married yet.'

Ridpath tore the envelope open as she spoke, scanning the contents. 'It's the post-mortem report from Dr Schofield. He states that in his view both men were killed before they were set alight.' He turned over the page. 'The accelerant used on both of them was the same: methylated spirits.'

'He's also confirmed a match between the dental bridge and one created for Joseph Brennan by his dentist,' added Sophia.

'Do we have the evidence now, Ridpath?' asked the coroner.

He nodded.

'It looks like you need to go and see Claire Trent again. I'll call her now.'

Ridpath's heart sank. If he couldn't convince her this time, his career was over. He was going to be as dead as the corpses in Dr Schofield's mortuary.

Only worse; he would still be breathing.

Chapter Forty

He was ready.

He had confirmed the address on the sex offenders' register and already scoped out the man's habits. Luckily, two of his victims had lived in the same town, as if drawn like moths to the same place or to each other. It had made life easier for him. He'd been able to kill two birds with one stone.

Or in his case, one lighter.

The television on the table in his room had just shown the news. They had found the psychotherapist on the moors above Marsden. Of course, they didn't know who he was yet, but he guessed they would find out eventually.

Not to worry. He would be finished soon.

He remembered the day he'd discovered the truth, found his meaning in life.

The psychotherapist had been treating him for six months using Eye Movement Desensitisation and Reprocessing, or EMDR as the man called it. Forcing him to tap his bloody leg while different sounds played through the headphones and he tried to remember what happened.

A waste of bloody time.

God, the man loved his acronyms. PHQ, PTSD, DIS, CBT, HRSD, IPT and MDD were just a few he used in their sessions.

These acronyms weren't meant to help him or explain his treatment. Instead they were used to cloud and confuse, to place the psychotherapist on a higher plane; the owner of secret, arcane knowledge. Like the priests of old mouthing their incantations in a Latin neither their congregation nor they themselves understood.

After two months, he started the RCT. A Randomised Clinical Trial to assess his depression. Not to help him, but to help the psychotherapist publish a paper for his next conference.

But whatever he was doing worked. One day, he was sat in his chair watching television and the song came on. Immediately, he was transported back to that time.

The pain.

The laughter.

Their taunts.

Everything he had buried for so long back with him as if it had only happened yesterday.

He knew then what he had to do.

Sunday evening was the beginning. The psychotherapist had to be the first, of course. He knew everything and it was all his fault anyway. If he hadn't meddled, the memories would have stayed hidden, buried beneath years of denial.

The man had been reluctant to get into the car initially, but a sharp tap with the ball peen hammer had soon made him understand it might be a good idea to obey.

'Don't hurt me. I'll do anything you say, just don't hurt me.'

He had forced the man to drive out from Manchester along the A62, through the wasteland that was Oldham and up past the delightfully named Delph, Diggle and Dobcross onto the moors above. He had mapped out the route the week before, knew the exact time it would take, the place to park and the length of time it would take to kill this man.

The psychotherapist didn't know he was going to die. Oh, he probably had an inkling, but in situations like this, the human brain refuses to accept the inevitable. It hangs on to hope like a man tiptoeing across a termite-rotten wooden bridge.

'Douse the lights and get out.'

The man did as he was told. They didn't have far to walk to the place he had chosen.

'Go down there. I'll follow you.'

'Where are you taking me? What are you doing? I'll pay you, pay you anything, just let me go back.'

'Go down there.'

'But it's dark, I can't see where I'm going. Release me, I'll pay you.'

He hated the pleading. The psychotherapist should have listened to him properly when he told him about the plan. Instead, he had said, 'You mustn't indulge these fantasies, they're not good for you.'

They weren't fantasies. They were real, as he was about to discover.

He took the backpack from the rear seat of the car and slung it over his shoulder. 'Move.'

The psychotherapist obeyed, slipping down the path to the old pack bridge crossing the stream. He had often come here in the past, sitting beside this small moorland rill, hearing the burbling of the water and the trills of the robins in the nearby trees. All the while thinking of murder: what it would feel like, what it would smell like, what it would taste like.

A wonderful time when a terrible beauty would be born.

The psychotherapist didn't understand when he was told. God, the man was stupid. 'If you persist in these, these morbid thoughts, I will have to report you to the police.'

The threat was the last straw. If the police knew, they would stop him.

And he couldn't be stopped. Not any more.

'Walk across the bridge and follow the path beside the stream. Seventy-five metres along you will come to a single rowan tree. Stop there.'

'Where will you go?'

'I'll be right behind you.'

He had chosen a moonlit night and the path was clear. The psychotherapist's mouth opened, flapped once, but no words came out. Then the man turned and walked over the bridge, taking the path towards the rowan.

He followed. Closer now; the man mustn't get away.

Not now.

Not when he was so close to being free. Free of the nightmares and of the dreams haunting him for so long.

This was simply the first step.

A week from now he would be free.

Once the plan had been implemented. Because freedom was never handed to anybody on a plate. It had to be seized with both hands and held aloft. Or in his case, seized back from those who had robbed him of it all those years ago.

The psychotherapist stumbled on the path, his comfortable loafers not really designed for walking along the barren moors. Myra Hindley and Ian Brady had loved this area too, burying their victims in the deep, peaty soil not far from here on Saddleworth Moor. Some of them must still be up here, their flesh ravaged by time and the acid in the soil. The quiet bleakness a perfect setting for death.

So it goes.

But he wasn't going to emulate those two. For one, he had a simple plan to avoid being caught. And secondly, there was a beauty to the way his victims were going to die. A terrible beauty.

The man was breathing heavily now. A combination of fear, the slight uphill gradient and obesity. Sitting down all day on his fat arse, passing judgement on the poor fools who believed in him, did nothing for his fitness.

'You can stop now.'

The psychotherapist slowly began to turn around.

He hit him with the ball peen hammer on the back of the head, just above the right ear. The man dropped like a sack of Spanish onions.

'Was he dead?'

No. A barely perceptible whine was coming from the man's mouth.

Never mind, he soon would be.

Putting his backpack down, he dragged the psychotherapist the rest of the way up the hill to the rowan tree. He should have made the man walk closer to it. Why expend energy uselessly? He would remember for the next one.

Propping him up against the tree, he adjusted the man's jacket so it hung correctly across his body and wiped the shoes clean. He couldn't stand dirty shoes, such a bad advert for any man's cleanliness.

He checked all the pockets were completely empty and returned to the backpack, admiring the symmetry of the man's body against the tree and the moonlit sky, like the logo on his Kindle. Except this man wasn't reading his book, he was about to die.

The can of spray paint was in the side pocket. He took it out and sprayed his message across the top of the gorse. 'PLAY THE GAME.'

Off in the distance a fox barked at the moon.

Then silence, a silence that called to him as it always had.

He let his head fall back and drown in its peace, before taking out the methylated spirits and sprinkling it all over the body.

He sparked the lime-green lighter and lit the end of the rag. It crackled for a moment and then burst into flame.

The flames took hold and he tossed the rag onto the man. There was a whoosh as the dry branches of the tree also went up in flames.

He checked the surrounding area to see if he had left anything behind and then walked slowly back down the path to his car.

Behind him, the night sky began to glow with a new source of light. Halfway down, he stopped for a second and listened to the sound of the tree crackling amid the dancing flames.

He couldn't resist it any longer; he glanced back. The man's body had dissolved into a roar of orange flame. The fire was spreading now through the dry grass and gorse, up the side of the bank and over the moor. An orange line sparking the night sky.

He sat back up in bed, drawn back from his memories to the small room in his boarding house by a familiar sound on the television.

They were playing the song.

He took it as a good omen. Not long to go before he would be free.

Chapter Forty-One

Mrs Challinor sat in the car outside the house in Bowden. She had just finished talking to Sandra Sykes, after returning as she had promised in the late afternoon. It hadn't been the easiest conversation.

'You said he was burnt to death?'

'Sorry, I should have made myself clearer. His body had been set on fire after he was murdered.'

The mother's hand went to her mouth. Her husband sat next to her, staring at *Antiques Roadshow* with the sound turned down, a half-finished bowl of soup on the table next to him.

'Oh, my poor son.' Tears appeared in the woman's eyes. 'Why would anyone do a thing like that to my son?'

'We don't know, Sandra, but the police are investigating the death as we speak. They will find out who did it.'

The woman was quiet for a moment. 'When can I see the body? I'd like to see the body.'

'I wouldn't advise it, Sandra. When a body is severely burnt, it—'

'I want to see him.'

'I'll check with the pathologist when it can be released.'

'Pathologist?'

'In all suspicious deaths, a post-mortem has to be performed.'

'You cut up my beautiful boy? You cut up Sam?' she shouted.

Her husband looked across at her but didn't move.

'We had to order a post-mortem, Sandra, it's the law.' Then Mrs Challinor reconsidered her answer. 'As the coroner, *I* had to order a post-mortem—'

Before she could finish her sentence, the woman was on her feet. 'Get out of my house. How could you cut up my poor boy?'

'Mrs Sykes, Sandra, I—'

'Get out. I want you out of my house.' The woman pointed to the door.

Mrs Challinor gathered up her briefcase, leaving her business card on the side table. 'Call me if you want to discuss anything. Call me anytime—'

'Get out!'

Those words still echoed in Mrs Challinor's ears as she sat outside their home in her car, staring out through the rain-spattered windscreen. She didn't know how long she had been sitting there. It could have been minutes or it could have been hours.

She thought about walking up the path, knocking on the door and trying to explain to Sandra Sykes that it was her job to investigate the dead, discover who they were and how they had died, but there was no point. Sandra Sykes would have to come to terms with her son's death in her own time. Intruding on her grief at this moment was not something that would help. In fact, it would only hurt the poor woman even more.

Mrs Challinor tried to do her job to the best of her ability, but it was at times like these she wondered if it was worth it. People were always going to die. Perhaps it would have been a better use of her life to save the living rather than explain the dead.

Enough. There was work to do.

She picked up her mobile and rang Ridpath. He answered immediately. 'Your meeting with Claire Trent is tomorrow morning at nine a.m. She was very reluctant to see you, Ridpath. What happened last time?'

'I may have pushed her too hard.'

'Well, don't do it again. Just take her through the evidence we've found.'

'Will do.' There was a pause at the end of the phone. 'Are you OK, Mrs Challinor? Your voice, it sounds—'

'I'm fine, Ridpath. Just don't let me down tomorrow, that's all.'

She switched off her phone. Perhaps she had been too harsh with him. Should she call him back and explain what had just happened?

'He's a grown man, he'll get over it,' she said out loud before switching on the engine, putting the car in gear and driving to the end of the road.

Instead of turning right, towards her own house, she turned left. She didn't know why, but she couldn't go home right now. Couldn't face the silence calling to her in that empty place. Both her children were away at university and her husband, well, he had found a younger model over five years ago now.

She couldn't face going back there.

Not this evening.

She turned right onto the A56 heading back towards the city centre. She knew where she was going, of course. It was something she sometimes did on a Sunday evening when the loneliness of home drove her onto the streets and no work remained to force her to stay inside.

Through Stretford, past Old Trafford with its floodlight towers standing dark in the rain, on through Hulme, rebuilt now after being devastated by the post-war plans of tower blocks and crescents that ended up as homes for the dispossessed and addicts. On up Deansgate, old Victorian buildings standing next to glass-and-concrete towers. Homes for the young and trendy and witless.

The streets were quiet, the roads deserted. The only illumination the harsh blues, yellows and reds of neon lights, stark in the rain.

In a few doorways, huddled heaps of clothing with a human being buried deep within sheltered from the downpour. She thought about stopping her car and asking the question she always asked on nights like this.

'Have you seen my brother? Have you seen Robert Challinor?'

But the answer would always be the same. A shake of the head. Or a quietly spoken 'Leave me alone.' Or worse, a shouted 'Fuck off', followed by a long drunken rant, rambling on incoherently until she returned to her car and drove away.

But in her heart she still held hope. Hope that one night she would find him. Hope that he would return to her. Hope that she could somehow save him from the life he had chosen.

She turned left at Bridge Street, heading as she always did towards the place she had last seen him. Over the River Irwell, the garish lights of the Lowry Hotel on the right, and straight on, stopping outside the New Bailey car park.

She knew she shouldn't be here. Ridpath had warned her it wasn't a safe place for a woman to walk alone at night, but she came anyway.

Out of the car and behind some billboards, looking for the arches beneath the railway. On a patch of derelict ground four homeless people were sitting out in the rain, huddled beneath a makeshift shelter.

As she approached, she saw there were three men and what looked like an old woman. She recognised the woman, she had met her before in this place. Her name was Sally and, although she looked well past sixty, her actual age was thirty-eight.

'Hello, Sally.'

The woman looked up at her with one eye. Plastic bottles of White Lightning were strewn on the ground around her. One of the men had his arm over her shoulders, his head resting against her body.

'Wha' you want?'

The mouth was toothless; pink gums surrounded by wrinkled, tanned lips.

Mrs Challinor knelt down in front of Sally. 'Do you remember me?'

Sally thought for a long time, nodded her head and then said, 'No. Who are you?'

'I'm Robert's sister. Robert Challinor. Have you seen him?'

Again, Sally thought for a long time before once again saying 'No.'

This time the man with his arm round her shoulders woke up. 'Who you? Why you botherin' my woman? Wha' you want?'

He swung his arm away from Sally's shoulders and stood up unsteadily. 'Leave us alone. Get away, go on, get lost.'

Mrs Challinor moved away quickly. For the second time that night somebody didn't want to have anything to do with her.

Day Seven

Monday, April 29, 2019

Chapter Forty-Two

Monday morning and Ridpath braved the commute into Police HQ.

He had already made breakfast for the girls. Eve ate hers in complete silence as usual, while Polly stared at him over the rim of her coffee cup.

Before he left, she helped him on with his jacket, adjusted his tie and kissed him on the cheek, whispering, 'Look after yourself. Remember, don't get too involved. It's just a job.'

He had told her all about it last night. They had gone to bed and she'd held him tight all through the night, holding him as if never wanting to let him go.

Thirty minutes later, Ridpath was sitting in front of his boss, taking her through the evidence, Mrs Challinor's admonition last night ringing in his ears. 'Don't let me down, Ridpath.'

Lorraine Caruso sat to one side examining her freshly painted nails, her face looking like she had been chewing on lemons.

'I'm doing this as a personal favour to Mrs Challinor, Ridpath. I'm not used to subordinates questioning my orders,' said Claire Trent.

'Or questioning mine,' chimed in Caruso.

Ridpath took a deep breath, it was now or never. 'You were looking for evidence, guv'nor, that the murders were committed by the same man. I believe both Joseph Brennan and Samuel Sykes were killed by having methylated spirits poured over them and then set alight.'

'A belief is not evidence, Ridpath,' said Trent.

'In addition, another John Doe who was burnt to death has been discovered in the moors above Marsden in Yorkshire.'

'So you're adding another body to the mix? Anybody who's died in a fire is now going to be a victim of your serial killer?' Caruso turned to her boss. 'Guv'nor, we've been through all this once, why are we wasting time going through it again? Ridpath is seeing connections where none exists.'

Ridpath realised they were tag-teaming him. He held up his hand, unfolding the index finger. 'One: Dr Schofield says the two Manchester men were both murdered.' He pulled out the post-mortem reports and placed them on the table.

Without looking at them, Trent asked, 'Does the pathologist say they were murdered by the same man?'

Ridpath shook his head. 'He's unable to say until more tests come in.'

Caruso smiled at him.

He continued. 'Two: spray paint cans were found near to all three men, with messages sprayed close to them. For both Sam Sykes and Joseph Brennan the message was "Play the game".'

'And the John Doe on the moor?'

'There was a message there, boss, but the fire destroyed it.'

Caruso suddenly sat up straight. 'Hang on, there have been fires on the moors recently. Are you saying one man was responsible?'

Ridpath shrugged his shoulders. 'I don't know. All I know is they found spray paint on the gorse near the body.'

Trent yawned. 'Any other evidence, Ridpath?'

'Three: both Sam Sykes and Joseph Brennan died after being doused with the same accelerant – methylated spirits. West Yorkshire police are waiting on lab tests for their body.'

'It's what the alkies drink on the streets and easy to buy if you're looking for a way to top yourself.' Caruso talked directly to her boss instead of looking at him.

Ridpath saved his trump card for last. If this didn't work, he could say goodbye to his job with MIT. The rest of his life would be spent as a coroner's officer with no hope for promotion or advancement. Worse, without any support from Greater Manchester Police, he might not even survive working for the coroner. Once you were out, there was no going back.

He took another deep breath. 'Four: at least two of the victims knew each other.' He pulled out the five-a-side team photos. 'See, here is Sam Sykes and next to him is Joseph Brennan. The three other boys are Tony Doyle, Tommy Larkin and Harry McHale. The man standing above them is the coach, David Mulkeen. We don't know who the other man is yet.' Ridpath touched the cropped arm and shoulder on the left.

Trent leant forward to get a closer look. 'Are you sure these are the same people?'

'I think so, the names and rough ages match.'

'You think so?' sneered Caruso.

'Why would two men who were burnt to death within days of each other both have the same photograph unless there was a link?'

'Circumstantial, not proof.'

Ridpath threw his hands in the air. 'A bloody massive coincidence, is it? But when you put everything together it adds up to one conclusion. We have a serial killer operating in Manchester who is killing people and then burning the bodies to destroy any evidence.'

Trent narrowed her eyes. 'If what you say is right, Ridpath, and there is a serial killer, but we haven't made the link yet, then there should be other victims.'

'I think you're right, guv'nor. One of them could be the body found near Marsden yesterday. I'm just waiting for the West Yorkshire pathologist to send through his report and tests to see if the accelerant used was the same as on Sam Sykes and Joseph Brennan, and discover if the victim was killed before being set alight.'

A long intake of breath from Caruso. 'It's still a long shot, boss. I just can't believe somebody is setting fire to people.' Ridpath noticed the change in tone from the DCI.

'Neither can I, but...' Trent sat back in her chair, spinning her pen between the tips of her elegantly manicured fingertips. She looked across at Ridpath and then at Caruso before lunging forward quickly to press the intercom on her desk. 'Chrissy, can you come in here?'

Five seconds later, a middle-aged woman wearing a Manchester City away shirt knocked on the door and entered. 'Yes, ma'am?'

Trent scribbled the names on a sheet of paper. 'Can you check these people out for me on the PNC? The first is probably in his sixties now, he's the adult in this picture. The others belong to the boys. They must be in their late thirties.'

'No problem, guv'nor. When do you want it?'

'Yesterday.'

'I'll get on it right away.' She left, closing the door behind her.

'The other thing we need to do is get onto HOLMES and see if—'

'You buying this guff from Ridpath, guv'nor?'

'We need to check it out, Lorraine. It's too much of a coincidence. Two people, possibly three, all being murdered with their bodies burnt afterwards. It could happen. But this,' she tapped the printout of the picture, 'this is the kicker. Two of the victims appearing in the same photo? The deaths must be related.' She stood up. 'We need to get onto HOLMES and cross reference any other deaths by burning recently.'

Ridpath raised his hand slowly. 'I have a confession, guv'nor.'

Trent's eyes narrowed again. 'What?'

'I already briefed Rob Johnson. He's working on it.'

'You did what?' erupted Caruso. 'You were given specific instructions, Detective Inspector, to drop this line of enquiry until compelling evidence came forward. Do you remember the conversation on Saturday?'

Ridpath nodded. 'But I thought the evidence was already compelling.'

'That's no excuse for ignoring the chain of command. You may have forgotten, Ridpath, but you report to me and I won't put up with your bloody maverick behaviour.'

Trent was quiet for a moment before speaking. 'We'll discuss this later. In the meantime, we'd better discover what HOLMES has found.'

Chapter Forty-Three

'This has been a fascinating exercise for HOLMES...'

'Let's have less of the self-congratulation, Rob, and just tell us what came up.'

But Rob Johnson wanted to build the suspense a little while longer. 'The key to using the system is the setting of the parameters you want it to search for. Most coppers don't use standardised language. A "slash" for a detective inspector in Liverpool might just be a "cut" for a constable in Cumbria. So the job is to create the standards and the facts so the programme can look for and discover links.' He chuckled. 'If you put rubbish in, you get rubbish out.'

'Can you just get on with it, Rob,' said Lorraine Caruso.

'Hold your horses. If you don't understand what it can do, how can you interpret the findings? Right? So shall I continue?'

Detective Superintendent Claire Trent nodded.

'Now, most times we just input the data from a victim: age, height, personal description and so on. Then we add lines identifying the nature of each crime. HOLMES then collates all the information, suggests possible links and identifies new lines of enquiry linking possible victims.' All the time he was speaking, Johnson was tapping away at his computer. A graphical interface appeared, followed by lines linking various victims. 'But in this case we didn't know who the victims were. Or even whether they were victims at all. Right?'

He looked across for confirmation from Trent and Caruso but received only blank stares.

'So when DI Ridpath briefed me...'

A glance that could kill from DCI Caruso to Ridpath.

'…I tried something different. I set HOLMES to look for parameters of all deaths reported to the police in the north of England for the last three months. I reasoned most deaths of the type Ridpath was looking for would be reported to the police.'

Caruso rolled her eyes extravagantly.

Johnson ignored her. 'What came up were twelve deaths by burning in the last three months for the area north of Birmingham up to Scotland.'

'You didn't do the whole of England?'

'I was briefed to just do the north.'

'Most killers have a limited range of operation. They tend to be either commuters moving in one direction from the site of the murder to home. Or marauders travelling out from the home in multiple directions searching for their victims. Serial killers are invariably the latter.'

'Thank you for those words from the Hendon Training Manual 2006, DI Ridpath,' Caruso said sarcastically. 'We've all been on the bloody course too, you know.'

'I then set HOLMES to search for the parameters of spray cans, orange message, burning, and accelerants, turning it into a search engine. Best keep it simple for the moment, hey?'

'Woe betide we do anything "complicated" like detective work.' Lorraine used her fingers to form quotation marks.

'Give it a rest, both of you. That's an order. As a senior officer, you should know better, Lorraine.' Trent's voice had a hint of steel and warning behind it. 'Carry on, Rob.'

He pressed a key on the computer and a different graphical interface appeared. 'I ruled out four of the deaths because they were definitely accidents. Three others were confirmed as suicides and one more in Newcastle was a fire-eater whose act went wrong, so I crossed him off too. That left four deaths, and guess what?'

'What?' said Ridpath.

'They've all occurred in the last week.' He pressed a button and links appeared between four icons. A Thomas Larkin on

April 22, a Joseph Brennan on April 23, and Samuel Sykes on April 24...'

All three detectives looked at each other at the mention of the name Thomas Larkin.

'...and one more last night. A John Doe found burnt to death with a spray can next to the body on the moors above Marsden. But this one could have been an accident. I've asked West Yorks for more information.'

Trent shook her head. 'You're telling me there have been four deaths from burning in the last week and we knew nothing about them?'

Johnson smiled. 'I'm not telling you nowt, guv'nor, HOLMES is.'

'Don't be a smartarse, Rob.'

Ridpath leant closer to the computer. 'What was that about a Thomas Larkin?'

Johnson clicked the icon. 'Thomas Larkin found on the roof of the registry office in Bakewell, Derbyshire. Cause of death: immolation. Age thirty-eight. Orange spray paint can found near body. Incomplete message on the wall above his head. Presence of accelerants unknown at this point in time. I could follow up and find out more if you want.'

'No, Lorraine is going to do it.' Trent turned to her DCI. 'Get onto Derbyshire police and find out all you can about the death. On second thoughts, drive over to Bakewell and check it out yourself. Find the pathologist and get a post-mortem performed immediately if one hasn't been done already.'

She looked at Ridpath. 'I want you to follow up on the Marsden death. We need to find out more and quickly.'

'Will do, guv'nor,' he replied.

'Rob, I want you to expand the search to include the whole of England. Find out if there have been any more deaths recently.'

'No problem, boss.'

A knock on the door. Chrissy Wright walked in. 'I thought you'd want to see the search results for the names you gave me, boss. That bloke, David Mulkeen, you asked me to check up on. Well, six months ago he was interviewed as part of Operation Hydrant, the investigation into child sexual abuse. Apparently, he used to run kids' football teams…'

Chapter Forty-Four

Dave Mulkeen was used to staying in the shadows, avoiding people's stares, keeping his head down.

It was the only way to live now.

Here he was new, nobody was aware he existed. The rented flat was under an assumed name, the rent paid a year advance so he would never have to see the landlord.

Bakewell was one of those towns where everybody kept themselves to themselves. They were friendly enough in a stand-offish sort of way, but that was why he had chosen to live here. Nobody was going to bother him or even ask who he was.

Tommy Larkin lived here, another reason why he came to this town. But Tommy didn't want anything to do with him any more. Not after the trial. At least Tommy hadn't ratted on him like some of the other boys.

Seeing those faces again after all these years had brought back memories. Of good times and bad. Mostly good, though, for him.

A time of innocence and the taking of innocence.

He parked up at the large car park next to the River Wye, as he always did. A beautiful place near the town centre; a soft trilling river running over rocks. Ducks paddling along the banks. A couple eating an ice cream, the man with his trousers rolled up to his knees and his bare white feet rediscovering the sun after a long, cold winter. He stood on the bridge for a while, looking down into the water.

The bridge had padlocks attached to it by lovers. An affectation on Bakewell's part, he thought, imitating the famous bridge in Paris. He'd thought about running away to live in Europe, hiding in the anonymity of a foreign country. But he didn't speak any languages other than English and somehow he never felt at home in any other place than England.

Finally, he decided to hide in the peace and quiet of a country market town. Nobody knew him here and nobody cared.

He glanced up at the sky. Ominous grey clouds were scurrying over the hills and into the valley. He would have to be quick today.

He hurried across the bridge and strode quickly into the local Co-op. He tried to avoid going out too much, spending most of his time at home with his telly and his memories.

It was strange how much he could remember when he thought about it. The police had asked him to remember too, but he was too smart for them. 'I can't remember' always being the safest answer to any question.

The doctor was easily fooled too. Early onset Alzheimer's, he had diagnosed.

Idiot.

He could remember everything, he just wasn't going to let them know. And his solicitor, clever man, picking holes in the boys' stories, casting doubt on their memories. They had been young and it was a long time ago.

He was sorry they testified against him. Didn't they know he could still control them after all these years?

He moved quickly through the aisles, buying the stuff he always bought: eggs, cheese (the cheapest available), pizza, teabags, bread and a curry puff. He always treated himself to a curry puff when he went to the supermarket.

Keeping his head down, avoiding eye contact, not recognising anyone or anything.

That was the way to do it.

He paid at the counter and thought about wandering around the market for some vegetables but decided against it. Too many people at this time of day and anyway, what was he going to do with vegetables? Could they be microwaved like the pizza?

Probably.

He shuffled back across the bridge with his shopping, stopping once more in the middle for a short while to look down at the ducks and drakes paddling on the river without a care in the world. He had been like that once, before the past caught up with him.

But not any more.

A wind sprung up from nowhere. A few drops of rain spattered on the water, followed by a few more, gradually increasing in intensity.

A quick glance over his shoulder and he hustled into the car park, feeling a welcome relief when he saw his car. Next time, he would have to make sure he brought an umbrella.

He pulled out his keys and was about to open the door when he heard a voice behind him.

'David, David Mulkeen.'

He froze for a moment, uncertain what to do.

Brazen it out, David. Nobody knows you're here. The rain became heavier.

He pasted a false smile on his face. 'I think you've made a mistake…'

And felt something sharp in the indentation beneath his ear where the end of his jaw met the neck.

'Just get in the car, David.'

Chapter Forty-Five

'Shit, just what we didn't need. Lorraine, forget Bakewell, start getting a team together now.'

'Include an ARU, boss?'

'Firearms? Yes. Make it happen.'

'Chrissy, find out the last known address of David Mulkeen as quick as possible. We've got to find out where he is. Rob, hurry up with the check for other deaths in England. I want to know if this bastard has killed anybody else.'

'On it, guv'nor.'

'Ridpath, you're with me.'

She left the room and, rather than wait for the lifts, hurried down the stairs to the MIT floor with Ridpath in close attendance. 'You think he's involved in the deaths, boss?'

'Could be. Getting rid of any of the boys who could testify against him in the courts. At his age, if he was ever found guilty, he'd never get out of prison alive. And that's before the other cons got hold of him.'

The clatter of her heels on the stairs created a counterpoint to her words.

'And if he isn't involved, he will know why it's happening. Two men from the same football team don't just die in three days without a reason.'

She stopped suddenly and Ridpath nearly bumped into her. She turned back to look him in the eyes.

'I'm sorry for doubting your judgement, Ridpath.'

'It's OK, boss, I'm used to it.'

She raised her finger and poked him in the chest. 'But if you ever go behind my back again in an investigation, you'll be out of the force, out of the coroner's office and out on your arse quicker than the chief constable awards himself a pay rise. Get it?'

'Got it, boss.' Ridpath didn't bother to explain that if he hadn't gone behind her back, they wouldn't now be chasing a serial killer.

He thought it, but didn't say it.

They reached MIT's floor and she burst through into the office. 'You lot, in the incident room now.'

The reaction in the room was electric. Two detective inspectors, three detective sergeants, five detective constables and three support officers stopped what they were doing, picked up their notepads and hurried after Trent and Ridpath into the incident room.

'Right, close the door.'

Harry Makepeace shut out the world.

'We have a major operation. Ridpath will take you through the details, but this is the most important case in these offices now. You drop everything else, is that clear?'

The assembled detectives nodded. One of them, Jill Carton, put up her hand. 'What's the operation called, boss?'

'I don't know...'

'How about Operation Douter?' suggested Ridpath.

Trent looked at him quizzically.

'It's the little instrument like a bell people use to snuff out candles.'

She shook her head. 'Sometimes you worry me, Ridpath.'

'Pub quizzes, boss, everybody knows that.'

'OK, Operation Douter it is. Brief the team, Ridpath.'

Chapter Forty-Six

'Just drive.' The voice came from the back of the car. It was followed by the touch of the knife on his neck. He couldn't see who it was. They were sat immediately behind him, their face hidden behind the headrest.

'But where?' he asked.

'Take the A6 towards Manchester.'

'What do you want? If you want money, just take my wallet.' He reached into his jacket pocket, pulling out the battered leather wallet his father had given him all those years ago. 'There's not much, but take it.' He tossed the wallet into the back.

'I don't want your money. Take the A6 towards Manchester,' the voice ordered.

David Mulkeen put the car in gear and drove out of the car park, turning left to cross over Bakewell Bridge and back into the town centre. They stopped at a pedestrian crossing. The windscreen wipers washed across the glass. A loud beeping entered the car and a young woman with a child in a pushchair crossed the road in front of them, her head down and her hand holding an umbrella over her child.

Mulkeen's eyes darted left and right.

'Don't even think about it. Before you could make a move, I would have slit your throat. Do you know what happens when you have a cut throat, David?'

Mulkeen licked his lips, saying nothing.

'I said, do you know what happens when I cut your throat, David?'

The beeping at the pedestrian crossing seemed to get louder.

'No…' Mulkeen felt his head being grabbed and the sharpness of the blade kiss his throat.

'I would draw the blade along your neck, starting below the ear and on the left-hand side, continuing round, becoming deeper as I pulled the blade across, severing the left carotid artery and spraying your blood across the windscreen and dashboard. Your windpipe would be cut so you wouldn't be able to cry out and the blood flow to your brain would cease. After that, you have just eight seconds to live. Not a pleasant way to die, David.'

A loud, long beep from a horn behind them.

Mulkeen visibly jumped in his seat.

'Just put the car in gear and take the A6.'

Nervously, he crashed the gears and the car jerked away, turning right onto the A6 after a busy roundabout.

They drove out of town, Mulkeen glancing continually in his rear-view mirror. 'Where are we going?'

'You'll find out when we get there.'

Silence.

The damp Derbyshire countryside raced past outside the car window. Wet grey limestone houses giving way to rolling green hills. An eiderdown of white cloud blanketed the top of the hills.

'Turn right at the next junction.'

'Ashford? Why are we going to Ashford?'

'Just do it. Then take the first left, following the road to Monsal Dale.'

'Why? Why are you going there?'

The knife against the throat again. 'Don't ask questions, just do it.'

Sweat dripped from Mulkeen's face down onto his shirt. The car's engine roared as they drove up the hill. The inside of the windows misted over. Once more the windscreen wipers swept across the glass.

'You really should have done something, David.'

'But I never touched you. You weren't my type.'

'What? Not pretty enough?'

Silence.

'But I don't care what you did with those boys. It's what you all did to me.'

'I don't understand.'

'Take a left at the hotel, and follow the road down into Monsal Dale.'

The car swung around and Mulkeen saw the beauty that was the dale laid out beneath him, a damp mist fogging the red-brick railway bridge.

'Drive slowly down into the dale. We wouldn't like to kill a walker in this weather, would we?'

He drove down the narrow, tree-lined lane. At the bottom it levelled out into a long straight road with the River Wye bubbling away over rocks on the left.

'You can pull up over there.'

He pulled into a small car park on the left, a hundred yards past some houses.

'I've chosen this place because it's so beautiful. You know Ruskin, the Victorian essayist, wrote about here. It was one of his favourite places on earth.'

Despite the rain sheeting from the left, Mulkeen saw the river and its overhanging trees, their branches dangling in the water like children dipping their toes before a paddle.

The windscreen wipers squeaked their way across the glass.

'It's so beautiful I decided it would be the perfect place to burn you.'

Mulkeen didn't hear the hammer being taken out of the bag.

He didn't see it swing from behind and smash into the bone above his ear. Again and again and again.

He didn't feel his body slump forward and his head strike the steering wheel.

He didn't feel anything any more.

Chapter Forty-Seven

Ridpath had just finished briefing the detectives when Chrissy Wright came into the incident room.

'That Mulkeen man is on the sex offenders register.'

'But I thought he was only interviewed,' said Lorraine Caruso.

'He had prior charge from 1995, exposing himself to children outside a school. Back then, a social worker wasn't convinced of his "cure" and thought he was at risk of offending again, so he's on it. Apparently he had been coaching schoolboy teams since 1983, had his coaching badges from the Football Association and everything. There's a note from the social worker that there were allegations, more "insinuations" as she put it, about his activities in the football teams. Apparently he concentrated on young teams, under-twelves and -thirteens. Unaccompanied trips away, sleepovers at his house, that sort of stuff. The social worker didn't follow up, though; nobody did back then.'

'Jesus. Between 1983 and 1995 he could have molested thousands of boys.'

'And that's just the years we know about.'

'Anything since 1995?' asked Ridpath.

'Nothing in the UK. Apparently he moved to the States soon after he was bound over to keep the peace in 1995. I can check with Interpol if there are any charges in other countries.'

'Do it, Chrissy,' ordered Claire Trent.

'He moved back to the UK in 2010 and, of course, had to inform the register of his whereabouts.'

'He's on the register. So what?' asked Caruso.

Chrissy smiled. 'It means we have an address. Even better, he's just informed them of a change of address. Two months ago, he moved to Bakewell in Derbyshire.'

'Shit, that's where Tommy Larkin's body was found.'

Trent was already on her feet. 'Come on, Ridpath, you're with me. Lorraine, you take Harry Makepeace. Text me the address, Chrissy, and check his car registration with the DVLA. Is there a telephone number?'

Chrissy glanced back at her printout. 'No mobile, just a home landline. You want me to ring it?'

Trent was putting on her jacket. 'Go ahead, but pretend it's a wrong number and do it from your mobile. I don't want him to know we're onto him.'

'Firearms, boss?'

Trent shook her head. 'Any record of violence, Chrissy?'

'Nothing in here, boss.'

'OK, we'll do without. And Chrissy,' she called over her shoulder, 'let Derbyshire know we're coming. I don't want them bleating about jurisdiction. Come on, Ridpath, what are you waiting for? Time you did some proper police work again.'

Chapter Forty-Eight

He was glad of the rain. It drenched his face and hair, cleansing his mind for the task ahead. It also meant there were no hikers out today to see him or what he was doing.

He had a choice, just as Mulkeen had a choice all those years ago.

The man could die at his flat in Bakewell. But the place was small and dirty, not the right location for such an important death.

Or he could kill him here, somewhere scenic, where a terrible beauty could be born. A fitting location for the last rites of Mulkeen. A place where the silence called.

He glanced across at the hire car he had parked here yesterday. The police would eventually check, but the car was hired in Manchester and it would take them a while to make the connection, if they ever did.

By then he would have vanished in the same way he had arrived. In a wisp of smoke-filled air.

Mulkeen was still sitting in the driving seat, his head slumped against the steering wheel. He had to die, they all had to die.

It was the only way he could be free. That was what the psychotherapist had told him. Kill the memories, erase them from your mind. He had meant it metaphorically, of course, because he never understood the meaning of his own words.

If he really wanted to be free, they all had to die. Not in the imaginary world of his mind, but in the real world. The world of cruelty, loss, sadness and desire.

Their world.

Only then could he be free.

He lifted the boot lid of the hire car to bring out the prepared kit for this job. He took out the blue plastic gloves and slid them carefully over his fingers.

The spray can was lying on its side. He shook it, hearing the widget inside rattling up and down. He bent down in the rain and wrote a large 'P' on the door, followed by the other letters.

He stood back and admired his handiwork. 'PLAY THE GAME.' A fitting epitaph for all of them.

The gallon container of methylated spirits was sitting in the back. He opened Mulkeen's door and sprinkled some of the pungent liquid over him and over all the seats. He wound down the window slightly before walking around the car, pouring the rest of the liquid over it.

He had to work quickly before the rain washed it off or diluted it too much. The meths inside the car should still create the effect he wanted, but it would be more spectacular if the metal was torched too.

He unwound the long cloth rag, stuffing one end of it into the open petrol tank and leaving six inches hanging down.

He was ready now.

He had always been ready.

Chapter Forty-Nine

'Alan, how long till we get there?' Claire Trent leant forward to ask her driver.

'About ten minutes, boss.'

Ridpath stared out of the window, his body tense. This is what he loved: the moments before an arrest when the adrenaline was coursing through his body like a drug and his senses were alive and alert, sensitive to the slightest sounds, the smallest movements.

They had blue-lit the drive all the way from Manchester, racing through traffic lights, dodging traffic, even ignoring a one-way sign near some roadworks in Dinting. The lights flashing a warning to all motorists and the sirens screaming at them to get out of the way. A drive that should have taken over an hour through some of the most beautiful countryside in England took less than thirty minutes.

Even after they hit rain near Hayfield, Alan kept the car's engine racing, staring out through the windscreen wipers with a fixed smile on his lips.

Inside the car was silence. Neither Trent nor Ridpath spoke to each other. Between them the tension was stretched as taut as a drum skin.

What would they find in the house? Was Mulkeen the killer removing all those who could testify against him? But why now? And what if he wasn't there?

Trent's mobile rang and she put it on speaker.

'Hi boss, it's Chrissy.'

'What is it?'

'I checked with the DVLA. A car is registered under Mulkeen's name. It's a Vauxhall Corsa, registration WU64 XHE.'

'Great, well done, Chrissy.'

'But there's more, boss. I passed the number to Derbyshire Police and one of their patrol cars spotted the vehicle near to a place called the Monsal Hotel just five minutes ago. A driver matching Mulkeen's description was seen at the wheel.'

'The Monsal Hotel is two minutes on the right, boss,' said Alan from the front seat.

'Great, Chrissy.' Trent ended the call. The car surged forward, pushing Ridpath further back into his seat. It roared uphill, cresting a rise in the road. All four wheels seemed to lift for a moment before coming back down to earth.

Up ahead a cluster of buildings, one looking almost alpine rather than English.

'The Monsal Hotel, boss.' Alan swung the car round to the right and it screeched to a stop. Trent and Ridpath jumped out, running towards the building on the left. A few bedraggled walkers, rain dripping from their bright yellow ponchos, stared at them.

No car.

Ridpath ran towards the car park. No Vauxhall Corsa.

He raced back to rejoin his boss, coming out of the hotel. 'Nobody called Mulkeen inside.'

Thirty seconds later, Lorraine Caruso's car arrived in a blaze of squealing brakes and flashing blue lights.

Ridpath ran to a low wall overlooking the dale. Down below, the river wound its way through a deep valley. On the left, a disused railway line and bridge. Trees grew in abundance and, despite the rain, the whole place had a stunning beauty.

He was joined by Trent and Caruso.

'No sign of the car any—'

Before DCI Caruso could finish her sentence a huge explosion erupted down in the valley, sending an orange-and-blue fireball up to the grey skies.

Chapter Fifty

He saw the blue flashing lights up on top of the bluff over-looking the valley, standing out against the louring sky.

How did they find us so quickly? Had he screwed up?

No matter. He was nearly done. Just one more to go and he would be finished for ever. The plan over, the job done. He would be at peace.

He glanced up at the blue lights reflecting off the hotel windows. They were still at the top, not moving down yet.

Mulkeen sat with his head resting on the steering wheel as if he were dozing after a long drive.

It was a good place for him to die. A beautiful place. Perhaps too good for a man who had brought such misery to so many children's lives.

So it goes.

He flicked the top of the cheap plastic lighter, seeing the flame dancing in the wind and the rain. He sheltered it with his free hand and lit the rag leading into the petrol tank. The cloth caught fire and began to burn upwards towards the petrol tank.

He ran back ten yards, taking shelter behind the hire car.

For a second nothing happened.

Then there was an audible swoosh as the burning rag reached the petrol cap and was swallowed by the car. An enormous bang exploded into the sky, followed by a fireball that grew and expanded as it rose heavenwards. The car lifted off the ground for a second before returning back to earth, black smoke pouring out of the open window.

Despite being behind the hire car, he felt a wave of hot air blast over his face and the roar of the flames inside the car reached his ears.

He stood up. The dark shape of Mulkeen's body was still sitting in place in the driving seat, unmoving as the flames consumed it.

The smells were wonderful. A combination of burning plastic, meths and roasting meat.

He checked the blue lights at the top of the hill. They were moving now, coming down towards him.

Time to get going.

He picked up the bag and threw it into the boot of the hire car. He put the car in gear and reversed out of the car park, taking one last look at Mulkeen's burning Vauxhall, flames and dense black smoke consuming it.

Then there was another almighty roar. The car almost jumped up from the road and another fireball of black smoke, orange and blue flames rose elegantly into the air.

The man pulled the hood over his head. The cops were sure to check the traffic cam footage for the area. But they were running out of time now.

He had nearly finished. Just one more to go.

This would be the best one yet.

Chapter Fifty-One

Ridpath and Claire Trent raced back to the car. Alan Hardisty had already beaten them to it. A Derbyshire squad car was blocking their way. 'Get that bloody thing out of here,' shouted Alan.

A nervous constable ran back and jumped in, trying to find reverse gear to go backwards.

'Get a move on,' shouted Alan again.

The car jerked once and then sped backwards out of their way.

They raced down the hill, sliding around the narrow, tree-lined corners. Luckily nothing was coming the other way. At the bottom of the dale, the road levelled out. In the distance a large plume of black-and-white smoke rose above some build-ings.

Alan gunned the car towards it.

They drove past the buildings and there it was. A Corsa burning brightly against the grey clouds and dull green of the trees.

They skidded to a halt. Trent and Ridpath jumped out and ran towards the car. In the front seat Ridpath could see the prone body of a man leaning over the dashboard.

Trent grabbed his arm. 'Stay back, Ridpath, this could go up again.'

Ridpath covered his face to protect it from the heat coming from the car, inching forward as he did. The smell was so powerful: the acrid tang of plastic mixed with the sweet aroma of burning flesh.

Alan appeared on his left carrying a small fire extinguisher. He banged the top and began spraying the white powder towards the Corsa. But it was like putting out a forest blaze with a water pistol; the flames just burned brighter.

Other coppers arrived also carrying red fire extinguishers. The Corsa was bathed in a cloud of white smoke, but still the blue flames leapt up towards the sky.

'Pull back to safety,' Trent ordered. She pointed to one of the Derbyshire officers. 'Get on your radio, I want roadblocks on all the exits leading out of here.'

'But... but we don't have the manpower. It'll have to come from Derby.'

'I don't care, just do it.'

He ran back to his squad car.

'And you,' she pointed to a uniformed constable, 'set up a perimeter down here and another at the top of the bluff near the hotel.'

'Yes, ma'am.'

They all stood and watched as the flames continued to consume the car. Less bright now, less ferocious, but still glowing strongly, the heat intense.

The car itself was just blackened metal; all the windows had been burnt or blown out, the boot had popped open and the paint had been burnt away. Only the number plate remained, hanging from one screw, its letters clear and bright: WU64 XHE.

'It's Mulkeen's car,' said Trent.

In the driving seat, a dark shape lay huddled over the steering wheel, looking almost subhuman in its form. But the smell it gave off was unmistakeable.

Roast meat.

Roast human meat.

Chapter Fifty-Two

They stayed at the scene for another hour as the fire gradually died down and the Scene of Crime team from Derbyshire Police took over. Ridpath and Claire Trent stood around, leaving the investigation to the local boys.

The car was a burnt-out shell, with twisted pieces of metal, springs from the seats, blackened metal doors and four rims all that remained. Everything that could burn was cremated, including the human body in the front seat.

The local head of Derbyshire CID turned up. A stocky man with a florid face, looking more like a prosperous squire than a copper. 'Remind me never to come to one of your barbecues, Claire.'

'Hello, John, you took your time.'

'I was on a stabbing in Worksop. Knife crime's spread out from the streets of London to our green and pleasant land. Who's the burnt sausage in the car?'

'We think it's David Mulkeen.'

'And who's he when he's at home?'

'Possible paedophile. Interviewed during a child sexual abuse investigation, but not charged yet.'

'Bloody CPS. It never moves quickly enough.'

'We wanted to question him regarding some other crimes in Manchester.'

'Looks like you were too late.'

A man dressed in white Tyvek moved away from the car and walked over to the detectives, pulling down his hood. 'I've pronounced him dead at 1:35 p.m.'

'We'll send you through the DNA results for David Mulkeen as a comparison for your lab.'

'Thanks, we'll rush the analysis for you. We've asked a fire investigator to take a look but even I can smell the accelerant in the car.'

'Was it a suicide, Doctor?' Ridpath spoke for the first time.

'I don't think so. Not unless he hit himself over the head first. Most of the rear side of his skull has been caved in, plus we found the remains of a ball peen hammer on the back seat.'

'So you think he was murdered?' asked Trent.

'That's my first guess. But I'll know more and confirm my initial finding as soon as I can perform the post-mortem, which I'll do this evening. You should have the report tomorrow morning.'

'Any fingerprints?'

'In that?' He pointed to the burnt-out remains of the car. 'You must be joking.'

Ridpath looked around. 'If it was a murder, how did the killer get away? This place is pretty remote.'

'He must have had a car waiting for him. Nobody passed us, so he used either of those two roads.' Claire pointed behind her before turning to the detective from Derbyshire. 'Where do they go to?'

'Both lead back onto the A623 eventually. Manchester is to the west and Sheffield or Chesterfield to the east.'

'Did the roadblocks stop anybody?'

'What roadblocks?'

'The ones I ordered to be set up.'

'I doubt it. There weren't any when I drove here.'

Trent looked around for the constable she had given the orders to, but couldn't see him. 'Can we at least get the traffic footage for both directions?'

'No problem.'

'Plus any ANPR footage of this Corsa. You have ANPR, don't you?'

'We're not quite in the Stone Age of policing out in the country. Nearly, but not quite. I'll check the number out and see what we've got.'

'And can we interview those hikers?' She pointed to a few of the wet, bedraggled people dressed in colourful gear who had clustered around the top of the hill, watching the entertainment below. 'See if they saw anything or anybody.'

'I'll get a team on it.'

'Thanks. We should head back, Ridpath.'

'What are we dealing with here, Detective Superintendent?'

Trent took a deep breath. 'We think it's a serial killer. And the bad news is, we think this is the second murder in your district, John.'

Chapter Fifty-Three

Back at Manchester HQ, the MIT office was a scene of frenetic activity. Ridpath and Trent were met at the door by Chrissy Wright. 'We've taken over the incident room for Operation Douter, boss. Let me show you what we've done.'

Lorraine Caruso and her team were already in the incident room, having left Monsal Dale as the pathologist arrived. Chrissy had been busy in their absence.

The walls were neatly divided into sections with dates printed clearly above each section, a picture of the victim and the details of each crime beneath. In the centre of the wall, the picture of the five-a-side team had been blown up with names placed beneath each player.

'Which photo is this?'

'The one given to us by Sam Sykes's parents. The other from Joseph Brennan's home is posted beneath,' answered Chrissy.

'What's N-A-B-G-C F...' asked Ridpath, pointing to the banner behind the heads of the boys.

Chrissy shrugged her shoulders.

'Find out,' barked Trent.

On the right-hand side, a detective constable was standing next to a whiteboard with 'Lines of Enquiry' printed across the top. He quickly wrote 'NAGBC?' on the top line.

Chrissy led Trent and Ridpath to the first section. It had a large question mark with the words 'John Doe' printed at the top.

'From the preliminary pathologist reports, we think the man on the moors was killed first, guv'nor. We can't be certain, but the pathologist has estimated the death as occurring on the 21st or 22nd of April.'

'We still don't know who it is?'

'Not yet, guv'nor.'

'Hassle the Yorkshire pathologist. It's critical we get the post-mortem report and know who this man is. Until then, we can't create a proper timeline of the deaths.'

Chrissy made a note in her book as she moved to the next panel. It was dated April 22 at the top. 'This is the latest shot we have of Thomas Larkin, taken three years ago when he was arrested for DUI in 2016. He was found on the roof of a registry office, burnt to death. The initial incident report put it down as a suicide, but we've now asked Derbyshire to reopen the case. Luckily the body hasn't been buried yet. The Derbyshire pathologist will perform the post-mortem this evening.'

'Make sure he shares his report with Dr Schofield,' said Ridpath. 'There may be a link between the murders we haven't found yet.'

'Do we know anything about him?'

'Not a lot, boss. Seems to be the quiet type, kept himself to himself. A loader in a warehouse. No girlfriend as far as we can make out, or next of kin. Derbyshire are checking for us.'

'Don't wait for them. Check him out yourself. Anything on the PNC? Where was he born? Did he grow up in Manchester? The usual stuff.'

Chrissy nodded and moved on to the next panel. 'This is where we start with Ridpath's involvement.' The picture from the flat had been blown up. 'Joseph Brennan, aged thirty-eight. We've put a question mark next to the face because we still don't have DNA confirmation. But Mr Brennan has not been seen since before the fire and the body matches his height and weight.'

'Dr Schofield told me they were going to check dental records?' said Ridpath.

'We haven't heard anything back from him. I'll follow up. We already have the medical records from your office. Somebody called Sophia Rahman sent them over by courier.'

Thank God she was so efficient, thought Ridpath.

Trent spoke. 'Let's assume it's him for the moment. Has DI Wharton been informed we are taking over the case?'

'Yes, guv'nor, and delighted he was too.'

'Why am I not surprised?' muttered Lorraine Caruso.

'Joseph Brennan was one of our own, boss. Well, sort of. Until three years ago he worked for one of the testing labs, Liscat Scientific. We put quite a lot of stuff their way, usually materials analysis, some DNA work and blood testing.'

'What did he do for them?'

'He was a lab technician as far as we know. Lost his job three years ago for unknown reasons.'

'Find out why,' barked Trent.

'What does the DWP say?'

'I don't know, Ridpath. They haven't returned my calls.'

'Bloody typical,' muttered Harry Makepeace.

Chrissy moved on to the next section. 'Victim number four. Samuel Sykes aka Soapy Sam. A long-term addict, street sleeper and one of the best-known homeless people in the city centre. I've asked Central to send us everything they have on his death.'

Next to the picture somebody had pasted up a shot of the message 'PLAY THE GAME' plus two blurry printouts of the CCTV images: the homeless man who was a possible witness and the man who attacked Ridpath.

'These are the best shots we have. The lads upstairs are working their magic to give us a better image. But they told me it's not going to get much better as the hard disk was knackered.'

'Is that the technical term?' Trent leant over to peer at the picture. 'Is this the man who attacked you, Ridpath?'

'I think so, but it all happened so fast and I didn't see his face.'

'You were lucky,' said Caruso.

'I don't think so. He knocked me out cold and could have killed me easily, but he didn't. Why?'

'I've heard they call you Catman, Ridpath – more lives than a bloody moggie.' Caruso looked around and all the other detectives laughed. Ridpath could see she didn't join in but stared at him, threateningly.

'We have reassigned this case as murder too,' said Chrissy. 'The SIO has been informed and is quite happy for us to take over.'

'I bet he is…' whispered Caruso.

Ridpath stepped forward and tapped the picture of the homeless man. 'Anybody recognise him? He may have seen the killer at the building site.'

The detectives all shook their heads.

'Can we ask the PCSOs who work in central Manchester? Perhaps they'll recognise him?'

'Harry, can you co-ordinate that?'

'Yes, boss.'

Chrissy Wright moved on to the final section. The picture area was blank with a large red question mark in a frame. 'Today's victim. We don't have a picture of David Mulkeen yet, but a mugshot is coming from the files. It should be here in an hour or so. He was a football coach, aged sixty-three. As we know, he was interviewed as part of the Operation Hydrant child sexual abuse investigation. I've asked the Child Protection unit for all the files. As I said, he worked with kids' football teams from 1983 to 1995, specialising in the under-fourteens.'

'Jesus. Nobody worked out what he was up to?' said Harry Makepeace.

Chrissy shook her head. 'None of the kids came forward, or, if they did, nobody believed them. It's only in the last couple of years that it's come to light, when some of the young men had the bravery to speak up. You have to remember what it was like then. These coaches, well, they wielded real power in these clubs. Places like City, Crewe, Newcastle, Chelsea,

Southampton and Peterborough have all had allegations made against them…' She stopped speaking.

'You sound like you know about it, Chrissy,' said Ridpath.

'My son, he was on the books at City when Barry Bennell was there. Nothing happened, but I…'

'We need to know more, Chrissy. Can you do the research?'

'Even better, I know the man in charge of the investigation. I'll ask him to brief us.'

'Great, well done, Chrissy.'

'There's a couple more things I need to show you.' She moved to another section which was headed 'Consistencies in the Murders'. 'Now, obviously we haven't got the complete information from the post-mortems or the incidents yet, but we have been able to find some of this killer's MO.'

Ridpath stared at the list.

All victims burnt to death, but killed first. (John Doe/Thomas Larkin ??)

Presence of accelerants. Methylated spirits ??

All victims knew each other. (John Doe ??)

All victims played on same team in 1994.

Orange spray paint can found at each scene ??

Most victims struck with a blunt object possibly ball peen hammer (except Sam Sykes)

All victims near the message 'PLAY THE GAME' ??

'I've put question marks where the information hasn't been confirmed yet.'

Trent nodded her head. 'This seems to be a comprehensive list of the consistent MO of this killer. Anybody disagree?'

No response from the detectives.

'Anybody have anything to add? Ridpath?'

He shook his head. 'I think Chrissy's done a great job in a short time.'

'There is one more thing I'd like to show you.' Chrissy Wright adjusted her City scarf and moved across to the final section. Two names were printed on it in large black letters, one above the other.

Tony Doyle
Harry McHale

'We've checked with the registrar of deaths and Doyle died of a drug overdose in 2010. Heroin. McHale died three years ago in a car accident. He drove his Ford into a wall. Another DUI.'

Trent took two steps back. 'But... but... that means all the people in the photograph are dead.'

A silence descended on the room. A clock ticked noisily on the far wall. The detectives stared at the picture of the smiling young boys kneeling in front of their coach, proudly displaying the winning trophy.

Ridpath walked towards the picture. 'You're wrong, guv'nor.' He tapped the cut-off arm and shoulder. 'This man is still alive.'

Chapter Fifty-Four

Trent brought the briefing to a close. 'Right, the priority is to find out who this man is or was. He's our most likely suspect. Somehow he has committed at least five murders in the last week and we've only just discovered he exists. If the newspapers ever find out, we'll be hung, drawn and quartered.'

Harry Makepeace coughed. 'That's what I was just about to tell you, boss. They've already got wind of it.' He held up a copy of the *Manchester Evening News*. The headline was in strong bold type: 'Is a serial killer stalking Manchester?'

He then read out the first paragraph of the article, detailing the deaths of Joseph Brennan and Sam Sykes, but not mentioning the other deaths, or the link to child sexual abuse.

'Shit, that's the last thing I need.' Then she fixed each detective in turn with a stare. 'If I find out any of you bastards have been leaking to the papers, you'll be out so quick your feet won't touch the floor. Is that clear?'

'It could have been Derbyshire, guv'nor, or the mortuary, or just an inquisitive reporter following up on a story. They haven't made the link to the other murders, but it will only be a matter of time.'

'Thanks, Ridpath. Any other words of wisdom?'

'I'm not sure this man is the suspect. It could be somebody else, somebody we don't even know about yet.'

'You really are a bearer of good news this afternoon, Ridpath.' She tapped the picture hard with her manicured fingernail. 'Unfortunately, this is the only lead we have at the moment. Lorraine, I want you to follow up on the two deaths

232

in Bakewell. Push the pathologist hard. I want the post-mortem and test results yesterday.'

'OK, boss.'

'Chrissy, I want the wall updated, there are quite a few gaps in it at the moment.'

'It's because all the information isn't in yet, boss.'

'I know, but I want it completed ASAP. Understand? And arrange that briefing from the head of the soccer investigation. We need to know more.'

Chrissy shrugged, the Man City scarf still around her neck. 'Yes, boss.'

'Lorraine, I want you to find out who this man is.' She tapped the shoulders on the cropped photograph. 'Was he another coach? A parent? Who the hell is he? And where was this five-a-side game held? Find out all you can about it.'

'Yes, guv'nor.'

'You might want to start looking at all the local newspapers for 1994. This looks like one of the shots taken by a staff photographer. Was there a stamp on the back? Local newspapers make extra money selling prints to happy parents and anyone in the shot.'

'Thanks, Ridpath,' Caruso replied without looking at him.

Trent sniffed. 'Harry, get on to Rob Johnson. I want those HOLMES results put in a report ASAP. I'll have to show something to the chief constable…'

As if on cue, a detective popped her head around the door. 'The chief constable's on the phone, guv'nor. Apparently he's read some newspaper article…'

'Just what I need. The bloody mayor will be on my back soon, you wait and see.'

'I've already put him on hold; thought you'd like to speak to the chief first.'

Trent started to pick up her files.

Harry Makepeace put up his hand.

'What is it, Harry?' she said brusquely.

'It may be nothing, guv'nor, but that's a song.'

'A what?'

'"Play the Game". It's a song by Queen. And now I come to think of it, the music video even has flames behind Freddie's head.'

Claire Trent stared back at the words written on the board. 'Follow up on it, Lorraine.'

'Yes, boss.'

The detective superintendent strode towards the door.

'What do you want me to do?' asked Ridpath before she could leave.

She stopped and then turned back slowly. 'I think you've done enough, Ridpath, don't you?'

Chapter Fifty-Five

Eve looked up guiltily from her iPad. 'Dad, you're home early.'

Polly came rushing out from the kitchen. 'Are you OK? Not coming down with something?'

Ridpath shook his head. 'I'm fine, just thought I'd come home early today.'

The truth was that after Claire Trent's curt dismissal of him, Ridpath had thought about going back to the coroner's office, but the idea of driving all the way out to Stockfield didn't appeal. Instead he gave Margaret Challinor a call to fill her in on what had happened.

'You weren't in today, Ridpath,' she said sternly before he had a chance to begin. 'Sophia did her best to cover for you but she didn't know where you were.'

'Sorry, Mrs Challinor, I got caught up in events. I should have let you know. The killer has struck again. This time in Derbyshire. You were right about the link to the Bakewell death.'

Her voice softened. 'Being right gives me no pleasure, Ridpath.'

Ridpath took her through the timeline.

'My God. I'll send an email to the coroners for West Yorkshire and Derbyshire to let them know. The inquest on Joseph Brennan is scheduled for May 7. I may have to postpone it until the police have completed their investigations.'

A strange feeling ran through Ridpath's body. 'Don't postpone yet, Mrs Challinor. For some reason this killer is working to a timetable. He's committed five murders in the last week.'

'So why is he killing now? And why use fire, Ridpath? What's the significance of fire?'

As ever, Mrs Challinor had reached the core of the investigation quickly. 'We don't know,' answered Ridpath honestly. 'I'll be in tomorrow morning, Coroner. I'll catch up with the backlog and brief Sophia on the new cases, if that's OK.'

'Of course.' And then a slight pause. 'Any news about my brother?'

In all the excitement, Ridpath had forgotten completely. 'I'll follow up straight away, Mrs Challinor.'

'Thanks, Ridpath. Sorry to hassle you about this, but I feel something has happened to him. It's like there's something missing and I don't know what it is.'

Ridpath knew what she meant. He always felt the same in the middle of an investigation when he didn't know where he was headed. That sense of loss, of absence, of something being missing. A piece of the puzzle they hadn't seen yet or didn't even know about. 'I'll follow up right now.'

He hung up the phone and immediately called Ted Jones.

'Hello, Ridpath, I heard you covered for me with Claire Trent.'

News got around quickly on the jungle drums of GMP. 'Yeah, you should have pushed the investigation harder, Ted. We now know this man has been killing other people in exactly the same way.'

'Shit, just what I needed on my record. A missed collar.'

'You'll be OK. You kept the investigation going, didn't you?'

'Well, yeah…'

'So that's how it will read – ongoing investigation into an unexplained death. Get onto Lorraine Caruso at MIT, find out the details from her, and then reclassify your case. It will be transferred to MIT anyway once they do the paperwork.' Ridpath didn't know why he was protecting such an empty suit as Ted Jones. It was just what they did in the police force. It was always 'us' versus 'them'. 'Them' being anybody who wasn't part of the tight bunch of people who worked at GMP. Including the bosses who sat in their ivory towers playing politics.

'Thanks, Ridpath, I'll get onto it right away. I owe you one.'

'And that's the other reason I'm calling. I need you to find somebody for me. A Robert Challinor, aged fifty-six. He's living on the streets.'

'A bit old for that sort of life. But I can check the shelters and the flophouses for you, plus get onto the local PCSOs. The mayor's on one of his clean-up drives again, getting the homeless off the streets.'

'Putting them where they can't be seen?'

'You got it.'

'Thanks, Ted, but get moving on your case. The sooner you get it across to MIT, the better.'

He switched off the phone and decided to drive home.

Now here he was, with his wife and daughter both fussing around him.

'Are you sure you're OK?' asked Polly.

'Dad, you're never home this early,' said Eve.

'There's always a first time,' said Ridpath, pulling them closer to him to give them a hug. 'Now, I thought I'd cook my super special spag bol, and then we could play a game of Scrabble. We haven't done that for ages.'

'Yay, great!' shouted Eve, dancing on the spot.

'I'll finish the marking and then I'm free. I fancy a spag bol tonight too.'

So for the first time in a long time they ate together as a family and played Scrabble. Eve won of course, with the connivance of her parents. Ridpath was particularly good at setting her up for a big score.

Afterwards, they watched a bit of telly, before sending Eve off to bed with the usual admonishment against being grumpy in the morning.

'I can't promise, Dad. I'm not really a morning person. But can I have pancakes tomorrow for breakfast?'

'Are you sure you don't want porridge?'

'Yeeeuuw, no way, pancakes would be great.'

'Pancakes it is then.'

Lying in bed later that night, Polly put her arms round him. 'I like it when you come home early.'

'I like it too.'

'Feels like we're a family again.'

As Ridpath drifted off to sleep, his mind inevitably returned to the murders and Mrs Challinor's questions.

Who was he?

Why had he started killing now?

And why use fire?

Before the oblivion of sleep drowned his thoughts, Ridpath realised with a sudden flash of clarity that the killer would kill again tomorrow.

Could he stop him?

Day Eight

Tuesday, April 30, 2019

Chapter Fifty-Six

As soon as he woke up, Ridpath knew what he had to do.

Polly lay snoring gently beside him, the spring light was just creeping through the curtains and the alarm clock had not yet buzzed its welcome to the day.

He knew what to do, but the question was, should he do it?

In that strange way the mind works, his brain had been mulling over the problem as he slept. He now saw that the key was the photograph of the young five-a-side team. Somehow that picture, or what happened at the time it was taken, was the catalyst for all the recent events.

But he was a coroner's officer, he wasn't a copper any more. He should tell them what he thought and leave them to do their job, working the case.

But what if Lorraine Caruso ballsed it up? Her track record hadn't been great so far. What if Claire Trent decided she'd had enough and wanted to get rid of him? Would he still have a job?

Then something Mrs Challinor said came back to him. 'Our job is to represent the dead in the court of the living.' He knew then what he had to do.

Find out who the man in the picture was. Maybe he was a suspect, as Trent thought. Or maybe he was something far more worrying.

The next victim.

He looked across at his wife sleeping beside him.

'Sorry, love,' he whispered.

Ridpath eased himself out of bed and crept downstairs. Over a mug of coffee, he worked out a plan. He knew Caruso would be far too busy running the investigation to get onto this right away. But if she didn't, he was sure another man would die today.

He rang Sophia Rahman on her mobile. 'Sorry for calling so early.'

A sleepy voice answered. 'Ridpath, it's... six thirty-five.'

'Sorry, but I've had an idea about the murders and I need you to help me. There's too much to go through on my own.'

The voice was sharper, more awake. 'Sure, what do you want me to do?'

'Meet me at Central Library as soon as it opens at nine a.m. I'll brief you there.'

'What about the coroner's office?'

'I'll send an email to Mrs Challinor explaining everything. She knows what's going on.' A slight white lie, but for Ridpath it was always better to act first and ask for permission later. He logged on to his laptop and sent the email.

It had been nagging him for a while what the 'NAGBC' stood for in the background of the photograph. He Googled it and immediately the answer was staring him in the face. It was the National Association of Girls and Boys Clubs and, even better, they held a national five-a-side competition every year as part of their activities. On their site was a link to the local association, the Girls and Boys Clubs of Greater Manchester. A name that just tripped off the tongue, but was known as the GBCGM.

Ridpath quickly scanned a history of the movement. It had been created amidst the squalor and poverty of Manchester's Victorian society as a solution to the growth of what were known as Scuttling gangs. He'd heard of these gangs, who used chains and belts to fight with other gangs in the late Victorian era. Ridpath laughed to himself. 'The more it changes, the more it stays the same.' Even in those days they had problems with street gangs.

Reading on, it seemed the founding clubs provided a means by which young lads could gain a basic education and vent their energies in a range of positive and purposeful activities. God, they needed them now more than ever. He looked through the rest of the website. The five-a-side picture must have been taken at one of these club events.

He checked his watch: 7:15. Time to get moving. He quickly cooked the pancakes, made coffee for Polly and left a note on the kitchen table telling them both he had to go to work.

He would miss the grumpy Eve enjoying her breakfast, but it couldn't be helped.

He closed the door as quietly as he could and drove into central Manchester. The roads were busy but he made good time. It would cost him a fortune to park in the city centre, but it couldn't be avoided.

At 8:50 a.m., he arrived outside Central Library to find Sophia Rahman already waiting for him, two Starbucks cups in her hands.

'I figured you'd need one of these, Ridpath. What's going on?'

By the time he had briefed her, a uniformed attendant was unlocking the big brass doors and opening them wide. Three students rushed in before them.

'You know this is a long shot, don't you, Ridpath? What happens if the photograph wasn't taken by a local newspaper? What if it was just a parent who made copies for the other families?'

Ridpath shrugged. 'You could be right, but at least we'll know and have exhausted one line of enquiry. At the moment we have nothing else.'

They walked up the wide marble stairs and entered the first-floor reading room. Ridpath sucked in his breath. The place always amazed him. He had first visited here as part of a school project when he was fourteen. Back then, the immense domed building with its eau-de-nil ceiling and the beautiful red marble pillars was dominated by stacks of bookcases and redolent of the peculiar damp smell that comes from old books.

But now, after the recent renovations, the place was bright and airy. The old bookcases had been removed to be replaced by reading tables, and the dome had been repainted in a brilliant white with gold corniches. The clock in the centre was still there, though. It had been regilded and cleaned and now dominated the surroundings.

Ridpath asked the attendant where they could find local newspapers.

'Try downstairs at local history, you'll find them there.'

Reluctantly Ridpath and Sophia left the reading room and stumbled downstairs to a far more practical place. He approached one of the librarians, showing them his warrant card. 'I'd like to look at the local newspapers for 1994,' he said.

'Which one?'

Ridpath shrugged his shoulders. 'We're not sure.' He showed the librarian the picture. 'We think this was taken by a local newspaper in 1994, but it's been cropped. We'd like to see the original if possible.'

The librarian frowned. 'It could be in any of the newspapers.'

'There are a lot?'

'About fifty at that time in Greater Manchester, maybe more. We hold a few here, but others are held in the local history libraries in districts like Bolton or Trafford.'

Ridpath's heart sank. This wasn't going to be as easy as he thought.

'I could take a look at GMLives for you. There might be something on the site.'

She went to a workstation and tapped in a code. Up popped a website with an old picture of Manchester. She typed 'five-a-side' into the search box. 'Just one result from Hulme in 1994, but it's not the same picture.'

Ridpath's heart sank for the second time.

'It looks like you'll have to go through them manually, I'm afraid. Do you want me to bring you all the local newspapers we have on microfilm for that year?'

'It looks like it's the only option.' He turned to Sophia. 'This could be a long day, Sophia.'

'And that's presuming this picture was taken by a local newspaper, and that they printed it, and there's more of the image to see. Have you thought this might be the original crop? Perhaps the man you're looking for was never seen in the picture.'

No, Ridpath hadn't thought of that.

Shit, this was going to be difficult.

Chapter Fifty-Seven

Ridpath was still thinking what to do when Sophia spoke up.

'Look, we know the tournament was organised by the National Association of Girls and Boys Clubs, right?'

Ridpath nodded his head slowly.

'Why don't I call the local branch and see if they have any records? They may have even taken the picture themselves.'

'It's called the Girls and Boys Clubs of Greater Manchester. GBCGM for short.' Both women stared at him. 'I Googled it this morning'.

The librarian finally spoke. 'I'll find the number for you.' She tapped her code into the computer and wrote the number down on a Post-it note.

'I'll get started on checking the local papers,' said Ridpath.

Sophia wandered off to the entrance to make the phone call.

'Do you have a date range?' asked the librarian.

Ridpath shrugged his shoulders. 'The whole of 1994?'

'It'll be a lot of reels.'

'Can't avoid it.'

'OK, but rather you than me.' She went off to the cabinets where the microfilms were stored, leaving Ridpath on his own in the middle of the library floor. All around him people were reading, checking maps, or staring at computer screens.

Off to the left, there was the buzz of a cafe. This was also different from the almost reverential atmosphere of the place when he was growing up. He remembered a cathedral-like silence where it was forbidden to talk except in a quiet whisper.

As he stood there, he wondered if this was just a wild goose chase and he had missed a clue he should have been following. A clue that would lead him to the killer before he killed again.

Too late now. This was the best thing he could do at this moment.

Sophia came back. 'I spoke to a Mrs Hargreaves. They probably have the records in their archives somewhere, but she said I should talk to a man called Steve Richards, who has run the five-a-side competition for donkey's years. He'll be in after ten o'clock.'

'Where are they based?'

'A place called Gritstone Mill out in Stockport.'

'You'd better go out there and interview him.'

'But I've never done an interview before.'

'Good time to start then. Just ask the right questions.'

'Thanks, Ridpath, that's a great help.'

'Find out all he knows about the picture. Take it with you.'

She waved goodbye as the librarian arrived back with an armful of microfilm reels. 'I'll start you on the *Manchester Evening News*, the *Manchester Advertiser*, the Sports Pinks, *Manchester Metro News*, and the *Middleton and North Manchester Guardian*. I'll come back with some of the district newspapers later.'

'How many of those are there?'

'Well... at least ten. But as I said, we don't hold them all.'

Ridpath's heart fell again. It was like looking for a payphone that worked. 'I'd better get started then.'

Two hours later and Ridpath had just about finished the *Manchester Evening News*. His eyes were tired from staring at the print on the cream screen. All the articles were blurring into each other in some vast sea of newsprint.

At first he checked the articles one by one, but quickly realised this was going to take him a year. Then he just checked the pictures. After an hour he worked out only the back pages held the sports news, so he whizzed through the microfilm until he reached that place.

Even though 1994 was only twenty-five years ago, and he had lived through it, the world and Manchester seemed like a very different place. United won the league and cup double, Keane was in midfield with Cantona up front, John Major was prime minister, Tony Blair became leader of the Labour Party, the IRA were still bombing Britain, and police were digging up bodies at the home of Rose and Fred West.

He remembered that time in his own life. His mother and his sister continually arguing, while he kept his head down and said nothing, burying himself in books or TV, or in the library to avoid their constant squabbles. His sister left home towards the end of the year, running away to London aged sixteen. Ridpath never asked her how she managed, but three years later she was serving time for theft and drugs, and had been in and out of jail ever since. They hardly saw each other any more; the last time was more than three years ago.

Ridpath had just switched off the machine to take a break when the phone call came through.

'It's Sophia. I met with Steve Richards and he remembers the time well. He was organising the tournaments in May every year. I showed him the picture and he remembered the team. They all thought they were going to be the next David Beckham or Paul Scholes.'

'Did he remember the man in the picture who's cropped out?'

'He didn't. Too many coaches and parents, he said, plus he was busy organising the event and had no time to talk to them.'

Ridpath's head sunk to his chest and he let out a long sigh.

'But he remembers the photographer. The same man used to come to all their events.'

Tentatively, Ridpath asked, 'Who was it?'

'He doesn't remember the name...'

Another sigh.

'…But he used to work for the *South Manchester Express*.'

Ridpath punched the air, shouting 'Yes!' The other library users stopped what they were doing and stared at him. Sheepishly, he nodded at them.

'Hello, Ridpath, are you there?'

'Well done, Sophia, you did great.'

'Not bad for my first interrogation.'

'Interview, Sophia, only the Secret Service do interrogations.'

'Do you want me to come back to Central Library?'

Ridpath thought for a moment. 'No, go back to the coroner's office and brief Mrs Challinor.'

He ended the call and hurried over to the librarian's desk. 'Do you have the *South Manchester Express* here?' Ridpath crossed his fingers behind his back.

'For 1994?'

He nodded.

She ran her finger down a list. 'You said the *South Manchester Express*, not the *South Manchester Reporter*?'

Ridpath said yes and crossed his toes as well.

Her finger stopped. 'We do have it, in cabinet 28. Would you like to see it?'

Would he like to see it? Would United like to win the league again? 'Yes, please.'

The librarian went off to the cabinet, returning with just one reel. 'Would you like me to load it up for you?'

'No, thanks.' Ridpath snatched the reel and trotted back to the microfilm reader. With fumbling fingers, he undid the box and put the microfilm on the sprocket, winding it through the gates.

He switched the reader back on.

It was upside down.

He unloaded it and threaded it on again properly. The typed message 'South Manchester Express Jan–Dec 1994' stared back at him. He pressed the lever of the reader and the newspaper whizzed past his eyes, a catalogue of house pictures, adverts and short articles.

He stopped. March 10, 1994.

He pressed the lever again, finally reaching May 1, then he slowed down, but kept the reader moving forward. More house pictures. A semi-detached house in his area was just 56,000 pounds. More ads for Tesco and Sainsbury. A cat stuck down a drain. Cricket team pictures. Even more houses.

He scrolled slowly through the month of May: nothing on five-a-side games or boys clubs. Back to the beginning and he started again, going more slowly this time. But the same reports remained in the paper right up to May 31.

Nothing.

A dark shadow appeared across his screen. He turned quickly, ready to strike out at whoever it was looming behind him. But it was just the librarian.

'How's the search going?' she asked.

'Not great. The five-a-side tournament happened in May but there are no pictures.'

'Have you tried June? The local papers were always a bit slow with the news.'

He pushed the lever forward.

And there it was on June 2. The full, uncropped picture.

His mouth dropped when he looked at the man's face and saw the name in the caption.

Chapter Fifty-Eight

He strode up to the door and rang the bell. He had spent most of yesterday afternoon watching the house and knew Charlie would be well into the Scotch by now.

'Who is it?' a querulous voice shouted down the hall.

Even after all these years, he still recognised the voice. 'It's me,' he shouted back.

He could see a shape coming closer through the mottled glass.

'I wish people would tell me their bloody names rather than shout "It's me". The door is open anyway.' As he said the last word, the door swung open and Charlie Whitworth stood in the hallway, leaning on a walking stick. 'Who the bloody hell are you?'

He could smell the whisky from here. 'You don't recognise me, Charlie?'

The man stared at him through unfocussed eyes. 'No, never seen you before.'

The door began to close but he was too quick, sticking his boot in the gap.

'If you don't remove your foot, I'm going to break it.'

He took the revolver out of his pocket and pointed it at Whitworth. 'Now, let's go inside and have a nice chat in your kitchen. We can talk about old times if you want, Charlie.'

The eyes creased up. 'Who the fuck are you?'

'I'm disappointed you don't remember me, but you'll find out soon enough, Charlie. Now why don't you turn around and hobble back to the kitchen on your walking stick. There's a bit of a chill in the air this morning and we wouldn't want you to catch your death. Not of cold, anyway.'

Charlie stared down at the metal barrel of the revolver then up at his face. He could see the man was trying to remember his face, going through the mugshot books in his mind to find out which criminal he'd put away had returned to darken his door.

After a few moments, the former detective gave up and slowly turned around, before limping down the hallway to the kitchen.

He entered the house, closed the door and followed him into the kitchen.

'Now sit yourself down, Charlie, and pour yourself a large Scotch. You're about to hear my life story. You'll know part of it, of course. But I'm sure you'll be delighted to hear the rest.'

'What do you want with me?'

'Not a lot, but you'll find out later. First things first. Sit down and pour yourself a Scotch.'

Reluctantly Whitworth took his seat at the kitchen table and poured himself a drink.

'I think I first met you in early 1994...'

Chapter Fifty-Nine

Ridpath stared at the article below the picture and the caption beneath it.

WINNERS FOR THE SECOND YEAR

Stockfield Boys Club came out tops once again in the Manchester and District Five-a-Side Competition hosted by the National Association of Boys and Girls Clubs played last week. They beat Harpurhey 3–1 in the final after trailing 1–0 at half time. The manager of the team, David Mulkeen, said, 'This is a special set of boys. My favourites after all these years coaching these age groups. After a lot of hard training, I'm going to take them out for a special treat this evening, so they can finally let their hair down and have some fun.'

Well done, Mr Mulkeen. We've just seen David Beckham and Paul Scholes break into the United team from the Juniors. Perhaps you are looking at a future star from amongst these talented boys.

Pictured above are the winning team: (from left to right) Thomas Larkin, Tony Doyle, Sam Sykes, Joe Brennan and Michael McHale, with coach David Mulkeen and his assistant, Charles Whitworth.

Ridpath looked again and again at the name of the man who had been cropped out. Charles Whitworth. It was definitely Charlie, a younger version but still his former DCI.

A second later he jumped out of his seat in Central Library and hurried past the startled librarian. Then he stopped for a second.

Think, Ridpath. What did he need to do?

Proof. He needed proof.

He raced back to the reader, got out his phone and took a picture of the screen. It was just about legible but the quality wasn't great.

The librarian was staring at him.

'Could you print out the page on my reader and send it to this email address?' He quickly wrote down the GMP contact address. 'Send it to Detective Superintendent Claire Trent.'

'Sure. Did you find what you wanted?'

'Yes, unfortunately.'

He ran out of the building, pulling the mobile phone back out of his pocket. Trent wasn't answering, the ringtone buzzing in his ears. He ended the call, nearly running into an old woman, but just dodging around her at the last minute.

He rang Lorraine Caruso. The phone was answered after two rings.

'Detective Chief Inspector Caruso.'

Ridpath bet she loved saying those words. 'Hi Lorraine, it's Ridpath. I know who the man in the picture is.'

'How? You're supposed to be back at the coroner's, not working on the case. I thought DS Trent made it clear.'

'It's Charlie.'

'What?'

Ridpath checked the traffic and ran across the road, down the side of the Midland Hotel. 'It's Charlie Whitworth, the man in the photo. The cropped man.'

'I don't understand, Ridpath. What the hell are you talking about?'

He slowed down to a walk. He had to explain it properly to her. 'I found the original of the five-a-side photograph. It was in a local newspaper and uncropped. The other man is Detective

Chief Inspector Whitworth. He must have been doing some youth work or liaison with the community back in 1994.'

There was silence on the other end of the phone.

'I'm going to end the call now and send you a copy of the page. I've sent one already to Claire Trent. We have to move quickly on this, Lorraine.'

Silence again.

'Hello, Lorraine...?'

'I'm just thinking, Ridpath.'

'There's not time. Send a squad car to Charlie's house immediately. I'm on my way there now. Hurry, Lorraine.'

'But... but...'

'Act now, for God's sake.' He ended the call and sent the picture to her address. He couldn't wait any longer.

Was Charlie in trouble? Was he going to be the killer's next victim? And then an idea struck him. Could it be Charlie? Could Charlie be the man who was killing people and setting them alight? The words of their last conversation came back to him. 'I'd burn the lot of them. There's so much fat there, it'd make the best bonfire night ever.'

He doubled his pace along the crisp packet strewn streets.

Chapter Sixty

'You have to believe me, I knew nothing about what happened.'

'So why did you ask me to keep quiet about it?'

Charlie frowned, trying to remember. 'Did I?'

'You visited me in hospital. You told me not to tell anyone, said you would have to arrest someone if the truth came out.'

'Well, I would. Playing that stupid game was asking for trouble. Why did you agree to do the dare? It was stupid.'

He smiled. Charlie Whitworth was good, no wonder he had finagled so many confessions out of reluctant cons. He could make anybody believe black was white. 'There was no game, Charlie. Mulkeen lied to you. They were doing it for him.'

The man's face went pale. 'That can't be true,' he blustered. 'They told me it was a game. I was a police constable. If I'd thought…' And then his eyes suddenly brightened as the penny finally dropped. 'They lied to me.'

'You wanted to believe the lie, Charlie. That's why you have to die.' He stood up and pointed to the door. 'It's time to go now.'

'Go? Go where?'

'You'll find out when you get there. Come on, get up.' He gestured with the revolver. 'Or I could shoot you here in the kitchen. I think your wife wouldn't like it, would she? Coming home to find her pots and pans and dainty china drenched in your blood. When is she coming home, Charlie?'

'Don't talk about my wife. Leave her out of this!'

'Then it's time to go.'

Reluctantly Charlie grabbed his walking stick and levered himself out of the chair, supporting his weight on it.

'You're going to drive us, while I sit in the back seat.'

'I haven't driven since the accident. I don't know if I can.'

'Looks like we're going to find out. If you can't drive, I'll kill you here.'

'Where are we going?'

'As I said, you'll find out. Come on, we don't want to be late.'

'Late for what?'

'Late for the fireworks. There's always fireworks at a celebration.'

'Let's get on with it,' Charlie said brusquely.

He stepped back as the ex-copper hobbled past him, just in case he tried to take a swing with the walking stick. He didn't, of course, the revolver made sure he stayed quiet.

He was quick, though. Nobody would have noticed the phone was no longer lying on the table next to the bottle of Scotch.

But he wanted him to take the phone. He wanted the police to track its movements through the phone towers.

After all, he needed an audience for this last party trick and it would save him ringing them later.

Charlie was quick, though, despite leaning on a walking stick.

Shame he was going to die.

Chapter Sixty-One

Ridpath reached his car, parked near the old Central Station, and immediately put it in gear. He reached down to switch on the blue lights before realising the car was no longer fitted with them.

Shit. He would have to drive like a lunatic and hope he wasn't stopped.

He raced out of the car park and down to the A57, weaving in and out of the traffic. Right onto the A6 and down through Levenshulme. On either side of the road, Manchester flashed past.

He stopped at a traffic light and picked up the phone again, ringing Caruso and putting her on speaker. She answered as the lights turned green.

'Have you sent the squad car, Lorraine?'

'I haven't received the picture yet, Ridpath. I'm not doing anything until I've received proof of what you are saying. We can't all be bloody mavericks!'

'Don't you realise he could be in danger?'

'There you go again. Always making a drama out of a crisis. Don't you realise we all can't—'

He cut off the call. He couldn't stand the woman's voice. Why didn't she do something?

Another red light. He tapped the steering wheel. What to do? Sod it.

He picked up his phone and dialled 999.

'Emergency services, what service do you require?'

'This is DI Ridpath. I believe a crime is being committed at Golddale Close, High Lane, off the A6. Please send a squad car immediately.'

'Sorry, what was the name and address again.

What was wrong with these people?

The lights turned green. He put the car in gear and accelerated away, overtaking a slow moving car on the inside.

He took a deep breath and spoke slowly. 'My name is Detective Inspector Thomas Ridpath. A crime is in progress at Golddale Close, High Lane.'

'What sort of crime?'

Ridpath thought for a moment. 'Murder. Somebody is being murdered.'

'Squad car dispatched, DI Ridpath. ETA seven minutes, over.'

'Thanks, Control.'

He was accelerating past Stockport Grammar School and the lights were just turning from amber to red. He put his foot down and felt the surge in the engine as the turbo kicked in. And then a flash in his rear mirror.

Shit. Shit. A traffic camera.

Sod it. He carried on accelerating, just managing to catch all the lights as they turned. Keeping left where the road split, he found himself behind a large Polish juggernaut. He overtook it, forcing it to move closer to the pavement. He was sure he heard some choice Polish swear words as he accelerated past.

High Lane was only a couple of minutes away now. He remembered driving here just a few days ago, to visit Charlie and bring him a bottle of Scotch. It seemed like an age and half a lifetime away.

Was Charlie the killer?

Impossible.

He had been bitter last time they met, but to go around pouring meths on people? Not Charlie, not in a million years.

He swung left onto Charlie's street. The squad car was nowhere to be seen. Ridpath stamped on the brakes and the car slid to a stop outside the bungalow.

Ridpath jumped out, hearing the sound of sirens in the distance. The bloody cavalry were on their way but late as usual.

The bungalow seemed quiet. No movement at the curtains.

The sirens were getting louder now, cutting through the sounds of birdsong in the quiet suburb.

He walked slowly down the driveway, checking for movement all the time. The door looked exactly as it had last time. He checked the handle and it opened. Charlie still wasn't locking it.

Ridpath stepped into the hallway, calling out, 'Charlie, it's Ridpath. Are you here?' Was Charlie drunk, sitting in his armchair, moaning about the world?

It was at times like this Ridpath wished he were armed, like American cops. At least then he would have some sort of weapon. Instead he picked up an umbrella from the hall stand. As his old instructor at the training college had said in his broad Scottish accent, 'Any weapon is better than nuthin' – remember that next time you're in a wee stramash.'

He moved slowly down the hallway, feeling the thick carpet under his feet, towards the kitchen where he and Charlie had sat just a few days ago.

'Charlie? Are you here?'

Outside, the squeal of brakes and the slamming of doors.

Would Charlie have gone out? But didn't he say he never left the house any more?

He reached the kitchen.

Empty.

'Charlie!' he shouted even louder.

No answer.

A banging on the door. Ridpath could see two enormous blue shapes through the glass. 'It's DI Ridpath, I'm coming to open the door,' he shouted, just in case some eager plod decided to take him down.

He walked back down the hallway and opened the door. 'Charlie's not here.'

They bustled past him.

'Do you have your warrant card, sir?' a sergeant asked.

Ridpath flashed it.

'You called it in?'

'I did. This is Detective Chief Inspector Whitworth's house—'

'Charlie? I worked with him in Prestwich.'

'He's missing.'

The sergeant turned to his men. 'Search the place.'

One ran upstairs and the other checked the living room and kitchen. After thirty seconds, the one in the kitchen shouted back. 'I think you should come and see this, Sarge.'

They both rushed to the rear of the house.

The constable was pointing to the far wall, hidden from the door.

High up, somebody had sprayed letters in bright orange paint.

'PLAY THE GAME,' repeated the constable. 'What does it mean, Sarge?'

Chapter Sixty-Two

Claire Trent stared at the wall. 'This wasn't here when you visited him?'

Ridpath shook his head. 'Definitely not.'

'Why those words? Has the song got something do with it? Chrissy told me Queen released it in 1980.'

'I don't know. It's been bothering me for a while. I saw it at Joe Brennan's house and at the building site where we found Sam Sykes. Both times sprayed with orange paint.'

'There must be some reason he sprays it on the wall. Is he letting us know it's him? Marking his territory, so to speak.'

'For me, it sounds more like an exhortation.'

Trent took off her glasses and wiped them with a paper handkerchief. 'What sort of nutter are we dealing with?'

She put the glasses on again and stared at the words on the wall, as if looking at them would reveal some hidden secret.

A white-coated Scene of Crime officer approached them. 'We've finished in the rest of the house. There's no sign of forced entry or any disturbance.'

'Thanks, Bert,' said Trent.

'Not surprising, the front door was always left unlocked so he didn't have to get up to let people in,' said Ridpath.

'A bit stupid for a copper.'

Ridpath shrugged. 'Did you find a walking stick, Bert?'

'Not in the house. The wheelchair is still here but nothing else. We've still got to search the garage but I didn't see it before.'

'Charlie told me he couldn't get around without it.'

Trent raised her eyebrows. 'So it's gone with him?'

'Looks that way.'

She was quiet for a moment. 'We're faced with two possibilities,' she said quietly. 'Either somebody else wrote this on the wall, or Charlie did. If it's the former, one of our own has gone missing, possibly abducted. But why?'

'He's the only one left alive in the photograph.'

'Perhaps… but it also begs another question.'

'Which is?'

'Do you think he could have done it?'

'What? Murdered all these people? Poured meths on them and set them alight, watching them burn to death? Not a chance, not Charlie.'

'But as you said yourself, he's the only one left alive in the photograph. Everybody else is dead. Joe Brennan, Sam Sykes, Tommy Larkin and David Mulkeen burnt to death recently. While Tony Doyle and Harry McHale died in accidents. Unless it's all a coincidence these people are dead, it only leaves one man in the photograph alive from the time: Charlie Whitworth.'

'You're forgetting one other death. Our man on the moors. John Doe.'

'You think he's important?'

Ridpath scratched his head. 'First, if we trust HOLMES, he's the only one who's linked to the killer but isn't part of the group photo. And second, he was the very first person to die. It's as if he somehow started it all off, if that makes sense.'

'None of it makes sense, Ridpath. It's a riddle wrapped in an enigma.'

Lorraine Caruso bustled into the kitchen. She avoided looking at Ridpath and spoke directly to her boss. 'West Yorkshire was just on the phone. They've got a DNA match to our John Doe on the moors. His name is Alistair Ransome and he worked as a psychotherapist. Well, at least that's what he called himself, but they've been onto Leeds University where he said he qualified and they've never heard of him. Seems to have been one of those so-called "consultants" who do a few courses and set themselves up in private practice. No clinical psychology degree or nothing but they think they can treat people. Usually do hypnotherapy and stuff like that.'

'Why was his DNA on file?'

'Spousal abuse about four years ago. The wife didn't press charges, of course, but we kept the DNA and he came up as a match.'

'Lorraine, get a list of his patients. Was he treating any of the football players or even David Mulkeen?'

'Will do, guv'nor.'

'Do you have an address?'

Caruso handed over a piece of paper. 'This is for his clinic but they haven't got a home address.'

'Find it.'

'Right, boss.'

'Ridpath, you're with me. We're going to the clinic. Lorraine, you stay and finish up here.'

'But this is just grunt work, I should be with you.'

Trent fixed her with a steely stare. 'And you should have discovered it was Charlie Whitworth in the photo, but you didn't.'

'But—'

'Enough with the buts, Lorraine. Finish up here.'

Just as they were leaving the kitchen, Ridpath had an idea. He collared the crime scene manager. 'Ron, did you find Charlie's mobile?'

The man shook his head slowly. 'Nah, definitely wasn't in the house. Could he have taken it with him?'

Trent smiled. 'Are you thinking what I'm thinking, Ridpath?'

'Charlie's still got his phone.' Ridpath dialled the number quickly and listened. 'It's gone straight to voicemail, guv'nor.'

'Lorraine, get onto his mobile provider. I want them to get the GPS details of the phone ASAP. I want to know where it is right now.'

'Yes, ma'am.'

Trent ignored the change in Caruso's voice. 'Come on, Ridpath, we need to visit the psychotherapist's office.'

'There's one other thing we haven't talked about, guv'nor.'

'What's that?'

'Last week we found a body virtually every other day. This man doesn't keep his victims for long.'

'You think he's working to a timetable?'

'Certain of it.' Ridpath glanced at his watch. 'Which means he only has seven more hours before today ends.'

Chapter Sixty-Three

Ridpath and Trent parked the car outside a large Victorian house in Didsbury, a trendy suburb of Manchester. In the paved-over garden a large sign proclaimed this was the 'Didsbury Wellness Center', along with a list of some of the treatments offered: traditional Chinese acupuncture, colonic irrigation, homoeopathy, reiki, Primordial Sound Meditation, aromatherapy and kinesiology, as well as common or garden yoga.

Ridpath noted the American spelling of the word 'centre' and smiled to himself. Polly would love this place – not. After their experience with the marriage counsellor, both she and Ridpath had a healthy disdain for the practitioners of the 'wellness' industry.

When he was first diagnosed with his cancer, some friends had told him in all earnestness he should ignore the doctors and go on special diets, visit Lourdes for a cure, drink herbal teas, smoke dope, or even try an Electro Physiological Feedback Xroid – some sort of device which you plugged yourself into and it magically cured you of piles and cancer. When he saw the cost, Ridpath shook his head and politely said no thanks. Christies and its tablets and chemo would do for him. Bastard things they were, but at least they had some sort of track record of success. Unlike the other stuff that promised the earth and delivered nothing but a hole in the ground.

They walked up to the old-fashioned portico entrance. The house had once been the home of some rich cotton merchant but was now divided up into twelve different clinics, each offering their own version of 'wellness'.

Each clinic had a separate number and doorbell to ring. Ridpath scanned down the names. Alistair Ransome was number six. Next to his name it stated he offered Repressed Memory Therapy, whatever that was.

Ridpath pressed the bell and waited.

No response.

Trent tried to turn the doorknob. It was obviously locked from the inside.

Ridpath pressed the bell again. Still no answer.

'Try number seven.'

The name on the bell was Hilary Smith, Herbal Menopause Treatments.

'Don't say a word, Ridpath.'

The detective held his hands up. 'Would I wind you up, guv'nor?'

'You would. And if I get a free gift card through the post, I'll know who to blame.'

Ridpath pressed number seven.

Instantly a voice responded. 'Are you my five thirty? Mrs Langan?'

'No, actually, we're the police,' answered Trent.

'Well, I give a ten per cent discount for all members of the armed forces, so I think I could extend it to the police. Come on up.'

The door buzzed loudly and Ridpath pushed his way into a large old-fashioned hallway with a high ceiling and a stairway leading up directly ahead. The smell was a combination of candle wax and incense. Not unpleasant but not one that made Ridpath feel better either.

A woman was waiting for them at the top of the stairs. 'Sorry, I don't do men. Not much call with my specialism. Though I often think some of them are so grumpy, there must be a male menopause.'

'We're not here for treatment, Mrs Smith. We'd like to ask you about your neighbour, Alistair Ransome.'

'Oh,' she said in a disappointed voice, 'it was him I was thinking about when I said about men being grumpy. You'd better come up, looks like my five thirty is late… again.'

Trent went up the stairs, followed by Ridpath. As they reached the landing, Mrs Smith pointed to a door next to hers. 'That's Alistair, number six.'

'How long have you known him?'

'Oh, I don't know him, we just work next door to each other.'

'You never talk?'

Her neatly pencilled eyebrows went up. 'Not much. Keeps himself to himself does Alistair, when he's not moaning about the rent or the lighting or the government or his bloody feet. I swear he could moan in the Olympics, could Alistair.'

'When was the last time you saw him?'

Mrs Smith counted on her fingers. 'Eight days ago, on the twenty-first. He'd been arguing with one of his patients. Their voices were raised and it disturbed my hot flushes.' She giggled. 'Actually, it was Mrs Jones, she's the one with the hot flushes who they disturbed.'

'So what did you do?'

'I tapped on the door and asked if everything was OK. He answered it was but didn't open the door.'

'Are you sure it was him answering?'

'Oh yes, I recognised his voice. He's from Somerset and has a peculiar West Country burr, like he's been drinking cider since six in the morning.'

'You didn't see who he'd been arguing with?'

Mrs Smith shook her head.

'Did you hear what they were saying?' asked Trent.

She shook her head again. 'Not really, I sort of zone out when I'm massaging people. I find it very therapeutic.' Then she paused a moment. 'But at one point it got very heated and

I heard Mr Ransome shouting "You must remember!" and his patient saying he didn't want to. Or words to that effect.'

'Anything else?'

'Not really, I don't listen to what's going on around me when I'm working. Focused I am, it's what my clients love about me.'

Trent's phone rang and she ignored it for a minute but the sound was insistent. 'Hello, Lorraine.' Trent was listening and nodding. She clicked the phone off, grabbed Ridpath by the arm and started to pull him back towards the stairs. 'Come on, they've found the phone. It's on the second floor of a building in central Manchester, Bruton Place.'

'We'll be back to interview you, Mrs Smith,' he called over his shoulder.

Trent was in front of him, clattering down the old stairs. 'Bruton Place is one of the blocks on the Greater Manchester list of high-risk buildings. Its cladding is worse than at Grenfell.'

'So that means...'

'If there's a fire on the second floor, the whole lot goes up, eighteen storeys.'

Chapter Sixty-Four

Lorraine Caruso ran up to their car as soon as it arrived outside Bruton Place.

Frenetic activity was happening all around: flashing lights from police cars and fire engines, firemen rolling out lengths of hose, police pushing onlookers back behind blue- and white-striped tape stretching across the street, PCSOs shouting orders.

'Boss, I've got the local plod to cordon off the area. More fire engines are on their way.'

'What do we know about Charlie?'

'The triangulation of the phone signal tells us he went into the building about two hours ago.'

'Which floor?'

'A kid said he saw a man with a walking stick going into Flat 2E.'

'Charlie?'

'She couldn't give us an ID of him, boss. Didn't look at the face, just noticed the walking stick.'

They marched towards the block of flats. Both ends of the street had been blocked and they showed their warrant cards to the constable guarding entry. Ridpath stared up at the orange-clad building towering above him.

'The block was constructed four years ago. That's when they added the cladding. To make it look prettier, someone said. Still looks like a tower block to me.'

'Which one is 2E?'

Caruso pointed to a window at the south-eastern corner. 'We're just checking who lives there now.'

'Have you requested an Armed Response Unit?' asked Ridpath.

The chief inspector looked at him for the first time. 'On its way. ETA four minutes.'

'Good, well done, Lorraine. Push the cordons further out. I don't want anyone to come close. We'll set up HQ here. Where's the incident commander?'

'Over there.' Lorraine pointed to a man in a bright yellow fire helmet. Ridpath recognised him as Dave Greene, from the fire at Joseph Brennan's flat.

'Have we tried to call Charlie?'

'He's not answering his mobile, boss.'

'Get a telephone number for the flat. We need to talk to him before he does anything stupid.'

'Yes, guv'nor.' Caruso hurried off to organise her team.

The incident commander marched up to them. 'It's you again, Ridpath, you turn up like a bad penny at these things.'

'Hi, Dave, there've been a few recently.'

'Are your men ready, Commander?' asked Trent.

'Ready for what?'

'Ready for anything and everything. We know there's at least one man in the flat. He could be planning to set this whole building on fire.'

'Shit.' Dave Greene's worst nightmares flashed before his eyes. 'We surveyed this building six months ago. Its panelling is potentially worse than at Grenfell. It could go up like a bonfire.'

'How long do we have?'

'Once a fire starts? If Grenfell's anything to go by, about ten minutes. But this stuff is even more flammable.'

'How could they build this crap?'

'That's what the fire service has been saying for years. But nobody was listening.'

Caruso reappeared with the head of the Armed Response Unit, James Fenton, and handed her boss a phone. 'We're dialling the landline in the flat now, boss.'

Trent listened to the ringing tone for twenty seconds. No answer.

She handed the phone back. 'Keep trying, Lorraine. If Charlie is in there, we need to get in touch with him.'

She turned to the ARU officer. 'We need to get in there before he starts a fire. Are your men ready?'

He nodded. 'We're ready.'

Ridpath could almost smell the adrenaline on the man. He glanced down at Fenton's black calf-length boots. The officer was shifting weight from one leg to the other like a runner desperate for the starting gun.

Dave Greene stepped forward. 'We need to evacuate the building before you send your men in. If he starts a fire, with this cladding it could spread out of control in a few minutes. You could have another Grenfell on your hands.'

'What do you suggest?'

'Evacuate the building now.'

Trent frowned. 'It may cause a panic and spook our fire-starter.'

Ridpath glanced at the hive of activity and flashing lights. 'If he hasn't been spooked already...'

Trent thought for a moment. 'You've got ten minutes to get everybody out of there and then we go in.'

Chapter Sixty-Five

Tenants began to stream out through the entrance of Bruton Place. Some were carrying their possessions: teddy bears, photographs, bedding, even an old bike. Others had nothing except the clothes they were wearing. Most were calm and collected, but some were agitated.

'When can we go back?'

'I need to go back to bed before my shift.'

'What about my dinner?'

Two old people, with their arms around each other, were looking tired and confused. 'Where are we going? What do we do?'

Ridpath detached himself from the group of officers surrounding Claire Trent. 'This way, come this way. The community centre is open, you can go and get a cup of tea there and a biscuit.' A PCSO ran up to help him.

'But we've never been to the community centre,' said the old woman.

The PCSO held out his arm for the woman to take.

'Where are we going? Is there a war on?'

'No, ma'am. There's just a problem with one of the flats. The police are evacuating everybody for their safety.'

'It feels like when I was a young girl and the Germans were bombing Manchester. Such terrible fires then...'

'Come along and have a cup of tea. There's some biscuits too.'

The three of them slowly walked to the community centre as Ridpath watched them go. He hurried back to Trent.

'We'll be ready to go in five minutes. Are your officers in position, James?'

The man in charge of the ARU nodded. 'We have snipers positioned overlooking the flat. A team will go in as soon as you give the order, ma'am.'

'Is everybody out, Dave?'

Ridpath glanced back to the entrance. A few stragglers were coming through the open doors, chivvied along by firemen and the police. One large, rotund man wearing a United shirt was shouting at the top of his voice. He was pushing against a uniformed sergeant.

'This ain't right, this ain't. You can't stop me from going into my flat. I know my rights.'

'It's for your own good, sir. You'll be allowed in as soon as we deem it safe.' The sergeant was trying to keep him moving away from the building.

'Safe? It's not safe? We told the council about the cladding two years ago and nothing was done. Now you're telling me it's not safe?'

'Please move along, sir. The community centre is open.'

'I know my rights, you can't stop me…' He tried to dodge around the sergeant and another officer.

The sergeant moved in front of him. 'You have a choice, sir. You either move along or I arrest you for obstruction. You can either spend some time in the community centre or a night in the cells. It's up to you.'

The man looked around for support and found none. 'Right, I'm going down the pub to write a letter to my MP. You can't treat people like this.' He stormed off in the direction of the King's Arms.

The sergeant ran across to the group around Trent. 'The building is clear, ma'am.'

'All the flats are empty?'

'As far as we can make out. We knocked on all the doors but there was no answer in some.'

'Thank you, Sergeant Harris.'

'Are your men ready, Dave?'

'The pumps are manned and the ladder is ready. We'll move in as soon as you give the order. But the safety of my men must be my priority.'

'Understood, Dave.'

'James, get your men into position.'

'Aye, ma'am. We'll move in at 6:30 p.m. exactly. That's in three minutes.'

'I want whoever is in there taken alive, if possible.'

'Yes, ma'am.'

'But remember, Charlie Whitworth is an ex-police officer and has received firearms training.'

'I understand, ma'am.'

'Charlie won't be armed. He would never use a gun against another officer.'

'We don't know that, Ridpath,' said Trent curtly. 'You have your orders, James, carry them out.'

'Yes, ma'am.'

'Can I go with them, guv'nor?'

Trent thought for a moment.

'I know Charlie and he knows me. If he's in there on his own, I can talk to him, get him to come out.'

'Right. James, have you got an extra vest?'

'Of course, ma'am'

'In you go, Ridpath, but you're under the command of Fenton. You obey his orders, understood?'

'Yes, guv'nor.'

Fenton took his arm. 'This way, we'll suit you up.'

A shudder went down his spine. He didn't have a good feeling about this operation.

Chapter Sixty-Six

James Fenton, the commander of the Armed Response Unit, adjusted his bulletproof vest, pulling it down over his stomach. It was a little tighter than it used to be. Either he had put on weight or the vest had shrunk. He was sure it wasn't the latter.

He gathered his five-man team around him. 'Listen up, there is one man, possibly two in the flat. At least one of them has received firearms training and is an ex-copper. Our call sign is Team Alpha, with me as one and the rest – two, three, four and five. And six.' He gestured to each man as he numbered them off, ending with Ridpath. 'I'll be on point with Trev as my second. When we get to the door, I'll be in first followed by Simon. Ridpath will be third. The living room is straight ahead with a bedroom and bathroom on the left and a kitchen on the right. Steve and Mike will go left and myself and Simon will go right. Once they are clear, we will go on to the living room. Is that understood?'

Each man nodded in turn.

'Only open fire if your life is being threatened. Understand?'

They all nodded again.

He checked his watch. 'We move in thirty seconds. Check your equipment. Be careful, people.'

All the men went through the ritual of adjusting the straps of their matt black helmets, pulling down the edges of their black ski masks to cover the tops of their jumpsuits and Nomex undergarments, tightening their stab vests and checking the safety catch on their Heckler & Koch rifles.

Ridpath stood there watching them, admiring the casual professionalism of their movements.

'Ready? Move.' Fenton raised his arm and pointed it in the direction of the lobby.

Like the well-drilled team they were, they entered the building in a long line, each man checking to his right and left, sighting along the barrel of his rifle. They reached the bottom of the stairs and began to climb, looking up at the flight above in case they were attacked. They moved quickly and silently up the stairs, their rubber soles making no noise on the tiled floor.

Ridpath stayed in the middle, following exactly in the footsteps of the man in front.

Fenton reached a fire door and stopped. A large red 2 painted on the wall next to his head. He gestured for Trev Davis to be point going through the door and for Ridpath to get behind him.

He listened for a moment.

Nothing. Just the creaking of the building.

He opened the fire door and peered out along the corridor. Empty.

The target flat was at the end of the corridor on the right.

He beckoned his men forward, with Trev leading, and silently they flowed through the door, separating into two groups, hugging opposite walls of the corridor.

Ridpath took the left side, sliding along the wall, keeping pace with the man in front.

Halfway along, a child's red fire engine had been left in the middle of the floor. Fenton gestured towards it, indicating his men should not touch it.

They carried on moving.

The silence was deafening now. An eerie silence in a building that should have been full of life and noise.

Fenton reached the door and hugged the wall next to it. He took three deep breaths and checked the men were all with him.

Ridpath looked down at this watch. Only thirty seconds had gone since they started. It felt like thirty hours.

Fenton shifted position, leaning closer to the door to listen for movement inside.

No sound.

For a second, the words 'as silent as a grave' flashed through Ridpath's head, but he quickly shook them off.

Focus. Concentrate.

Fenton called Trev Davis forward. Trev was their biggest officer so he was in charge of the Enforcer, known as the 'Big Red Key'.

Silently the man positioned himself in front of the door. He raised the battering ram and waited for his team leader's signal.

Fenton listened once more.

Ridpath leant in to listen too.

Nothing.

Three deep breaths and Fenton raised his arm, bringing it down in a swift chopping stroke.

Trev crashed the Enforcer into the point where the door lock met the surround. The door crunched and smashed open wide.

'Move. Move. Move,' shouted James Fenton.

Chapter Sixty-Seven

Outside the tower block, Claire Trent looked across as the snake of Armed Response Unit officers vanished into Bruton Place, Ridpath an incongruous figure in the middle. She wished she were with them, it would be so much easier than being stuck out here.

She glanced over at Lorraine Caruso. Her DCI was standing still, not a trace of emotion on her face, her forehead uncreased, unworried. Only the set of her jaw betrayed her tension. In her hand, an Airwave relayed the sounds of the operation.

The last words of James Fenton before they began to move.

The breathing of the man as he climbed the stairs.

The creak of the fire door as it opened.

Next to her, Dave Greene crossed himself, moving his hand quickly across his chest.

The rest of the team, including Caruso, just stood and watched.

To the rear, the noise of the crowd was getting louder behind the police tape. Off to the right a reporter was interviewing the man wearing the United shirt on camera, in front of a white van with a large satellite dish on top.

Other reporters and their photographers had decamped off to the left, hoping to get a better view of the action.

The light was still perfect and, for once, Manchester had decided this was not the time for rain.

As one person, the team around Trent shifted its gaze to the window on the south-eastern corner of the building.

The radio in Caruso's hand still relayed the sounds of the operation.

More breathing.

The soft swoosh of rubber soles against tiled floors.

The thud of a body landing on a wall.

Followed by a loud crash and the shouted words 'Move. Move. Move.'

The door crashing against a wall again.

Shouts of 'Three. Bathroom, clear. Over.'

A few seconds later, 'Five. Bedroom, clear. Over.'

More banging. A shout. This one louder and from Fenton himself. 'One. Kitchen, clear. Over.'

Then a slight pause, punctuated by heavy breathing. 'Going in.'

Then Ridpath's voice. 'Jesus Christ.'

Chapter Sixty-Eight

Ridpath stood at the entrance as the ARU teams flowed to the left and right, checking the kitchen, bathroom and bedroom.

'Three. Bathroom, clear. Over.'

'Five. Bedroom, clear. Over.'

The banging of the door at the end of the corridor, followed by a loud shout at the end of the corridor, this one from Fenton himself. 'One. Kitchen, clear. Over.'

The team assembled in the short corridor that led to the living room. Fenton beckoned Ridpath forward and positioned him directly to his rear. Then he whispered, 'Going in' into his Airwave and inched his way forward. Ridpath followed close behind. On the opposite wall, Trev advanced so he was level with them, his Heckler & Koch pointing the way.

Fenton stuck his head round the corner and immediately jerked it back. He pulled Ridpath close to him, whispering, 'One person, sitting in a chair, his mouth is covered. Is it your man?'

Ridpath edged forward in front of Fenton. 'Charlie, is that you?' he said calmly.

A muffled sound was the only response.

'Charlie, it's me, Ridpath. I'm going to come forward slowly. Don't do anything rash, Charlie, we don't want anybody to get hurt.'

As Ridpath moved forward, Trev, the ARU man, inched level with him, the Heckler & Koch covering his every move.

'I'm going to look round the corner now, just so you can see it's me.'

More muffled noises from inside.

Ridpath took a deep breath. His heart was beating so fast it was ready to burst out of his chest. His legs felt weak and his mouth was dry. 'I'm looking now, Charlie.'

He counted to three and leant slowly out so he could see round the corner.

Charlie was sitting in a chair, his mouth bound with flesh-coloured masking tape. His wrists were handcuffed to the metal arms and his legs bound with more tape. His eyes seemed to be imploring Ridpath to do something, to help him. He struggled in the chair, muffled sounds coming from his mouth.

'Is anybody else here, Charlie?'

The man violently shook his head.

On Ridpath's right, Trev took a step forward, covering Charlie all the time with his rifle.

Then another step.

Suddenly the whole room erupted with noise. A wall of orange flame headed straight for Ridpath, throwing him backwards into Fenton and onto the floor.

Trev, who had stepped forward, was thrown up into the air, coming down on his back against a wall.

Ridpath's ears were ringing and a strong smell of burning meat assaulted his nostrils. He shook his head, trying in vain to get rid of the smell.

Inside the flat, a scream of pain cut through the noise and sound and smell.

Ridpath tried to pick himself up but his legs were like jelly.

Through the noise, he heard Fenton shouting, 'Back, back.'

A pair of strong arms pulled him out through the door and down the corridor, away from the screams, away from the smell of burning flesh.

Chapter Sixty-Nine

Trent stared up at the window of the flat.

A ball of orange flame suddenly erupted like a fireball from the middle window of the flat. The windows shattered, sending shards of glass falling to the ground below.

'Shit,' shouted Trent. She snatched the Airwave from Lorraine Caruso. 'What's happening? Fenton, are you OK? Come in, Fenton…'

Flames licked out of the windows and up the outside wall of the building.

'Are you OK?'

The Airwave crackled.

'Come in, Team Alpha.'

More crackling, before a breathless voice came over the comms. 'Team Alpha all A-OK. A bit shook up but all present and correct. Something exploded as we were advancing into the living room. Flames everywhere. We've pulled back to the corridor. A man sitting in a chair before the explosion…'

'Pull your men back, Fenton.' Trent turned to the incident officer. 'It's your call, Dave, do you send your men in?'

Dave Greene stared at the outside of the building. Flames were beginning to lick the walls, blistering the thin metal covering of the cladding. Black smoke was drifting up into the sky.

Would there be any other explosions? Was it safe to send his men in?

'Dave. What's your decision?'

More orange flames leapt out of the window and up the side of the building.

He turned to his waiting fire teams. 'Move in,' he shouted. 'Offensive Oscar mode. Repeat, Offensive Oscar mode.'

Instantly men raced forward with hoses and began playing water on the outside of the building. An engine with a telescopic ladder reversed into position. Within thirty seconds a stream of water was being poured into the interior of the flat.

For a second the flames leapt higher out of the window as if struggling with the streams of water, before vanishing back inside the flat.

Within minutes the fire was under control. No more flames threatened to ignite the flammable cladding. All that remained was a thin stream of grey smoke coming from the interior.

'Send in a team. Check the interior of the flat,' ordered Dave Greene.

A fireman wearing breathing equipment formed his team up and they went into the lobby of the building, following exactly the same route taken by the ARU just minutes earlier.

Ten minutes later the same man came out, walked over to the command group and took off his mask.

'The heat is savage, but the fire's out, boss. There's just one body sitting on a chair in the middle of the room.'

'Is he dead?' asked Claire Trent.

'He's toast… literally.'

'Lorraine, get a forensics team in there ASAP.'

'Yes, boss.'

'Alan?'

'Yes, guv'nor.'

'Interview all the neighbours, anybody who lives in or near the block, even the kids. I want to know if anybody else saw a man, or men, going into the flat this afternoon. Start now, while memories are still fresh.'

'Will do, guv'nor.'

'And check CCTV. It might let us see who went up to the flat.'

'I think it's out of order, boss, the kids on the estate…' Alan's voice trailed off.

'Check it anyway. And get onto the local council or the management committee. Find out who owns the flat or if there's a tenant.'

'Anything else, boss?'

'Nah, just get moving.'

Trent looked back at the scorched outside of the tower block. They had just prevented a major fire, but another man had died.

Chapter Seventy

He watched as the fireball exploded out of the window and up the side of the tower block. Now he would see some action as the fire caught the composite tiles and ignited them, turning the whole building into one giant Roman candle.

The firemen rushed forward and reversed an engine close to the flat, water already pouring from a nozzle on top of a ladder. Other men were rushing in with hoses, training them on the tiles, making sure they didn't ignite.

Shame, he would have liked to see the whole lot go up in flames. A fitting end to his work. A celebration bigger and brighter than bonfire night.

No matter, he was finished now.

They were all dead.

He felt an immense weight lift from his shoulders.

After all these years, they were dead.

So be it.

His work was finished. For now.

One day, he would let the world know what he had done and why he did it. The urge to tell everything was strong in him now, he had held the secret for too long.

But not yet.

Maybe later, when he had rested and recovered, he would start planning again. After all, there were hundreds of Mulkeens in the world. Adults who preyed on children for their own gratification. They would be easy to find and punish.

And then there were the Whitworths, the ones who allowed it to happen. By doing nothing, letting it continue and pretending it had never happened, they were just as guilty. Maybe even more so.

Next month he would start planning again. The sex offenders register would give him all the clues he needed to find them.

He knew now he had finally found his role in life. He was Shiva, the destroyer. And when he was ready, Shiva would rise again from the flames.

Chapter Seventy-One

Three hours later and Ridpath was struggling into a Tyvek suit a size too small for him. He had been checked by the medical team and given the all-clear. The only thing he had lost was his left eyebrow, singed off in the first explosion.

Terry Dolan was next to him, also putting on a suit. 'Don't often do this. Usually forensics have long gone before they let me anywhere near.'

'Get a move on, we haven't got all day,' shouted Trent.

'Impatient woman, your boss.'

'You've just seen the good side.'

Ridpath pulled up the hood and placed a mask over his mouth. 'Ready, guv'nor.' His voice was muffled but still clear.

Trent made a show of looking at her watch. 'If we could get on? It's 21:55 already and I have a management meeting tomorrow morning and a briefing at noon. You will attend that, Ridpath.' The last sentence was an order rather than a request.

Terry Dolan rubbed his hands. 'Let's get on then.'

They climbed the stairs to the second floor. The forensics team had set up lights powered by a generator to illuminate their work. The power to the building was still out, with engineers from the local electricity board attempting to restore it.

Outside, people were still not allowed back into their homes. The mood was becoming restless, the crowd working themselves up into anger.

The corridor on the second floor was awash with water. Soot stained the white-painted ceiling. A child's toy fire engine stood forlorn and lost in the middle of the floor, its red-painted sides now smeared by smoke.

As they splashed through the water and approached number 2E, the walls became darker.

They were met at the door by the crime scene manager, who signed them in.

'Hiya, my name's Tracy.'

'Detective Superintendent Claire Trent.'

'Ooh, I've never had a Super on one of my jobs before. I thought your lot never left the office.'

'This one does.'

Ridpath leant forward and held out his hand. 'DI Ridpath, attached to the coroner's office.'

'Weren't you in the explosion?'

Ridpath nodded.

'A glutton for punishment.'

'Can we get a move on?' said Trent.

'Terry Dolan, fire investigator.'

'Hiya, Terry. Right, let's get on with it.' The woman had a no-nonsense informality which Ridpath found refreshing but he could see it was already beginning to annoy Trent.

'The pathologist is with the victim. He should pronounce time of death soon.'

'Who is it?'

'The young'un, Dr Schofield.'

They stepped across the threshold into the flat. Most of the water had drained away inside but there was still that peculiar smell of damp and mould mixed with smoke that seemed to enshroud all fire scenes. From the living room came a lingering warmth left over from the explosion and the fire.

'As you can see, the kitchen, bedroom and bathroom were relatively untouched by the fire itself. Most of the damage is from the water used to put the fire out. We're currently dusting for fingerprints and any trace elements.' As she spoke a large man carrying brown envelopes walked past them, heading into the corridor. 'But with an explosion and so much water, we're not expecting to discover much.'

They walked down the short corridor towards the living room.

'What caused the explosion?'

'We don't know.'

As the crime scene manager answered, Terry Dolan knelt down and pointed to the skirting board. 'I think this may answer your question, Ridpath.'

His gnarled finger pointed to a tiny pinhole. He then crawled across to the other side of the entrance and pointed to another small dot of dark on the opposite skirting board. 'I bet you found a thin length of wire with two picture hooks attached, didn't you?'

The crime scene manager's mouth opened. 'How did you know? There was another wire leading into the living room.'

'Did you find a battery too?'

She nodded. 'One was burnt out on the floor near the door. We thought it may have been involved.'

'The battery would have sent an electrical charge which caused a spark, igniting an accelerant on and surrounding the victim.'

'A booby trap?' asked Ridpath.

'That's my bet,' answered Dolan. 'The Armed Response Unit in their size tens checked out the other rooms, advanced through the door and boom...' He mimed an explosion with his hands.

'Why was nobody injured?'

'The blast was contained in the living room, it didn't make it into the corridor. You were lucky, Ridpath.'

'Or that's how it was planned.'

'What do you mean?'

Ridpath touched his burnt eyebrow. 'Well, guv'nor, haven't you noticed nobody else has been hurt in any of these fires except the victim? In the Brennan fire somebody called it in before it even started. In the Mulkeen death, the fire and explosion was set miles from anywhere. And here, in a tower block with flammable cladding, nobody is hurt.'

'That's not strictly true, Inspector.' The high-pitched voice of Dr Schofield interrupted Ridpath in mid flow from inside the living room.

They went in. The doctor was bent over a charred corpse. On the far wall, bright orange spray-painted letters shouted 'PLAYED THE GAME'.

The doctor stood up and took one last look at the corpse before walking towards them. 'In here, one person died.' He turned to the crime scene manager. 'Tracy, I'm calling the death at 22:05 for your logs.'

'Thanks, Eugene.'

Eugene? It was funny but up until now Ridpath had never heard Schofield's first name. Doctors didn't have names, they had titles. Or that was his experience on the cancer wards.

The doctor stepped aside to reveal a charred body. The face was blackened and the mouth twisted into a rictus grin, the lips pulled back and the teeth bared. A burnt moustache like hay stubble on the top lip. The charred arms still with their metal handcuffs around the wrists. Nothing was left of the eyes or hair.

Ridpath stepped towards the corpse. The stench of burning flesh was strong in his nostrils despite the mask. He stared at a shiny metal object sitting against the charred skin. A St Christopher medallion.

'It's Charlie.'

Chapter Seventy-Two

Ridpath finally reached home at two a.m. Polly was sitting up waiting for him, just a single lamp illuminating her face.

'Sorry I didn't call,' he said quietly.

'We were worried about you. Eve has only just gone to bed.' She spoke without looking at him.

'Sorry, there was a—'

'I saw the explosion on the news. You closed off most of Manchester.'

Before he could apologise again, she stood quickly and ran to him, wrapping him in her arms. 'We were so worried...'

He buried his face in her hair. 'I'm sorry, I should have called, but we were so busy...'

She pulled away from him, putting her hand over his lips. 'I'm just so happy you're safe. They said one man died, we were scared it was you.'

'It was Charlie.'

'What?'

'Charlie died. We think he was abducted this afternoon by the killer and placed in a flat next to an explosive device.'

'But why?'

Ridpath shrugged his shoulders. 'We don't know. It seems to be something to do with a football team in the 1990s.'

'A football team?'

'I know, I know. It doesn't make sense. None of it makes sense.'

'Oh, Ridpath.' She buried her face in his chest and held him tighter.

For a moment he forgot about Charlie and the deaths and the blackened bodies, losing himself in her warmth and her touch.

After a while, she pulled away again. 'You need to get out of these clothes and into the shower. Everything smells of burning and smoke. I'll pour you a nice big Glenmorangie while you shower.'

He kissed her on the forehead. 'Sounds just what I need.'

She stroked his head. 'Ridpath, what happened to your eyebrow?'

He took off his jacket and handed it to her, pretending he hadn't heard, then climbed the stairs slowly. God, he felt old and tired and drained.

On the landing, he popped his head around Eve's door, ignoring its bright orange 'keep out' sign.

She was curled up in bed, the duvet pulled up to her face, clutching the stuffed rabbit she had loved since she was a baby.

Her face had that wonderful serenity and peace only children have when they sleep.

For a minute Ridpath stood there and watched her. The slow, rhythmic rise of her chest. The quietness of her breathing. The way her dark fringe fell across her eyes.

The last image of Charlie flashed into his mind. A blackened, charred corpse sitting handcuffed to a chair. That was no way for any man to die.

And then he imagined it was his body sitting in the flat. How would Eve feel? And what about Polly?

He shook his head, trying to get rid of the images flashing through his mind. You can't think of them, it doesn't do anybody any good.

He closed the door to Eve's room.

His job was to find out who killed Charlie. That's all there was and all there would ever be.

Day Nine

Wednesday, May 1, 2019

Chapter Seventy-Three

At noon the detectives were assembled in the incident room for Operation Douter, waiting for Claire Trent.

Chrissy Wright's panels held two pictures of each of the deceased now: one from the five-a-side picture and the other a more recent shot. The only exception was Charlie Whitworth. His panel only held a blown-up version of the picture on his warrant card, Charlie staring out as if he were still alive, still in the incident room with them, working the case.

Ridpath couldn't look at it. Instead, he looked out of the windows at the bleak landscape of northern Manchester, the floodlight towers of the Etihad Stadium shrouded in the mist. As ever, it was raining; a steady drizzle that continued for days on end without hope of respite.

Trent eventually arrived fifteen minutes late, Lorraine Caruso in her wake. 'Sorry, everyone, dealing with the fallout from last night's incident. The press seem particularly interested in Charlie Whitworth's story.' She sat down at the front while Caruso took up position next to Chrissy Wright.

The DCI spoke first. 'As you can see, we have entered the information we have so far on the panels, updated to reflect the new findings. I'll let Chrissy take you through the developments since our last meeting.'

Chrissy stepped forward. 'The West Yorkshire pathologist has completed his post-mortem of Alistair Ransome.' She moved to the first panel. 'The pathologist puts the death of the psychotherapist at late on Sunday April 21 until early on Monday April 22. Which makes him our killer's first victim.'

'Have we checked his patient list and appointment book, Lorraine?' asked Trent.

'The lads on the fifth floor have cracked the password on his laptop. With their latest kit, it took less than five minutes. There are 173 names on his list, none of which match any of our victims. We're going through them as we speak, boss, contacting each of them one by one. As you can imagine, it's a laborious process.'

'You need more resources?'

'It wouldn't hurt, boss.'

'You'll have them.' She turned in her seat to face the other detectives. 'I have the chief constable's promise that nothing will be spared in the hunt for this killer. Understand? And that includes you lot. Continue, Lorraine.'

'The appointment book just had a time on the relevant date but no name so wasn't much use. We haven't found his mobile. We presume it was taken by the killer.'

'Has his next of kin been informed?' asked Ridpath.

'That's been taken care of by West Yorkshire,' she answered dismissively.

Chrissy continued. 'The second victim was a Thomas Larkin. He was found on the roof of Bakewell registry office, burnt to death. Derbyshire police initially logged it as suicide...'

'Has the designation been changed?'

Chrissy nodded. 'They've also handed the case to us. A Detective Sergeant Frobisher is our liaison if we need it.' Chrissy checked her notes. 'The registry office was closed that day.'

'CCTV?' asked Harry Makepeace.

'The system was not operational. Somebody sprayed the lens with orange paint.'

Caruso stepped forward. 'We think it could have been the killer.'

'No shit, Sherlock,' whispered Harry to Ridpath.

Trent swung round sharply in her seat and stared at both of them.

Caruso carried on. 'We're checking other CCTV in the area, but Bakewell isn't as well covered as Manchester.'

Chrissy moved past the panels showing Joseph Brennan and Sam Sykes, across to the picture of David Mulkeen. 'The Derbyshire forensic pathologist has completed his examination of both Thomas Larkin and this man. Both were hit over the head with a blunt object, probably a ball peen hammer, and both were dead when they were set on fire. The accelerant used in each case was methylated spirits.'

'What was the accelerant in West Yorkshire?' asked Ridpath.

Chrissy checked her notes once more. 'Also methylated spirits.'

Ridpath glanced at the MO board. The question marks had been removed.

'It seems the only method of killing that was different was Sam Sykes. I wonder why?'

'Let's not get ahead of ourselves, Ridpath. Continue with Charlie Whitworth, Lorraine.'

'Yes, boss. As I said earlier, we found Mr Whitworth's car in a nearby car park. In the boot was a large container of meths and some rubber gloves. The car has been dusted for fingerprints and the only set we found belonged to Mr Whitworth.'

Ridpath noticed she no longer called him Charlie. He was now just another picture on a panel.

'Dr Schofield is performing the post-mortem as we speak. He's promised to ring through his results ahead of the formal report.'

'Good. Who's with him?'

'I've sent Jill Carton, boss.'

Ridpath knew about the post-mortem as Dr Schofield had invited him. He couldn't face watching his friend and mentor being reduced to a pile of skin, bones and discarded organs. Sophia had volunteered to represent the coroner's office.

For a second, a memory of Charlie flashed into Ridpath's mind. His way of licking his moustache with his tongue when he was thinking, as if tasting his thoughts as they dripped from the bristles. Then another image muscled its way to the front of his thoughts. Charlie's eyes as he sat in the chair, struggling against the handcuffs. Scared, frightened eyes, full of pain and hurt.

'Do we have a confirmed ID it was him?' Trent's voice cut through his memories and he focused back on the meeting.

'The lab has promised to rush the DNA test, boss. As a serving police officer, we have Charlie's DNA on the database.'

'Good, it's key we get confirmation.' She nodded her head at the man sitting next to her. 'Before we go any further, I've asked Detective Chief Inspector Lionel Smith, the man in charge of GMP's investigations into the sexual abuse at football clubs, to brief us this morning.'

A tall, thin, ascetic-looking man stood up. He placed his hands in front of him as if leading a congregation in prayer. 'The abuse of young players at football clubs in the United Kingdom first came to our notice in mid-November 2016. A few former professional footballers waived their rights to anonymity and talked publicly about being abused by former coaches and scouts in the 1970s, 1980s and 1990s. This led to a surge of further allegations, as well as allegations that some clubs had covered them up.'

He glanced down at a piece of paper he held in his hand. 'To date, Operation Hydrant – as the nationwide police investigation is known – has received 2,807 incident reports from police forces and the NSPCC and 300 alleged suspects have been identified, with 340 football clubs named. Ninety-five per cent of those identified as victims were males aged between four and twenty.'

A hush enveloped the room, broken by one word from Harry Makepeace. 'Jesus.'

'Two thousand, eight hundred referrals? Does that mean nearly three thousand victims?' asked Ridpath.

'No. The actual number of victims gathered so far is 849.' He stopped for a moment and looked down. 'My feeling is the number of victims is actually far higher. Many of these young men are still too ashamed to come forward.'

'Jesus,' repeated Harry.

Trent glared at him. 'Please continue, Detective Chief Inspector Smith.'

'Within a month of the initial reports, the Football Association, the Scottish Football Association, several football clubs and over twenty UK police forces had established enquiries into these allegations. GMP initially co-operated with Cheshire Police as the enquiry involved a man called Barry Bennell who had worked at both Crewe and Manchester City. He had previously been charged with sexual abuse offences in the US and the UK. In 2019, he was convicted at Liverpool Crown Court of fifty offences against twelve boys and sentenced to thirty-one years in prison.'

'Best thing the Scousers ever did,' whispered Harry.

Lionel Smith ignored him. 'Since then another ninety-seven offences have come to our attention. The CPS is considering whether to prosecute him as we speak.'

'Is he the only one charged so far?' asked Trent.

'No, thirteen other men have been charged, with twelve convicted. All except one have received custodial sentences. Many of the men involved have already died.'

'What about the Football Association, what are they doing?' asked Chrissy.

'They have set up an independent enquiry which found no evidence of institutional cover-up. The final report has been delayed.'

'Why doesn't that surprise me?' said Harry.

'Locally, Manchester City opened an investigation regarding Bennell's association with the club in the 1980s and that is still ongoing. It has also created a compensation fund for victims of historical child sexual abuse at the club, with forty potential claimants and more expected to come forward.'

Ridpath glanced across at Chrissy, still wearing her City scarf and standing next to the picture of the five-a-side football team from 1994.

Lionel Smith continued speaking. 'Operation Hydrant has now expanded to include other sports: basketball, rugby, gymnastics, martial arts, tennis, wrestling, golf, sailing, athletics, cricket and swimming. The Ministry of Justice has also agreed changes to the law to make it illegal for sport coaches to have sex with sixteen- and seventeen-year-old children in their care.'

Without saying any more, Lionel Smith sat down.

A hush descended again. Finally Trent stood up. 'I think it's time for a break, ladies and gentlemen. Five minutes please, and then we need to work out the next steps in the case. Five minutes.'

Chapter Seventy-Four

After everyone had returned and sat down in the same places, Lorraine Caruso went over the evidence one more time, ending her speech by pointing to the picture of the five-a-side team.

'Up until now, our investigations have been guided by the assumption the killer must be one of the people in this picture. But they are now all dead, including the photographer. Did we go wrong from the beginning? Was the picture just a coincidence and nothing to do with the deaths?'

Trent thought for a moment. 'It's a fair question, Lorraine. You're saying there could be other links we don't know about?'

'There could be, boss. Maybe they went to the same school. Or the same cub scout group. We don't know.'

'Find out.'

'Yes, boss.'

A buzz went around the room as the detectives offered other places to look.

'But the picture must be the key. How can five people in it die in one week? All were murdered and then set alight. It's too much of a coincidence. We need to know more about the team and about each of the people in the photograph. Did David Mulkeen abuse one or more of them? We all heard DCI Smith, there must be something we're missing.' Ridpath raised his voice above the chatter of the other detectives. 'This has to be the link.'

'But they are all dead, Ridpath, or hadn't you noticed,' said Caruso from the front. 'And dead men can't be killers last time I checked the Hendon handbook.'

A support officer knocked on the door and entered, passing a note to Caruso. She opened and read it. 'This is from the DNA lab. They confirm the body we found in the flat last night was Charles Whitworth.'

A murmur went round the room as the detectives absorbed the information.

Trent stood up with her arms outstretched. 'Calm down, people. This is now a murder investigation of Charlie Whitworth, who was still a serving police officer at the time of his death.' She looked around the room before continuing. 'All efforts must be made to find this killer. No stone left unturned. Somebody must know who he is. Shake every tree, question every informant. This man must be found.' She pointed to the picture taken from the CCTV of the man who had attacked Ridpath.

Caruso raised her hand. 'I have a different possible explanation, boss.'

'Let's hear it, Lorraine.'

'It could have been suicide. Mr Whitworth could have killed himself last night.'

'What?' shouted Ridpath. 'The man was handcuffed to the chair.'

'He could have fastened the cuffs himself to make it look like he was murdered.'

'Why the hell would he do that?'

'And he could have placed the booby trap himself. We have him attending an explosives course in 2012. Plus the forensics have only found one set of prints in the apartment and they belonged to Mr Whitworth.'

'But forensics have found no prints at any of the other scenes. Fire has either destroyed them or our killer is savvy enough not to leave any behind.'

'What about the accelerant found in Whitworth's car?'

'That's stupid. It could have been placed there by the killer.'

Trent held her arms up again. 'Enough,' she shouted, 'this is not the forum for you two to air your personal differences. And

Ridpath, you will not speak to a senior officer in those terms, do you understand?'

Ridpath looked straight ahead.

'I said, do you understand?'

'Yes, ma'am.'

She glared at him for a moment before turning back to Lorraine. 'Continue, Detective Chief Inspector.'

'Guv'nor, despite our affection for Mr Whitworth—'

'It's Detective Chief Inspector Whitworth.'

'Ridpath, I won't tell you again. You are to remain silent.'

Caruso continued. 'Despite our affection for DCI Whitworth, we must keep all avenues of investigation open until we discover evidence to the contrary. This morning I spoke with his wife. She had recently split up with DCI Whitworth and moved back to her mother's.' She glanced over to Ridpath. 'There was no heart attack as has been reported. Maureen Whitworth told me that since the accident he'd been increasingly difficult to live with, and drinking far more than he should. In addition, we requested DCI Whitworth's financial records from his bank. Apparently he was undergoing financial difficulties: failed investments and problems with a property he had purchased.'

'Interesting, Lorraine.'

'But not proof he murdered five people and then killed himself,' said Ridpath.

Caruso looked to her boss, who simply stared straight ahead, clenching her jaw.

The DCI shrugged her shoulders and continued with her speech. 'And given his acquaintance with a known paedophile in David Mulkeen, we are going through his service records to see if there are indications of any reports of unnatural activities towards children.'

Ridpath stood up. 'You can't be serious. Charlie Whitworth, a paedophile? Never in a million years—'

'That's enough, Ridpath. Please wait for me in my office.'

Ridpath stayed where he was, with all the detectives watching him.

'That is an order, Detective Inspector Ridpath.'

Reluctantly Ridpath gathered up his files and marched out of the room. As he was closing the door he heard Trent say, 'These are valid areas of enquiry, Lorraine, we must leave no stone unturned. What else are you doing?'

Chapter Seventy-Five

After he'd waited for half an hour like a naughty schoolboy in the headmaster's office, Trent finally appeared.

'You were out of order, Ridpath. Lorraine Caruso was simply pursuing all possible lines of enquiry.'

'Including Charlie Whitworth was a paedophile?'

'Yes, including that. Unless we investigate everyone, including our own, we're never going to discover this killer.'

'But the whole idea it could be Charlie is crazy. The man could hardly walk, for one thing. Never mind the fact that for twenty-five years he was probably one of the best natural coppers Manchester has ever seen. The idea such a man is both a killer and a paedophile is...' Ridpath spluttered, looking for the right word, and finally ended up with '...ridiculous.'

Trent sat back in her chair and played with a pencil. 'Ridiculous or not, I've asked DCI Caruso to continue her enquiries. If nothing else, they will eliminate Charlie from our investigation.'

'But Caruso isn't a copper any more, guv'nor. She's a bureaucrat. She sees the spilling of blood, the suffering of people as statistical entries in a computer or costs on a balance sheet, not real men and women who used to be alive and have dreams and wants and desires.'

'Have you finished, Ridpath? DCI Caruso will continue her investigation into DCI Whitworth and anybody else I think is a possible suspect.'

'But it's a waste of valuable time and manpower we could be using to chase the real killer.'

'Manpower? You may have noticed half of MIT is now composed of women, Ridpath. I'll ask you to use the correct language in the future.'

'I'm sorry, but you know what I mean. We could use the resources far more effectively elsewhere.'

'I don't agree, Ridpath. And last time I looked it was my name on the door to this office, not yours, and it's my reputation on the line if this goes wrong.'

She suddenly sat forward and the tone of her voice changed. 'Look, Ridpath, I think you have a gift for police work, you understand what needs to be done intuitively. You're a natural copper, as you said about Charlie Whitworth. You make connections where others see nothing. It's one of the reasons we thought you'd be brilliant in the role of liaison between the coroner's office and GMP. To find those crimes that slip between the cracks in the system, going beyond jurisdictions and police boundaries. It's down to you we even knew there was a killer out there in the first place. But...'

He was waiting for the 'but'.

'But sometimes you can't see the wood for the trees. You don't know when to keep your mouth shut and be a team player. You've just pissed off your boss in front of the whole team. How do you think she's going to take it?'

'So I'm supposed to keep quiet if I see something I think is stupid.'

'The short answer is yes. We work best together as a team, not as a collection of individuals. Sometimes you have to get your head down, do as you're told and work the case. You're been a copper for ten years, you should know this.'

'It's twelve years, boss.'

'Whatever. You're not a kid, you're a detective inspector in GMP.' She sat back. 'And there's one other thing...'

Ridpath waited to hear what it was.

'You're too emotionally invested in this case. You can't distance yourself. You're not taking a step back, looking at the evidence, working out lines of enquiry to satisfy the CPS standards for conviction.'

'That's hard to do when the man who was my mentor and friend for all my time in GMP has been murdered.'

She nodded slowly. 'I understand. That's why I'm taking you off the case.'

'But—'

She held up her hands to stop him speaking. 'It is DCI Caruso's case now. You are not to get involved, Ridpath. If you do, I will consider it a serious breach of police discipline and will have no hesitation in recommending your dismissal from the force. Do you understand me?'

'But—'

'Do you understand me?'

'Yes, ma'am.'

She took a letter from her in tray and began to read it. 'We're done,' she said without looking up.

For the second time that day, Ridpath gathered up his files and marched out of a room.

Chapter Seventy-Six

'So that's where we are, Mrs Challinor. All the people in the image from 1994 are now dead. Five murdered in the last week and two who died years ago. One from a drug overdose and the other in a car crash. Not forgetting a psychotherapist who was somehow involved.'

'What is MIT doing?'

He shrugged his shoulders. 'Lorraine Caruso seems to be obsessed with the idea Charlie Whitworth was somehow involved—'

'You don't agree?' she interrupted.

'Charlie Whitworth could never murder five people, nor would he ever kill himself. The idea is unthinkable.'

'What other lines of enquiry are they following?'

'Your guess is as good as mine. I've been thrown off the case and sent back here with a flea in my ear.'

Ridpath finished informing the coroner of the latest developments in the case, including the noon meeting with Trent.

'Should I postpone the inquest into the death of Joseph Brennan? It's scheduled for a week on Thursday, May 9. Sophia has found a relative, an aunt, living in Devon. She won't come to the inquest but would like the body transported down to her so it can be buried in the family plot. Apparently she was close to his mother but hadn't seen him for years.'

'I don't think the police will have finished their enquiries by then, unless they manage to find the killer.'

'Do you think he will strike again?'

Ridpath thought for a long time. 'I don't think so. I might be wrong, but with the death of Charlie, it feels finished. He was the last person left alive in the photo. Plus the message changed at his death. It wasn't 'Play the Game' any more, but 'Played the Game'. I feel it's all over. He's done now.'

She looked at her laptop and pressed a key. 'We'll proceed with the inquest. I can always leave it as an open verdict pending further police enquiries. Afterwards, at least we can release the body back to her.'

'I think it's the right way to go.'

'What are you going to do, Ridpath?'

'About what?'

'The investigation.'

He frowned. 'To be honest, I don't know. Claire Trent is right – I am emotionally invested in this case. Charlie Whitworth was one of my best friends. We may not have always seen eye to eye, but he was a bloody good copper and an even better man.'

'You can't get involved, Ridpath.'

'I don't want to, but Lorraine Caruso is not understanding that the whole case revolves around the picture. Why kill all the people shown in it? Understand why and you can find the killer.'

Mrs Challinor brushed a lock of curly grey hair off her forehead. 'You don't understand me, Ridpath. That was an instruction, not a piece of advice. You can't get involved.'

'You're telling me the same as Detective Superintendent Trent?'

She nodded. 'Claire rang me after she had finished talking to you. She made it clear your continued existence as a police officer was dependent on understanding this instruction.'

'But he was my friend...'

'You have to let it go, Ridpath. If you leave GMP, we can't afford to keep you on here. It's only because Claire Trent pays your cost that I'm able to employ you.'

He stood up. 'I get the message, Coroner.'

'It's probably the wrong time to ask, Ridpath, but any news about my brother?'

'I'll follow up with Ted Jones.'

'Thank you.'

He turned to go, stopping briefly at the door. 'Mrs Challinor, whatever happened to being on the side of the victims? Charlie was a victim too.'

Chapter Seventy-Seven

'What are you going to do, Ridpath?'

They were both lying lengthways on the couch with his arm around her, holding her close, watching the fifth series of *Line of Duty* on BBC iPlayer. Polly loved it but Ridpath could only see faults in police procedure. What particularly annoyed him was the way every investigation seemed to collapse time, missing the hard slog of collecting evidence and following through lines of enquiry.

'I think I'm going to leave it, Polly.'

She sat up. 'Leave the police force, quit your job in the coroner's office?'

He smiled. 'Nah, leave the investigation to MIT.'

She pounded his chest, shouting, 'You bastard, why do you tease me?'

He pulled her to him. 'Shhh, Eve will hear you. Can't have her repeating words like "bastard", can we?'

'Are you serious? You're just going to leave it alone?'

'I can't see anything else I can do. They've both made it clear they don't want me involved. I'm not stupid, I can take a hint.'

He didn't tell her that he kept seeing Charlie. The man would pop up at the strangest times, at the edge of his vision, but when he looked round nobody was there. In his dreams, in the deepest part of the night, the last image of Charlie's eyes kept coming back to him. What would have happened if he had told Charlie about the message on the wall? Would Charlie have been able to tell him something? Would he still be alive?

She reached over to grab her glass of wine. 'It's the right decision, Ridpath, for you and for us.' She took a large sip of Sauvignon Blanc, passing the glass to him to share.

'I know, but it doesn't feel good. It feels like I'm letting Charlie down. I keep asking myself what he would do in my place.'

'And?'

'He would probably say, "Sod 'em. Do what you want, Ridpath, and sod the bloody lot of 'em".'

'That's what he might say, but he would do something completely different; he would toe the line. He managed to survive twenty-five years in GMP after all.'

He kissed her head. 'You're not as daft as you look, Mrs Polly Ridpath.'

'I'll take that as a compliment, Ridpath. I'd support you whatever you decided, but I think you've made the right decision.'

She nestled back against his body and continued to watch another tense interview between AC10 and a corrupt copper.

He couldn't help thinking about the case and about Charlie.

Had he missed something? Was there a clue to the killer's identity which had somehow escaped everybody? What was the meaning of the photograph? Why was everybody dead who had been involved in a five-a-side team way back in 1994? Was there a link to the child sexual abuse cases?

For a few minutes he focused back on the TV. For some reason there was a Mexican standoff with guns between two policemen. How had that happened?

But soon he found himself drifting back to the real-life case. One simple question kept coming back to haunt him again and again.

If they were all dead, who committed the murders?

One Week Later

Wednesday, May 8, 2019

Chapter Seventy-Eight

Detective Inspector Thomas Ridpath tried to get into the car park near Manchester Crematorium on Barlow Moor Road, but gave up after twenty minutes waiting in the queue and eventually parked illegally on the grass verge next to the road.

There was no likelihood he would get a ticket today. Any copper who had the balls to try would be a pariah for the rest of his time in the force.

Ridpath walked up the road to the yellow-brick temple to the dead that was Manchester Crematorium. Next door was Southern Cemetery, one of the largest urban burial grounds in Europe. A constant reminder death was alive and kicking.

A crowd of black-dressed men and women milled about the entrance waiting for the ceremony to start. He adjusted his black tie, bought from Marks and Sparks that morning, and strode through the gate.

He saw Claire Trent immediately, wearing a very stylish black coat with bright red trim. She was in earnest conversation with DCI Lorraine Caruso. She acknowledged Ridpath's greeting but Caruso turned away without looking at him.

For once, Ridpath had kept a promise to himself and his wife. He had stayed away from the investigation into the deaths of the football team and of Charlie, concentrating instead on his work as a coroner's officer. He had even left the liaison with the families to Carol Oates.

It hadn't stopped him thinking about the case, though. Each night, he lay in bed with Polly snoring gently beside him, going over the details in his mind, re-examining anything and every-thing to see if he had missed the one snippet of information that would reveal the killer.

Nothing came.

And when he did sleep, Charlie was there, staring at him.

He shook his head. Must stop thinking about it.

Beside the door of the chapel stood John Gorman, the former head of MIT, now retired after Ridpath had pointed out the mistakes he made during the Beast of Manchester investigation. He was surrounded by the MIT old school. Coppers Ridpath had worked with and respected when he was one of the up-and-coming lads, one of the bright boys. John Gorman pointedly looked in the opposite direction when he saw Ridpath approaching.

On the right, held back by a hastily erected orange barrier, was a phalanx of reporters and photographers. He supposed this funeral was still news.

Next to them, Ridpath recognised some well-known Manchester villains come to show their respects. A strange world, Manchester. On any other day the crowd here would have been trying to kill each other. But today, at the funeral of a respected copper, it was as if the crematorium was a no man's land in the eternal battle between good and evil in the city.

The only people absent were the top brass. They had been told in no uncertain terms they were not welcome at the funeral and there were to be no uniformed police present.

In the centre, the woman who had given them their orders was wearing a black veil over her face and was supported on either side by her son and daughter. Maureen Whitworth looked frail but Ridpath could see a core of steel there. She was going to get through today, whatever happened.

He walked over to one of his old mates who was standing all alone. 'Hello, Dave, sad day.'

'Didn't ever think it would end like this.'

'Nobody ever imagined…' Ridpath didn't finish his sentence.

Dave Hardy shook his head. 'I always thought he was inde-structible and they'd have to carry him kicking and screaming out of his office when he was ninety, still looking for one last nutter to put away.'

'How're you doing, Dave?'

'I'm good, got my transfer out of MIT, couldn't stand working for Claire bloody Trent, and have now got a cushy number with force liaison. Regular hours, regular pay and a regular retirement in two years.' He looked up at Ridpath with bright eyes. 'I thought you'd have moved back into MIT by now.'

'Still with the coroner, and working for Claire Trent too, but we manage. For me, it's like doing old policing with none of the bullshit.'

Dave Hardy nodded towards Claire Trent. 'I heard they bolloxed the case. Thought Charlie was a suspect only to discover he had alibis for two of the killings. He was getting drunk with a detective super and a former chief constable.'

'Alibis don't come any better than that.'

'You don't say. All the other lines of enquiry have turned up blanks too. Both are heading for the chopping block.'

'Not Claire Trent, she'll survive. DCI Caruso on the other hand…' Ridpath shrugged his shoulders. Despite his disagree-ments with her, he didn't want to see Caruso fail. It was far more important to catch the killer than for him to see himself vindicated.

The undertaker approached John Gorman and the men around him and led them to the back of the hearse. They began to slide the oak coffin out through the rear door, stooping down to place it on their shoulders and march solemnly into the Old Chapel. A wreath of flowers with the single word 'Charlie' created out of white roses lay on top.

Organ music began to play. Ridpath recognised it as 'I Love You Because' by Jim Reeves. Had Charlie chosen this music? Was he having a last laugh at all the people assembled for his funeral?

Probably, knowing Charlie.

Ridpath followed the coffin and all the other mourners as they filed into the chapel.

It was time to say goodbye.

Chapter Seventy-Nine

Ex-Detective Superintendent John Gorman walked up to the pulpit, his head down.

The wooden pews were full of a sea of black-clad men and women. Ridpath and Dave Hardy had secreted themselves on the far left, out of the way.

Ridpath noticed the swagger with which Gorman had dominated the Major Incident Team for so many years had gone, to be replaced with a diffidence, an uncertainty. He looked older now, more frail, as if retirement had sapped his strength. He was a small man so he adjusted the microphone downwards. His trembling hand placed a single sheet of paper on the lectern and he coughed once to clear his throat.

The Old Chapel of Manchester Crematorium was small. The coffin lay on a conveyor belt in the centre of the far wall, surrounded by curtains the colour of blood. Above the coffin, a stained-glass rose window allowed light to enter from outside. Light which, through accident or design, illuminated Charlie Whitworth's family on the front row.

John Gorman coughed again and began speaking. 'We are gathered here today to celebrate the life of Charlie Whitworth. A man, a copper, my friend.'

At the last word, Gorman sucked in air through his teeth. 'I knew Charlie for over twenty years. He graduated from the police training college in Edgeley Park two years after me. We struck up a firm friendship when we were both based in Moss Side in the 1990s. And anybody who knew the area then knows the coppers used to go around in threes for safety.'

Dave Hardy leant over to Ridpath and whispered, 'If they ever left the station...'

'This was the era of Gunchester, of course, a time of great stress for most coppers, but not for Charlie. He quickly built up a rapport with the locals and by the time he left, after completing his detective exams, I can truly say he was missed by the people of the area. He wasn't missed by the thugs and low-lifes, though – they were happy to see him go.'

'I bet he was missed by the shebeens too,' Dave whispered.

'When the Major Incident Teams were created and I was asked to lead them...'

'Is this about Charlie or John Gorman? He always was full of himself.' Dave Hardy's running commentary continued under his breath.

'...The only person I wanted as my number two was Charlie. I couldn't trust anybody else to do the job...'

'Or to do your dirty work.' Dave Hardy spat the words out a little louder than he should have done. Unfortunately, this coincided with a moment of silence as John Gorman paused in his speech.

A few of the mourners on the bench in front turned round to stare at Ridpath as Dave Hardy kept his head down. For a second Gorman stopped and glared at him before continuing.

'...The Gooch Gang case, the Highland Road murders, the Post Office robberies, the Feelan killing, the Canal Street rapes, all were solved, and solved quickly by Charlie and his team under my guidance.'

Ridpath noticed he didn't mention the one case which had led to his retirement. The Beast of Manchester.

'...Charlie was that rare thing in this world. A copper who never gave up, one who doggedly pursued his man, or woman, till the very end. A copper's copper. His dedication meant he was eventually injured in the line of duty, an injury which would have meant spending the rest of his life in a wheelchair or hobbling around on a walking stick. Not something Charlie would have enjoyed.' He paused for a second and looked at Charlie's family in the front row. 'He died last week, killed by a brutal murderer. A murder that must not go unsolved by Greater Manchester Police…'

Ridpath glanced across at Claire Trent. She had her head down and wasn't looking at Gorman.

'…The reputation of the police force and justice is at stake. Charlie Whitworth's killer must be found and found fast.'

'He's really sticking the boot in,' whispered Dave Hardy.

A loud 'shush' from the pew in front.

After this exhortation, Gorman softened his tone. 'Charlie Whitworth will be missed. By his wife Maureen, his daughter Angela, and his son Charlie Junior. But most of all, Charlie will be missed by the people of Manchester. He dedicated his life to preserving the peace of this city and now he deserves to rest in peace. Thank you.'

The ex-detective superintendent left the pulpit and, after a few desultory words from one of the local vicars, the Smiths' 'Shoplifters of the World Unite' blared out from the speakers.

Ridpath smiled. Charlie *had* chosen the music. Only he would have the balls to make fun of everybody at his own funeral. As Morrissey's voice belted out the chorus, the curtains parted and the doors opened in the back. Slowly the coffin began its last journey into the heart of the crematorium.

'Bye, Charlie,' Ridpath whispered.

Chapter Eighty

Ten minutes later and Ridpath was outside the crematorium, smoking. It was his first cigarette for nearly six months and it tasted rank. He had cadged one from Dave Hardy.

'I thought you'd given up.'

'I have, but after the funeral I need the reassurance of tobacco.'

'I know what you mean.' Dave lit both their fags. 'You coming to the pub? A lot of the old team will be there, having one last drink on Charlie. Not that he paid for many when he was alive. You didn't often see Charlie's wallet.'

Ridpath shook his head. 'Can't face it. And anyway, I have work to do back at Stockfield.'

'The coroner driving you hard?'

'She's OK. We have an inquest tomorrow on one of the victims.'

'Fair enough.' He stubbed the half-smoked cigarette out with his heel. 'I'm off. See you around, Ridpath.'

As soon as Dave left, Ridpath was approached by Claire Trent. 'Morning, Ridpath, a sad occasion.'

'It is, ma'am,' he answered stiffly.

'Is the inquest on Joseph Brennan tomorrow?'

Ridpath nodded. 'It starts at 9.30 a.m. Should be finished by noon, though. In the absence of any new information, it's simply to facilitate the release of the body to the family.'

'What will the verdict be?'

'You'll have to ask the coroner, she's the one who will make the decision. But my bet is either murder by persons unknown or an open verdict. Either way, it leaves the investigation free to continue. Will you be there?'

'Yes. I've promised the coroner. I'm sure the vampires of the press will be too, so I'll have to face more questions. Or give them more blood, whichever is easier.'

'I'll make sure they keep a seat for you.'

Trent looked down at her feet. 'Ridpath, we're having a review of the case at Police HQ with the chief constable on Friday, the day after the inquest. Could you attend?'

Ridpath couldn't resist. 'Are you sure you want me there?'

Trent looked up at him. 'Don't rub my nose in it, Detective Inspector. Make sure you're there. Eleven a.m. on the sixth floor.'

She then strode back to a waiting Lorraine Caruso.

Ridpath smiled to himself. What goes around, comes around.

He glanced up at the clock.

Time to get back to work. He turned once more towards the chapel and made the sign of the cross, whispering 'Bye, Charlie. I hope you enjoy your time in heaven or hell, wherever you end up.'

Once a Catholic, always a Catholic.

Chapter Eighty-One

'How was the funeral?'

Ridpath frowned. 'Like all funerals. Sad and bewildering.'

Margaret Challinor sat back in her chair. 'I'm not my best at them either. I never know what to say to people. I find I end up talking about the weather. Terribly English, I suppose.'

'It was a funeral full of coppers. We talked about work.'

'Still nothing on the murders?'

Ridpath shook his head. 'Claire Trent is holding a review of the case on Friday. She's invited me.'

'You're pleased?'

'Not really. It means they have nothing. I'd much prefer we'd arrested and charged somebody. It gives me no pleasure to see us floundering around, desperately looking for a way to solve the case.'

Mrs Challinor changed the subject. 'Are we ready for tomorrow?'

'Sophia is just putting the notes together for you to review this evening. We'll call Dr Schofield to the stand first—'

'Oh, why?'

'He has a backlog of cases and can only spare us the morning. Followed by Brennan's GP, Dr Marshall, then Dave Greene and finally the fire investigator, Terry Dolan.'

'Good. Our job is to establish the who, what and how of the case. We'll leave it to the police to discover the why and the perpetrator. Even though it sounds like they are no nearer to bringing somebody to trial than they were a week ago.' She touched her grey hair, always a sign she was about to change the subject. 'How's Sophia working out?'

'Fine. Best thing I ever did was hiring her. After a rocky start, she and our pathologist seem to have bonded over haematology. And thank you for the recommendation. Her biomedical and organisational skills are becoming indispensable.'

'Bureaucracy isn't your forte, Ridpath.'

He smiled. 'That's an understatement, Mrs Challinor.' He gestured towards the door. 'I'll see how she's getting on.'

'Ridpath, I know it hurt, but it was the right thing to do.'

'Taking me off the case?'

Mrs Challinor nodded.

'I know, but there's still an emptiness there that won't be filled until they find the man who did it.' He paused for a moment. 'What I don't understand is why. What would drive anybody to set fire to another human being?'

'Pain, Ridpath, immense pain.' She reddened and looked down. 'Have you heard anything about my brother?'

'Ted Jones has put the word out. People living on the streets are always hard to find. As you can imagine, the last thing any of them want to do is talk to the police. As soon as they hear anybody asking questions, they lose themselves in the under-world or they move on. I'm sure we'll find him soon, though.'

'Thank you, Ridpath.'

He gestured towards the door again, both of them slightly embarrassed by their sudden closeness. 'I'll check on Sophia.'

Mrs Challinor nodded once and opened a file on her desk. 'Thank you, Ridpath,' was all she said as he left her office.

Chapter Eighty-Two

Lying in bed that night, Ridpath couldn't fall asleep. Images of Charlie's body kept leaping into his mind.

The St Christopher medallion sitting on the scorched skin.

The handcuffs encircling the blackened wrists.

The mouth twisted into a rictus grin of sheer pain.

What remained of the hair smouldering on a blistered, charred scalp.

And Charlie himself disturbing his dreams when he did nod off. Always asking him questions. Questions Ridpath couldn't answer.

'Who did it?'

'Why did they do it?'

'What are you doing?'

Finally Polly woke up too. 'Are you all right?'

'Yeah, just can't sleep.'

'Thinking of the case tomorrow?'

He checked the alarm clock beside the bed: 3:40 a.m. 'No, thinking of the case today. You go back to sleep. I'll go and make myself a coffee. What does Eve want for breakfast?'

'Eggs, I think. She needs the protein. A growing girl.'

'No problem. Coddled eggs it is. Go back to sleep. I'll wake you before I go.'

'Ridpath, you did your best. Nobody could have done more.'

'Aye, but was it good enough? Charlie's killer is still out there and I'm organising inquests and filling in forms rather than pounding the streets to find him.'

Polly put her hand in his. 'You did your best.'

He kissed her on the forehead. 'Go back to sleep.'

Ridpath padded downstairs as quietly as he could, switching on the light in the kitchen. He made himself a coffee, choosing the strongest espresso capsule they had for the machine. 'This should keep me going,' he said out loud to fill the silence.

Then he sat down at the table and mentally went through the case from the beginning, exploring every detail, re-examining everything he knew and everything he could remember.

As dawn's grey light seeped over the city, he was no closer to an answer. He had written down a few more lines of enquiry to suggest during the review on Friday.

Did we ever find the tramp on the CCTV coming out of the building site?

Was anyone else involved in the five-a-side team but not in the picture?

Why was Sam Sykes the only one who had his throat cut rather than being struck with a blunt instrument?

Had they checked the CCTV between Charlie's house and Bruton Place? Did it show more than one person in the car?

What happened to the psychotherapist's phone?

He looked down at his notes again. They were just areas to follow up rather than new lines of enquiry. And he was sure Claire Trent and Lorraine Caruso had already covered them.

He slumped back in the chair, exhausted. 'Sorry, Charlie,' was all he managed to whisper.

Outside, the quiet of the early morning was broken by the sounds of a magpie cawing from a nearby tree.

To Ridpath, it sounded like the silence was calling.

Thursday, May 9, 2019

Chapter Eighty-Three

The witnesses and a solicitor arrived at the first-floor courtroom one by one. First there was Dave Greene, dressed in a suit and tie. Ridpath realised it was the only time he had seen the fire officer in civilian clothes. Normally he was wearing his helmet and heavy-duty gear. Somehow, he looked more human, more frail, less of a superman in a suit.

'Hello, Dave, I think the coroner is going to call you to the witness stand after the pathologist. Have you attended a coroner's court before?'

'Only once.'

'Just remember, it's not adversarial like a criminal court. All the coroner is seeking is the truth. Who died, when they died and how they died. If you sit over there, you won't have far to walk to the witness stand.' Ridpath pointed him in the direction of a chair behind a velvet rope.

The next to arrive was Terry Dolan, sporting a jacket, jeans and an open-necked shirt.

'You'll have done a few of these, Terry,' Ridpath greeted him.

'Not that many,' he answered, scratching his bald head.

Ridpath checked outside the window. It was drizzling as usual. The sort of rain that seeped into every pore, leaving the soul damp and miserable. 'Sit next to Dave, you'll be called after him.'

'Right-o.'

A pair of black-garbed solicitors representing the family came next, followed by Claire Trent and Lorraine Caruso.

'How long is this going to last, Ridpath?' asked the detective superintendent.

'Your guess is as good as mine, but it should be finished before lunch. Just five witnesses.'

'Good, I have to brief the mayor at two this afternoon.' She glanced at Caruso. 'The shit has hit the fan. You saw the funeral pictures in *The Times* this morning?'

Ridpath shook his head.

'The case has been picked up by the national newspapers. The tabloids are having a field day and even the quality papers have joined in.'

'I'm sure the mayor is happy.'

'As happy as any politician who sees his name attached to a negative story.'

Ridpath raised his eyebrows. '*That* happy?' Then he put the boot in. 'The coroner may need to call you.'

She looked surprised. 'Oh?'

'I don't think she will, but before she decides the verdict, she may want a statement on the progress of the investigation.'

Trent nodded, glancing once more at Caruso. 'Seems like everybody wants to know the status of the investigation, including me.'

They moved off to sit at the back of the court.

As if on cue, four reporters entered the courtroom, all chattering loudly, accompanied by a PCSO in uniform. Ridpath gestured towards them. 'Press, over there.'

They all sat down in their reserved seats, still chattering away.

He took hold of the PCSO's arm. 'Can I help you, sir?'

The man looked flustered. 'I just thought I'd stop by to see the inquest.'

Ridpath raised his eyebrows.

'I was there that night,' he stammered, 'the night the flat caught fire and Joe Brennan was burnt, helping with the crowd.'

'Your name is…?'

'Clive Tennant. Can't stay long, though, my shift starts at noon.'

'OK, Mr Tennant, you can sit close to the door in case you need to leave.'

Dr Marshall was waiting at the door. 'Will this take a long time?'

Why did everybody want to rush this inquest? 'Should be finished before lunchtime, I think. The coroner will call you last for an opinion on his state of mind.'

'But I hardly knew him.'

'You were his doctor...'

The man rubbed his nose before answering. 'I hadn't seen him for three years.'

Ridpath noticed the telltale giveaway that somebody was lying and decided to risk a stab in the dark. 'That's not strictly true, is it, Doctor?'

The man looked down at his feet. 'He rang me six months ago and asked for a referral to a psychiatrist, but the NHS ones were all booked up for months...'

'So you referred him to your friend, Alistair Ransome?'

'Something like that.' He then looked up and stared at Ridpath. 'But you can't prove anything.'

The wrong answer. 'I'm sure the coroner will ask about it now. And I'd just like to take this opportunity to remind you the penalties for perjury apply in a coroner's court as much as they do in the rest of the judicial system. You can sit over there, next to the other witnesses.'

The doctor sidled away, sitting by himself, away from the others.

The last to arrive were Dr Schofield and Detective Constable Ron Pleasance. The pathologist was carrying a large medical bag and looking flustered. 'I hope I'm not late, Ridpath,' he said in his high-pitched voice.

'It's OK, we're just about to start. Are you prepared?'

'As I'll ever be. I just hope Mrs Challinor doesn't ask me to explain everything in layman's language again. It's so imprecise.'

Ridpath looked over the court. 'I'm sure she will.'

'Damn, I'd better check my notes.' He paused for a second. 'You haven't seen Sophia this morning?'

'She's in the office. Do you want to talk to her?'

'No, no,' he said hurriedly, blushing slightly, 'I was just wondering if she would be here. I'd better go and check my notes.'

'How is Inspector Wharton treating you, Ron?'

'Same as usual. Like a piece of shit he found on the sole of his shoe. His bromance with me didn't last long once the Brennan death was reclassified as murder.'

'Not your fault, Ron. You did everything right.'

'Tell that to Wharton. The only saving grace was MIT taking the case off his books. He still hasn't forgiven me, though.'

'He's an arsehole, remember that, but if you can survive him, you can survive anything GMP can throw at you.'

'Why do I not find your words encouraging, Ridpath? And sorry for what I said about Charlie Whitworth. I read about the funeral this morning in the papers. Not a great way to die.'

'None of them are, Ron.'

More reporters drifted in, accompanied by a few members of the public alerted to the case by the interest from the tabloids. Ron Pleasance went and sat down next to the doctor.

As the clock ticked over to 10.00 a.m., the door at the rear of the court opened and Mrs Challinor entered.

A hush descended – even the reporters stopped chatting – as she took her place behind the coroner's desk.

Chapter Eighty-Four

Mrs Challinor was dressed in a formal black suit, and Ridpath noticed her grey hair had been tied back into a bun, the curls encased in a net. She began to speak in a voice commanding silence. 'Today we open the inquest into the death of Joseph Brennan.' She pointed to the empty jury box on her left. 'There will be no jury present at this inquest.' A quick glance down at the papers in front of her. 'Representing the family is Mr Rupert Stead.'

The solicitor stood up and bowed his head once.

'Is the family present, Mr Stead?'

'They are not, ma'am.'

'They have appointed you to represent their interests?'

'They have, ma'am.' He bowed once again and sat down.

'A gentle reminder to all those present, including the ladies and gentlemen of the press I see before me.' She gestured towards the group on her right. 'This is not a court of law. I will ask each witness questions as I see fit. The legal representatives of the family will then have the opportunity to question the witnesses when I have finished. As the pathologist has an urgent appointment we will take the unusual step of calling him first. Jenny...'

The office manager stepped forward.

'Please call the first witness, Dr Eugene John Schofield.'

Did Ridpath see a small smile cross the coroner's face as she pronounced the pathologist's full name?

The man strode to the witness box and took the oath on a Bible held by Jenny Oldfield. As Margaret Challinor began questioning him, he ran his finger around the inside of his shirt collar, as if giving himself more room to breathe.

'Please state your name and occupation.'

'Dr John Schofield. Forensic pathologist attached to the Western Manchester Regional Health Authority.'

'You were called to an incident on April 24 of this year, were you not?'

'I was. A fire on the top floor of a building at Stockfield Road in Wythenshawe.'

'And what did you find? Please explain your findings in layman's terms.'

The doctor glanced over at Ridpath. 'A deceased male, aged between thirty-five and forty years. He had suffered fourth-degree burns over ninety per cent of his body.'

'Did these burns cause his death?'

'I thought so at the time, but when I performed the post-mortem on him, I reached a different conclusion.'

'And what was it?'

'He had actually died from three blows to the head from a blunt instrument, a ball peen hammer or something similar. The blows struck the junction between the occipital, parietal and temporal regions of the skull.'

'Could you show us where on your own skull, Doctor?'

'Around here, just behind the right ear.'

'Thank you. And did you ascertain the time of death?'

'It is notoriously difficult to give an exact time of death for any fire victim, but in this case he died at least eight hours before the onset of the fire.'

'We will hear from the incident commander, Mr Greene, about the timing of the fire later. But you seem to be suggesting he died before the fire started?'

'I am stating exactly that, Coroner. At least eight hours before the fire began. In my professional opinion, the fire was started to cover up the crime, not to kill the deceased. He had already been dead long before it started.'

'Thank you, Doctor. And did you manage to make a positive identification of the deceased?'

'We did. No DNA of Mr Brennan was on the national database and unfortunately, the fire had resulted in sloughing of the skin around the fingertips, removing the possibility of fingerprint identification. However, despite the fire having a deleterious effect on the skull, face and body, the forensic team managed to find a dental bridge that had fallen out of the mouth. When we compared this to Mr Brennan's dental records, we discovered a match.'

'Thank you, Doctor. Any questions from the family?'

Mr Stead stood up. 'None, ma'am.'

'Thank you, Dr Schofield, you are excused. Jenny, can you please call the incident commander, Mr David Greene?'

Dave Greene walked to the witness stand. After the usual formalities, he answered the coroner's first question. 'We received the call at 22:02 and arrived on the scene at 22:12.'

'That's very quick, Mr Greene, you are to be congratulated.'

'Thank you, ma'am.'

'And what did you do?'

'Luckily, the fire was in its early stages. We immediately evacuated the rest of the building and I evaluated the risks of the operation, deciding we would go into Offensive Oscar mode.'

'What does that mean?'

'It means we will proactively fight the fire. I rationalised it had not spread to the roof yet, so there was little danger to my men. Plus if we could put it out quickly, we could restrict the fire to the living room of the flat.'

'And that is what you did?'

'Yes, ma'am. It took us about fifteen minutes to put it out.'

'And then you entered the flat?'

'Yes.'

'And what did you find?'

'The body of a man sitting in a chair facing a burnt-out television. I informed the police and they called their station requesting an investigative and forensic team.'

'Thank you, Mr Greene. Have you anything more to add?'

'Just one thing, ma'am. The fire hadn't taken hold when we arrived on the scene. It was almost as if we were called before it started.'

'Thank you, Mr Greene, we will hear from the fire investigator later on this theory. Any questions, Mr Stead?'

'None, ma'am.'

She checked her watch. 'This would seem to be a good time to take a ten-minute break. We will return at 11.15 precisely.'

Mrs Challinor stood up and exited through the same door she had entered. Ridpath looked around. Dr Schofield had already gone and Dave Greene was sitting at the back of the court. Ron Pleasance was the next witness up and he was looking a little nervous. Only Terry Dolan seemed relaxed and confident.

The reporters had resumed their gossiping, laughing at each other's jokes and generally making noise.

Claire Trent approached him. 'Are we on time, Ridpath?'

'I think so, just three witnesses to go. Terry Dolan may take a while but the family solicitor isn't asking any questions so I think it will move rapidly along.'

'Good, I've just received a text from the mayor. He's confirmed our meeting at two p.m.'

'Lucky you.'

As Ridpath spoke, the door at the rear of the court opened again and Mrs Challinor entered, walked quickly to sit behind her desk, and waited for everyone to settle down, before saying, 'Let us continue with the inquest. Please call Detective Constable Ronald Pleasance to the stand.'

Chapter Eighty-Five

'You were called to a fire on the evening of April 24?' the coroner asked Ron Pleasance.

'Well, yes and no, ma'am.'

Ridpath saw Mrs Challinor's eyes roll towards the ceiling. 'What do you mean, Detective Constable?'

'I had been working the late shift at Cheadle nick, I mean station, when a call came in from Foxtrot Alpha...'

'Could you speak English, Detective?'

'Yes, ma'am, that's what I'm doing.'

A roll of the eyes again. 'Please avoid police acronyms if you can.'

'OK, will do. A call came in from a squad car that a body had been found in a burnt-out flat just off Stockfield Road. I arrived at the address at 00:05, so technically it was April 25, ma'am.'

'Yes, Detective, please get on with it.'

'I will, ma'am,' he said, clearing his throat.

'And what did you see?'

'There was a dead body in the living room, so I cleared the area and asked the duty pathologist to come out, plus I asked for forensic support.'

'Why did you do that?'

The detective looked surprised by the question.

'Let me rephrase it to help you. You saw a dead body and you felt it should be investigated.'

'Yes, ma'am, exactly. I talked with the incident commander, Dave Greene, and he thought an accelerant had been used to start the fire. The pathologist arrived, pronounced death, and the body was removed by the morgue attendants at four a.m. In the morning, I contacted my boss, Inspector Wharton, and he informed your department. DI Ridpath arrived around noon and we examined the scene of the crime together with Dave Greene, the crime scene manager Helen Charles, and the fire investigator Terry Dolan.'

'Thank you, we will be hearing Mr Dolan's evidence shortly. Your initial report states you were unable to ascertain the reason for death. Why is that?'

'After a discussion with all the participants, we decided there was no possibility of the fire being an accident, but a strong possibility of either suicide or murder.'

'Why?'

'Because of the presence of a fire accelerant at the scene.'

'Yes, we will be asking the fire investigator about this later. What else did you do?'

'I questioned the neighbours, who had hardly seen Mr Brennan for the last three years. I also visited his doctor, who had prescribed antidepressants for him since losing his job, and I checked out the local B&Q. Mr Brennan went there on the morning of the fire.'

Ridpath noticed his own involvement in the investigation had been completely omitted by Pleasance. The young lad was learning fast how to get ahead in GMP.

'What happened next?'

'I was inclined to think it was suicide, but then the pathologist reported back he believed it was murder. And when it was linked to another death, the file was handed over to MIT.'

'That's the Major Incident Team, isn't it?'

'It is, ma'am.'

'Thank you, Detective Constable. Any questions, Mr Stead?'

'None, ma'am.'

'Jenny, please call Mr Terry Dolan to the stand.'

The fire investigator stood and ambled over to the witness stand. He sat down confidently, adjusted the microphone and then swore his oath without looking at the card offered by Jenny Oldfield.

'Mr Dolan, you are an accredited fire investigator?'

'I am, ma'am. I've been working in this field for my whole career since leaving university, firstly as a lab technician and later working as an investigator. I have been working for Adelphi Consultants, one of the accredited fire investigators to Greater Manchester Police, for the last three years.'

Ridpath stared out of the window as Terry Dolan gave his evidence. Outside, the rain had become heavier. Manchester looked like it was drowning.

'Were you called to investigate a fire occurring in the home of Joseph Brennan on April 24?'

'I was. I received the call at six a.m. and went to the scene immediately to make a preliminary investigation, returning at noon to explain my findings to the police and your officer, DI Ridpath.'

At the sound of his name, Ridpath turned his head. What had he just heard? Three years. Had Terry Dolan only worked for Adelphi for three years? Where was he before then?

As the rain beat against the glass of the windows outside the court and Mrs Challinor continued with her questioning inside, a series of images flashed through Ridpath's mind.

The neighbour, Mrs Finnegan: 'He was some sort of lab technician.'

Helen, the crime scene manager: 'Hello, Terry, you're out again, must be nice to get some air.'

He thought about it more, raking through his memories. Wasn't it Terry Dolan who suggested they look for the dentist and ID the body through dental records? Almost as if he knew the DNA wasn't on file and there were no fingerprints. How did he know about the condition of the hands if the body was moved at four a.m. but he didn't arrive until six a.m.?

Ridpath took a step forward, staring at Terry Dolan as he gave evidence.

More memories flashed through his mind. At Bruton Place, it was Terry Dolan who spotted the tiny holes in the skirting board. It wasn't great eyesight, he already knew what he was looking for. He wanted people to know about the booby trap.

But why? If he was the killer, what link did he have with the children in the picture? They were all dead, weren't they?

And then the answer hit with a clarity he had never known before, like looking at a painted miniature through a magnifying glass and seeing each tiny brushstroke, each minute dot of colour.

The whole crime revealed in one flash of insight. It was the only answer that worked.

But how to prove it?

He needed time.

He took out his notebook from his inside pocket and hastily scribbled a message for Mrs Challinor.

He strode up to her desk, feeling as if all eyes in the court were watching him. She stopped questioning Terry Dolan for a moment and stared at Ridpath.

He approached her desk and reached up to pass her the note.

She took it, put her reading glasses on and scanned the message. 'Are you sure, Ridpath?'

He nodded.

She raised her eyebrows. 'OK. Ladies and gentlemen, let us adjourn for another break of ten minutes. We will reconvene at eleven forty-five exactly.'

A buzz went around the courtroom.

Mrs Challinor leant across the table and whispered to Ridpath, 'I hope you know what you're doing.'

'Trust me, Mrs Challinor. I'll see you in your room. I won't be long…' the last words were shouted over his shoulder as he rushed out of the doors of the court, down the steps and up into his own office.

Chapter Eighty-Six

Sophia Rahman was sitting at her desk, collating the work in progress for the meeting at the end of the week. Carol Oates was standing in front of her, talking.

'Sophia, can you—'

'Excuse me, Ridpath, I am briefing Sophia on an urgent job. Please wait your turn.'

'Sorry, Carol, this is critical. Sophia, did we check Terry Dolan's credentials and work history before we asked him to attend the inquest?'

She shook her head. 'No, why would we? He's just a witness…'

Carol Oates stared at Ridpath before tossing her head and stomping off.

'Can you check them now?'

Recognising the urgency in his voice, Sophia dropped what she was doing and opened Google on her computer. 'What was the name of his company?'

Ridpath racked his brain for the answer and then it came to him. The name of a theatre in London. 'Adelphi, Adelphi Consultants?'

Sophia's fingers moved across the keyboard rapidly. 'Here it is.'

Ridpath moved round to look at her screen.

'Adelphi Consultants, specialists in fire investigations for insurance, valuations, civil and criminal cases. They are one of GMP's registered agencies.'

'Can you find their personnel?'

'Seems to be a small company; three investigators. The founder, an ex-fire chief of Manchester called Ronnie Whelan, and two others, Terry Dolan and George Lincoln.'

'Where did Dolan work before?'

She clicked on Dolan's page. 'It doesn't say. Just deals with his career since he joined Adelphi three years ago.'

'Nothing earlier?'

She shook her head.

'There must be something. Google him.'

Her fingers rattled the keyboard. 'Nothing, just his Adelphi profile and links to reports he has written.'

'Any written before he worked for Adelphi?'

She checked the list of reports, shaking her head. 'All written in the last three years.'

Ridpath let out a long sigh. Had he been wrong about Terry Dolan? But why were there no reports from before 2016? He scratched his head. He had to get back to the court; Mrs Challinor would be waiting. He sighed once again and began to walk towards the door.

Then he stopped.

What had Dr Schofield said? The dental bridge was found by the forensic team and then tested, finding a match to Joseph Brennan.

Ridpath scrolled through the contacts on his mobile and dialled a number. He crossed his fingers – she had to pick up.

The phone rang on and on and on.

No answer.

Ridpath was about to give up when there was a click as the call was forwarded.

A tinny-sounding voice from an answering machine came on. 'This is Helen Charles, I'm probably working a job at the moment, but if you leave a message, I'll get back to you just as soon as I can.'

'Helen,' Ridpath shouted, 'this is urgent. If you can hear this, please answer your phone… please.'

Silence.

Ridpath waited.

Then, 'I'm on a job, Ridpath, can't it wait?'

'Sorry, Helen, it's urgent. Remember the Brennan case? The fire in Wythenshawe? Who discovered the dental bridge of the victim? Can you remember?'

'Yeah, I remember it well. We were really lucky. The bridge must have fallen out of the mouth when the morticians moved the body. My lot missed it, but the fire investigator, Terry, saw it beside the chair and called us over before he touched it.'

'Bingo.'

'Sorry, what was that, Ridpath?'

'Nothing. You've been a great help, Helen. One more thing. Do you know Terry?'

'Course I do, he's worked a couple of fire investigations for us. The team call him Scarman, after the judge.'

The hackles on the back of Ridpath's neck rose. 'Why's that?' he asked tentatively.

'He's got scars on his arms and body. He said they were from a fire when he was young.'

'Thanks, Helen, you've been really helpful.'

'Can I go back to the job?'

'Of course, and I owe you a drink.'

He switched off the phone. Sophia was on her landline. She held her hand over the speaker and said. 'It's Mrs Challinor, she wants to know where the hell you are.'

'Tell her I'll be there in two minutes, just one more thing to do.'

Sophia relayed the message and put down the phone.

Ridpath crossed his fingers once more. It had worked last time, why not now? 'Sophia, the medical report on Joseph Brennan. His doctor said he had an accident when he was young. Do we have the report?'

Sophia reached across her desk to grab a file. She leafed though a dozen pages before finding Brennan's medical history from Dr Marshall. Her finger followed the dates and times of illnesses, vaccinations and routine check-ups. 'Here it is,' she finally said. 'He suffered third-degree burns all down the left side of his torso and arm from an accident in a fire when he was fourteen years old...' She looked up. 'In 1994. The burns left extensive scarring and involved grafting of skin from his thigh to his torso.'

'Got you.'

Chapter Eighty-Seven

By the time Ridpath had finished explaining everything to Mrs Challinor it was already 12:05 p.m. The people in the court were becoming restless, the news reporters anxious to get away to file their reports and Claire Trent pointing to her watch.

Terry Dolan was the calmest person in the room, still sitting in the witness chair as if nothing had happened.

Trent strode over to see Ridpath as soon as he re-entered the courtroom. 'What the hell is going on? I'm going to be late for my meeting with the mayor.'

'You'll see now, guv'nor. Can you ask Lorraine and Dave Greene to be ready?'

'Tell me what's bloody going on, that's an order.'

As she spoke, Mrs Challinor entered and sat back down at her desk.

Ridpath moved away to stand in front of the entrance to the court.

The coroner began speaking. 'My apologies to everybody; I was unavoidably detained by an urgent matter. We will continue with Mr Dolan's testimony. Now, Mr Dolan, you were saying how you knew an accelerant had been used.'

Terry Dolan adjusted the microphone in front of him once more. 'Actually, its presence had already been indicated to me by the incident commander, Dave Greene. He reported the smell of an accelerant, what we now know was methylated spirits, when he first entered the living room of the flat. But the signs were obvious to see.'

'And what were those signs?'

Dolan was speaking confidently, obviously a speech he had rehearsed often. 'There were scorch marks above the chair suggesting a source of intense heat. Plus the chair itself had suffered fierce and extreme burning, destroying most of the fabric and the foam stuffing inside. Not an effect one would see from a cigarette or a dropped match.' He smiled and looked around the court.

'And who found the dental bridge later used to identify the victim?'

The smile suddenly vanished from the man's face. 'I... I did. It was me,' he stammered.

'Where did you find it?'

'At the side of the chair, beneath the metal leg.' He was recovering his assurance a little.

'How do you think it got there?'

'I wouldn't know. The crime scene manager, Helen Charles, thought perhaps it had fallen out of the victim's mouth when he was moved to the morgue. Apparently the body was extensively burnt during the blaze.' He smiled once more.

'Yes, we will be calling Ms Charles as a witness later,' pronounced the coroner, looking over the top of her glasses. 'Now, Mr Dolan, have you ever been in an accident?'

The smile vanished again. 'What do you mean?'

'I think the question is pretty straightforward. Have you ever been in an accident?'

'Not that I can recall.'

'Never been in a fire?'

'No.'

'Never experienced the pain of burning?'

'I'm a fire investigator, Mrs Challinor, I don't have to experience it to understand what is happening.'

'You misunderstand me, Mr Dolan. I wasn't calling into question your competence. I was calling into question your identity.'

'I... I... I don't understand.'

344

'Could you take your jacket and shirt off, Mr Dolan?'

A buzz went through the courtroom. The reporters were all sitting on the edge of their seats, scribbling furiously. Even Trent was staring at Dolan.

'This is outrageous,' he blustered. 'You have no right to ask me.'

Mrs Challinor smiled for the first time. 'This is my court, Mr Dolan. I have every right to ask anything I wish. Detective Inspector Ridpath, in your role as the coroner's officer, could you help Mr Dolan off with his jacket and shirt?'

Dolan had been slumped forward staring at his folded hands resting on the witness stand.

Ridpath took two steps forward before the man jumped up. 'That won't be necessary, I am quite capable of undressing myself.'

Ridpath stood still. To his left, he saw Trent, Caruso and Dave Greene had already moved round behind the witness stand. He held his breath. In the next five seconds, he would find out if he was a good copper or the biggest fool on earth.

He reckoned the odds were 50–50.

Dolan removed his jacket, laying it carefully against the back of the seat. He pulled out the tails of his purple shirt and slowly began to unfasten the buttons.

Ridpath watched as his fingers deftly undid each one, starting at the top.

Then he removed the shirt and stood upright in the dock.

'Please remove your undershirt, Mr Dolan,' ordered Mrs Challinor.

A hush had descended on the court. The stenographer had stopped tapping away at her machine to record the proceedings. The reporters had stopped writing in their notebooks. Ridpath had even stopped breathing.

Dolan smiled ruefully and pulled the T-shirt over his head.

He stood there with his arms open wide. 'See, see what they did,' he shouted.

Ridpath stared at the puckered and scarred skin stretching from just beneath where the shoulder met the arm, extending down to the belt of the trousers and round to the back. The skin was distorted and discoloured as if writhing in pain.

Chapter Eighty-Eight

Terry Dolan slumped down in the witness chair. His eyes flickered from side to side, before his shoulders finally relaxed and he began to speak in a quiet whisper. 'This is what they did to me.'

'Who?' asked Mrs Challinor gently.

There was a long pause before he answered. 'Mulkeen and the rest of them.'

'Mulkeen abused you?'

The man's head rose for a second before dropping down onto his chest once again. Ridpath saw no defiance in the eyes, just sorrow and resignation.

'He never touched me. I wasn't one of his favourites. Not one of his special boys.'

'What happened?'

'It was supposed to be a celebration, we had just won the five-a-side cup. Best day of my life it was, until then. I scored the winning goal.'

He lifted his head. Ridpath could see he was no longer in the courtroom but back in that day in 1994, slotting the ball into the net past the goalkeeper and raising the cup above his head.

'Mulkeen had arranged for us to go camping if we won, out near Dunham Massey. He'd bought beer and food and wine and vodka. We lit a fire in front of the tent and all sat around it, drinking and eating. It was a special treat for his special boys.' He paused for a moment, remembering and reliving the past. 'Sykes and Doyle were his favourites, the ones he called "his pretty boys". He promised them trials with United, meetings with scouts, everything. All they had to do was let him touch them…'

He fell silent for a long time. Inside the court nobody moved. The reporters didn't say a word. The stenographer had stopped typing again. Ridpath held his breath.

'It all started when we drank the vodka. Somebody, I think it was Mulkeen, decided to play Truth or Dare. Sam Sykes went first and asked the coach who was his favourite footballer. He chose truth and answered Eric Cantona. When it was Mulkeen's turn, he asked me to choose truth or dare. I chose truth and he asked me a question…'

'What did he ask you?'

Dolan's voice was quiet now, almost inaudible. 'He asked me if I fancied any of the boys in the team. I didn't know what to say. I went bright red and didn't answer. Mulkeen pointed at me and shouted, "He does, he fancies Sam." I still didn't answer.' He looked up for a second and Ridpath could see a film of tears in his eyes. 'You see, Mulkeen had sussed me out. He knew what I thought every time I saw Sam.'

'What happened next, Mr Dolan?' asked the coroner.

'Mulkeen started clapping and shouting and dancing around me. "PLAY THE GAME, PLAY THE GAME." All the rest, except Sam, joined in. "PLAY THE GAME, PLAY THE GAME, PLAY THE GAME." Then, Sam picked up a stick and began to prod me with it. Telling me I was useless, hopeless, each word followed by a poke with the sharp point of the stick. Mulkeen egged him on.' He stopped for a second and swallowed. 'I knew what Sam was doing. He was hoping Mulkeen would choose me that night instead of him. So I snatched the stick from his hands and began to hit him with it. I knew Sam was stronger than me but I had to protect myself, didn't I? I had to fight back. We struggled for a few moments, the others formed a circle around us as we fought, encouraging Sam to hurt me. "Kill him, Sam. Show him who's boss."'

He swallowed again and stared down at his hands. 'Sam forced me to the ground and used his weight to pin my shoulders down. Then he pulled a knife and held it to my throat. I couldn't move. I could feel the cold of the hard steel against the soft skin of my neck. I closed my eyes and he leant in close, whispering into my ear. "Play the game, Brennan, play the game." I felt his weight lift off my shoulders as he stood up. I lay on the ground unable to move. Then I felt a stream of liquid being poured over me. Sam had picked up the petrol can used to start the fire and poured it over me. I can still smell it now, the harsh, acrid aroma of petrol...'

'What happened next?'

'I tried to get up to run but Tommy Larkin came forward in his orange anorak. He was laughing. He picked up a burning stick from the fire... They were all shouting "PLAY THE GAME. PLAY THE GAME. PLAY THE GAME." Mulkeen was the loudest.'

His head lifted and he continued speaking. 'Tommy Larkin threw the lighted stick on me.'

There was a sharp intake of breath from the stenographer. The rest of the court stayed silent.

'I spent two months in the burns unit. I never played football again. They killed me that day even though I didn't die...'

'You murdered all the boys from the football team?' The coroner was encouraging him to say more, but by now, he didn't need any more encouragement, the story was pouring out of him.

'Not all of them, just those who deserved to die. The other two had already been taken.'

'And Charles Whitworth, why did you kill him?'

His face reddened with anger. 'He was the worst. He was police, he was supposed to protect me, but he didn't. Visited me in hospital, told me to forget it, just a stupid accident, he said. Mulkeen and Sykes lied to him, but he knew what really happened, just didn't want to admit it to himself. My body tells the truth…' He ran his fingers over the puckered, malformed skin.

'When did you decide to take revenge?' Mrs Challinor's voice was gentle, coaxing.

'About a year ago. I'd been recommended by my doctor to Alistair Ransome, a psychotherapist. By then I'd buried the memory of what happened very deep. It was as if the fire had cauterised that area of my mind. Ransome brought it back, though. All the pain and the hurt and the anger. I decided then I had to kill him and they had to die for what they did to me.'

Caruso and Trent silently moved closer to the witness box, accompanied by Dave Greene.

'But you survived, Mr Dolan… Or should I call you Mr Brennan?'

'You can call me what you want. I'm dead anyway.'

'Why did you fake your own death?'

'Joseph Brennan had to die like all the others. It was the only way I was going to be free.' He laughed. 'It was easy to fool the police and the rest of them. I'd worked in forensics all my life. I knew they'd look for dental records for a burn victim. Planting the bridge from my own mouth was simple.'

'But who was the body in the flat?'

'An interfering postman. Kept asking why I was getting mail with two different names. He was the same size and shape as me, so the morning before the fire I finished him off. I'd already created my new identity when I joined Adelphi, shaving my head but wearing a wig when I went back to the flat.' He paused again. 'I suppose that was the real start, when there was two of me.'

Trent stepped forward. 'Joseph Brennan, I am arresting you for the murder of Samuel Sykes, anything—'

Before she could finish, Brennan jumped out of the witness box and pulled a knife from his pocket.

Everybody in the court stood up, chairs fell over, a woman screamed.

Brennan backed towards Mrs Challinor's desk, waving the knife in front of him.

Trent shouted, 'Put it down, Brennan.'

She began to move towards him with Dave Greene on her left. Caruso stood where she was, her mouth covered by her hand.

Trent shouted again, 'PUT IT DOWN.'

Brennan looked at her, then around at the rest of the court. He smiled and turned to face Mrs Challinor, bringing the knife up to his throat and driving the point into his neck beneath the ear. A spray of blood erupted over the desk.

Ridpath jumped towards the coroner.

Brennan brought his knife slowly across his throat, a thick red line appeared and blood poured over his scarred body. A strange vacancy appeared in his eyes and he sank to his knees, falling forward onto the wooden floor of the courtroom.

Friday, May 31, 2019

Chapter Eighty-Nine

'Where are you taking me, Ridpath? I thought this was supposed to be your day off.'

'It is, Mrs Challinor, but the train to London isn't until twelve thirty so I still have time. And we don't have to go far.'

They were in Ridpath's car heading towards Stockport. He had picked her up early from the coroner's court, asking her to come with him to meet somebody who was key to a case they were working on. She had grumbled but agreed to go.

'I hear you're off to see BTS in London.'

The two women, Polly and Mrs Challinor, had been talking again. 'True, Eve's a fan. More than that, a BTS maniac. I can't wait to be surrounded by ten thousand screaming twelve-year-olds... not.'

'I can imagine. The Halle is more my scene.' She paused for a moment. 'Anything more on the Brennan case?'

'The papers are with the CPS and he's locked up in a secure mental health facility at Ashworth Hospital in Liverpool. He missed his carotid artery with the knife. Just a little bit deeper and he would have drowned in his own blood. The doctor saved his life.'

'I never asked you how you worked out that Terry Dolan was Joseph Brennan?'

'I didn't.'

'But you passed me a note in court and told me you were certain they were the same person.'

'I know, sorry. It was an educated guess. You see, it was the only possibility that explained everything. It was when he said he'd been working for Adelphi for three years that it suddenly came together for me. When I discovered it was Dolan who found the dental bridge, I knew what he had done.'

'But that still doesn't explain how you knew he was also Joseph Brennan.'

'As I said, it was the only explanation that fit the facts and the evidence.'

'So when you wanted me to get him to remove his shirt, you weren't absolutely sure what we would see?'

Ridpath ignored the question, turning into the driveway of a big Victorian house. 'We're here.'

'Asure Rehab Services,' Mrs Challinor read the sign over the door. 'What is this place, Ridpath?'

'It's what it says it is. A drug and addiction rehabilitation centre.'

Then the penny dropped for the coroner. 'My brother?'

Ridpath nodded. 'He checked himself in three weeks ago. Ted Jones rang me late last night and told me he'd been found. I called them this morning and they said you could come and see him.'

Mrs Challinor sat in the car, staring out of the windscreen.

'He's waiting for you.'

'I can't go in, Ridpath.'

'He wants to see you.'

Her fingers fluttered to her hair. 'What do I say?'

'You could start with hello and take it from there.'

She took a deep breath. 'Come in with me?'

He nodded. 'If you want, but wouldn't you prefer to be alone with him?'

'Not this time.' She took another breath and opened the door, stepping out onto the gravelled driveway.

They walked to the front door and were let in by a member of staff. 'He's in the community room. He's looking forward to meeting his sister.'

They walked into a large room on the left. A thin, unshaven man was sitting by himself at the table, staring out of the window. He stood up and turned to face his sister.

Mrs Challinor ran over to him, hugging him close to her as if she would never let him go.

After a long while, he pulled back. 'I saw a man burning, Margaret. I knew then I'd have to change.'

Ridpath recognised her brother. He was the homeless man from the video, the one who had entered the building site. He would have to be questioned, but it could wait until after the weekend.

Mrs Challinor hugged her brother again, whispering words of comfort into his ear.

Ridpath walked out of the room, leaving the two of them alone.

For some reason, he was desperate for a cigarette, just one. He wanted to taste the past one last time.

He searched in his glove compartment and found an old half-empty packet sitting amongst Eve's discarded chocolate wrappers and Polly's sticks of chewing gum.

He lit it, took a long drag and watched the blue smoke drift hazily up towards the canopy of the trees. Above his head, a single magpie squawked, its call breaking the silence of the morning.

'Bye, Charlie,' said Ridpath softly, before stubbing the cigarette out with the heel of his shoe.